MURDER ON THE ILE SAINT-LOUIS

Cara Black

CHIVERS

British Library Cataloguing in Publication Data available

This Large Print edition published by BBC Audiobooks Ltd, Bath, 2008.
Published by arrangement with Soho Press Ltd.

U.K. Hardcover ISBN 978 1 405 64508 9
U.K. Softcover ISBN 978 1 405 64509 6

An Aimée Leduc Investigation Series

Printed and bound in Great Britain by
Antony Rowe Ltd., Chippenham, Wiltshire

MURDER ON THE ILE SAINT-LOUIS

In memory of the deportees on Auschwitz-Birkenau convoys 37 and 38, September, 1942, the real Stella, and all the ghosts.

Immense debts of gratitude go to Leonard Pitt; Dorothy Edwards; Max; Stephen; Grace Loh for opening my eyes; Manon Noubik; Jessie; Barbara; Jan; Maggie, midwife extraordinaire; Stacy; Lt. Bruce Fairbarn, Special Investigative Unit, SFPD; George Fong, FBI; Dr. Terri Haddix; Roland Fishman above and beyond, in Sydney.

In Paris, Chris and Colette Vanier, for their generosity; Daniele Nangeroni, who told me her story; Captaine de Police Michel Constant of Brigade Fluviale; Jacques Valluis-Avocat; Alain Dubois; Bella and John Allen; Gilles Fouquet; Jean-Damien; Anna Czarnocka of the Société Historique et Littéraire Polonaise; Flora Pachelska; Pierre-Olivier; Madame Wattiez; Jean Caploun; Paris Historique; Cathy Etile, little Zouzou; toujours Sarah Tarille; little Madelaine; and Anne-Françoise Delbegue.

7

And nothing would happen without James N. Frey; Linda Allen; Laura Hruska; my son, Tate; and Jun.

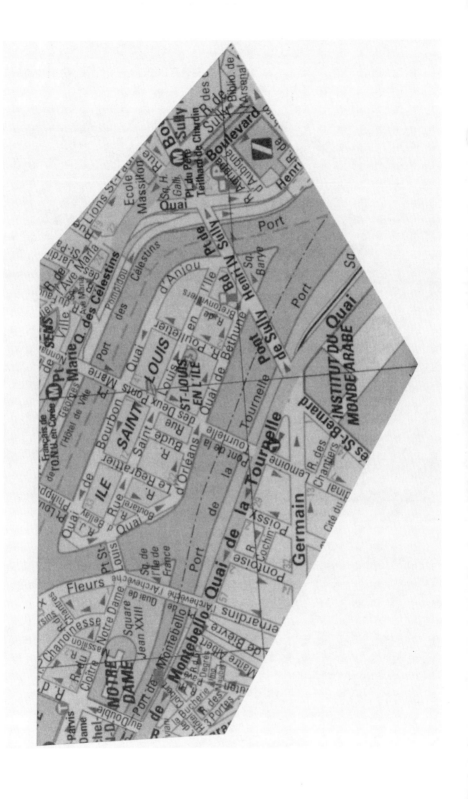

It is dangerous to be right in matters on which the established authorities are wrong.

— Voltaire

Paris, February 1995, Monday Night
Aimée Leduc sensed the scent of spring in the air rising from the Seine and spilling through her open balcony doors. A church bell chimed outside; leaves fluttered in the breeze and couples ducked into a nearby *brasserie.* It was a beautiful night on the Ile Saint-Louis, the island in the heart of Paris.

She ran her chipped gigabyte green fingernails over the laptop keyboard; she had to finish system maintenance and get her client's network up and running online by nine-thirty. Only twenty-seven minutes to go and she was exhausted, but she knew she'd manage it. All she had to do was concentrate, but after five straight hours, her brain rebelled. She rubbed her black-stockinged calf with her foot. One more system to check, then *voilà.*

From somewhere under the papers piled on her desk the phone trilled. Miles Davis, her bichon frise, who was nestled at her feet, awoke with a bark.

"*Allô?*" she said.

She heard someone panting and the sound of a wailing siren in the distance.

An obscene phone call?

"*Oui?*" she asked, in a brusque tone of voice.

"You have to help me!" a strange woman said.

"Who's this?"

"Go to the courtyard. If they catch —"

"Wrong number, *désolée,*" Aimée said, about to hang up.

"They want to kill me." It was a young woman's voice, rising in panic. "They want my —" Static obscured the rest of her sentence. "Please, now!"

"What do you mean?" Aimée leaned forward, shoulders tensed.

"I can't explain. . . . There's no time and they'll hear me."

"What kind of joke . . . ?"

"Please, Aimée."

She still didn't recognize the voice.

"Do I know you?"

"They'll kill — I trust you."

Aimée gripped the phone harder. "*Me?* Look, if you're frightened, call the *flics.*"

14

A car engine started. "No *flics*, no hospital."

"Who is this?"

"You're . . . you're the only person who can help me now. . . . Go to the courtyard. It'll just be for a few hours. Please! And don't tell anyone."

The line went dead.

The hair on Aimée's neck rose. She hit the callback symbol and got a recorded message saying that the public phone she'd reached couldn't accept calls.

Twenty-four minutes to her work deadline. But the call had unnerved her; she couldn't concentrate. It would only take a moment to reach the courtyard. She pressed *Save* and slipped her feet into the black kitten heels under her desk.

The parquet floor of the long hall in her seventeenth century town-house apartment creaked under her feet. She rooted through take-out Indian menus in the drawer of the *secrétaire* near the front door, found her Beretta, and checked the cartridge. She went downstairs to the courtyard, shivering as she kept to the shadows, gripping the pistol in her pocket. The glint of the half-moon spread a luminous glow over her building's ivy-covered walls. The soft air was almost palpable; it was a rare, clear night, with stars thick in the sky. An aroma composed of algae mingling with wet stone wafted from the Seine, which was swollen with melted snow. They had endured freak Level 3 snowstorms in January, and now, courtesy of El Niño, a seductive February warmth had forced half the population into tank tops and the cherry trees in Jardins du Luxembourg into early bloom.

Apprehensive, she paused to scan the courtyard.

Who was her unknown caller and why had she been picked, Aimée wondered.

She made out the shapes of the green garbage containers in the corner and edged closer to them, treading warily over the damp cobblestones. By the light of her pocket flashlight, she looked around for someone hiding in the courtyard.

"*Allô?* Anyone there?" she called.

There was no answer. No movement in the shadows. No one was concealed behind the gnarled pear tree encased by a circular metal grille that stood near the bins. Then something behind the containers moved.

She raised the Beretta, stepped closer, and took aim. A denim jacket with a collar embroidered with blue beads was wrapped around a bundle of some sort. The jacket trembled; a mewling sound came from it.

16

She shook her head. A sick joke? Kittens? Had the roaming orange tabby that the concierge fed produced another litter? Like the one the concierge left scraps for in the rear garden of Notre Dame across the footbridge? She'd been stupid to take the telephone caller's bait with her deadline looming! Most likely she'd been lured here by a rival, a competitor who knew what was at stake. Her fingers relaxed their grip.

She leaned down and parted the lapels of the beaded denim jacket. A tiny, pinched red face stared up at her.

A baby.

The baby's eyes blinked; the oval mouth widened. Its cry wavered, echoing off the stone walls. She slipped her hands under the baby's neck, wondering how to hold it. The head lolled back and she pulled it to her, cradling the infant in her arms, amazed at how light it was. No heavier than her laptop.

Pink mottled skin, a russet fuzz of hair. Yellow scallop-edged shirt. But no diaper. She peered closer. A girl, with the stump of a cylindrical, pinkish umbilical cord still attached. A newborn.

The cries mounted; the little mouth now wailing with all its might. She rocked the baby and the cries subsided.

Aimée looked around again, wondering why the mother had picked her, how she could entrust her baby to a stranger.

Tiens, she couldn't take care of a baby. She was on deadline. She ran a computer security firm, dealt with viruses, deciphered encrypted code. She knew nothing about babies; she couldn't take on such a responsibility. Half the time she missed Miles Davis's appointment at the dog groomer. No one, no one who knew her, would peg her as maternal.

The long toot of a passing barge rose from the Seine.

The baby was making sucking motions with its mouth. The little pink hands flailed, brushing her like butterfly wings. She extended a finger toward the hand and the tiny pink fingers grasped hers, clutched it. She saw the perfectly formed, minuscule, pearlescent pink fingernails.

Nothing had ever been so tiny, so exquisite. So helpless.

The cries started again. *Merde!* Crying brought attention, the neighbors, or . . . whoever was after the mother.

"What should I do with you?" she asked aloud.

The cries dwindled. She could have sworn the fuzzy head, hardly bigger than her fist, turned toward her voice.

"Where's your mother, little one?" she asked.

Dampness radiated from the courtyard's surface. The baby might catch cold! She disengaged her finger and flicked on the Beretta's safety. Then she noticed the striped baby bag on the ground next to the dirty jacket. She picked them both up.

Cradling the baby close, she mounted the worn marble steps to her apartment. And then a warm wetness began to spread over her arms and chest. It — she — was wetting on Aimée's vintage Chanel black dress! It was a flea-market treasure she'd bargained down to five thousand francs.

She unlocked her door and strode to the kitchen, thoughts of a hungry baby, her deadline, and the cryptic message from the mother churning in her head. Something terrible had happened. She had to think.

She unzipped the baby bag, searching for a note. In it she found disposable diapers, a bottle, and a tin of powdered Lemiel formula *"premier age"* — for newborns to four months.

Boil water, she told herself. People boiled water in the movies when babies were concerned. Sterilize everything. *Bon,* she poured a bottle of Evian into a saucepan and read the formula label. There had to be instructions.

She spread a towel on her bed's duvet cover, laid the baby down, and took a disposable diaper from the bag. She studied the Velcro tabs, the flat white panel with yellow ducks resembling an origami puzzle.

Miles Davis whined and cocked his head.

"We'll manage, right, Miles?" Too bad he only had paws; she could use another pair of hands.

She went to work. When the diaper encased the baby, Aimée wrapped her in the chenille throw that lay across the foot of her bed. She kicked the radiator several times until it sputtered to life. And kicked it again.

Aimée leaned down, studying each pale chestnut eyelash, the daintily formed kiss of a mouth, the nautilus-shell ears. The pearlescent glow of her skin. She was perfect in every way. Aimée searched for a resemblance to someone she knew. She drew a blank.

Her eye was caught by the photo on her spindle-legged dresser. A photo of Aimée herself, aged six months, in a white onesie, lying on a blue flannel blanket. But she looked huge compared to the little one lying on her duvet.

The face of her long-vanished mother rose

in her mind: carmine red lipstick and huge doe eyes. Her American mother, who hadn't been home when eight-year-old Aimée returned from school one rainy afternoon. Or any afternoon after that. No explanation, no good-bye. Gone. Leaving her father to cope. He'd thrown away her mother's things and refused ever to talk about her.

The smell of burning plastic came from the kitchen.

The bottle.

The saucepan's plastic handle had melted onto the burner. A mess. Her culinary skills didn't even extend to boiling water.

She salvaged what she could, filled the bottle with boiled water, measured out the formula, added it to the water, and shook the bottle just as the instructions directed. Her hand bumped the Beretta in her pocket. *Zut!* Ninety-nine percent of all household accidents happened in the kitchen!

Somehow she had to feed this baby and get her work done. She stuck the Beretta in the closest drawer with serving spoons and looked at the time. If she didn't hurry she'd miss her deadline.

She tested the formula on her wrist. Too hot. She added cool water, shook the bottle again.

She could do this, she had to, she told

herself. In her bedroom, she put the nipple of the bottle to the baby's lips. But the little thrusting mouth just emitted screams. "Cooperate, can't you? Try, please," Aimée begged.

Little blue eyes stared back at her.

Aimée shook the bottle and giant air bubbles filled it but no formula flowed. Aimée sucked on the nipple in desperation and swallowed a mouthful of bland milky slush. It was not the sweet, velvety drink she'd expected. Formula dripped down her front and she stuck the now-flowing bottle into the baby's mouth.

The laptop alarm beeped; she had set it to signal three minutes before the system needed to go up. She panicked, grabbed a pillow, and rushed to her laptop, propping the baby with the bottle in the crook of her arm.

One last system check to make. But she needed to verify the algorithm. She had it *somewhere.* Scrabbling through the papers on her desk, she finally found it.

The bottle was empty now. She hefted the baby, white fluid dribbling from its mouth. Aimée had to burp her. Of course, they had to be burped after a bottle. But she just had to finish this . . .

And the baby spit up all over the desk.

Monday Evening

Krzysztof Linski hurried past the piano-shaped ice sculpture in the vast salon of the Polish Foundation's seventeenth-century town house on the Ile Saint-Louis. He'd just make it if . . .

"Where's your dinner jacket, Krzysztof?" Comte Linski, his uncle, demanded.

Caught! Krzysztof played with the zipper of his hooded sweatshirt. *Merde!* He'd be imprisoned at the gala the foundation was sponsoring if he didn't maneuver his way out of it.

"But, Uncle, I'm late. . . ."

"The crown prince of Poland, dressed in Levi's?" His uncle frowned as if in disapproval of the moisture-beaded magnums of champagne standing in ice buckets, ready to be poured for the assembling guests.

Leaning on his cane, his uncle blocked Krzysztof's escape from the somber room, which was decorated with bookcases filled with leather-bound volumes whose spines were molting and crackle-surfaced oil paintings of nineteenth-century Warsaw. Everything here reeked of the past.

"Our committee's donating Chopin's death mask to the foundation's collection; we expect you to say a few words to our assembled guests, but not dressed like that."

Dream on, Krzysztof refrained from saying.

"We're marching tonight to stop the signing of the oil agreement," Krzysztof said, hoping to avoid an argument. "If I don't hurry —"

"Not that silly business again!" In the chandelier's light, his uncle's medals gleamed. The ones he trotted out for occasions like this were all pinned to his waistcoat: ribbons earned in the Polish resistance and his French Légion d'Honneur medal, on its red ribbon.

"But I helped organize the protest, it's vital that I be there. I need to leave now, Uncle."

"Your duty's more important, Krzysztof," his uncle told him.

In Krzysztof's opinion, preventing global pollution and the poisoning of the seas was more important than paying tribute to a man dead one hundred years.

"Your duty lies here, Krzysztof," his uncle continued. "This is *your* culture, *your* heritage. These are your people. How can some abstract cause compete?"

Strains of a Chopin piano sonata drifted over the white-haired crowd. The old folks came out in force for a gala and free meal.

No one here was under seventy. Their formal attire emitted a whiff of mothballs, Krzysztof noted.

The comte grabbed his elbow. "Think of what you owe your ancestors."

The monarchy had ended in 1945, and their land and castles had been seized. Krzysztof took catering jobs now to supplement his living expenses while he attended the Sorbonne and his uncle, a glorified gofer, organized receptions in return for a free room at the foundation. Yet his uncle insisted that Krzysztof remember that he was descended from a princess, the Infanta Maria Augusta Nepomucena Antonia Franziska Xaveria Aloysia. That and five francs would get him an espresso, Krzysztof knew. His uncle overlooked the fact that the infanta had died in the last century and that Krzysztof was only the offshoot of an illegitimate branch.

Krzysztof knew his stories by heart. The past was like yesterday to hear his uncle and his cronies talk. They were the descendants of Polish *émigré* nobility who had fled to Paris from nineteenth-century insurrections and, later, tsarist troops. Still they clung to their visions of a noble past and their hopes of a restoration while they dealt in antiques to pay their rent.

Murmurs rose above the piano sonata.

"It's time." The old man gripped Krzysztof by the elbow. "Please, stay until the unveiling. For me," he said, his voice softening.

Krzysztof hated to hear his uncle beg. The last thing he wanted was to disappoint him. Reluctant, he nodded.

"Mesdames et messieurs," a voice announced from the rear of the salon, "join us for the unveiling of Chopin's death mask, our tribute to a great musican and son of Poland."

A bit late, Krzysztof thought. When Chopin, tubercular and estranged from the Polish aristocrats, died, his lover, George Sand, had footed the bills.

"The monarchy lives," his uncle whispered. "You're in the line of succession. Be proud."

Proud? What were obsolete titles compared to toxic oil spills, killing wildlife, and depleting the ocean of oxygen? The lies of Alstrom, the guilty oil company, had to be exposed; the Ministry prevented from signing the proposed agreement.

"Pour me some champagne before it's gone, young man."

He turned to see an old woman, wearing a fur stole, too many pearls, and too much makeup for her age. She was feeding the Chihuahua at her side from her plate with a fork. He would humor her and then escape, Krzysztof decided.

"With pleasure." He executed a small bow, his manners ingrained. On weekends he did this for a living. "Your dog has a good appetite, Madame." He poured and handed her a Baccarat flute of fizzing champagne.

"Tiresome, this reception fare. Always the same," she said. "But Bibo loves *pommes dauphinoise.*"

He repressed a sniff. The old woman hadn't washed in a while or maybe it was Bibo, a bulging-eyed thing whose teeth were bared at him.

The old woman said in Polish, "You're the comte's —"

"I speak French" he interrupted.

"Hardly a trace of an accent either," she said. "So you're the troublemaking prince he complains about. Highstrung, a rebel." She smiled at the little dig she'd managed to inflict.

"My mother taught me French," Krzysztof said. "And the system of kings and aristocrats is dead."

To his surprise, she beamed. "Dead? Try telling *them* that, young man." She waved her arm in a vague gesture at the crowd.

27

"But I see, you're like me."

He doubted that.

"Believe it or not, in my day we were enthralled by the anarchists, idealists with letter bombs, all very romantic and exciting. I raised hell, too." She patted his arm and left her hand there. "Isn't that the expression?"

Krzysztof cringed. She still thought of herself as a *coquette.*

"I'm just a student." He glanced at the hand of the Sèvres clock. "There's a protest against North Sea pollution . . ."

"Marvellous," she interrupted, noticing his gaze. "The young always protest, that's your job. I find those who stir things up fascinating."

"Stir things up?" She made it sound as if it was a lark. If they didn't bring the facts to the world's attention, the Ministry would sign an oil rights agreement with Alstrom the day after tomorrow.

She let out a meaningful sigh. "Boris Bakunin. Now if he'd put as much energy into revolution as he did between the sheets . . . our movement would have succeeded." There was a wicked grin on her face. "We learned how to build, set, and defuse *explosives.* It was my idea — that book bomb — not that anyone cares these days."

He shifted his feet. He wanted to slip out before his uncle noticed.

"I hope you're involved in something illegal and thrilling." Her eyes sparkled, amazing green young-looking eyes revealing traces of the beauty she must once have been. "It's the only way to live, young man." She fed Bibo a forkful, then leaned forward. "Just watch your back. If Trotsky had paid more attention to what was going on behind him, he wouldn't have been assassinated in Mexico."

"Pardon?" He stood, eyeing the door, distracted.

"They hatched the plot here; we knew the saboteur. I warned him myself."

And then he realized who she was. Jadwiga Radziwill, the once notorious revolutionary, double agent, and rumored lover of a Wehrmacht general. *Zut,* he'd thought she was dead.

Darkness shaded the narrow cobblestone surface of the Left Bank street. Fewer than a hundred had gathered for the march; Krzysztof had expected more. And the press? Not a camera crew in sight.

Disappointed, he wiped damp hair from his forehead, passing a candle to the next demonstrator. The march would culminate two blocks away in a peace vigil on the grounds of l'Institut du Monde Arabe, the cultural foundation where the conference was being held. A multistory building part library, museum, and seminar center, l'Institut du Monde Arabe's countless bronze light-sensitive shutters imitated the *moucharabiya,* an Arab latticework balcony. Another Pompidou design project not working half the time.

He looked for Orla, who'd promised to provide them with more information, but she was late as usual. A camera truck from France2 pulled up. He brightened; now they'd get coverage on the television news. The word would spread.

Fellow Sorbonne students wearing bandannas strummed guitars, and the old Socialists, always ready for a demonstration, circulated bottles of red wine among those standing in loose ranks. Handheld candles illuminated expectant faces. He smiled at his fellow organizer, Gaelle, who had draped a red-and-white Palestinian scarf over her tank top. She raised her fist in a power salute, grinning back as he dumped an empty candle box in a bin.

"My press contact's coming. I told him you'd convinced Brigitte and the Monde-Focus to sponsor this demonstration,"

Gaelle said, her face flushed with excitement.

Perfect, everything was running according to plan. His nervousness evaporated. Now he was sure everything would work. He'd followed the right channels, applied for and obtained a permit. There was not even a *flic* or a police car in sight.

A girl with long blonde hair smiled and kissed him on the cheek, her scent of patchouli oil surrounding them both. "Comrade, help out a minute, won't you?"

He caught a whiff of kerosene and hoped no one had brought a lantern. Their march was supposed to end in a silent protest illuminated only by hundreds of flickering candles as they submitted their alternative proposal. A lantern would ruin the effect.

She smiled up at him and slung her backpack strap over his shoulder. "Take this, will you? I've got to carry the rest of the candles." The clink of bottles came from within the backpack. She winked. "I've brought something to quench our thirst while we keep vigil."

He hesitated and shrugged. "Why not?" He hefted the bag. Voices around him rose in song and he recognized "The Internationale," the old Socialist anthem. He found himself stepping out in time with the singing. And then she vanished, dropping behind the ranks of marchers, as someone hugged him.

The group linked arms and strode over the cobbles. Beside him, Gaelle held the green STOP THE OIL DRILLING banner aloft.

As they marched, their voices and laughter echoed off the stone buildings. Their candles flickered in the soft breeze from the Seine. His uncle's speech came to his mind. Proud of his ancestry? *This* made his heart swell with pride.

They reached the corner and rounded it. Ranks of uniformed CRS, Compagnies Républicaines de Sécurité, an armed riot squad, stood in front of l'Institut du Monde Arabe.

This made no sense to Krzysztof. They were marching peacefully to protest oil pollution.

He paused in midstep, as did the others. The CRS was drawn up in riot formation. The revolving police-car lights cast a bluish light that was reflected by the clear shields they held positioned in front of them.

This was only his second demonstration and he almost jumped out of his skin as a Mercedes limo screeched down the institute's exit ramp and tore off toward the Seine.

"Merde," Gaelle said at his side, "the bigwigs are taking off before we can present our proposals. The pigs!"

Krzysztof exchanged a confused look with Claude, a tall, leather-jacketed documentary filmmaker who stood on the sidelines.

"Get this on film, Claude!" he called.

Claude raised his fingers in a V, video camera crooked between his neck and shoulder. "Got it, from the beginning!" Claude considered himself a master of *cinéma vérité.* His ten-year-old documentary of activists fighting the building of African oil platforms was already considered a classic.

The marchers were at a standstill. Strategize, Krzysztof told himself. They had to strategize and keep the momentum going.

"Gaelle. Over here." He made his way through the crowd, toward plane trees with peeling bark. Amid the planters holding bushes he set the backpack down.

The CRS loudspeaker broke the silence. "Advance no further."

"Everything's legal," Gaelle shouted back, "approved by the —" Her voice was drowned by the clanking of the metal-heeled boots of the CRS scraping against the cobblestones.

"This is an unlawful assembly. Your permit has been revoked," the loudspeaker blared. "Put down your weapons."

Their permit revoked? Weapons?

"We're conducting a sanctioned peaceful assembly," Krzysztof shouted. MondeFocus only countenanced peaceful lawful demonstrations.

All of a sudden, a figure ran toward the front line of marchers, cradling something to her chest. "Wait . . . !"

Before he could see who it was, the stark white glare of police searchlights blinded him. He shielded his eyes.

"Krzysztof!"

He recognized Orla's voice. But more blinding light prevented him from seeing her.

"Look, Orla's arrived," Gaelle said.

"This is your last warning." Static crackled from the loudspeaker.

He stepped back in a panic. "But I obtained the permit. How could they revoke it?" he asked, dazed.

"They can't do this," Gaelle told him.

"Of course not. No one informed me!"

"Lies!" The crowd started chanting, their voices mounting in the humid air.

"They'll have to understand," Gaelle said,

desperation in her voice, as she broke past the marchers and ran ahead.

The CRS advanced in a single rank, clear shields positioned in front of their faces.

Gaelle raised her candle and took a step forward, into the boulevard.

What was she doing? The CRS came closer, truncheons raised. He could see their features behind their clear shields. He sprinted forward. She took another step.

"Gaelle, *non!*" He reached for her arm.

People behind him shoved forward and he tripped, losing his balance. The banner fell. He was pressed against a stone bollard.

"We're presenting a peaceful petition —"

The rest of Gaelle's words were lost in the bone-cracking whack of a truncheon. She crumpled to the ground. For a moment, all was silent, then cries of horror rose around him. Blood spurted from Gaelle's head, drenching her scarf. And Krzysztof was pushed to one side in the melee as the crowd surged around them.

MONDAY NIGHT

Aimée answered the door, her hands shaking. The Chanel dress she wore was now caked with clumps of beige formula.

"About time, René!"

35

Her partner, René Friant, a dwarf, all of four feet tall in his tailored Burberry raincoat and custom-made shoes, stared at her.

"Interesting fashion statement. Sorry I'm late," he said, hanging his coat on a chair. "They cordoned off the bridge because of some MondeFocus demonstration." He sniffed. "Did Miles Davis have an accident?"

"I need your help, René," she said.

"System up and running, right? Is this about tomorrow's meeting . . . ?" He paused, his eyes searching hers. "Don't tell me you missed the deadline."

"Come here." She took his hand and led him down the hall.

The baby's mauve-hued eyelids were closed, the small chest rose and fell. She was at peace, asleep on the duvet.

"A baby? Instead of playing house, we need to monitor Regnault's security update."

Miles Davis cocked his head at the baby's gentle breaths.

"René, it's not like that."

He took a step back. "Did I miss something during the past nine months?"

She shook her head. "No cracks about the Immaculate Conception either."

"Shouldn't her mother come for her?"

For once she agreed.

He sat, his eyes intent on the screen. "What's this 'system down for maintenance'?" he asked. "You *didn't* get the system back online."

"I indicated we had maintenance issues because I needed to buy more time. Everything's up and ready. I checked."

"We can't use that delaying tactic again, Aimée. We have to get the system admin done in time, every time. Our clients have to have confidence that we'll get the job done. Otherwise we'll lose our big account because you're babysitting. Have you gone soft in the head?"

Soft in the head . . . never. "I got a mysterious phone call, I went downstairs, and found this baby."

He turned in the chair, his legs dangling. "What?"

"*Sssh*, it took forever to get her to sleep." She pointed to the second laptop screen displaying the system program. "Tell you later. Once I go back in, we've got seven minutes. Ready?"

Her fingers ached by the time they'd checked the last user configuration but they finished with two minutes to spare.

"Close, Aimée. Too close."

"Just listen, René."

"It better be good."

And she told him.

He frowned. "Somehow the woman found your name and your phone number," he said, his tone matter-of-fact. "It's some scam. Now she'll demand money."

Aimée doubted it. The desperation in that voice had been real.

"Wait a minute," she said, running her hands through her spiky hair. "I didn't have time to check earlier, too much was happening." She dumped out the diaper bag's contents, spread them on the parquet floor: diapers, wipes, another tin of powdered Lemiel formula. She turned the bag inside out and noticed stains. Earlier, she hadn't paid attention to the rust-colored smears on the lining. She leaned down and sniffed.

"Dried blood, René."

René sat back, open mouthed for the second time.

"The woman said someone was trying to kill her. And they may have threatened . . . the baby."

She stared at the duvet. The infant's tiny nose crinkled, and the little mouth yawned, revealing a glistening rose tongue.

Almost two hours had passed since the telephone call that had summoned her to the courtyard. She had to do something.

"You still have that friend in Centre d'Écoute Téléphonique, René?"

"Martin?"

She handed René her cell phone. "Ask Martin to locate the public phone booth from which my land line was called. The number was 01 33 68 42 18."

"Look, Aimée . . ."

"Talk to him nicely, René. Tell him you'll owe him big-time."

Ten long minutes later, René handed her the address scribbled on the back of an envelope.

"*Alors,* asking him didn't hurt, did it?"

"My promise to overhaul his motherboard helped."

She looked at the address: 5 Boulevard Henri IV, only two blocks away, near the tip of Ile Saint-Louis. "But that's close by. She could easily have been here by now unless . . ."

René blinked. "Isn't she coming to get the baby?"

"This bloodstain's in the baby bag. . . . She may have been hurt. What if she can't?"

"I don't like this, Aimée," he said.

"René, it's just two blocks away. Do me a favor. Watch the baby a few minutes."

"Me?"

She handed him a bottle of formula. "All

babies do is pee, cry, eat, and sleep." She remembered this line from a late-night program on the *télé.*

"But what if she wakes up?" Alarm showed in René's eyes.

"You'll figure something out, René."

Aimée slid into the warm night. She saw white wavelets hitting the opposite bank of the Seine. Flooding threatened if the thaw kept up.

She'd lived here most of her life, yet the neighbors in her building were only nodding acquaintances. Not one was someone to go to for help. Of course, she was aware, as they all were from the concierge, that a retired doctor of L'École de Médecine lived on the first floor with his dog. An actor and his family resided on the second floor. An old aristocrat owned the top-floor *pied-à-terre,* handed down through the generations. Hers had been inherited from her grandfather. God knows she couldn't have afforded to buy a place on the Ile Saint-Louis on her earnings from Leduc Detective.

Along the quai, a few lit windows, like eyes peering into the darkness, showed in the *hôtels particuliers,* narrow limestone-facaded town houses with delicate wrought-iron balconies and high arched entrances. Most, like hers, were attributed to Le Vau, the architect of Versailles. She knew other worlds existed behind the massive carved entry doors leading to double- and triple-deep courtyards and gardens that could never be glimpsed from the outside. Life on this island took place in the courtyards, in the hidden back passages that had changed little since medieval times. The Ile Saint-Louis was a feudal island fortress, its fortifications the town houses built for the aristocracy. Five bridges spanned the comma-shaped island, which had once been a cow pasture in the Middle Ages. It was eight blocks long and three blocks across at the widest, yet so self-contained that long-time Ile Saint-Louis inhabitants — Ludoviciens — still referred to the rest of Paris as "the Continent." Stubbornly reclusive, the inhabitants ignored the tourists, aware that they inhabited the most desirable streets in Paris, keeping themselves to themselves. They were proud of having allowed a post office to open only a few years ago, of having neighbors like a minister or two and like the Rothschilds, whom one was unlikely to visit to borrow a cup of sugar. Who was she to criticize? She'd never live anywhere else.

A woman in trouble wouldn't knock on the Rothschilds' door in the middle of the night. Was that why she'd been chosen?

She reached Pont de Sully, the bridge connecting Ile Saint-Louis to the Left and Right Banks, just as a lighted, half-empty, Number 87 bus passed her, then made a U-turn to avoid the looming police barricade. An ambulance siren wailed and she saw its red light streaking down the quai across the river. The demonstration must have gotten ugly, she thought.

She located number 5, Boulevard Henri IV. It was the garage next to the fly-fishing shop that had been patronized by Hemingway. A black-lettered sign reading STATION DU SERVICE DE PONT SULLY stood above a blue-and-white metal representation of the Michelin man. A yellow gas pump stood on the pavement, an incongruous object for an island in the middle of the Seine with no Metro stop, no cinema, no police station, and only one *café-tabac.*

The garage lay dark, doors locked, windows semishuttered. Puzzled, she took out her penlight and shone it through a crack in a shutter. Before she could knock, she saw the blinking red light of an alarm system and stopped. With her penlight she examined the garage, seeking a side entrance, without success. The premises were shut tight as a drum, yet the woman had called her from here.

What if the woman had been part of the nearby demonstration? Aimée filed that possibility away. But if the woman was hurt, and being chased, it seemed unlikely she'd run across the bridge to reach this island. Too exposed.

Aimée strode over the zebra-striped Pont de Sully crossing to Place Bayre, the one green space on the island. Miles Davis's favorite walk. And a good place to hide among the chestnut trees, deserted gravel paths, and slatted benches. In its center, a stone statue of a naked man straddling a lion replaced the original bronze animals melted down by the Germans during the Occupation. Diffused light from green metal street lamps filtered through the branches of the trees, casting sticklike shadows on the gravel. She flicked on her penlight. And then she noticed scattered gravel; it looked as if it had been kicked. Or as if there had been a scuffle. She followed the scattered gravel behind a tree trunk. Her foot stepped on something soft. She stopped.

Please don't let it be . . . ! She didn't want to finish the rest of her thought.

Cautiously, she shone the penlight in an arc, poking the leaves with her high heels, expecting to find a human hand or foot. She ground her teeth. *Non,* only soft mud.

A twig crackled behind her. The baby's mother? She spun around.

The path lay deserted.

"Allô?"

The only response was the flapping of a seagull's wings overhead. If the woman was here, surely she'd show herself. Hiding from Aimée made no sense.

She had to calm down. The noise could have been made by squirrels or chipmunks or even a less desirable member of the rodent family.

She walked toward the path and heard the crunch of gravel. She stopped in her tracks. An assignation? In the seventies this spot had been notorious for cruising gays waiting for cavalry soldiers from the nearby Arsenal. Maybe they were still active? But the footsteps padded on, keeping pace with her. Stupidly, she'd left the Beretta in her spoon drawer.

She speeded up, then took cover behind an ivy-draped tree on her right. She inhaled, wishing her heart wasn't beating so hard.

Something moved. She parted the glossy green ivy leaves and peered around the trunk of the tree. Behind her, bushes rustled and she froze, holding her breath. Silence.

And then she saw . . . a shadow, the silhouette of a raised arm holding a bar with a hooked end. As quietly as she could, she backed away until a branch snapped beneath her feet. Then, behind her, more rustling noises in the bushes.

She slipped off her heels, stuck them in her pockets, and sprinted through the bare trees, her heart thumping. If she could make it to Boulevard Henri IV, people might be standing at the bus shelter. At least there would be passing cars.

Sharp pebbles cut her feet but she kept going, past the stone wall, and made it out to the street. She didn't look back as she ran across it, despite flashing headlights, a car swerving, brakes squealing, and blaring horns.

She kept close to the buildings, rounding the curve into Quai d'Anjou, passing the red wall tile marking the height of the 1910 flood that had devastated Paris.

Now her apartment was just a few doors away! She leaned against a carved stone portal, her shoulders heaving, trying to catch her breath. Perspiration dampened her dress; her black stockings torn to shreds.

Yellow light from the street lamp filtered through the budding branches of a plane tree onto the deserted pavement. She could see no one.

She counted to ten, then walked on.

The footsteps came again, this time closer.

The baby. Was there a threat to the baby? She tried to recall the mother's words. Whoever was after her, Aimée couldn't lead them to her doorstep and the baby.

She started to run.

MONDAY NIGHT

On the boulevard, Krzysztof stumbled in front of the advancing boots of the CRS. Candle wax had spilled, scorching his arm. Thick white foam sprayed by the silver-helmeted *pompiers,* the firemen, clung to his pants. A man in a flak jacket with EX-PLOSIF — bomb squad — printed on his vest was operating a remote-control device. The crowd surged from all sides, shouting angrily.

"Clear the area," said a voice from the loudspeaker.

Whistles shrilled. Krzysztof watched, astonished, as behind them a metal robot on small grinding tank treads tore apart empty candle boxes and the backpack he'd set down by the nearby planters.

"Get away from those boxes. Move!" one of the CRS barked. From the crushed backpack, broken wine bottles cascaded onto the ground, but no liquid pooled in front of the shards of glass. They had been stuffed with yellowed rags that emitted a pungent kerosene odor.

"Bottle bombs . . . stand clear."

"We didn't bring those," Krzysztof shouted. "We've been set up!"

High-pressure blasts of frigid water from a Karcher, a water cannon mounted on a police-truck roof, drenched him and the others. People near him scattered, slipping as they ran away. He saw a red flashing light as an ambulance braked to a halt near where Gaelle had fallen.

He found himself pushed and shoved under a pile of wet bodies, limbs flailing. Panicked, he tried to crawl out from under on his hands and knees, gasping for air. He couldn't see Gaelle; he couldn't see anything with water hitting his face.

Visions of his father in Warsaw's Bialoleka Prison flashed before his eyes: the dingy cell holding political prisoners, the hacking coughs of fifteen men to a cell, the vomit-tinged corners. He vowed that he'd never let himself get caught and end up in prison.

Pulling himself forward on his hands and knees, he clawed dirt and vines with his fingers. The water still pelted him; he was soaked.

He'd caused this disaster. And he couldn't stop it.

"This way," a man called, "over here."

Shaking, Krzysztof followed the voice, burrowing behind some planters. Then he was through and he straightened up behind an idling police truck and wiped his eyes. Peering around, he saw two white-coated medics lifting a stretcher on which Gaelle lay into the ambulance.

More people were crawling behind the planters, shoving the hastily erected barricades down.

He followed a police truck down an adjoining street. He ran, dodging a taxi. His thin-soled, lace-up suede boxing boots made little sound as he pounded the pavement. Sirens echoed as more police trucks approached. He turned right and almost ran into a patrol of blue-uniformed *flics* guarding the street. He ducked into an arched doorway, thankful that they hadn't seen him.

He caught his breath. Terrified, sick to his stomach, he waited. Five, ten long minutes, dripping and shivering in the humid air.

He had to salvage their campaign. To do something. They'd been sabotaged but he wouldn't let whoever did this get away with it. They had proof of the oil company's falsifications, but the evidence they'd compiled wouldn't be safe at the MondeFocus headquarters. After finding bottle bombs, the *flics* would obtain search warrants and search the office.

Who could have set them up? He pulled out his cell phone, tapped in the MondeFocus number . . . he had to warn Brigitte. There was no answer and the machine didn't pick up. She must not have returned yet from the protest at La Défense. He couldn't wait any longer. He peered out again. One of the *flics* ground out a cigarette with his foot.

If only they'd move on. He needed to safeguard the files at the MondeFocus office, and he'd have to enlist help. His mind raced. When Brigitte returned, they'd put their heads together and come up with a new plan. Tomorrow was not too late to submit their alternatives to the oil executives. And after this near riot, they would certainly get press coverage. Something could still be salvaged.

The office was close, just over the short Pont de la Tournelle, on Ile Saint-Louis. Almost where he'd started from on this disastrous evening. His jacket had half dried by the time the *flics* left to patrol the next street. He hugged the walls, crossed Boulevard Saint-Germain with his head down, then paused on the bridge leading to Quai Tournelle at the floodlit, needle-like monument of Sainte Geneviève. The Seine ran dark and viscous below.

Ahead lay a few lit windows in the Polish Foundation and he debated for a moment seeking refuge there. But his uncle would ridicule him after berating him for leaving the reception in the first place. His adrenaline had surged when he'd had to get away, and now his emotion had turned to anger. The CRS had beaten Gaelle, lied about the permit, and dispersed their march. Someone had set them up by planting bottle bombs. The blonde's face flashed in front of him. He had to be sure not only of who had betrayed them, but of why.

Krzysztof's lungs heaved as he pressed the numbers on the digicode for the office of MondeFocus. The olive green door clicked open and he ran past a wheeled shopping cart, taking the stairs two at a time as he raced up the winding staircase. The MondeFocus office door stood ajar, a slant of light illuminating the black-and-white diamond-patterned tiles of the landing.

Too late. He was too late.

He leaned against the door, his shoulders

sagging. Inside, desk drawers had been dumped on the floor, papers strewn. The floppy-disc box was empty; the copy machine that stood on a makeshift slat of lumber across two sawhorses was open. Had they gotten to the file cabinet? A brief ray of hope flickered inside him. He rooted in the drawers of the cabinet: all their vital evidence, oil platform drilling statistics, petroleum percentages, all gone.

Then he heard voices and footsteps and looked up. Brigitte, the director, burst into the office. Fine lines webbed the corners of her mouth and she looked tired, showing the age she normally managed to hide. She stopped when she saw him, surprise and fear on her face. "We heard on the radio . . . what are you doing?"

A long-haired man in overalls and a stocky woman followed behind her, carrying armfuls of leaflets. Brigitte turned and exchanged looks with the man.

"I just got here," Krzysztof said.

"Just got here?" Brigitte said. "You're rummaging in the files. How did you get in?"

He stepped back in alarm. "Someone has ransacked the office — the door was left open."

The look on Brigitte's face chilled him.

"I think you did this and now you're trying to make it look —"

"Brigitte," the woman said, stepping forward. "Give him a chance to speak."

"You think I'd do this?" He choked. "The movement's my life, you know that."

"You're a dilettante who's been hanging around here for a few weeks," Brigitte said. "A student fired up with big ideas for a peace vigil that backfired. Did you know that Gaelle's in the hospital?"

"Gaelle tried to talk to the CRS, I wanted to stop her . . ."

Brigitte shook her head. "Our coalition formed MondeFocus years ago. Since then we've done painstaking, backbreaking work, building our reputation for factual opposition to the destroyers of the environment, careful never to become involved in violence, and you've shot it all to hell in one night!"

"You have to listen to me," said Krzysztof. "The files containing the evidence were stolen."

Brigitte asked, "Why didn't you obtain the permit for the vigil?"

He nodded. "But I did . . . they revoked it."

"Then you supplied false information, didn't you? To make sure they'd revoke the permit," Brigitte said.

Where was the copy of his application? Where had he put it? He raked his pockets with shaking hands but only came up with a used Metro ticket and a few centimes. He looked at the long-haired man. "Pascal, you showed me how to apply and gave me the form to fill out. You saw the application!"

Brigitte turned to Pascal.

"Eh, get your facts straight," Pascal said, his voice charged with anger. "Giving you a form isn't seeing how you filled it out and whether you submitted it."

Krzysztof reeled at the look of doubt in Brigitte's eyes. "But I told you, they granted the permit," he said. He appealed to Pascal again. "You and I were together the day I picked up the permit at the Préfecture, Pascal. We've been sabotaged!"

"And pigs have wings. Remember the first thing I said? Get the *Préfet's* signature. Bet you didn't follow through, eh?"

He'd tried so hard, fought with his uncle, even missed his physics exam. And now Gaelle was hurt and he was being blamed for everything that had gone wrong. And if they didn't do something to find the real saboteurs, the agreement would be signed.

A man stumbled into the office, his shirt wet and bloodied. Blood dripped from his swollen nose. He stared at the mess, then his gaze settled on Krzysztof. He pointed his finger, stabbing the air. "You, you're the one!"

"Hold on, Franck, you're bleeding," Brigitte said, grabbing a first-aid kit from the items scattered on the floor.

"It's him," Franck said. "The TV crew showed me the video."

"What do you mean?" Brigitte asked.

"He carried the bottle bombs in his backpack," he said, pointing a shaking finger. "It's on film, I saw it."

Krzysztof was terror stricken. He struggled to breathe. "A blonde asked me to carry her backpack. I didn't know it held bottle bombs. She was a plant, don't you see?"

"No, I don't see," Brigitte said. "You came here as a volunteer. We have other causes you could have worked on but you've been fixated on the oil conference. Only that interested you."

Orla. He had to tell them about the information she'd promised.

"Le Pen's right wing hired you," Brigitte accused him. "They'll stop at nothing to discredit our movement. I should have suspected! You have all the hallmarks of the scum *intello* student saboteurs the right wing plants to disparage us."

Perspiration dampened his sweatshirt. "Le Pen, that fascist . . . you're calling me a saboteur?"

He banged his fist on the littered desk, sweeping papers onto the floor.

Brigitte's eyes flashed. "And as soon as you could, you headed here and ransacked the office!" She grabbed his arm.

He had to calm down. If they didn't believe him, the oil companies, led by Alstrom, the worst one, would get away, implicating him as a spy, a saboteur. "I'm sorry." He took a deep breath. "But you must believe me: we were all betrayed."

Four pairs of eyes stared at him.

"We had them dead to rights; the evidence was here, in black and white. So they sent someone to steal the files after setting me up," he told them. "If we don't find those files or get hold of Orla — who has more information — the oil companies will be able to push their agreement through. We can't fight among ourselves; we have to act against them before it's too late."

Instead of nodding in agreement, Brigitte reached for the phone. "You stole the files. You've worked things perfectly so the agreement can't be stopped," she said. She picked up the receiver and dialed 18. "You can tell your story to the *flics* when they arrive."

His pulse raced. He'd been framed but they wouldn't believe him. He was cornered. He made his feet move, backed out the door, and ran down the stairs.

MONDAY MIDNIGHT

Aimée pushed open the gleaming green door of the *Chambre Professionelle des Artisans Boulanger-Pâtissiers,* the bakers' union and academy, and rushed past bread sculptures, ancient kneading tables, and a turn-of-the-century wooden bread cart in the foyer. Woodcuts of bread ovens lined the walls. The door clicked shut behind her. Now if she could just . . . The door buzzer sounded and she jumped. Her hands trembled. To get in, you had to know the door code, like she did; few buzzed unannounced at night. The buzzer sounded again, echoing off the stone-paved foyer. She leaned down, trying to catch a glimpse of the person who was buzzing for admittance through the crack in the four-hundred-plus-year-old door. But no one was visible in the dim sodium yellow of the streetlight. A car engine started, and she heard the motor idling on the quai. She hoped it was the person who had followed her, about to drive away. Then a muffled cough came from right outside the door. She had to hurry and get out of here.

Pungent warm yeast smells filled her lungs. In the rear, she saw a group of men in the kitchen wearing white cooks' shirts buttoned on the side, like a culinary military uniform, she always thought. Indeed, the baking master ran the academy with precision rivaling the nearby Arsenal's cavalry exercises.

A row of bullet-like moist white baguettes sat on the marble kneading table, poised for insertion into the wall oven.

"Escaped again, eh?" Montard asked, measuring cup in hand, his wide brow and flushed face beaded with perspiration.

The buzzer sounded again. Montard shot a look over his flour-dusted shoulder. "Another man who wouldn't take no for an answer? This one's persistent."

She'd used the academy's back exit before. It came in handy when a date turned sour. She shrugged, sticking her shaking hands in her pockets.

"The espresso is on me, Montard."

"Someday . . . you're always asleep when I'm working."

The oven timer beeped and Montard

sprang into position, reaching with a long wooden paddle to hoist the baked loaves onto cooling trays. She walked past the industrial-sized aluminum mixer and hundred-kilogram sacks of flour and bins of Maldon sea salt to open the fire exit door. Threading her way through the courtyard, past a dormant rose trellis and hedges winding by an old well, she emerged by her own courtyard's old carriage house. She paused until she was sure that no one was following her. Shining her penlight in the corners, she checked her courtyard again. And then trudged upstairs. In her apartment bedroom, René, his sleeves rolled up, sat on the floor working on his laptop. The baby cooed on the duvet.

She pulled the gauze draperies aside and peered out the window. Shadows wavered on the quai below.

"Someone followed me."

"So you led them here?"

She pulled a crisp, warm baguette from her pocket. "I took a minor detour at the baker's."

She needed a cigarette. Too bad she'd stopped smoking last week. Again.

"Did the mother call yet?" she asked.

René shook his head, grabbed the nub end of the baguette, and chewed while he scanned the computer screen. His flexed his toes in their black silk socks. "You might want to put the tabs right."

Curious, she sat next to him cross-legged, scanning the report displayed on the screen of the laptop, and asked, "Didn't I?"

"The diaper tabs." He pulled the blanket away to show her the cooing baby's legs.

She stared at the now properly arranged diaper.

"You put the diaper on backward," René said.

A kitchen towel wreathed the baby's neck like a bib. Aimée's large lime bath towel propped her on her side.

"I checked with my friend, a pediatric intern. He said it's better for their digestion for them to lie like that. I'd say she's ten days to two weeks old."

Surprised, she bent forward, scanning the baby's face.

"How can you tell?"

He shrugged. "See." He lifted some sheets of paper covered with blurred black-and-white images. "He faxed these photos of umbilical cords from his textbook. And told me to check the soft crevice on her head, the fontanel. It's much too early for it to close so don't drop her on her head."

René pulled on a corner of the blanket

and the baby stiffened, her arms shooting out, fists clenched.

Like a fit, or a convulsion. Aimée's mind raced ahead to the emergency room, huddled doctors, forms to fill out. Inconvenient questions.

"What's the matter?" she asked, worried.

René thumbed through the faxed pages.

"Let's see, I read about it . . . here, it's a Moro reflex, it says here. It's normal. If she didn't have reflexes then you would worry."

"How can you — ?"

"Stroke the sole of her foot," he interrupted. "From heel to toe."

She brushed her fingers across the warm foot. The baby's toes flared upward and then her foot curled inward like a wrinkled peach.

"Eh *voilà,* the plantar reflex," he said. "They're just little bundles of reflexes when they're not poop machines. My friend said they even have an *en garde* fencing reflex."

She stared, amazed. There was so much to know. And it was such a responsibility.

"Notice her perfectly shaped head?" The baby's nose crinkled in a yawn and her eyelids lowered, and a moment later they heard her little snores of sleep.

Every baby was cute, she thought.

"They don't all come out like that, my

friend said. Probably a C-section."

René put the faxed sheets down on the parquet floor.

"How do you know you were being followed?" He didn't wait for her answer and shook his head. "It's your overactive imagination as usual."

"I didn't imagine a tire iron!" she said. "Or ruin a good pair of silk Chantal Thomas stockings for fun. Hold on, I've got to change." She went into the bathroom, peeled off her shredded stockings, and wiggled out of the Chanel. By the time she rejoined René, she'd put on leggings and a denim shirt.

"It doesn't make sense, René, unless someone's watching for her outside."

"What do you mean?"

She told him about the shuttered garage, the figure with the tire iron chasing her across Place Bayre.

René's eyes widened.

"That's why the mother hasn't come back — she's afraid." She paused. "Or more than afraid. She may be injured. Or worse."

"Call the *flics*," René said.

Aimée had to make him understand. "I don't know how, but this woman knows me, René," she said. "And I believe her; she was fearful for a reason. Would you feel better if the baby was at social services when she shows up? Then she would be hauled into jail for abandoning her infant, all because she begged me to watch the baby and I wouldn't help her for a few hours."

"Did I advise that?" He averted his eyes.

That's what he'd meant.

"I'll tell her — *non,* convince her — to speak to the *flics* once she turns up."

"But you don't know how to care for a baby."

Like she needed him to remind her!

"I'll do what I can." The rest, well . . . she stared at the phone, willing it to ring.

TUESDAY MORNING

Penetrating the fog of sleep, Krzysztof heard a long, piercing whistle. He blinked awake, panicking, grabbing at what enfolded him. The stinging welts on his back flamed. He realized he was lying inside a sleeping bag on the floor. The memory of last night's surprise attack came back: the CRS truncheons, sirens, revolving blue lights, Gaelle's blood, their group scattering. The peaceful organized march shattered. Running, escaping through the wet bushes. The ransacked MondeFocus office and Brigitte's anger and accusations.

62

Something clanged and sputtered. He inhaled the aroma of fresh-ground coffee and just-baked bread. His eyes cleared and he saw a red-haired woman sipping a soup bowl-sized *café crème* at a worn farm table. Despite the frigid air, she wore a lace halter top and torn jeans, and her feet were bare.

Now he remembered finding this safe place, a squat the others had told him about. No one would bother him here. He checked his cell phone for voice mail. Nothing. Why hadn't Orla returned his call? He'd left three messages on her phone last night.

"Coffee, Prince Charming?" The woman grinned. *La rouquine,* the redhead, they'd called her. A steam kettle boiled on the stove in the squat's industrial-sized kitchen.

He saw her blowtorch leaning against the battered Indian-style sandalwood screen. Gaelle had told him last week about this *artiste* who was sympathetic to their cause. She welded metal sculptures and could hold her wine. Last night's empty bottles filled a corner. He had seen how much she could drink before he'd passed out.

The files were gone, Gaelle was in the hospital, MondeFocus was against him. Very well, he would act on his own.

He winced as he got to his feet, still in his Levi's and half-buttoned shirt, and joined

63

her by the stove, from which heat slowly emanated. She kissed him on both cheeks and handed him a bowl. Her hands, he saw, were rough with blackened fingernails. From the blowtorch, no doubt. The squat was on the site of what used to be an old farm, now scheduled for demolition. The last farm remaining in Paris, it was the abode of artists, political types, and immigrants without papers who hid there. Like him. No one would trace him here.

"I'm late, *ma rouquine,*" he said, glancing at the salvaged train-station clock hung on the peeling plastered wall.

"Come back, Krzysztof," she said. "We'll have a long lunch."

He saw the dancing look in her gray-speckled eyes. But he had no time for that.

Krzysztof got off the Number 38 bus by the Sorbonne. The headline of *Le Parisien* read RIOT BY MONDEFOCUS AT L'INSTITUT DU MONDE ARABE OIL CONFERENCE: TWENTY JAILED. He took a deep breath; if he hadn't known what to do before, he knew now.

His student ID folded in his back pants pocket, he walked between the pillars of the entry gate and hurried up the wide stone staircase to the library. The wood-vaulted reading room smelled of age — antique mahogany had warped with time and the walnut oil that had been rubbed into it for years had given the wood a rich patina. Krzysztof eyed the room, which was covered floor to ceiling with books but vacant except for a few older scholarly types bent over their work. Most of his fellow students were attending lectures.

He had to find proof. The proof that had been stolen from the MondeFocus office.

The librarian took his ID and he sat down at a computer terminal. He logged on using "Sophocles," the user ID and password of a philosophy professor that he'd found taped under the desktop in a deserted office last week at noontime. It was so easy to steal passwords and IDs. Krzysztof imagined that professor abhorred computers and preferred contemplating his navel, as did most of the tenured staff.

Last week he'd accessed Alstrom's Web site. Alstrom was the oil conference's major sponsor. Their external site displayed nothing but blatant propaganda about how their oil exploration enriched the world. Enriched their pockets, more likely.

Now he was going to try the site of Regnault, Alstrom's PR firm. Operational files might contain telltale documents under a code or project name. He'd seen parts of environmental reports that had been withheld from the media, suppressed. And they'd made him sick.

He logged into a privileged user account and told the system to add a new user, Sophocles. So far, so good.

Ready for the plunge, he logged into Regnault with Sophocles. If Alstrom had bribed ministers to overlook discrepancies in its environmental reports and he could find evidence of this, he could salvage their protest and stop the execution of the proposed agreement.

His fingers tensed on the keyboard, feeling that particular rush, the crackle of expectation. In seven keystrokes he'd be inside Regnault's network, scanning their operational documents. They'd never know their system had been infiltrated. Nine out of ten times they didn't recheck privileged user accounts or monitor their firewall.

But a message flashed on the screen: *If you read this, you're dead.*

Krzysztof froze. Someone was on to him. Or . . . ?

He logged off and grabbed his hooded sweatshirt. He kept his head down, grabbed his ID, and passed through the turnstile before the librarian turned her head.

Tuesday Morning

Aimée stared at the clock. It was 6:00 a.m. Still no word, no call from the baby's mother. The dried blood on the baby bag, the figure who had chased her in Place Bayre — these thoughts had kept her up half the night. Yet the responsibility for this small human terrified her most of all.

Streaks of an apricot dawn sky filtered in through the tall window, showing her vintage Chanel, now filthy, hanging from the armoire door. She envisioned the dry cleaner, hand on her hip, rolling her eyes, saying, "Miracles, Mademoiselle, cost more." Reports were stacked on the desk, talcum powder dusted the duvet. All night she'd listened, alert to the breathing of the sleeping baby beside her, afraid at every hiccup that it would stop.

For a moment she imagined the room strewn with baby-care manuals, plush toys, dirty diapers, and a fine spray of pureed carrots decorating the cream *moiré* wallpaper. And herself, with sleep-deprived eyes and a misbuttoned sweater dotted with spit-up, like the bookstore owner's wife around the corner who had three young children.

Next to her on the duvet, a little fist brushed her arm. The phone receiver stared her in the face. She had a business to run: a client meeting to attend, office rent to pay, and the sinking feeling she'd run out of diapers.

The phone rang. She picked it up on the first ring.

"*Oui?*"

"You sorted things out, right?" René said. "Had a good sleep?"

"Snatched an hour or two, René."

The sound of a coffee grinder whirred in the background, a kettle hissed.

"You mean . . . the baby's still there?" René asked. "Are you all right?"

She rubbed her eyes, torn between alternatives. She didn't know what to do.

"I'm fine," she said.

The coffee grinder sputtered to a halt.

"You know, and I know, that you're an innocent party, Aimée," he said. "But you could be accused of kidnapping."

"Me, René?" she asked. "Her mother asked me to keep her for a couple of hours."

"Don't wait to read about a missing or kidnapped baby in this morning's paper. It's time you called Brigade de Protection des Mineurs, the child protective services," René said, his voice rising. "You don't know what's going on. The longer you keep her . . . well, why get yourself in trouble?"

She gazed at the baby's fingers, so small, curled around hers. She stroked the velvet fuzz on the baby's head, like the skin of a peach. All night she'd racked her brain, trying to figure out who the mother could be and how she knew Aimée and had gotten her phone number.

René made sense. But she couldn't send the baby away. Not yet. The woman had been in fear for her life and for the baby's; she hadn't even diapered her infant. Aimée knew she had to give the woman more time.

"She knows me, René, and she'll be back," Aimée assured him, wishing she felt as certain as she sounded.

"You'll have to wing the Regnault meeting on your own, Aimée. Can you manage?"

"What?"

"I'm off to Fontainebleau," he said. "The client likes the proposal but has questions to be answered before they sign a contract. This morning. You know how skittish they've been."

A big, fat contract, too, if he could seal the deal.

"Don't worry, I'll think of something."

There was a pause.

"Think of the baby. The mother could be in jail, or on the run. Or . . . gone."

She heard a *thupt* from a gas burner.

"Hasn't that crossed your mind, Aimée?"

Just all night long.

"Promise me you'll call child protective services."

"I'll take care of it, René." She hung up.

In the stark daylight his words made sense. She should call the agency. Go through proper channels. But visions of a dreary nursery, short-staffed like all government institutions, filled her mind. Crowded, babies crying, indifferent social workers and judges and reams of bureaucratic red tape. She couldn't bring herself to turn this tiny mite over to them.

Dulcet tones came from the covers. The little mouth was smiling like a cherub. Aimée lifted her arms up to tickle her and the yellow shirt rose on her birdcage chest. Bluish marks showed by a fold of skin under her armpit. Bruises. An awful thought struck her: this newborn might have been mistreated. Had an abusive mother abandoned her child, thrusting her into Aimée's care? René was right. She was an idiot; she should have checked the baby more closely last night. Come to think of it why hadn't René noticed?

Sick to her stomach, she peered closer. What she had thought were bruises — blue marks — looked more like scribbling with a pen. She could make out letters and numbers, a part of a word — *"ing"* — a name? Then *"2/12,"* part of a date? Odd. The mother hadn't had the time to diaper her, yet she'd written. . . .

She grabbed the first thing she saw on her bedside table — a chocolate-brown lip-liner pencil — and copied into her checkbook the letters and digits she could make out.

The fax machine groaned as a page began to emerge from her machine. *Due to scheduling conflicts, the Regnault meeting has been moved up to 8:00 a.m. Please bring the programming reports. Nadia Deloup, secretary.*

Aimée thanked God she'd downloaded them last night. She glanced at the old clock and panicked. She had an hour. There was only one person she could call on.

"You do need help," Michou said. He pulled off his red wig, stepped out of a sequined sheath, and hung it on a hanger under plastic. "You don't know the first thing about them, do you?" He rolled his mascaraed eyes. "Sealing a diaper with packaging tape?"

She'd ruined three diapers and ended up taping one together.

Michou, René's transvestite neighbor,

stepped out of his pantyhose and into sweats. "You said it was an emergency so I came straight from the club." He slathered his face with cold cream, using a counterclockwise motion. "I won't be a minute."

"Does Viard know about your maternal talents, Michou?" He and Viard, the crime-lab head Aimée had introduced him to, had been together for eight months . . . a milestone for both of them.

"Every man wants Paul Bocuse in the kitchen, Mother Teresa to care for his children, and a whore in the bedroom."

No wonder she had no man. "What kind of dinosaurs think like that?"

"Not that we get it." He grinned. His face wiped clean, Michou reared back in horror. "What did you do to this formula? It's like cement, *nom de Dieu!*"

Aimée rubbed her eyes. "I was up all night, Michou, watching her, afraid she'd stop breathing. I couldn't figure out that damn diaper. And this formula . . ." She shrugged. "You get it in and it comes right up again."

Michou patted Aimée's arm. "You need some coffee."

Aimée showered, slicked back her hair, hoped that concealer would cover the rings

72

under her eyes, then rimmed her lids with kohl. She slid into her pinstriped suit, a Dior from a consignment shop, and picked up the daily *Le Parisien* from outside her door.

In the kitchen Michou hummed, hot milk frothing on the stove as he held the baby in his arms. Rays of sun haloed the baby's head. Through the open window, Aimée saw sunlight glinting on the Seine, a tow barge gliding under the Pont de Sully's stone supports. Another warm day. She scanned the quai for someone surveilling the apartment but saw no one lingering behind the plane trees or the stone wall. Just the man she recognized from the first floor walking his dog, a plumber's truck idling out front. A morning on the Ile Saint-Louis, like any other. No sign of a stalker.

Michou stroked the baby's cheek. "Notice how she turns toward my finger — she's 'rooting.' " He placed the bottle between her lips and she sucked. "*Voilà,* she's a pro! Tilt the bottle up so the formula fills the nipple, otherwise . . ."

"Some kind of baby voodoo, Michou?"

"I'm serious, air's the enemy," he said. "If air gets in, she gets gas. Gas you don't want."

"*Merci,* Michou, you're a lifesaver."

"Such a little beauty, Aimée."

She was.

He looked at her. "So she's on loan, to see if you want to order a model?"

"Do I look the type?" Aimée gave him a brief version of how she had gotten the baby.

"*Et alors,* the minute the mother calls, I'll let you know," he assured her, rocking the baby, blowing air on her toes, eliciting a gurgle.

"You have the touch, Michou." Some people were born with it . . . a woman's touch, a maternal side.

"Maybe you do, too, Aimée." He gave a knowing wink. "It comes with practice."

"They should come with instruction booklets . . ."

"Like your computer? If only it were that easy," he said. He grimaced at her chipped lacquered nails. "If you waited long enough for your nails to dry properly, they wouldn't chip like that."

As if she had time. She was lucky when she could grab a manicure at all. Still . . . "Gigabyte green, Michou, it's the new color."

"*Quel horreur.* Without that, you're naked, Aimée." He pointed to the tube of Chanel Stop Traffic Red on the counter.

As she wiped the lipstick over her lips, she

checked *Le Parisien* for a mention of an abandoned baby or of a woman being attacked on the Ile Saint-Louis. But the headline was about the MondeFocus protest erupting into a riot. The accompanying story alleged that the CRS had provoked the demonstrators. She turned to the short articles from the police blotter, but saw nothing about a woman having been assaulted or a kidnapped baby. The crime section continued on the next page. There had been incidents of purse snatching and an attack in the Châtelet Metro. Strange, nothing about . . . then she saw a short notice in the lower corner: *Body of a young woman found in the Seine by Pont de Sully near Place Bayre.*

Her hands clutched the rim of the steaming *café au lait* bowl as she read: *"Police request help in identifying a young woman, early twenties, recovered from a drain in an overflowing sewer in the Seine."*

The public was allowed into the morgue in such cases in hopes that someone could identify the victim.

Her skin prickled. She recalled the figure with the tire iron who had chased her in the Place Bayre, across from the Pont de Sully. So close by, almost outside her window.

Her cell phone trilled.

"Taxi downstairs, Mademoiselle." The meeting would start in twenty minutes.

"Go. Buy more diapers on your way back." Michou kissed her on both cheeks. "What about *bisous* for the little peach, eh?"

Aimée leaned down into the baby smell, kissed the soft cheeks, and swallowed hard. She tucked the newspaper under her arm and headed for the door, walking faster than she had to. Then she turned around, came back for the denim jacket, thrust it into her backpack in a plastic bag, and ran.

Aimée nodded to Vavin, Regnault's head of publicity, a man in his mid thirties, trim, with wide-set eyes. He was cradling a cell phone at his ear.

"*Bonjour,* Monsieur Vavin."

He flashed her a quick smile and raised a finger, indicating that he wanted her to wait a moment.

She knew his type: a harried blue-suit who traveled all the time, delegating and supervising ten publicity campaigns all running at once.

Beige carpet, beige walls, beige cabinets. He stood behind his desk. Also beige. The only personal touch was a framed photo on his desk, a smiling child on a wooden hobby horse.

Vavin clicked off his cell phone. "We've been hacked," he said, punching the thick stapled pile of computer printouts on his desk. "Our system's compromised, Mademoiselle Leduc."

"Not since last night, Monsieur Vavin. Remember, you only hired us yesterday." She opened her laptop and brought up the report on her screen, forcing herself to concentrate and ignore the article about the drowned woman she'd reread three times in the taxi. "As contracted, you hired my firm temporarily to maintain your operating system. Shall we go over what I've accomplished so far?"

If he'd hired Leduc Detective last week when she had presented the security proposal to him, instead of yesterday, the hacker would have been foiled. But she thought better of pointing this out.

"You can see from these results, it's running smoothly. The system is secure." She smiled. "For now."

He studied her screen and calmed down. "Excellent, Mademoiselle. I like the way you've streamlined user functions and smoothed out the glitches in the interface. You're as good as you claim. A small independent security firm like yours is what we need right now."

She decided to seize the opportunity to reoffer the comprehensive security design he'd hedged about committing to the previous week.

"My firm found vulnerabilities in your system during our comprehensive security overview. We did a minor patch last night. With hackers, you can close the door but they'll look for an open window. In our proposal we noted that . . ."

"We pay you to keep them out." He gave her a tired smile.

He wanted a finger to plug a hole in the dike but sooner or later it wouldn't be able to hold back the flood.

"As outlined in our proposal, your system has numerous flaws and we recommend stronger firewall protection." She paused for effect, consulting the file in her hand, which she'd memorized. "My report shows that twice last month hackers took advantage of your vulnerability. It's not in your interest or ours to apply Band-Aids to an old system."

"Correct," he said. "But my manager's overwhelmed. I put your proposal on his desk but he was off to Johannesburg. This year our accounts have tripled. And, as with many companies enjoying a growth spurt, our auditing and computer services have been neglected."

"I suggest you start fresh."

"In the meantime, Mademoiselle Leduc, we need to operate and keep our systems functioning and secure."

She turned to the window overlooking the Jardin des Plantes, the botanical garden, while she thought. A few protesters with banners reading STOP OIL DUMPING stood on the pavement below, fanning themselves in the heat. She wondered why there were protesters in front of Regnault.

"I'm not up to speed on your client accounts yet but . . ."

He noticed her gaze, shrugged. "The environmentalists don't understand. Our premier oil company account is Alstrom. They have recently acquired some small companies that have ignored regulations. But Alstrom has already taken steps to cure these infractions."

Typical spin from a PR man. She thought back to the article about the MondeFocus riots in *Le Parisien.*

"From what I understand about the MondeFocus allegations —"

"All blown out of proportion." His eyes snapped. "They jump on any bandwagon, smear 'the big, bad corporations.' Uncalled for. They've targeted us, not knowing our client is already cleaning up toxic waste. They're misinformed — that's putting it in polite terms." He shook his head. "Look, I'm progressive, so's our firm and those we represent. Bottom line, my firm's integrity means more to me than a huge contract. I've got a family and like every parent I want my child to grow up in a clean world. Believe me, pollution's a great concern to all of us."

His intercom buzzed and he glanced at his watch. "Excuse me, I've got a meeting."

She smiled and tried once more. "Our joint package of security and system administration makes economic sense for you."

Vavin reached in his drawer. "Right now I need you to continue maintaining our systems." He slid a new addendum extending their contract across the desk. "Our sysadmin's been hospitalized with acute appendicitis and we've lost two of the contract staff to a crisis in Milan. Count on me to recommend your comprehensive package to my manager when he returns."

One didn't say no to a client. Especially one with *this* much potential. Better more work than no work, René would say. She scanned the contract, signed it, and shut down her laptop.

"Last week, when we met," Vavin said, his

voice lowered, "I didn't realize the ongoing nature of our system issues." He flipped open a file, studied it. "A few areas . . . well, they concern me."

Of course, he wanted to look good to his boss, to appear to be on top of his projects. Or was there something else she couldn't put her finger on?

"Do you foresee more problems, Monsieur Vavin?"

Nadia, his assistant, peered around the door and smiled at Aimée. "Your car's here, Monsieur Vavin."

"*Merci,* Nadia," he said. Then he turned to Aimée.

"In our line of work, we call them issues, Mademoiselle."

Aimée nodded. She noticed a stack of environmental reports, pamphlets bearing the MondeFocus logo by his key ring and briefcase.

Before she could ask him if he had studied them, he'd put on his coat, dropping his key ring into a pocket, and shouldered his case. Pausing at the door, he said, "Mademoiselle Leduc, I appreciate your help but there is one more thing. Any problems, you deal only with me."

She detected something behind his words. "Of course, Monsieur Vavin."

As a system administrator, their firm would monitor Regnault's network, deal with glitches in the staff's computers, but rarely, if ever, would this involve the managerial staff. His request was strange. Unless Vavin was watching his back.

"Only me, *comprends?*" he repeated.

Outside, Aimée stared at the khaki-colored Seine lapping against the mossy stone. Two years ago, a *clochard* — now termed *sans domicile fixe* (SDF) — the politically correct phrase for "homeless" — who'd slept under a bridge had fallen in, his foot catching in the branches of a tree carried on the swollen water. The current had swept his bloated body past her window. She shivered. More often corpses sank, drifting along with the bottom currents until they were caught in the locks downriver at Sceaux.

She ran her fingers over the stone wall fronting the L'Institut médico-légal's brick facade, *Le Parisien* under her arm, her laptop case slung over her shoulder. She had a bad feeling in her bones.

She wondered if the young woman found in the Seine might be the baby's mother. Her father always said, Think like the criminal, find the motive. If that didn't work, go with the victim. Retrace her steps.

In this case, she imagined a young woman looking over her shoulder, seeing the light in Aimée's window, trusting Aimée to keep her baby safe. Safe from whom and what, she had no clue. And how had the woman known her name and phone number?

Aimée tried to think the way she must have. Scared, running away from someone, something, she sees light, finds the digicode broken, as it had been for a week, and enters the town house through the front door. Before she can go upstairs, she hears noises; someone's followed her. Quickly, she takes off her denim jacket — now she looks different. She wraps the baby in it. She runs through the courtyard, sees the garage, which is open late, and uses the pay phone to tell Aimée that the baby's downstairs. Then she runs to the Place Bayre.

But the attacker has recognized her. Did they have a confrontation on the quai? Was he the father of the baby, demanding his child?

Questions . . . all she had were questions.

To her right, the Ile Saint-Louis glimmered in the weak sun. Her apartment stood past the curve of the quai. She turned to face the rose-brick médico-légal building.

If she didn't check out her hunch, she'd

kick herself later. She hated this place — the odors of body fluids that were hosed down the drains in the back courtyard, the miasma of misery and indifference surrounding the unclaimed corpses. She couldn't forget identifying her father's charred remains after the explosion in Place Vendôme as the bored attendant scratched his neck and checked his watch, as her tears had dropped into the aluminum trough by her father's blackened, twisted fingers.

She took a deep breath and opened the morgue door.

Aimée stood alone in the green-tiled viewing cubicle of the morgue basement. On the other side of the window lay a young waxen-faced corpse, a white sheet folded down to her neck, livid stains appeared on the skin of her cheek and neck, but Aimée could see that her eyes were deep set and her cheekbones were prominent. Unforgiving, stark white light bathed her features; there was a bruise on her temple, a mole on her chin, and she had straw blond hair that hadn't been completely combed back, falling in greasy strands over her temple. Her partly visible ear showed raw, jagged edges and there was a frothy blood bubble on her neck. Weren't they supposed to clean up the corpse to protect the family's feelings?

Aimée didn't recognize her. She'd had a hunch, but she'd been wrong. Why had she expected a corpse to sit up and talk, to give her a clue to the baby's identity? Nothing tied them together.

"I'm sorry," Aimée whispered, her breath fogging on the glass, "whoever you are."

The door opened and she heard shuffling footsteps behind her. A blue-uniformed *flic* from whom the telltale aroma of Vicks emanated — used by new recruits to combat the odor — approached her.

"Mademoiselle, can you identify the victim?"

"I am so sorry but I can't help you."

A young man in a zip-up sweatshirt, brown hair curling behind his ears, edged into the room.

"Then if you'll follow me, Mademoiselle, I'll see you out," the *flic* said.

She turned to leave, heard a small gasp, and saw the man clap his hand over his mouth.

"Monsieur, do you recognize the victim?" the *flic* asked.

He shook his head, looking away. He had a copy of Le Parisien in his back pocket.

"You seem upset," the *flic* said, gauging his reaction.

"It's unnerving to see a dead person," he replied.

Aimée followed the *flic* but not before she noted that the man had recognized the corpse.

"Mademoiselle, this way please," the *flic* said, hurrying her past several other sad-eyed people standing in the hallway.

Aimée inquired at three offices before she found Serge Leaud in the morgue foyer, which was lined with busts of medical pioneers, talking with a group of white-coated technicians. She hated bothering Serge, her friend as well as a medical pathologist, but she had to clear up the nagging doubt she felt. "What if?" kept running through her brain. She had to find out if the woman had recently given birth. She caught Serge's eye, mouthed, "Please." And waited.

Serge shifted from foot to foot, his gaze flitting from her to his colleagues, one hand in the pocket of his lab coat, the other stroking his black beard. A moment later, he excused himself and joined her.

No customary kiss on the cheek greeted her; instead, he displayed a harried frown.

"The chief's here and my blood-screen panel's waiting," he said. "I've only got a minute, Aimée."

"Can you show me an autopsy report, Serge," Aimée said, lowering her voice, "for the young woman found in the Seine by Pont de Sully."

Serge nodded to a white-coated staff member who passed them.

"Let's talk over there." He jerked his thumb toward the corner. "You mean for the Yvette?"

She knew that was what they called all unidentified female corpses.

She nodded.

"I'm not supposed to do this, Aimée."

"Help me out," she said, "and we'll call it quits."

He owed her. His mother-in-law and wife both down with *grippe,* Serge tied up at work, and no Sunday babysitter available, she'd answered his plea and agreed to take his toddler twin boys to the Vincennes Zoo. The highlight of the day had been the ride on the Metro, and the twins, fascinated with trains, had refused to leave the station. The afternoon was spent greeting trains and saying good-bye to every engine. She'd finally bribed them with Mentos to go home. She'd been exhausted, wondering how his wife coped every day.

"The autopsy's later this afternoon," Serge

said. *"Désolé."*

First she felt disappointment, then relief. Of course, the baby's real mother was alive and would return; she might be at Aimée's now. Yet Michou would have called if she had turned up. A prickling sense that it all connected troubled her.

"No ID, and waterlogged fingerprints."

"Was the skin on the hand so sloughed off she'll need the 'treatment'?"

Serge shrugged.

She knew the treatment, a technique used on waterlogged corpses that consisted of slicing the wrist to peel back the skin of the hand so the technician, inserting his own gloved hand inside the skin, could exert sufficient pressure for a print. Gruesome.

"It's a hard call," Serge said. "Creatures have nibbled on the fingertips and there are injuries on the hand from the buffeting of the waves. We'll inject saline for the soft tissue pads to plump them out. And if we're lucky, we'll get prints."

He shook his head. "A sad case, I'd say." He pulled a sheaf of papers from his pocket. "I have a prelim report. It indicates suicide. So young." His brow furrowed as he thumbed through the pages. He flipped one over and read on.

"But the bruise I saw on her temple might

mean she was attacked," Aimée said.

"It could have been caused by contact with the stone bank after she hit the water."

"And the blood froth?"

"I'd say blood pooling in the ear first, associated with drainage. Or feasting by the river creatures."

Aimée suppressed a shudder.

"You mean they showed that side because . . ."

"The other side was worse." Serge exhaled. "The river squad, well . . ." he paused. "Let's say the turbulent current and sewer grate against which she'd lodged made it difficult to pull her out."

He shook his head again. "I've seen it before. *Suicide d'amour,* a love affair gone wrong, depression. No one to talk to." Serge read further. "Where was her mother, her aunt? That's what's so sad. She's like any twenty-something you see on the street: lace camisole, espadrilles, jeans."

Her ears pricked up. "Jeans? What kind?"

"Hmmm . . . Lick, some designer brand my wife wears."

"That's all?"

He riffled through the pages of the preliminary report. "It says here that she wore earrings . . . beaded. No, my mistake. No beads on the earrings, sorry. Blue beads were embroidered on the jean cuffs."

Like the ones on the denim jacket? Aimée's pulse raced. There it was, the link she had sensed.

"Look, Aimée, I've done you a favor, and I haven't asked you any questions, but what's this woman to you?"

"A baby was left in my courtyard. Someone called me and begged me to protect her." She pulled the plastic bag from her backpack. "Look, Serge, this denim jacket is embroidered with blue beads; it was wrapped around the baby."

Serge stared. *"Et alors?"*

She controlled her apprehension. "What if these beads match the ones on the cuffs of the jeans?"

Serge's beeper, pinned to the lapel of his white lab coat, vibrated.

"Can't you check, Serge?"

"Aimée, you're asking me to wade in deep water for a few beads," he said. "And I'm late."

"If the beads don't match, no one will be the wiser," she said. "But if they do . . ."

"Why would I stick my neck out?"

Feelings in her bones didn't count with the *flics*. She couldn't involve them until she knew positively that the beads were identical.

"Ballet tickets, Serge. Opening night. Isn't your anniversary coming up?"

His wife loved ballet.

"Eh? You could get tickets?"

With enough francs and her friend at the FNAC ticket office, she could. She nodded. Across the foyer she saw the *mec* she'd noticed in the viewing cubicle mounting the stairs, then entering the restroom. She had to talk to him.

"You'll inform me of the autopsy findings when you get them, Serge?"

He took the plastic bag with the denim jacket from her. Nodded.

"Of course, you'll babysit the twins," Serge said. "We'd make an evening of it, dinner . . ."

"Don't press your luck, Serge."

Below the stern gaze of Pasteur, Aimée tapped her fingers on the blue plastic chair. She'd checked with Michou; still no word. She was waiting to question the *mec,* who she could have sworn had recognized the corpse. The woman might have been the baby's mother.

She'd formulated her questions by the time he emerged from the restroom.

Typical student attire: Levi's, hooded sweatshirt. He had a thin face with a jutting jaw, sharp nose, and sallow complexion. A crowd of blue-uniformed *flics* paused in the foyer, blocking her view, and by the time they'd moved on, he was gone.

Hurry, she had to hurry, to catch him before he reached the Metro or hopped on a bus and disappeared.

She saw him, already half a block ahead of her, crossing Pont Morland, and she ran to catch up with him. Below her, the anchored houseboats creaked, shifting in the rising Seine. She finally drew level with him, gravel crunching under her heels, two blocks further on, on Quai Henri IV.

"Excuse me, I need to speak with you," Aimée said, gasping for breath.

His eyes darted behind her as he fussed with the zipper of his hooded jacket. Eyes that were red rimmed and bloodshot. Had he been crying?

"Why?"

"I'm sorry but in the morgue —"

"Who are you?" He shifted his feet.

Young, no more than twenty, she thought. "Aimée Leduc," she introduced herself. "Did you know . . . the victim?"

"Know her?" He averted his face. "My cousin's missing, but that wasn't her." His agitation was noticeable as he zipped and unzipped his sweatshirt. There was a slight compression of syllables at the ends of his words. Was he a foreign student perhaps?

"You saw the article in the paper. Are you sure this woman wasn't your cousin?"

He backed away. "Yes."

She handed him her card.

" 'Leduc Detective, Computer Security'?" He stiffened. "What do you want?"

"Didn't you recognize her?"

"As I told the *flic*, I didn't know her."

"*Non*, you said your cousin was missing."

And she even doubted that. She wished he'd stand still. A bundle of nerves, this one.

"Please, I'm not a *flic*, but I need to establish her identity. It's vital."

He broke into a run. She sprinted and finally caught him by his sleeve. Ahead, an old man scattered bread crumbs to a flock of seagulls by the *bouquiniste*, the old secondhand bookseller's stand.

"Maybe I can help you," she said, panting and clutching his arm.

"A computer detective can help me with what?"

He pulled away, knocking her shoulder bag to the ground. The papers in the Regnault file spilled onto the pavement.

"Sorry. Look, I'm in a hurry." He bent down, picked them up, and then stared at the pages he held, before slowly handing them back to her.

She caught his sleeve before he could take off again.

"If you're illegal, that's not my business. But if you know her identity, that is my business."

Instead of showing fear at the intimation that he might be an illegal immigrant, he bristled. "I'm an *émigré;* I have been granted political asylum. But the manipulations of ministries and business here are just as bad as it was under the Communists. You call this a corporate economy, but it's all the same."

What was with the political jargon? Though he had a point.

"Tell me her name, tell me where she lived."

A bus crossed Pont de Sully, slowing into the bustop on their right.

"I don't know what you mean."

How could she reach this stubborn kid? She wanted to grab him by the shoulders and shake him. Two nearby matrons holding shopping bags paused in their conversation and moved away from her.

She stepped closer to him, so close she could see small beads of perspiration on his brow.

"You work for them! I've seen the names in your papers," he accused her. And he took off, jumping into the rear door of the bus before it took off.

Them? Regnault? What was going on? He knew something. But she couldn't chase him on the bus. She had another idea. He wouldn't get away so easily next time.

Back at the morgue, Aimée spoke to an older man with a handlebar mustache who sat at the reception center. Behind him were shelves of files and a barred cage in which a bright green parrot perched. Since the morgue's reception floor wasn't a sterile environment and due to Ravic's seniority he managed to bring his feathered pride and joy to work. "*Ça va,* Ravic?" she asked. "Pirandello got any new languages under his beak?"

Ravic grinned. "Esperanto — he took to it like his mother tongue."

His claw-footed wonder had won prizes, even talked on an RTL radio pet show once.

"Do me a favor, Ravic. Let me see the visitors' log."

"Eh? Didn't you sign in?"

Of course she had; she'd had to show her ID. The student would have done so, too.

She leaned closer over the chipped Formica counter. "It's embarrassing. I just saw an old friend, but I've forgotten his name."

Ravic, one of her father's old poker crowd, smoothed his mustache between his thumb and forefinger. "Regulations, Mademoiselle Aimée. I can't."

"Of course, I understand. But you could just slide the book across." She flashed a big smile, lowering her voice. "We're meeting for coffee and I feel stupid."

"A chip off the old block, like they say," he said. "I'd like to, eh, but I'm sorry."

Ravic had aged little in the five years since she'd last seen him. She wondered how her father would have looked, had he lived.

"If I let you, everyone else and their mothers will want to . . ."

"Ravic, no one has to know." She grinned, wishing he'd relent. A line had formed behind her; someone cleared his throat. "Just turn the log a little more to the right so I can read his name. That's all."

He glanced over his shoulder. "For old time's sake then." Ravic slid the register in front of her. There was a blue scrawl under her signature but it was undecipherable.

She thought hard. She'd shown her ID; he would have had to do so as well.

"Ravic, it's not legible," she said. "Remember anything from his ID?"

"A student card, that's all," he said. "I'm sorry, Mademoiselle Aimée." He raised his hand to beckon to the person in line behind her.

She had to persist, couldn't leave without something. Ravic had been a formidable poker player; he always remembered all the cards that had been played.

"You need to see an ID with an address," she said. "Remember anything from this one?"

He scratched his cheek. "Polish?" Then he shook his head. "I'm not sure. So many people came today."

"That looks like an L at the beginning and it ends with an I," she persisted.

"Maybe it's a Polish name," he said.

She took a guess. "Lives near the Sorbonne or he used to."

"That's right. Rue d'Ulm." He grinned. "My wife's father worked on rue d'Ulm, I remembered thinking that."

She pointed to the scrawl. "Look again, Ravic. Does anything jog your memory?"

He shrugged. She heard shuffling. A long line stretched behind her now. He didn't remember. Disappointed, she turned as an irritated woman edged in front of her.

"Aha . . . that actress," Ravic said. "Sounded like that actress."

She paused and looked back. "Which actress . . . You said it sounded Polish."

"Rhymes with Nastassja Kinski."

"You mean Linski?"

He winked. "Got it in one."

Krzysztof Linski was the name she'd found listed in the phone directory at an address on rue d'Ulm. He lived in a sand-colored stone building near the Panthéon, a few doors down from the Institut Curie and the Lebanese Maronite Church. The ground floor contained a bar/pub with posters advertising heavy metal and rockadelic nights. Bordering the nearby Sorbonne, this was a student area, the Latin Quarter. The building had no elevator but there was a flight of wide red-carpeted stairs with oiled wood banisters, leading to apartments containing lawyers' and psychiatrists' offices. The staircase narrowed to bare wooden steps as it reached the sixth floor, which held a row of *chambres de bonnes,* former maids' rooms.

Typical cramped student accommodations. Hovels was more descriptive, she thought. A shared hall toilet; the odor of mildew coming from the dirt-ingrained corners. Peeling floral wallpaper illuminated by a grime-encrusted skylight that let in only a sliver of light. Dust motes drifted in it and she sneezed. The chords of an amplified electric guitar reverberated from down the hall.

She knocked on the third door. No answer. Knocked again.

"Krzysztof Linski?"

The guitar drowned out her voice, her knocks. Either Krzysztof hadn't returned yet or he was ignoring the raps on his door. His attitude had become belligerent; she doubted he'd welcome her. She'd have to convince him to trust her, open up.

The guitar stopped, someone swore. She heard footsteps below, slapping on the stairs.

A red-haired, pale-faced tall scarecrow of a *mec* edged past her and inserted a key into the lock on Krzysztof's door.

She thought fast. "So you're Krzy's roommate."

He nodded.

"I'm supposed to meet him."

He shrugged.

Unsociable, and no conversationalist. Or was he mute?

"Mind if I wait?"

"Suit yourself." He actually spoke as he started to shut the door.

"Inside?" She didn't wait for an answer.

Once she was inside she realized the

problem. The attic room wasn't much bigger than a closet. Two people standing in it would touch shoulders. She hoped the *mec* wasn't about to change his clothes.

Orange crates with slats for shelves supported piled textbooks and a Polish-French dictionary. On one side of the tiny room there was a sleeping bag crumpled on a Japanese straw futon. The *mec* stooped; still his shoulders touched the sloping wood ceiling. She could imagine him sticking his head out the skylight, like a giraffe, to breathe. A pair of black denims and a tuxedo under plastic wrapping hung from the rafters. Perhaps Krzysztof moonlighted as a waiter at fancy restaurants or catered affairs as many students did. She filed that thought away for later.

The *mec* set his backpack on the floor, sat down cross-legged, and pulled his damp sweater over his head, then started on his T-shirt.

"Sorry, I'll turn around . . ."

In answer, he pulled closed a little curtain suspended on shower hooks — like those in the sleeper compartments of trains — for privacy. His welcoming skills rivaled his conversation for charm.

The small corkboard on the opposite wall, pinned thickly with photos, ticket stubs and fliers, caught her attention. She looked closer. Photos of a demonstration, Krzysztof carrying the banner of MondeFocus, groups of young people handing out leaflets clustered around a pillar that she recalled; it belonged to the Panthéon.

No one she recognized. Another dead end. She glanced at her Tintin watch.

"Any idea when Krzysztof will get back?"

"Not anytime soon," the *mec* said from behind the curtain.

"Why's that?"

"His stuff's gone. Guess he forgot to tell you."

"But the tuxedo?"

"He hated that tuxedo."

Done a runner. Lost him. Again.

As she was about to stand up, she saw several MondeFocus pamphlets stuck halfway into a dictionary. She'd take one, get the address, and ask around for him there. She coughed to cover her actions as she slid a leaflet out.

A photo fell to the floor. A group shot of student types sitting in front of the Panthéon. And then her heart skipped a beat. She saw the dead girl — straw blonde hair, wearing jeans and a denim jacket, a serious expression on her face. Sitting next to her were Krzysztof, two other women, and two men. But the blonde girl didn't look pregnant.

The curtain was pulled back. "Jealous type, aren't you?" he said.

She thought quickly. When caught, brazen it out. And pointed to the blonde girl. "Then she *is* his girlfriend!"

"What else?"

"For me, eh, it's casual." She shrugged. "I met Krzysztof two days ago," she said, improvising. "But he owes me two hundred francs. Do you know his friends or where he hangs out?"

"You know him a day longer than me." He shrugged. "No clue."

This one was really helpful!

All the way down the stairs she thought of Krzysztof's look of recognition as he saw the dead woman's face, his reaction to the pages of the Regnault files that he'd picked up and scanned, his parting shot, "You work for *them*." It all tied together . . . but she didn't know how.

She caught the bus, sat in the rear, and turned the photo over. "Orla, Nelie, me, Brigitte, MondeFocus antinuke" was the inscription, but there was no date.

So Orla was the blonde woman in the morgue, his girlfriend, and both were involved with MondeFocus. Strange that he'd refused to identify his girlfriend. Then she wondered if the dead woman might have been the mother of his child. And why would Orla have telephoned her for help and entrusted her infant to Aimée? But now that she had the MondeFocus address, she had someplace to start.

Aimée debated calling the *flics* and dropping the information she had so far into their hands. But she knew what they'd say. No proof this Orla was the mother or Krzysztof, the father. Why wouldn't the dead woman have left the baby with Krzysztof if he was the father? She decided to postpone making any decision until she received the results of the autopsy. First she had to go shopping.

She stared at the Monoprix aisle crowded with diapers, formula, teething rings, bibs, nonirritant soap . . . endless. How could tiny babies require all this? Every package bore labels color coded to age and weight. Endless varieties of formula, including soy and lactose-free. A large display printed with symptoms and arrows cross-referenced photos of homeopathic herbs for diaper rash, floral remedies for colic, a veritable rainbow of products for ages zero to five; it resembled the duty-free brochure on an Air

France 747. Her mind balked; she was overwhelmed. Unless it was for shoes, shopping wasn't her forte.

Did it have to be this complicated, did she need to take courses? In Madagascar, women squatted by thatched huts, letting their diaperless babies do their business in the white sand, then rubbed them with coconut oil. No vast crowded Monoprix aisle for them.

Her hand brushed a booklet, *Using a Pacifier or Not . . . the Hidden Traumas.* Here was a new world, new worries . . . pacifier trauma?

She had to get a grip; it couldn't be that difficult. She looked for the newborns section, figuring the baby weighed less than five kilos, like her laptop. But she stood devastated by the array of baby wipes, scented and unscented; shampoos; vitamins. She would need hours to read the labels, to compare and match them to the baby's skin condition and digestive disposition. She didn't have that kind of time; she had work to do — a body that had been found in the Seine to identify, her security programming assignment to complete . . .

She needed a method to bring order out of confusion.

Within three minutes she'd located several

women with infants. One held a baby in a carrier across her chest, its pink knit cap with rabbit ears poking up, who looked the right size. She trailed the woman to the baby aisle. Every time the woman selected an item from the shelf and put it in her cart, Aimée followed suit.

With a full cart she stood at the cash register.

"You sure you want the night-control protection diapers for a newborn *and* for a ten-month-old?" the cashier asked with a wink. "Had them close together, eh?"

Aimée reddened. "*Oui . . . non,* I mean you can't be too careful at night."

A woman chuckled behind her in the long checkout line. She stammered *merci,* grabbed her change. Ran out and hailed a taxi, jumped in, and piled her bags on the seat.

She was late. Ahead, a snarl of buses and cars sat in midday stalled traffic. Pedestrians filled the zebra-striped crosswalks; the outdoor café tables on the sidewalks spilled over as the lunch crowd took advantage of the unexpected heat.

"Quai d'Anjou. Fifty francs extra if you skirt the traffic on rue Saint Antoine," she said, perspiration dampening her collar.

The driver grinned and hit his meter.

Ten minutes later, she set her bags down in her sun-filled kitchen, where the wonderful scent of rosemary filled the air.

"Bought out the whole baby section, have you?" Michou pulled out pureed broccoli tips, yellow squash in small jars. "Quite the organic gourmet . . . but a thing this little won't eat solids for a few months."

She was useless. She couldn't even buy the right food.

The baby cooed, wrapped in Aimée's father's soft old flannel bathrobe. Michou had improvised a bassinet from an empty computer-paper box resting on the table.

A surge of protectiveness overwhelmed Aimée. Duty — no law — required her to turn the baby over to the authorities. But the mother knew her name and had begged her not to tell the *flics*. Until the autopsy result revealed whether Orla was the baby's mother, she'd keep her and care for her.

She put the future out of her mind. She planned to monitor Regnault's system, deal with their other contracts, *and* master diapers this afternoon. She lifted the lid of the copper pot simmering on the stove, swiped her finger across the surface, and licked it. "Ratatouille!" The last time she'd used the stove had been for heating up takeout. For her, that counted as cooking.

The wavering slants of pale light pouring through the window, the aroma of *herbes de provence* perfuming the kitchen, reawakened a warm familar feeling she remembered from the deep recesses of her childhood. Good homemade food had been as much a given as breathing in her grandmother's kitchen. She recalled the hazy summer heat in her grandmother's Auvergne garden; her mother's laugh, her sun-warmed pockets filled with fragrant fresh-picked raspberries — red, glistening jewels exuding a scent that was so sweet. Her laughter as she popped them into Aimée's mouth. Her mother . . . where had that memory come from?

"Take a cooking class, Aimée."

"I'd do better to get a wife, Michou. Like you."

Michou grinned. "Try cuisine dating. It's for singles. You cook together, eat, and see if any sparks fly."

Baby products, cooking classes . . . what next? As if she had spare time after completing her job: computer security, sysadmin, and programming. Let alone time to discover why a baby had been left in her courtyard, and why the mother, if indeed it was she, was lying in the morgue.

"At least you bought diapers. That's a

start, Aimée." Michou shouldered his bag, rubbed his chin. "I need to wax my chin and iron my gown. We're playing in Deauville tonight."

She caught her breath. "Deauville? You'll be that far away?"

"The casino." He smiled. He patted her on the back. "You'll do fine. Oh, by the way, the phone rang in the middle of her bath, but when I answered they hung up."

She wondered if the mother had tried to make contact, then had hung up, scared by a man's voice answering Aimée's phone.

"Michou, did you hear voices?"

"Only in my head, *chérie*."

"Wait a minute, Michou. You answered the phone, said, *'Allô'* —"

"Common courtesy, of course," Michou interrupted, putting his wig case into his tote bag.

"Try to think, Michou. Repeat what you did and said. There could be a clue, some way to —"

"You mean like in Agatha Christie?" Michou's plucked eyebrows shot up on his forehead. "*Mais oui,* I looked out the window." He took a mincing step. "I showed *la petite* the birds nesting in the . . ."

"I mean when you answered the phone?"

"I bathed her in the kitchen sink, wrapped

her in a towel, of course, but *oui*, right here."

He took another step, gestured with wide arms to the open kitchen window. "*Allô, allô* . . . I kept saying *allô*, that's all."

From below came the churning of water, the lapping of waves against the bank as a barge passed them on the Seine.

"Michou, think back," Aimée said, trying to keep her foot from tapping. "Did you hear anything in the background? Maybe traffic, indicating the call came from a public phone, or was it quieter, like in a *resto* or from a home. . . ."

"That's why it seemed so hard to hear — it was the water."

"Water?"

"*C'est ça!*"

"You heard water like the sewers being flushed or —"

"The river."

Aimée controlled her excitement. "You're sure?"

Michou's eyes gleamed. "Over the phone, I could hear a barge whistle . . . that's right. Like someone was calling from right down-stairs."

Hope fluttered in Aimée's chest. There were no public phones on the quai down-stairs but the mother was nearby, and alive, she sensed it. She would surely make contact again.

Michou shouldered his bag.

"Don't forget, Aimée, keep the baby's umbilical stump out of the water for at least two weeks."

"But I don't know how old . . ."

"I rubbed off all those ink marks. An infant's skin is very delicate. Why in the world would anyone . . . ? But it doesn't matter. She didn't have an allergic reaction and they're gone now."

Good thing she'd copied them.

Aimée eased the pink bunny-eared hat she'd bought over the baby's fontanel. "Never too early for a fashion statement, *petite*."

"You'd like to keep her, Aimée."

She froze.

"It's written all over your face," Michou said.

"She's not mine, Michou."

He sighed. "You're becoming involved; it's impossible not to with a baby. Aimée, don't let yourself get hurt. . . ."

Of course she wouldn't. She kissed Michou on both cheeks. "You're a lifesaver, *merci*."

A tinge of color swept over Michou's cheeks. He paused. She'd never seen him tongue-tied before.

"All in a working girl's day, *chérie*."

There had been no call. Aimée rubbed her eyes, strained from monitoring Regnault's system. Boring, tiring, drudge work. Several hours of it. The most lucrative in the business. The baby, on a pillow in a hatbox on the floor, gurgled.

She entered her old student ID number on a second computer and combed the Sorbonne student directory. She accessed the administrative files using the technique a savvy friend had shown her — useful for altering grades. She accessed the personal files of all the students, then narrowed her search to *émigré*-status students with the name Linski.

Voilà. Krzysztof Linski was an engineering major. She even found his class schedule, which she downloaded. Twenty years old, born in Kraków, Poland. Member of the chess club and an above-average student. And he knew about computers.

She copied the information, put it in a file. The baby let out a bleating cry and Aimée picked her up and rocked her.

With the baby in the crook of her arm, she hunted online for Orla, a search by first name. But the program, an old one, indicated that the last name was required. No go.

At least she could contact MondeFocus and seek some answers there. She telephoned the number given on the flier but a generic recorded message was the only answer: *Sorry we missed your call. Leave a message.* Frustrated, she left her name and cell-phone number and hung up.

Right now she should be questioning the garage owners for information about the woman who had used their phone. Again she wondered why the woman hadn't called back. She stood the baby in her arms and reached for the group photo she had stolen from Linski's room. Too bad there were no last names written on the back. She sniffed as she caught a rank whiff, then gasped in horror at what leaked from the baby's diaper all over the keyboard of her computer.

As she reached for a tissue, beeping came from her computer. *Error code. GX55 flashed on the screen with respect to Regnault's system. The beeping was a counterpoint to the baby's cries. A system glitch. Perfect timing. Everything happened at once.*

Bon, Hélène thought, counting eighty-four glasses. She hadn't broken even one washing up! Her quavering hands rubbed the linen towel over the last champagne flute stem. She felt the warmth of satisfaction as she aligned the glassware in sparkling rows on the shelves just so. The Comte liked everything in order.

From the Polish Foundation's kitchen window she could look out over the manicured garden in which trellised ivy climbed the courtyard walls. She imagined last night's gala — the wax-encrusted candelabra she'd cleaned blazing with tapers, platters of hors d'oeuvres dotted with caviar she'd washed, the gowned and tuxedoed crowd milling in the high-ceilinged salon under carved gilt boiserie. Each detail to savor and recount later to her sister, Paulette.

"Hélène?"

She paused, startled. Listening, she took a deep breath. She suppressed her fear, the fear that was always with her, the fear that never went away.

"Hélène?"

Non, the voice was different, it was not the bad man. She gathered herself. "*Oui,* Monsieur le Comte?"

Comte Linski leaned on his cane, a strained smile on his gaunt face. "Please, no need for formality," he said. "I'm the *chargé d'affaires,* only a glorified watchman, you know. And I'm even too old for that now, Hélène."

Hélène folded the towel. Always too modest, the comte. "They're lucky to have a cultured man like you. A decorated war hero."

And she was lucky, too, that he asked her to work odd jobs after receptions and gave her the leftovers.

"A Polish community that's dying out and a heritage to protect; it's not an easy task." The comte went on, "If only the young generation . . . ah, that's another discussion. But I must thank you for your efforts."

She beamed, smoothing down her apron, until he held out an application form to her.

"Hélène," he said, "write down your address so I can process your paycheck."

Paperwork . . . why did people always need paperwork? She avoided all banks, forms, bureaucracy.

"*Mais,* Comte, you've always paid me in francs before. I prefer cash. I don't trust banks."

"Now I must pay you by check," he said.

"We have to protect our nonprofit status should we be audited. Just fill this out, Hélène." He set the form on the counter.

She untied her apron, folded it, backed away. No paper trail . . . never leave a way to trace her.

"I'm late, pardon," she said.

The comte's eyebrows rose.

A tall woman rushed into the kitchen and shot a withering look at Hélène. She was puffed up with self-importance, this one, Hélène knew.

"Comte, the director needs to speak with you about the Adam Mickiewicz display in the library. As he was the leading poet of Polish romanticism, the director deems it fitting that we —"

"Pardon, Hélène," the comte interrupted. "Talk to me before you leave."

Hélène nodded but she had no intention of doing so. She knew she could never come back here again. In the coatroom off the courtyard she gathered her shopping bags and put on her woolen jacket.

She paused at the glassed-in temperature-controlled storage salon, where paintings to be cataloged were stacked. She recognized the portrait in a gilt frame on the very top. A young girl on a swing, skirt trailing over the sun-dappled riverbank grass, painted by a Polish Impressionist. One of Paulette's favorites, it had hung in her family's *brocante,* once the only secondhand shop on the island.

Out on the quai, Hélène knotted her scarf over her white braids, picked up the shopping bags that held most of her earthly possessions, and tried to ignore the pangs of hunger. No leftovers this time.

Somehow she'd have to feed them.

She turned onto rue des Deux Ponts. At least the *bainsdouches municipaux* were free. And warm. Inside the white-tiled bathhouse she set her bags down. The bored middle-aged attendant listened to the weather on the radio as he handed her a key. "Take cabin three," he instructed her.

"Merci." She took a towel from the pile on a plastic chair and shouldered her bags again, ignoring the curious look that he didn't bother to hide.

She turned on the chrome shower faucets. Hot water steamed out into the warped wooden stall, which was like the one in which she and Paulette had changed their bathing suits at Dieppe. But instead of coarse sand underfoot, there was a slick tiled floor.

"I'll wash all our socks," she said. "It's so hard to keep clean where we live." She wondered how much longer they could stay there; the waters kept rising.

She undid her long white braids and pulled out the cheesecloth bag that held bits of Marseilles lavender soap. She'd saved these soap chips, like her *maman* had taught them to do during the war. Les Boches would like it if we were *all* dirty *all* during the Occupation, Maman had said, but they would save soap scraps and keep clean. So there.

"Hey, what's going on? Only one person to a stall," someone said.

She overheard the bath attendant. "She comes every week, keeps herself clean. Harmless."

Not again. Another one of those hurtful people who ignored Paulette, never even offered her a *bonjour* as they entered a shop. These days only Jean, their schoolmate before the war, exhibited any manners. Most of the others were gone. Up in smoke.

She soaped up with the cheesecloth and lathered her hair.

"Paulette, don't be afraid," she whispered. "No one will hurt you. What? The bad one? We'll never see that bad one again. *Non,* the bad one won't hit you. I won't let him push you in the river like he did the girl. I promise, Paulette."

"So go farther down. Take cabin six," the bath attendant said. "She talks to herself but she's not dangerous, believe me."

Why did people say that? Talk to herself? Not she.

"Paulette, stop that," she said. "I told you. You're fifteen now; act like it."

Clear hot water ran over Hélène's face. "*Méchant!* You are naughty, Paulette. Give me the towel. *Bon.* Eh? You're safe. How do I know? Oh, I took care of him. I had to."

Tuesday Afternoon

Aimée stared at the small bundle that was keeping her hostage in her own apartment. Her laptop had cleaned up well and apple vinegar had dispelled the odor. Wonder of wonders, it still functioned. But there were still deposits of baby spit-up dotting her father's old flannel bathrobe, the sagging bunny ears of the cap, all over. Should she feed the baby again? Or maybe it had gas? Aimée needed a step-by-step manual.

The baby flexed her pearl pink toes and unfurled her small fists. Her hiccups reverberated against Aimée's chest. Then a big burp and a sensation of warmth filling the diaper. Again.

"So that's the problem. Warn me next

time, eh?"

A gurgling stream of bubbles trailed from the side of the little mouth. "That's your answer then?"

More bubbles.

Aimée changed her, becoming increasingly efficient with the help of the aloe-scented baby wipes and Michou's detailed diaper diagram.

The group picture was burning a hole in her pocket. She needed to show this photo around, figure out the mother's movements, and why she'd left the baby. And, of course, who she was.

But Aimée was loath to take the baby outside and possibly endanger her. This tiny thing with feathery lashes, whose chest rose and fell softly against her, who smiled in her sleep. "Gas," Michou had informed her. "It's gas. They don't smile until three months." She disagreed.

She couldn't keep calling her "it" or "the baby." She thought of the stars patterning the night sky when she'd found her. Stella meant star; she'd learned that on a holiday in Italy.

"Stella," she breathed. "I'll call you Stella because you glow like a star."

René was working in Fontainebleau, Michou had gone to Deauville. She needed to get to the dry cleaner's and to give Miles Davis another walk. Most of all, she needed a nanny.

Errands would have to wait. Other things couldn't. She'd change her style, cover up Stella, and hope to blend in with the stroller crowd. From the collection in her drawer she chose large dark sunglasses, Jackie O style; a cap with STADE DE MARSEILLES printed on it; a black corduroy miniskirt; and metallic red Puma trainers.

She left her cell phone number on her answering machine. That done, she found the newly purchased baby sling, a striped affair of blue ticking, nestled Stella into it, and grabbed the dog leash.

Downstairs in the courtyard, she paused before the concierge's loge. A warm breeze ruffled the potted geraniums on the steps leading to the concierge's door with its lace curtain panel.

"*Bonjour,* Madame Cachou," she said, peeking inside, where a woman with steel gray hair was punching in figures on an adding machine.

"May I ask a favor, Madame? I've got to take Miles Davis out. Would you mind watching the baby, just for an hour?"

Madame Cachou's lips pursed. "Mademoiselle Leduc, did you get the notice? The second notice, to move the items from your space in the *cave?* I put it in with your mail."

Aimée groaned internally. Clearing her storage area was a task Madame Cachou deemed of highest importance due to the plumber's whining that he needed more space to refit pipes under their building. On her return from a several months' absence helping her sister, ill in Strasbourg, Madame Cachou had resumed her responsibilities with vigor. Aimée hoped the broken front door digicode would make her priority list.

"This weekend, Madame. My cousin Sebastian will help me."

Madame Cachou, a widow, pushed her glasses up on her nose, then folded her arms over her ample chest. In her light blue smock, flesh-toned support stockings, and clogs, she personified the traditional concierge captured by Brassaï in old photographs. She was a rumormonger who delivered the mail twice a day. But Madame Cachou was one of the handful of concierges still working on the island and one of the fewer still who weren't Portuguese. The new immigrant Portuguese women not only managed multiple buildings, they also juggled cleaning jobs and raised families, but rarely spoke much French.

"*Tiens!* Today, *s'il vous plaît.* Tomorrow they're off and then . . ." Madame Cachou shrugged, as if to ask who knew when they would return. "The plumbers' union is strike prone; it could be next month, next year."

Aimée had to stall the concierge and convince her to watch the baby. "As I said . . ."

Madame Cachou expelled air from her mouth. "*Bon.* Then you must sign the release to absolve the building of liability. No guarantee of responsibility, you know, but at least then they'll move things aside and finish the work. It's covered in your agreement, Mademoiselle. The leaks affect the water pressure in the whole building. We've had complaints."

Aimée hadn't been down there in years and had forgotten what her grandfather had stored in his underground compartment. She'd sign. That would give her one less thing to deal with.

She stepped inside the neat and narrow concierge's loge, one wall lined with calendars stretching back to 1954, the other with romance novels. A large-screen television took up the back wall. Madame Cachou pointed to a release form next to a state-of-the-art laptop.

It occurred to Aimée that Madame Cachou might have seen the baby's mother.

"Monday night, Madame," she said. "Were you here around 11:00 p.m.?"

"What's this question and answer?" Madame Cachou shook her head. "Monday's my night off. It's in my contract, eh? I go to my writers' group."

Aimée had lived here for years and had no idea.

"I earn a little money, you know," she confided. "On the side."

More than a little, Aimée thought.

"I see." But she didn't, surprised that a concierge who minded the building and mopped the floors also attended a writers' group.

Madame Cachou ignored Stella.

"Never interferes with my duties here, if that's what you're implying, Mademoiselle. At 8:00 a.m., I'm here on Tuesday morning. Mop the stairs, wax the foyer. Before that, I'm where I want to be on my own time."

There was a stack of Xeras, a line of "liberated" women's romance novels, by the side of the laptop. Those novels were really soft porn, Aimée thought.

"Sign, please."

"Do you study these . . . kinds of books in

your writers' group?" Aimée asked.

Madame Cachou's chin jutted forward. "I write these books, Mademoiselle."

Aimée wondered if she was in the wrong line of work. No wonder Madame Cachou could afford the laptop and a high-end *télé*.

Before she could ask more, a plumber in blue overalls appeared. "If we're not going to measure for the pipe fittings, I might as well go home."

"I'm coming."

Aimée's idea of begging the concierge to babysit evaporated.

Madame Cachou turned toward Aimée. "You young women have babies and expect the world to take care of them. But it's your responsibility."

"Madame Cachou, it's an imposition, of course, but just for —"

"*Et alors,* leave my friend Miles Davis," Madame Cachou interrupted. Her expression softened as she petted him. "We'll go to the park later."

Miles Davis wagged his tail and sniffed the treat bag she kept hanging from the door.

Now she'd have to take Stella with her. Put Plan B into action. She'd use her disguise, cover Stella with the blanket. The baby should be safe so long as they remained anonymous. She put on the dark glasses and cap, draped the blanket over Stella, and opened the ivy-covered back door, then wended her way through the dark rear courtyard.

She pushed open a small door cut into a larger wooden portal that filled the archway and stepped over the sill to stand on bright and busy rue Saint Louis en l'Isle. This narrow commercial artery, the principal one on the island, lay full of trucks unloading and of scurrying passersby. It was sheltered from the Seine breeze. She emerged onto the pavement in the midst of several women with strollers blocked by a moving van unloading furniture.

"Bonjour," a woman greeted her. She bent down, smiling, to look at the baby, then shook her head. "Impossible."

"What do you mean?" Aimée asked, nonplussed. Was it obvious that Stella wasn't hers?

"A newborn and you with such a flat stomach. How do you do it? That grapefruit diet?"

Relief flooded her and she nodded. She was eager to get away and question the garage owner, but she couldn't move quickly. The narrow pavement was blocked, as usual at this time of day. Overhead were wrought-iron balconies accessed via open doors with fluttering curtains behind them. The tall doors open to catch any breeze in the unusual heat, through which the murmur of conversations reached her.

At least, she could blend in. Nothing for it but to smile, join them, and eavesdrop on the discussions around her concerning playgroups, mother and baby yoga, errant nannies who took more than one day off. These were the conversations of women engulfed in a world ruled by little people who couldn't even talk. And for a moment, with the sun hitting her back with a slow delicious warmth, she wondered what it would be like to have the biggest crisis of the day be deciding which park to go to.

But that was not her life. A body lay in the morgue and the baby breathing warmly against her chest was in danger. She thought back to the marks under Stella's arm, the mother's frantic plea — *"no flics"* — and she knew the mother was depending on her.

Two blocks later, having passed leaning soot-stained buildings with paved courtyards big enough to hold carriages and horses — now relegated to storing green garbage containers and the occasional truck — she entered the dimly lit garage across from Place Bayre.

"Monsieur, Monsieur?" A generator thrummed and she jumped, hearing shots. She ran behind a Renault on a lift and clutched Stella tightly. She felt foolish when she saw that the noise had come from a mechanic in an oil-stained jumpsuit who was shooting lug nuts onto a tire rim with an air-powered wrench.

A man wiping his hands on a rag appeared from behind a small cage in which two yellow parakeets trilled.

"We're full up," he said. "No more appointments until Thursday, Madame."

"It's Mademoiselle. And I don't own a car."

She walked, biked, or Metroed everywhere. She would never understand anyone having a car in Paris. Yet she knew René couldn't envision life without his customized Citroën.

"A woman made a call from your garage last night. Late, around ten . . ."

He shook his head. "Impossible. We close at 8:00 p.m."

How could she explain that she'd had the call traced?

The other mechanic handed him a power wrench. "Stas, I forgot to tell you. The baron called. He wanted special treatment. As usual. He'd punctured a tire."

"Again, eh?" Stas rubbed his cheek, leaving an oil smear. "You keeping other things from me, too, Momo?"

Looked like she'd opened a can of worms.

"You know those aristos." Momo shrugged. "I tried to say no but —"

The phone rang in the small office and Stas ran to answer it.

"Do you mean you opened the garage last night after hours?" Aimée asked.

Momo rolled his eyes. "Just for him. He knows I live upstairs. Can't seem to get away from doing him favors."

More than one baron lived on the island. "The baron lives near here?"

Momo jerked his oil-encrusted thumbnail toward Hôtel Lambert's high stone wall. "Rents his wing out most of the time. Stays with the owners in the country."

Aimée took the photo from her bag, pointed to Orla's face. "Did you see her last night?"

Momo shook his head. "Why should I have?"

If Orla had sneaked in while he was busy working, she was no further than before. Perplexed, she pulled her cap lower. Unless he was keeping his knowledge close to his chest. She pointed to the pay phone that stood under an oil-stained Michelin map of

Burgundy.

"Come on, Momo. I'm sure she called me from here last night."

Momo looked down, reaching for his tools. If she pushed him a little more she thought he'd admit it.

"We'll keep it just between you and me," Aimée said, coaxing him.

He glanced at Stas, who was still speaking on the office phone, then turned toward her.

"He's a tightwad. He makes the customers use the pay phone. And I'm not supposed to let people in." Momo lowered his voice. "But" — he pointed to the dark-haired girl seated next to Orla in the group photo — "she said her cell phone battery had run out."

Surprised, Aimée looked again at the names on the back. Nelie. She guessed Momo liked a pretty face and leaned closer. Birdseed from the parakeets cage crackled under her feet.

"So you let her in. What did she say?"

"She was walking funny. Her face was white as a sheet," he said. "She seemed nervous. That's all."

"Was she by herself?"

"I didn't see anyone else. I changed the tire and when I looked up, she'd gone," he said.

Stas had returned. "Hey, Momo . . . you're on the clock."

"How old's your baby?" Momo asked.

Aimée gulped. "Close to two weeks."

She walked past an air pump, her mind spinning. The dark-haired Nelie, not Orla — who was now lying in the morgue — had called her. She stared at the face in the photo and felt a fleeting sense of familiarity. Had they passed in the street, stood in line at a shop? But if it was Nelie who had called her, why had Stella been wrapped in Orla's jean jacket?

She turned around. "Momo, have you lost any tire irons, those things you use to change a tire?"

He rubbed his chin. The moons of his fingernails were rimmed with black. "I've got to get back to work."

"Would you mind checking?"

"The equipment's kept in back," he said. "Sorry."

She pulled out twenty francs, put it in his hand. "Does this make it any easier?"

He nodded. She put her card in his grease-rimmed pocket. "Let me know, Momo."

Pungent aromas wafted from the white-walled cheese shop on rue Saint Louis en l'Isle. Runny cheeses perched on the marble counter leaked onto their straw beds. The old orange cash register sat by the wall, as always. Bernard, *le maître de fromage,* was also *le maître de gossip.* Most people on the island passed through his shop. And if anyone knew anything about them, he did.

"Haven't see you in a while, Aimée. Try a piece." Bernard, compact in his white coat and apron, pared the rind off a Reblochon and offered her a taste. "Perfect for after dinner tonight." His eyes widened when he noticed the baby. "I had no idea . . . you've been busy, eh?" He grinned. *"Quelle mignonne!* I can hear it now — all the old biddies on the island discussing you and your baby. Why, just the other day —"

"I'm babysitting, Bernard." She slipped some francs over the counter to him along with the photo.

"Do you know her?"

He pulled on his glasses. "Who?"

"Either of these girls. They're MondeFocus activists."

Bernard shook his head.

A dead end. If Bernard didn't recognize her, well . . . Disappointed, she picked up the ripe slice of Reblochon in its white waxed-paper wrapper, slipped it inside the baby bag, and turned to go.

"Attends," he said, scanning the photo

more closely. "*She* seems familiar." He pointed to Nelie, sitting next to Orla.

"Did you see her yesterday?"

"Those students sneak cigarettes at the café. Try there."

Aimée nodded to the older woman, wearing a green sweater set and wool scarf knotted around her neck despite the heat, behind the zinc counter of her corner café. One of the handful on the island sure to stay open late in winter. A few empty tables and booths stood in the rear room, which normally catered to the lunch crowd. Now only a single couple sat there, deep in conversation over a carafe of wine. The decor, redone in the seventies when smoked-glass dividers were introduced, didn't hide the Art Nouveau banister of the staircase leading down a flight to the phone and bathrooms.

"*Bonjour,* Sabine, *un café, s'il vous plaît.*"

"Right away," Sabine said, rubbing the milk-steamer wand with a wet dishcloth. She was a typical Auvergnat — brusque, born into the business, accustomed to watching every franc.

"Nico still on vacation?" Aimée asked. Nico, the co-owner, took February off.

Sabine nodded, setting down a demitasse of steaming espresso with a respectable tan

132

foam head and pushing the aluminum ball holding sugar cubes toward her. Stella was asleep, her soft breaths just audible to Aimée.

"Merci," Aimée said, unwrapping two sugar cubes and letting them plop into her cup. She moved the baby sling to the side, leaning toward her, as if to speak in confidence. As in Bernard's cheese shop, not much went on in the café without Sabine's knowledge.

"Not your usual style," Sabine said, glancing at Stella.

"I'm helping my friend. You know how that goes!"

"Thought so," Sabine said.

"Et alors, but I've got to work, Sabine."

"Bit off more than you could chew this time?"

Little did she know.

"You could say that, Sabine." She slid the photo onto the zinc countertop. "I need to find these girls to babysit for me. Bernard said he's seen them here. You wouldn't happen to have seen her this morning, would you?"

She pointed to Nelie.

Sabine shook her head. "Not this morning."

"I hope they're not out of town." Aimée paused as if in thought. "What about last night, did you see either one last night?"

"Janou closed up as usual," Sabine said, rinsing dirty cups in the sink and stacking them in the small dishwasher under the counter.

Janou, her brother, wearing a blue workman's coat and his habitual frown, wheeled a handcart of stacked Orangina cartons past the staircase leading down to the bathrooms and phone.

"*Ça va,* Janou," Aimée called to him. "Remember seeing either of these girls last night?" She held out the photo.

"A lot of students come here." He straightened up, paused, pulled his chin. "A blonde, a young *fille,* with a baby thing like yours. Could have been her last night."

"Was she wearing a jean jacket with blue beads embroidered on the pocket?"

He shrugged. "I didn't pay much attention. The *mecs* were watching the motocross rally replays on the *télé.* You know how loud they get."

That meant a bunch of beer-swilling motorcycle enthusiasts and a crowded, steamy café if Janou hadn't noticed much. But she wouldn't give up. A sharp-eyed Auvergnat, Janou reminded her of a crow, a nice crow with his close-set black eyes, who'd spot the shine of a franc lying in the gutter a street away.

Sabine, now with her glasses on, stared at the photo. "That blonde one. I remember now. She wiped her denim jacket sleeve on the fogged-up window. Her jacket was trimmed with funny blue beads in the pattern of a whale." Sabine's finger stabbed Orla's face in the photo. "That I noticed before I left."

At last!

"She left streak marks all over." Sabine pointed to the window. "Like those." Outside, a group of students stood in line at Bertillon's to choose from more than forty flavors of ice cream, blocking the café door. This was a sore point for Sabine. "Gave me the job of cleaning the whole window this morning, inside and out."

She'd washed away any fingerprint evidence then.

"Sabine, do you think she was looking for someone?"

Sabine shrugged. "Hard to say. Tell her to leave the window alone next time, eh?"

Aimée stroked the fuzz on Stella's head.

"Did she meet anyone?"

Janou leaned down and hefted a crate. "I served the *mecs,* and when I had finished, she'd gone. When I stacked the café chairs outside, she was just leaving the ATM across the way."

"Alone?"

"Some girls were running. She could have been one." Janou pointed to the dark-haired girl in the photo, then opened the cabinet door, which concealed a dumbwaiter to the cellar, and slid a carton of Orangina onto it. "But I'm not sure."

"Running?"

Janou scratched his cheek. "One of them kept looking back over her shoulder."

"In what way?"

"Like everyone does after they take cash from the machine, *alors!*"

Or had she been scared and running for her life?

"She limped. Stopped every so often."

"The blonde?"

"The dark-haired one."

Nelie.

"Does she live around here?"

"You're curious this morning." Janou paused, his head cocked, watching her.

She had to think fast. "Count on me to lose her number and I have a meeting. I wish I hadn't told my friend I'd watch her baby."

Janou shook his head. "Try the women's hostel! You'd think they might order a sandwich to eat, just once, eh, since they

136

make this place their living room."

"The woman's hostel on rue Poulletier?"

He nodded.

Aimée knew the place around the corner from her apartment that sheltered students and troubled young women.

Aimée set some francs on the counter. *"Merci."*

She left the café and walked down the narrow street thinking. Unease filled her.

Had she looked at this all wrong? She stared at the photo, concentrating on the dark-haired girl, Nelie. Momo had let her use the phone in the garage. Bernard, Sabine, and Janou had recognized her.

Had Nelie, though limping and injured, met Orla after the demonstration at the café? But then why hadn't she used the telephone downstairs in the café rather than the one at the garage? On top of that, why hadn't Nelie explained the situation calmly and clearly to her over the phone? Instead, she'd spoken frantically, almost incoherently. She had seemed desperate, sure that someone was after her. And now Orla was dead.

There was still no clue as to why Nelie had chosen to telephone Aimée. Nor any explanation of the writing on Stella's skin.

Questions swirled in Aimée's mind as she tried to fathom a frightened woman's thought processes. But now at least she knew whom she was looking for. She had to find Nelie, get answers, and resolve the baby issue without involving the authorities. She turned into rue Poulletier, feeling a frisson in her bones as she passed the words carved in worn limestone — SAINT-VINCENT DE PAUL ÉTABLIT LES FILLES DE LA CHARITÉ 1652. A reminder of the time when priests found babies abandoned on church steps and the parish provided social services that the king didn't. A newer sign, hanging near the ancient metal S-shaped hinge, which compressed the inner beams and held the floors together, read WATCH OUT.

In a few minutes, she imagined, she might be handing Stella over to Nelie. Stella stirred and Aimée felt a pang of regret.

Get on with it! she told herself. Resolutely, she pressed the digicode at the entrance to the soot stained stone building. The door buzzed open. Now she'd find out why Nelie had entrusted Stella to her.

"No babies allowed, Madame." A honeyed voice belied the sharp expression of the stout woman at the window of the reception area.

In the crowded alcove behind the woman, faxes hummed and a phone console lit up with red lights.

"I'm meeting Nelie," Aimée smiled, determined not to let this dragon of a sentry put her off. "Can you ring her room?"

"We're a busy office. You'll have to call her yourself."

"Her room number, please?"

"We don't give out that information," the receptionist said warily. "You should know that."

Had the *flics* sniffed her out and come for Nelie already? She doubted that.

"I'd appreciate your help, Madame."

"You'll have to excuse me, it's our busiest time. If you're meeting her, she'll come down," said the woman. A red light was blinking on the switchboard. Several young women entered the vestibule, crowding around the window asking for mail.

A brunette with a long braid down her back leaned down and cooed at the baby. "What's her name?"

"Her name . . . Stella." Aimée seized the opportunity. "You don't know Nelie, do you? We're supposed to meet and I forgot her cell phone number."

"I'm sorry." The brunette shook her head.

Aimée showed her the photo. "Maybe you're on the same floor."

The girl shook her head. "I'm in the exchange section, just here short term." She smiled, a milk-fed provincial girl. "Sorbonne students occupy the second floor, that's all I know."

Aimée found a seat near a table bearing old magazines. Another group of girls in tracksuits carrying soccer balls in a net assembled by the desk. On the back wall Aimée saw room numbers next to linen assignments on a blackboard. She stood and scanned the numbers until she came to one for Nelie Landrou on Staircase C. Finally! That had to be her.

She edged through the glass doors to the courtyard while the receptionist was busy. Charcoal gray tiles formed the slanted rooftop overlooking the grass-covered rectangular courtyard. There were no blue zinc roofs on this island; that would have been too modern.

Stella nestled closer in her arms, radiating warmth. "Such a good girl," Aimée whispered. If only she'd stay that way.

Staircase C lay at the back. Aimée mounted a flight of covered stone steps. She faced a line of planked doors. There was a name holder outside each room, next to the door.

Nelie's resembled the others. At least no police crime-scene tape was visible. She took a breath before she knocked. "Nelie, it's Aimée Leduc. I can help you." There was no answer even after she knocked repeatedly.

She'd never picked a medieval lock before. Certainly never picked a lock of any sort with a baby in her arms. She didn't think her credit card would work so she inserted her miniscrewdriver into the lock, swiveled it around, and then heard the tip snap. Great! Propping a gurgling Stella on her hip, she reached in her bag for her key ring, found the long old-fashioned keys to her *cave,* and used one as a lever to prise out the broken screwdriver shank. That done, she slid in the narrow lock-picking tool with a quick twist and upward shove.

She heard laughter from down the hall; she had to hurry. She jiggled the lock-picking tool, heard scraping metal and a click. She pushed the door open.

"Allô?"

No Nelie. Empty and like a monastic cell, spartan; narrow, white-washed stone walls, a small coved window filled with old blue bubbled glass with bars across it. She saw a poster of a munitions site with the legend: *One nuclear bomb can ruin your whole day* on the wall, a textbook on the floor, and an Indian cotton print bedspread on the single bed, which gave the room a student feeling. But it was an unlived-in feeling.

Her hopes dashed, she debated what to do. She picked up some notices left on a chair. The one on top was for a mandatory house meeting dated a month ago. A brief message in an opened envelope read: *Madame needs to meet with you regarding the balance owing on end-of-term rent.* It was dated three weeks before.

She'd been here, opened this envelope. Or someone had. Aimée wondered if she'd left when she couldn't hide her pregnancy anymore.

Aimée didn't have much time. Clutching Stella in the baby sling, she searched under the bed. Nothing. She examined the sheets, the pillow, and the gray sweater tossed down on an orange crate. This girl had left little more than a textbook and that sweater.

She hadn't just moved out, she had fled. Aimée felt it in the pit of her stomach.

She opened the window. In the courtyard, several uniformed *flics* stood talking to the woman from reception. The woman pointed up at the window. Nelie's window.

Her pulse raced. She had only minutes. Forget searching, she had to get out. Her foot slipped on a rag rug and she cushioned Stella with one arm, grabbing the metal bed frame with the other hand. It was a cheap tubular frame, typical of dormitories. Hollow tubed! And the screw where the tubes joined was loose. A good place to hide something, Aimée realized. After two turns, the screw came off and she wrenched the tubes apart. Inside, her index finger found a rolled-up plastic folder. Empty. The name *Alstrom* was embossed on the cover.

Their client, Regnault, ran Alstrom's publicity campaign. The protesters she'd seen from Regnault's window, the blue lights that had illuminated the demonstration last night just across Pont de Sully . . . somehow they were related to the victim Orla, Nelie, and the baby.

She rerolled the folder, stuck it back in the bed frame, scrabbled to her feet, and draped her jacket over her shoulder. By the time she'd closed the door behind her, the jacket covered Stella as well. She heard footsteps and the murmur of voices from across the courtyard.

A single file of *flics* tramped up Staircase C on her right. She ducked behind a pillar. But not before she'd seen the leader point to Nelie's door. The other officers fell back, in position. A keening cry came from her arms. Aimée wiped her finger, stuck it in Stella's mouth, praying it would pacify the baby until she could give her a bottle.

She padded down Staircase B, keeping close to the wall of the arcade. Stella's mouth gummed her finger. She reached in the bag, found the bottle, and shook it. Thank God, the formula line reached the top.

Head down, she threaded her way through the soccer team crowd, made it to the covered entryway, and opened the vestibule door.

"Excuse me, Madame?" said a blue-uniformed *flic.*

She froze.

He smiled, and handed her a diaper. "This fell from your bag."

"Merci," she said. "Excuse me." She edged past him, eager to get away.

Rain pattered on the warm stone buildings turning to steam in the unseasonable heat. She shielded Stella with the baby bag, quickened her step, and turned the corner onto Quai d'Anjou. Mist curled under the supports of Pont Marie. Then the spring-like drizzle turned into a downpour before she could take shelter in a vaulted doorway.

Drops beaded her eyelashes. She took a few more steps, then caught her breath. An unmarked police car blocked her building entrance.

TUESDAY AFTERNOON

René, holding a dripping umbrella, paced over the gravel by the statue in Place Bayre as he debated what to do.

He reached for his phone and the stuffed toy in his pocket squeaked. The unmarked police car parked in front of Aimée's door indicated that she'd given in and called the authorities. Guilt racked him.

The way she looked at the baby, the way the baby turned toward her voice. All she noticed was the baby. Now it had infected him. He'd found himself noticing babies in the bank that morning, comparing stroller prices in the window of a shop in Fontainebleau. Ridiculous.

He'd insisted she call social services, demanded she do what he thought was right. Then why the queasiness in the pit of his stomach?

He pulled out his cell phone. "Aimée, do you have company or shall I come up?" He tried to keep concern out of his voice. She might be in real trouble with the authorities.

"Hurry," she said. "Come in through the back, you know the way. I have to tell you something."

Aimée paced by the sputtering radiator. Nothing seemed to add up. She'd sneaked back the way she'd left, via the back passage. Stella was sleeping in the hammock she'd fashioned from an Afghan throw, suspended between the eighteenth-century *recamier* and the protruding window hasp.

By the time René draped his damp Burberry raincoat by the fireplace she couldn't wait any longer. She thrust the photo in front him. "See, René."

René tore his gaze away from the baby.

"Notice the woman wearing a jean jacket?"

"Who is she?"

"Orla. She's on a slab in the morgue."

René stepped back in alarm. "What have you gotten yourself into now?"

"Her body was found in the Seine by Pont de Sully. I think either she left the baby, or it was Nelie, her friend. I don't know which one is the mother." She took him by the arm and led him to her laptop.

"Wait a minute," he said. "Start from the

beginning."

"I won't know more until I can get hold of the autopsy report. But I can't figure out why either of them trusted me." She rolled up the sleeves of her silk shirt. "There's no way I'm going to contact social services until I know."

"Know what, Aimée?" he asked. "This gets more complicated every minute."

She showed him the newspaper article and described her visit to the morgue and Krzysztof's reaction — despite his denial that he knew the dead woman. Then she told him that later she'd found this photo of both Krzysztof and the blonde, Orla, with some others, in his room.

"Don't tell me he handed it to you after denying he knew her?" René tapped his stubby fingers on the chair.

"OK, I 'visited' his room and he happened not to be there," she said. "He's gone."

"Breaking and entering, some would call it."

Now René would know she was crazy if he didn't already. "His roommate let me in."

"You're guessing there's a connection. You have no facts to go on, Aimée."

"Guessing? Janou at the corner café recognized Nelie from the photo." She pointed to the dark-haired one. "The two women were seen together last night with the baby."

"Let the *flics* handle this."

"Not only that, Nelie lives around the corner — literally — in the student hostel. But she wasn't there when I went there just now. Somehow she looks familiar, but I can't place her. She must know me, otherwise . . ."

Apprehension filled her. This felt all wrong. "If the dead girl is Stella's mother, why hasn't Nelie come back or tried to reach me?"

Pedestrians scurried below on Quai d'Anjou. Every other woman seemed to be pushing a stroller or holding a toddler's hand. Had there been a baby explosion that she hadn't noticed before? Wind chased the silver puffs of cloud across the sky, leaving pewter puddles on the pavement. Aimée felt more confused than ever and weighed down by responsibility. She couldn't call social services and abandon the baby, like her own mother had abandoned her. At least not until she knew who Stella's mother was and why the baby had been entrusted to her.

René tugged his goatee. "Why must you be involved? What's it got to do with you?"

"I don't know," she said. "But for some reason Nelie didn't trust the *flics*."

"The baby's not your responsibility. Under the circumstances, you've done more than enough."

"If only it were that simple! Say Orla was murdered, René, as she was trying to hide something . . . and Stella . . ."

"Stella?" René looked at her quizzically.

"Well . . ." She searched for the words. "She's not an inanimate object. I can't keep calling her 'it.' "

"None of this is your job. Turn the baby — Stella — over to people who can take care of her. Let the *flics* find the mother."

Aimée's gaze rested on the pink bundle swaying in the hammock.

René slumped and put his head in his hands. "*Tant pis!* Don't tell me you want to run the office with a crib in the corner? Be realistic, Aimée."

"Realistic?" She realized that she did possess some facts. Maybe when she laid them out, they would lead to a conclusion. "Nelie, the dark-haired one, had information on Alstrom, the oil company," she began.

"Did I miss something here?"

His words jarred her. Miss . . . missing . . . what if Nelie couldn't contact her?

If Nelie knew that Orla was dead . . . again Aimée came back to Krzysztof.

A vital piece was missing from the puzzle.

She started over. "Nelie hid an Alstrom file in her room at the women's hostel around the corner. I found the cover of the file. The contents were gone."

René stood openmouthed. "How? Breaking and entering again?"

"The *flics* will have found it by now. They were right behind me." She pulled out her checkbook. "Look, René." She showed him the marks she'd copied from the baby's body. "Doesn't it look like an equation?"

He turned away.

"It doesn't hurt to look; it won't bite you."

"It's bitten you already." He rolled his green eyes. "I don't know. Where did you find this?" He pulled out his handkerchief, monogrammed RF, and wiped his forehead.

"This was written under Stella's arm, René," Aimée said. "The mother's protecting not only her baby but this, too. Whatever it may mean. Stella's the key."

He shook his head. "I don't want to have anything more to do with this. Neither should you."

She reported Krzysztof's look of recognition when he'd scanned the papers in the Regnault file.

"Why didn't he identify his girlfriend in the morgue?" René asked.

Good question.

"There is a reason, René." She sat down at the laptop. "I have to find out what it is."

"Wait, you're not suggesting — Aimée, we work for Regnault, Alstrom's publicity firm. So, in the first place, delving into Alstrom's affairs is unethical," René said.

"Did I say I was going to do that?"

"You don't have to," René said. "Second, if Alstrom suspects you are checking on internal procedures in their company . . ." He cleared his throat. "We'll never land another computer security contract, Aimée."

She stared out at the arms of the Seine, then back at her laptop screen, trying to figure out where Orla would have entered the water. "The Net's an open door if you know how to navigate, right? We do it all the time, René. How do you think *Libération* scooped the bribes camouflaged as campaign contributions to the Socialists? Some geek on the inside fed them the information."

He shrugged. "We're in the computer security business, we're not muckrakers, Aimée. We have enough trouble of our own. The tax refund due since last year still sits on a bureaucrat's desk, not to mention the fact that we have to eat and pay rent. Our security contracts pay our bills. Focus on our problems. Leave the rest to the activists."

Right. Of course he was right. "Good point. But it's the tip of some iceberg, René. An iceberg of scandal."

"And Regnault? The company that pays us? I'll ask you again, do you think what you intend to do is ethical?"

"Vavin begged me this morning to sign a new contract."

René opened his briefcase. "And that would consist of?"

"Patching their firewalls, which were hacked right before we came on board. Continued system administration. See. Boring, routine and . . ."

"With a nice check in payment for our work," René interrupted, scanning the contract. His eyes brightened. "We need it right now."

"Vavin's desperate, his sysadmin's in the hospital. He tripled our fee."

"Glad you took the initiative. I've handled the firewall, for now," René said.

"With your usual threat to hackers, I suppose."

René nodded. "If you read this, you're dead," was his signature threat.

Stella stirred, her eyes blinking open. Time for another bottle. Aimée opened the baby bag, then glanced at the mail on the table she'd picked up from downstairs.

In the pile of bills lay a smudged, unstamped manila envelope bearing her name: Aimée. Hand delivered. Visions of the tire iron filled her mind, of the figure who had chased her on the quai. Her arm shook so much she dropped the envelope.

René asked, "What's the matter?"

Her face paled. "Everything or nothing." She took latex gloves from a drawer, slit the envelope, and shook it. A page torn from a magazine fell onto the table. It displayed a crossword puzzle filled in with smeared ink. The capital letters ran off the page.

Aimée recognized it as the back page of *Mots Croisés,* the weekly crossword magazine sold at street kiosks. Underneath the puzzle were words printed in the same scrawling block letters: *WAIT ONE MORE DAY. HER MOTHER BEGS YOU TO TELL NO ONE, OR THEY'LL KILL HER, ME, TOO. HER LIFE AND THE BABY'S ARE IN DANGER, DON'T CONTACT THE FLICS, OR TELL ANYONE.*

Aimée's hands trembled.

Kill her, me, too. The shaky letters recalled old penmanship books from the thirties. She wondered what she should do . . . could do.

"You believe this?" René asked. But she

saw fear in René's eyes, too.

"Do I have a choice?"

Her buzzer sounded. Nelie? She ran to the open window to gaze below. Morbier, her godfather, who was a commissaire, stood on the cobblestones. Alone.

"Leduc, thought I'd stop by for a cup of coffee," he shouted up. A cloud passed over and briefly shadowed his corduroy jacket with its leather patches on the sleeves, his salt-and-pepper hair, his basset-hound drooping eyes.

He hadn't "stopped by" in five years.

"What's the occasion?"

"Invite me up. As I was in the *quartier* . . ."

In the *quartier* . . . an interesting way to put it. No doubt he had been called in to investigate Orla's death.

The last thing she needed, Morbier up here with the baby. "*Un moment,* Morbier. There's plaster and stucco all over. I'll come down, we'll go to lunch. My treat."

She ducked back inside. "Can you give Stella a bottle, René . . . please. Watch her for a little bit."

"Again?"

"She's so good. Never a peep from her."

And then Stella contradicted her by crying. Aimée picked her up, patted her back. The cries subsided.

154

"She likes to be held, René, that's all."

"But Regnault's firewalls need more protection . . ." She heard the doubt in his voice.

"Program the new safeguards while she drinks the bottle. When I get back I'll handle the rest." She had to get his mind off her predicament and on to work. "Vavin assured me he'd propose our new package to his boss. Count on his support."

René looked undecided.

"You saw the note. Morbier's fishing. But I have to find out what he knows. Please, René!"

She thrust Stella into his hands.

"Do I have a choice?" he asked.

She grabbed her bag.

Aimée willed her shaking hands under the red-and-white-checked oilcloth to be still. She'd steered Morbier to the bistro around the corner. It had a dark seventeenth-century timbered ceiling and a stone fireplace big enough to walk into. Now the fireplace held a gas heater piled with menus.

"Still remodeling your apartment, Leduc? Business must be good."

Morbier stored information, compartmentalized it in a way that put a database to shame. Old style and with the human touch, better than any profiler could do with a computer.

"Good? The ancient gas lines in the ceiling are still live; that was our latest setback." She had to divert him and get him off the track. Then maybe she could discover what he knew. "Every time they drill a hole I end up in the bank manager's office. Asking for credit."

She reached for the bread basket at the same time he did. Their hands touched. Age spots she'd never noticed showed near his knuckles.

And not for the first time she wished that their relationship had been different. Or that she could share things with him as she had with her father. But five years ago that had changed.

"So, Morbier, you're hobnobbing here with the nobility and just dropped in to visit me?"

"That's me all over." Morbier grinned. A dyed-in-the wool Socialist, Morbier had lived until the year before in the working-class slice of Bastille he'd grown up in, in the same fourth-floor walk-up apartment over the old metal foundry he'd been born in.

"The special looks good." He gestured in the direction of the blackboard and raised two fingers at the man behind the counter.

"*Oui,* Commissaire, two specials."

Morbier tucked the napkin into his collar. Sniffed and cocked his eyebrow. "New perfume?"

Eau de baby, instead of her usual Chanel No. 5. "I'm trying new fragrances," she said. She looked down, noticed a clump of clotted formula on her blouse, and flicked it off. "Last time you 'stopped by' was for Papa's funeral."

The pitiful affair she'd organized with his colleagues and neighbors in attendance. *Flics,* the baker, the priest recounting Pernod-fueled stories until dawn smeared the sky. Reminiscences hadn't brought him back. The wake remained hazy but the hangover had hardened her resolve. She'd quit criminal work.

Morbier blinked, caught off guard. A rare occurrence.

"That long?" Morbier said. "Well, Ile Saint-Louis is my turf, too, Leduc." No need to remind her he was a commissaire in the fourth arrondissement who worked at the Préfecture one day a week, keeping the nature of his duties there close to his chest. "The Brigade Fluviale found a female student in the Seine by Pont de Sully early this morning."

"I'm sorry for her family," she said. "A suicide?"

"You're local, Leduc. Trouble's never far behind you. I wonder if you saw anything?"

Now he was getting to the real reason he was here.

"You're asking me for help?"

A good *flic* baited hooks, and sometimes got a bite. That's how it worked. She'd have to give him something to find out what he knew. "A student?" She leaned back as if in thought. "Not many can afford to live here. *Mais non,* there's a women's hostel."

"We know about that."

They'd worked fast. Unusual. They had discovered Orla's identity, but how had they traced Nelie to the hostel so quickly?

"So she lived in the hostel . . . then you know more than I do."

"She — I don't know where she lived." He shrugged. "Her friend's hostel laundry receipt was found in her pocket."

"Who is she?"

"More important, what's her angle? That's where I hoped you'd help."

That didn't make sense. Unless Morbier knew Aimée had already been at the hostel.

"Me? Don't you even know her name?"

"Orla Thiers. It's her friend at the hostel, Nelie Landrou, we're interested in now. She was involved in a theft from a nuclear fuel processing site in La Hague." He retucked his napkin into his collar. "She's on the wanted list."

"What?"

"That's all I can say."

Wanted. No wonder she was hiding.

Wanted like Aimée's own mother, a seventies radical, who'd disappeared years before, gone into hiding, or on the lam. Only Aimée's mother had been imprisoned, then deported, before she vanished. The only trace of her mother she had discovered years later was a letter in a faded envelope with a blurred U.S. postmark. Her hand clenched and unclenched.

"Leduc? You with me?"

She had to control her nerves.

"Does that strike a chord? Hit close to home?"

Cruel, he would hurt her deeply and then feign ignorance.

"Students stealing nuclear secrets, Morbier? Unlikely."

"Did I say that, Leduc?"

Or maybe he was casting a wide net, unsure. Fishing.

"Wait a minute — was she one of those MondeFocus protesters at l'Institut du Monde Arabe? The article in *Le Parisien* stated the CRS beat up the demonstrators."

"Those reporters . . . climbing the wrong tree as usual, Leduc. No truth to that report."

If she believed that, she'd believe the earth was flat.

"Do you deny that students were beaten?" She tore the dark crust off the bread and chewed.

Morbier shook his head. "Their permit was revoked, the CRS found weapons, warned the crowd twice, did their job. Only one was hospitalized. But they never approached the Seine."

"Only one? Guess that makes it OK."

"The brigadier's been called on the carpet by the minister. He's chewing nails, insisting the CRS was set up." Morbier tore off a hunk of bread. "I think he's right."

"How's that, Morbier? Sounds to me like you're toeing the party line."

A bowl of steaming mussels in garlic butter broth with a side order of crisp golden fried potatoes appeared.

She wouldn't let him wiggle off the hook. "The CRS squeals when its brutality's exposed."

"Who said they're ballerinas?" His thick eyebrows rose up his forehead. "The brigadier is Ciel's kid, Viktor, the one who used

160

to chew his lip so it bled. Remember?"

She did. Remembered a fifteen-year-old Viktor's short woolen pants and thin white legs as he delivered his father's lunch to the Commissariat. He'd been teased mercilessly. An odd choice for the CRS, or was the agency getting in touch with its sensitive side?

Morbier speared a mussel. "Because of Alstrom's high profile, the CRS was careful to adhere to regulations. They did everything by the book. Last thing they'd do would be throw a body in the Seine."

"Face it, Morbier, they'd deny it anyway."

"You're interested in ecology, global warming, and all that kind of thing?"

Where did that come from?

"I recycle," she said, going along with him. "The haze of pollution clinging over La Défense bothers me as much as the next person. What's the connection?"

"There's more to it, Leduc."

Her shoulders tensed. The baby? She tried for a casual tone. "Like what?"

He set his fork and knife down on the tablecloth and pulled out a pack of unfiltered Gauloises. He lit one with a wooden match.

"It's about cooking a wolf, Leduc." He blew smoke out the sides of his mouth.

One week, three days, four hours, and thirteen minutes since she'd quit. Not counting, was she? She pulled a pack of stop-smoking patches from her bag, stuck one under her blouse.

"A wolf?"

He set his burning cigarette in the Ricard ashtray, deep in thought, his fingers on his lip, removing a flake of tobacco.

She stared at Morbier over the steaming plate of mussels. He'd gone mystic . . . cryptic remarks, first about ecology, then wolves. "Getting philosophical in your advancing years, eh?"

He cupped the cigarette, ignoring her comment. "Winter of 1943, the wolves in the countryside outside Paris descended on the Bois de Vincennes."

"Wolves in Paris? Not since the Romans. Tell me another one, Morbier."

"Aaah, but the wolves were starving, they smelled fresh meat. The zoo animals, the city's pigeons and cats were, let's say, depleted."

She'd heard those stories. Rationing during the Occupation had reduced Parisians to hunting what lived in the city.

"We heard them howling at night and my father kept saying wolf tasted like venison. We hadn't had meat on the table for a year.

Hungry, we were hungry for that taste."

She waited, tapping her fork. Morbier never talked about his childhood or his life, for that matter. "There's a point to this story, I gather."

"I figured you'd skin a wolf like a rabbit. Concocted plans with my schoolmates. But when I asked my father, 'How do you cook a wolf?' he paused and grinned. 'First,' he said, 'you have to catch the wolf.' "

"The moral escapes me, Morbier." She forked a succulent parsley-laden mussel into her mouth.

"Sounds like there's a wolf out there." He stubbed the cigarette out. "We heard it; now we've got to catch it."

"We?"

"You said you're into environmental issues, *non?*"

Sharp as ever. All this time he'd been leading her where he wanted her to go and she'd thought he'd lost it.

"Right now, Morbier, I'm into a boring and highly lucrative system administration contract with a network just aching for a rehaul." And minding a baby who spit up, pooped, and cried at the most inopportune times. But she kept that to herself. "My contractor's always sticking out his hand for money."

"How many tight spots have I pried you from, eh?"

His influence, albeit exerted with reluctance, had helped her more than once. And his tone had changed. Deepened.

"What are you saying Morbier?"

Morbier leaned back, tenting his fingers. "Get involved with saving the ecology of the planet. Sniff around 38 Quai d'Orléans."

"But that's . . ."

"Two blocks away, the MondeFocus office," he interrupted. "In your backyard."

She had planned on questioning the organizers at MondeFocus. Yet if she gave in without a fight, Morbier would be suspicious.

She wanted to trust him, to confide in him. But he withheld things from her, doling out information sparingly. And he had kept his distance since her father's death.

"Don't you have undercover cops for that?"

"Not like you."

"Meaning?"

"You can worm your way in and find a connection we'd never think of. I've seen you do it before."

Was Morbier complimenting her?

"Should I take that as a compliment?"

"I'd consider it to be repayment for some

favors, Leduc."

Her thoughts flashed to the man with the tire iron in the park close to Pont de Sully, the footsteps following her.

A wolf. Maybe he was right.

Aimée paid for lunch, said good-bye to Morbier on the corner, and with misgivings walked through the pelting rain. The carved wooden door of Saint-Louis-en-l'Ile stood open, and she took shelter in the church.

The dark vestibule was hung with heavy velvet curtains to keep out drafts. They opened to the rear nave and marble holy water font. Flickering shadows and an aroma of wax came from the votive candles. The ribbed struts of the vaulted ceiling had witnessed Jean Racine's baptism and the time Henri Landru, the *belle époque*-era serial killer, had spent as a choirboy.

She nodded to the restorer in overalls who was testing the organ pipes, hitting D notes that reverberated in the air, then faded away.

She dipped her fingertips in the ice-cold water, crossed herself, and murmured a prayer for her mother, as she had ever since she was eight years old, when her grandfather brought her here every Sunday. But years of earnest Sunday devotions and her little confessions apologizing for whatever she'd done wrong hadn't brought her mother back.

Aimée had watched the Dassaults in the pew ahead of them — the father in his Sunday suit; Madame Dassault's arms filled with an infant; Jeanette and Lise, her classmates, nudging each other and pretending to sing. After mass, Monsieur Dassault and her grandfather would stop at the *pâtisserie* for the *tarte* they'd carry home in a small white box tied with ribbon. Monsieur Dassault, Jeanette, and Lise would return to their waiting midday meal and Aimée and her grandfather to a long table with *charcuterie* tidbits or a cassoulet her father had prepared the night before, if he wasn't on duty. Most Sundays, she remembered, he was. Afterward, the rest of Sunday was spent at a *cinéma* on one of the grand boulevards. A voyage to other worlds, lost in a celluloid fantasy. Her grandfather and father had done their best.

Aimée would hear the Dassaults through an open window. Once Lise had knocked, inviting her and her grandfather for birthday cake. Entering their apartment had been like visiting another world. Beaming, Madame Dassault had hugged her infant and helped Lise fill a bag with party favors, and welcomed Aimée. Monsieur Dassault had set up the domino table, and for a time she had felt as if she were part of this family, a real family. Not an outsider.

But afterward, from the open windows, she'd heard the harsh tone of Madame Dassault's voice escalating to screams, then slaps and crying. At school the next day, Lise had bruises on her arms and swollen cheeks. She'd never been the same laughing tease.

Even seemingly perfect families had secrets.

A deep chord issued from the organ, startling her and bringing her back to the cold air, the stiffness in her knees, and the knowledge that she couldn't take care of this baby.

She had to reject her wish to become the mother she'd wanted to have. Life didn't work like that.

She stood, brushed off her knees, and wended her way past the pews toward the confessional, a dark, vaulted wooden closet reeking of holy water and damp. Inside, she pulled out her cell phone and punched in Serge's number at the lab. He'd have the autopsy results by now.

"Serge?"

"Sorry, we're backed up, Aimée." She heard water running. "I've never figured out why warm weather brings out the psychos and suicides."

The whine of a saw erupted in the background. She cringed. A bone-cutting saw.

"What did you discover about Orla Thiers?"

"So you know her name," he said. "The bruise joined a laceration behind her hairline."

"But you said the bruise could have come from hitting her head as she fell . . . wait a minute. You're saying there was a blow to the head before submersion?"

"A skull fracture as evidenced by the pooling of blood over her brain. That indicates a blow to the head prior to death."

A door shut. Footsteps echoed. There was a clinking sound, then a long pause.

"This machine coffee tastes like river water," Serge said, disgusted. "The canteen sandwich is a slab of dry Gruyère between pieces of stale baguette."

She figured Serge had changed the subject because someone had come in.

"Who eats four star every day, Serge?" She heard him chewing. "Can't you talk somewhere else?"

Echoing footsteps. The sound of a door slamming shut.

"It's quieter here in the hallway," he said.

"Have to grab lunch while I can."

How he could eat while performing a postmortem was beyond her. Her stomach turned. Yet in her brief year in premed she remembered students keeping their yogurt in the refrigerators with body parts.

"That's the conclusion. A deep laceration and a fracture of the skull beneath a bruise, caused by a heavy instrument."

She thought of the figure in Place Bayre with his tire iron.

"Lots of interest in this victim. What do you know about her?"

More to the point, what had he found out? "You're the pathologist, Serge, you first."

"Two cavities, a healed femur fracture, and stunning good health for a dead person. I'm just curious since the *flics* and DRM hovered like bees."

The Direction du Renseignement Militaire? Did that explain Morbier's interest? She shoved that aside for later. Her fingers tensed on the worn satinlike wood of the confessional railing. She had to know.

"Had Orla given birth recently?"

Serge cleared his throat, and paused, as though reading from a report. "No evidence of cervical enlargement, distortion, or a C-section."

Medicalese for no, she recalled that much.

Relief and surprise filled her. Still, she had to be sure.

"Had she ever been pregnant?"

"Never. According to traces in her blood-stream she took the pill," Serge said.

So Nelie, a fugitive, was the mother. She hated to ask the next question, yet the dead had no privacy once they'd succumbed to the big sleep. "Her stomach contents . . ." she paused, hesitant, thinking of the open organs with their overflowing contents.

"Oh yes," Serge said, gusto in his voice. "Crêpes Provençal for lunch and a last espresso, though I doubt she knew it was her last one. With sugar. But the river water diluted . . ."

"Serge," Aimée interrupted, "was she dead before she hit the water?"

"The water in the lungs indicate respiration. The blow would have stunned her, rendered her unconscious. Her natural reflex to breathe caused her to open her mouth and swallow. That's the usual way. The bruise came from the drain grille later. I'd say, according to the type of discoloration, that it was inflicted after death."

Serge cleared his throat. "I'm coming, Adjutant General," he said.

The big brass must have stepped in to listen. She heard shuffling footsteps, the clang of dropped metal on the floor, and someone saying, "*Merde* . . . my foot! The rib spreader fell on my foot!"

"In our report we concluded she had been a victim of foul play," Serge said.

"But did the beads on Orla's jeans match the jacket?" Aimée whispered, seeing a black-cassocked priest standing nearby.

"According to my tests, Inspector," Serge said into the phone, "the results correlate."

"*Merci,* Serge," she said and hung up.

Tragic and puzzling. The beads matched. Orla had left the baby wrapped in her denim jacket in Aimée's courtyard, been murdered, and dumped in the Seine. She thought back to the rust-colored bloodstains, the garage mechanic saying Nelie looked odd, Janou's observation of her limping. It might make sense if Nelie, injured and desperate, had gone into hiding and sent her a message on the crossword puzzle that she feared for her baby's life. Aimée thrust the phone into her bag. What had she written on her baby's skin?

She imagined the two women, wanted, trying to escape from the police — or someone — unable to keep the baby at the hostel. Again she drew a blank. Pieces of the puzzle were missing — the why and who.

She left the church. Would she have the heart to turn Nelie in? Turn her in like someone had turned her own mother in, to go to prison?

And then . . . foster care, or that of distant relatives, or adoption for Stella? She was rationalizing.

She shivered in the rising wind and rain, called her friend Martine, and left a message. On the narrow street, a man brushed by, a small child atop his shoulders. The wet-haired child, laughing, ordered, "Gallop faster, Papa!"

"*Chocolat chaud* to the winner," the red-cheeked mother said, bringing up the rear.

She couldn't test René's already frayed patience any longer. She, too, ran.

She found her apartment as warm as an oven, the printer running. René's voice came from the kitchen.

"The database, *oui*," he was saying. "I've entered the information. *Bien sûr*, the framework's been redesigned. You'll appreciate the new ease of use."

He was talking into the speaker phone. A laptop screen displaying an antivirus program stood on the kitchen counter. His gold cuff links were in the soap dish by the sink.

She stared, openmouthed, watching him

stand on a chair to reach into a high cabinet, the sleeves of his handmade Charvet shirt rolled up, a lace-fringed apron tied around his waist. Steam rose from the kettle humming on the stove. Miles Davis lay curled, his tail wagging, next to Stella, who was sleeping in a computer paper box together with a stuffed pink pig. Where had that come from?

The domestic scene, the result of fortuitous circumstance, gave off a sense of family. For the moment, it felt like her family.

In her room she took off her wet blouse and skirt. She searched her armoire and found jeans, a black cashmere sweater, and an old Sonia Rykiel lined khaki raincoat. Urban chic? *Non.* She decided on a warm waterproof parka from her Sorbonne days. Nondescript and utilitarian. She picked items from her computer tool kit and stuck them in her backpack.

Back in the kitchen she said, "We have to talk, René."

Startled, he reached to untie the apron. "I didn't hear you . . ."

"You've got it all under control," she said. "Amazing."

René's large green eyes took in her outfit. He frowned. "You didn't tell Morbier, did you?"

"He called in favors I owe him. So I've agreed to assist him."

"And somehow neglected to mention Stella." He jerked his thumb at the baby. Relief or something else filled his eyes.

"Her mother's alive. And wanted."

René lost his balance and grabbed the cabinet handle. She reached him before he fell and helped him down. He took off the apron, summoning a stern look.

"What do you mean 'wanted'?"

"Martine's checking on that. But if students can 'steal' from a secure nuclear fuel processing site, military security's in trouble."

René gave a wry smile. "And I'm six feet tall."

"I've got to find her first, René. With you here, I will. Here's the deal — I'll take the late shift —"

"And put our work in jeopardy?"

She ignored his reproach. "Tonight I'll continue monitoring the network and finish the firewall protection. Hell, we can do this half awake."

She squeezed the stuffed pink pig at Stella's side and it squeaked. A price tag on the floor caught her eye.

"She'll love that, René."

He turned away but not before she saw

the funny look on his face.

As she raced down her worn marble steps, she wondered why René hadn't admitted where the stuffed toy had come from.

TUESDAY NIGHT

In the galley kitchen in the back of his *brocante*, or secondhand shop, Jean Caplan sighed and smeared a knife full of Nutella onto a warm baguette. Better humor her as usual, he thought. The poor thing.

He shuffled past a chair piled with melamine ware, cracked Ricard ashtrays, and old Suze liquor bottles, all layered with a film of dust.

"*Voilà*, Hélène." He set the chipped Sarguemines plate on the marble-topped table next to which the old woman sat. Rain pattered outside on the courtyard, streaming from the gutter, beating a rhythm on the metal well cover.

"So thoughtful, Jean!" Hélène said, reaching a thin blue-veined hand out to help herself. Her nearly transparent paper-white skin barely covered her protruding bones.

He'd been sweet on her then, he was sweet on her now. Hélène had sat in the wooden school desk in front of him and he'd dipped the tip of her ribbon-tied braid in his ink-

175

well. He still saw traces of that feisty young girl although the long braids were now white and tied together at the back of her head with string.

"Haven't seen you for a few days," he said, combing back his thick white hair with his fingers. He'd worried with all the rain . . . where was she living now? He pressed a wad of francs into her hand.

"Jean, *non!* This kind of money I can't take from you."

"I sold the armoire — you know the seventeenth-century one the baron gave me on consignment, eh? And you never let me take you for a meal."

"Merci." She rolled her dark blue eyes, violet ringing the irises. There wasn't a wrinkle on her smooth face; her skin was that of a young woman, only her jaw was more pronounced than it had once been. She was clean and neatly dressed . . . only, if one looked closely enough, the shopping bags gave her away as a street person. Yet for periods of time she'd stay in a city-run *pension,* hold a job, and blend in with the anonymous older generation.

"The baron? Up to his tricks again. Tell me more."

Someone had to show her kindness, Caplan thought. She'd been traumatized during the Occupation. Out of sync, out of step, after the war. But then, deep down, who wasn't?

Her family had owned this store on Ile Saint-Louis until Libération. Now he did. The Wehrmacht's fault. Their boots had strutted over the bridge, back and forth, between the town house they'd requisitioned — now the Polish Center — and the shops on rue Saint Paul in the nearby Marais. Those were all gone. The bordello, whose attic his family had hidden in after the 1942 raid, was gone, too. The whole block of stores had been torn down and it was a manicured garden now.

"Well, our playboy baron keeps asking me to sell his lower-end furnishings, if you call seventeenth century low end, piece by piece to finance his rent boys." He leaned back on the marquise chair, his weight straining the curved legs. "He needs more money to attract them the older he gets."

"You remember the parties . . . the Polish diplomatic receptions and how we'd peek at the guests over the hedge?" she asked.

Jean grinned. A memory they shared from before the time of the marching jackboots. She loved talking about the island as it had once been, long ago.

"If those walls could talk! Remember the

masked costumed party, the servants dressed as Nubian slaves?"

She was mixing the eras up. This party had taken place in the seventies; it was still a legend but a legend for a set that was dying out. None of the very rich lived like that anymore. Today socialites mixed Cartier diamond watches and designer jeans. It was another world now, *déclassé,* common.

Jean looked down at the worn soles of his brown shoes. A decade ago Hélène had turned up and walked into the shop only to ask with a vacant smile if he had her schoolbooks.

" 'Hélène . . . where were you?' " he'd asked.

"Down south," she'd said.

He'd recognized the burns on her temples. She'd had shock treatments. The part of her brain they hadn't burned out was living in the past. Guilt had racked him.

"Mustn't be sad, Jean," she said now. He came back to the present as she took his chin in her hand, searching his face. There was a puzzled, warm look in those violet-tinged eyes.

"Stay here," he offered.

"I can't. The bad one might catch us." She leaned closer, whispering, "We have to hide."

"Who are you afraid of? Did someone threaten you or call you names again? I told you I'd take care of —"

"The bad one," she repeated. "You know, the one who threw the girl in the river. Paulette's ever so afraid the bad one will toss her in."

Paulette? Her sister Paulette had been taken in 1942.

"She's afraid that he'll kill her, too."

"What do you mean, Hélène?" Jean had overheard talk at the *café-tabac* counter that morning and read the newspaper article: a young woman's body had been found in the Seine. "You witnessed this?"

She nodded mutely.

In her own way she never lied. But he couldn't credit this.

"So I took care of the bad one, Jean," she said, her mouth set in a thin line.

Jean controlled his shudder. He gripped the chair's threadbare armrest. "Took care . . . how?"

"I couldn't let the bad one do it again," she said, shaking her head. "Now I've made it safe."

He wanted to shake information out of her. As he leaned toward her, his foot hit the shopping bag at her feet and he looked down. Inside one of the bags he noticed the

179

black handle and ornamental bee of a Laguiole knife.

"Did you use that knife . . . to protect yourself?" he asked her.

She stood, gathered her bags and broken umbrella, and went to the door.

He followed her, putting his arm around her shoulders. "Wait, Hélène. What did you see?"

"*Merci,* Jean." Her eyes clouded. "There's a break in the rain. I have to go."

He stared after her as she padded down the rain-soaked street, mumbling to herself. She'd gone over the edge, he concluded. Next it would be UFOs.

But he couldn't get her voice out of his head. What if someone had attacked her and in self-defense she'd retaliated? She might have hurt someone. Worse — someone might be attacking women and the homeless on the island. He thumbed through the the phone directory, found the listing he sought, and, with shaking fingers, dialed the Commissariat.

TUESDAY LATE AFTERNOON

Martine's red-soled, black-heeled Louboutins clicked across the creaking floor of the Musée des Hôpitaux de Paris. She was wearing an orangey peach wool suit and matching blossomlike hat. Breathless, she still managed to kiss Aimée on both cheeks.

"Nice place to meet! These old operating theaters look like torture chambers." Martine pointed to an exhibit — a gray, tubular iron lung. "Trying to tell me something, Aimée?"

Martine smoked a pack a day.

"You? Never."

Martine, her best friend since the *lycée,* did investigative reporting now after her stint at a defunct fashion magazine. She was tamer than she'd been in her student days. Martine shared a huge high-ceilinged flat with her boyfriend, Gilles, and his assorted children, overlooking the Bois de Boulogne in the sixteenth arrondissement. *Haute bourgeois,* too staid for Aimée.

"Charming." Martine stared at the enlarged sepia turn-of-the-century photos of barefoot children in line at a milk bar. She grinned. "Gilles's kids only stand in line at FNAC for the latest CD."

"What did you find out?" Aimée asked.

Martine opened her pink alligator bag and thrust a batch of printouts at Aimée. "Not much. Last week, certain allegations surfaced. There was enough there for the Army to put Orla Thiers and Nelie Landrou on

181

their wanted-for-questioning list."

"What kind of allegations?"

Martine consulted a printout. "Sexy stuff," she said, with a moue of distaste. "Apparently, they acquired knowledge of truck schedules — arrivals and deliveries."

A far cry from nuclear secrets.

"That's all?"

"Looks like it," Martine said. "It's a favorite tactic of MondeFocus to set up a roadblock to stop a fleet of semis, tanker trucks carrying hazardous materials."

"The Army steps in if there's any activity threatening radioactive materials, Martine," Aimée said.

Martine shrugged.

Aimée stuck the printouts in her bag to study later. If Krzysztof Linski was implicated as well and on the run, too, it would explain his behavior.

"I've got to rush." Martine took Aimée's arm and they walked through the hall under the painted ceiling showing eighteenth-century surgeons in panels encircled by *trompe l'oeil* pillars. "The oil conference . . ."

"Wearing that?"

"First, my niece's baptism. You know Liliane, my youngest sister."

"You're a godmother how many times over?"

"Three, or is this one the fourth? Can't keep track of all of them." Martine had three married sisters, all with children. "She's hired another babysitter. To supplement her other nannies."

Aimée suddenly perked up. "Liliane's got a babysitter, too?"

Martine nodded.

"I need one. Think she'd share?"

Martine stared at Aimée. "Don't tell me! You're pregnant?"

Aimée's gaze rested on an exhibit with an explanatory placard: *Circa 1870. Often the desperate parent left a bracelet, beads, or some other token with the infant being abandoned, hoping to reclaim the child in the future.*

"The color's drained from your face," Martine said, steering her to a bench. "You're paler than usual. Sit down. Morning sickness?"

Aimée was stuck on the phrase "or some other token . . . hoping to reclaim the child." Had those marks on the baby's chest been meant as identification?

Aimée shook her head.

"Tell me, Aimée."

"It's not that, Martine, it's worse." Then she told Martine everything: the phone call, finding the baby, the body in the morgue, the matching blue beads, Morbier's demand, and finding René wearing an apron, buying a stuffed animal without admitting it.

"René's nesting," Martine said.

"What do you mean?"

But she knew.

Martine dug into her bag and uncapped a small brown bottle with red Oriental characters on the label, took a swig, and passed it to Aimée.

"Drink this. Oronamin-C, a Japanese energy drink full of electrolytes. You need it."

It was dense, viscous, and tangy, with an aftertaste like a children's liquid vitamin drink. Her cheeks puckered.

"René's exhibiting the classic signs: cleaning, cooking, feathering the nest for the new baby, Aimée," Martine said, outlining her lips with a brown pencil. "Instead of you. He's a gem."

"My best friend next to you, Martine."

"A lasting relationship can be built on friendship, but it is rare in life."

What was Martine getting at?

"Knowing what they look for in adoption court, I'd say you've got a good start. René could help —"

"What?" Aimée caught the bottle before

she dropped it.

"Don't tell me adopting this baby hasn't crossed your mind."

"What's crossing my mind is what Nelie may have found in the Alstrom file, how MondeFocus is involved, and where she might be."

"Phhft," Martine said. "Everyone hates oil companies. You've got an in — hacking or whatever it is you two do on the computer — and . . ."

"Tunnel into Alstrom?" Aimée finished. "Easier said than done."

They were working for Regnault, Alstrom's publicity firm. There was a definite conflict of interest, as René had quickly pointed out. She reached in her back pocket for another stop-smoking patch, handed one to Martine, and stuck one above her hip.

"This should get you through the christening."

Aimée saw a gift certificate inside Martine's pocket.

"What's this?" She looked at the name. Jacadi, a baby store carrying top-of-the-line frivolous baby clothes.

Martine shrugged. "I'm always going to a christening these days, have to keep them handy! What's with your grunge outfit . . . infiltrating the Sorbonne?"

"Close."

And then it hit her — Martine was going to the oil conference. "Can you e-mail me your notes on Alstrom's participation in the oil conference?"

"I'm lead article editor, I write the overview, gluing everything together for *L'Express*. We're doing a four-page supplement in this week's issue."

Impressive. Martine had risen above straight investigative journalism.

"A young Turk's covering Alstrom, doing the nitty-gritty."

Aimée stood and they walked into the next cavernous room. "You've got the perfect reason to request his notes. To verify sources, legality, et cetera."

"It's better if I introduce you. He's a dish."

Martine never stopped trying to set her up.

"Pass."

Martine pulled out a parchment-paper envelope that contained an engraved invitation and dangled it in front of Aimée.

"The Institut du Monde Arabe reception for the Fourth International Oil Conference?" Aimée said. "How'd you get that?"

"Press corps," Martine said. "Come with me. You'll get more out of him that way."

She had a point.

"It's formal, Aimée. Bring a bottle of Dom Pérignon, too," she said, a shrewd twinkle in her eye. "The slush they serve's undrinkable."

Martine always had deluxe ideas concerning payback.

"Right now I'd appreciate an entrée into MondeFocus."

"Not again. I've only got my old press pass . . ."

"Brilliant idea, Martine."

Aimée leaned on Pont de la Tournelle's stone wall, scraping Martine's name off her old press card with her nail file. She used manicure scissors to snip her name from a business card and glued it and her photo from her Metro pass on top of Martine's. She sealed the result with wide, clear tape. Not bad. A quick flash of credentials and with luck it would work.

She crossed the bridge and reached Ile Saint-Louis. She gazed to the right at Quai de Béthune which Marie Curie and Baudelaire had once called home and where President Pompidou's widow still lived, and hoped the sky didn't open up.

At the MondeFocus address on the Quai d'Orléans, she pressed the buzzer. The door clicked open. Inside the dark *port cochère* entryway, another door opened. A dark-curly-haired woman wearing a blue smock stuck her head out the loge door.

"MondeFocus office, please."

"Don't think they're open."

Had the MondeFocus, wary after the demonstration, instructed the concierge to vet visitors?

"I'm with the press," Aimée said. "They must have forgotten to inform you."

The woman looked over Aimée's jeans, shapeless trench coat. Shrugged.

"*Bon.* Third floor left rear."

The door slammed shut.

On the third floor, a woman wearing pink capris and a striped man's shirt opened the door. She paused in her conversation, a cell phone held to her ear, scanning Aimée up and down. "Oui?"

Aimée smiled and flashed the press card and a folded copy of *Bretagne Libre.* "I'm working on an article. May I talk with you?"

"*Un moment.*" She motioned Aimée toward a worn blue-velvet window seat. Silver rivulets of rain ran outside the window, condensation fogging the corners and a draft hit Aimée's back. Her face looked familiar but Aimée couldn't place her.

The office was not a hive of activity. No

one sat behind the desk or worked at the computer that rested atop a narrow slat over sawhorses. An Andy Warhol silk screen of Yves Saint Laurent hung on the wall; an orange modular couch stood in the interior of the salon. It looked like a makeshift office had been set up in this woman's apartment. Warm, close air filled the room. Aimée took off her coat and scanned a pile of brochures. The World Wildlife Movement's story about rhino abduction competed with pamphlets about other causes piled up on the parquet floor.

And then she saw the vinyl record jackets in the corner and recognized the woman. Brigitte Fache, a seventies pop icon who'd had a handful of record hits. She came from an aristo background and was still well connected with the *gauche caviar,* society liberals. She was older and her eyes were devoid of her signature black eye liner. The *gauche caviar* had been lampooned in the daily *Le Canard enchaîné* for lending a sympathetic ear and sending hefty checks to Brigitte's pet causes until she had founded Monde-Focus and gained credibility and grudging acceptance in the ecological movement.

Brigitte resumed arguing into the cell phone. "They had no search warrant . . . what do you mean, who? I call that more than intrusion — it's breaking and entering," she said. "Not just harassment, it's illegal." She listened, then laughed, a short sardonic laugh. "So who raided our office, Brigadier, if you didn't, eh? The sandman?"

She held the phone away from her ear, rolling her eyes at Aimée, who heard indecipherable words tumbling over the line. Brigitte exuded an air of entitlement. "We've organized a dozen rallies for which we've always obtained permits, put in place a first aid corps and a contingent of legal aid, but of course, that's standard for a demonstration. Now, this candlelight march! We never sanction weapons. You've made a mistake."

She listened to an explanation, then Brigitte's palm slapped the metal file cabinet. "Proof? You call that proof, Brigadier?"

But her brow knit in worry. Outside the window, needles of rain beat down on the rising Seine.

"Krzysztof Linski's not in our organization," she assured the caller.

Her blunt-cut, unmanicured nails drummed the cabinet. The woman was lying, Aimée sensed it. But now she was forewarned; she wouldn't mention Krzysztof as a contact.

Barefoot, Brigitte padded into the other room. By the time she returned, wearing a wool trouser suit, with a cigarette and without the cell phone, Aimée had her makeshift card ready.

"Aimée Leduc, freelancer, referred by Léon Tailet of *Bretagne Libre*." She stood and handed Brigitte the card.

"How is Léon?"

Thank God she'd prepared and actually spoken to him on the phone.

"Rheumatism bothering him. As usual. You know, the damp in Brittany. But it didn't stop him last week from attending the demonstration."

Brigitte nodded, set the card on the desk, and rummaged through a worn black Day-Timer. Good thing she had a lot more on her mind than delving further into Aimée's credentials.

"What do you want?"

"Tell me about Krzysztof Linski."

"No comment."

"Were you at last night's march?"

Brigitte shook her head. "I couldn't be there. I had to march in a protest at La Défense."

Too bad.

"A young woman's body was recovered from the Seine. She and Nelie Landrou were in your organization —"

"Who's this article for?" Brigitte interrupted.

"Whoever will print it; the truth must come out. I've got contacts at *L'Humanité,*" Aimée hastened to add. It was a Communist rag, but that should appeal to Brigitte.

Brigitte's phone rang. She glanced at her watch. "*Merde,* the meeting started five minutes ago," she said, grabbing her bag and keys. "Sorry."

Aimée couldn't let her make her escape without getting any information. "A meeting concerning . . . ?"

"Alstrom's filing a suit against us. They're asking for an injunction and that's just for starters." Brigitte shook her head.

"Shouldn't it be the other way around?"

Strange that an oil company would file suit against MondeFocus and seek an injunction. Had things changed so much that an oil conglomerate could silence protests against it?

"Those with the most expensive lawyers win. We're attempting to negotiate to prevent their enjoining our campaign." Brigitte opened the door to the cold hall.

"How well did you know Orla Thiers?"

Brigitte looked down and when she did meet Aimée's eyes, a sadness filled them. She started to speak then caught herself and sighed. "I'll have more to say later."

"Wasn't she involved in the roadblock near the nuclear facility at La Hague? I'd like to speak with her friend, Nelie."

"Nelie . . . the hanger-on? I haven't seen her for a while."

Odd. It sounded as if Brigitte didn't know that Nelie had had the baby.

"How does Krzysztof Linski fit in?"

Brigitte's eyes blazed back in fighting form. "He's not part of our organization anymore."

"But I thought . . ."

"He got us into this mess. He was a right-wing plant. That's all I have to say." Brigitte's keys jangled in her hand. "Look, if you don't mind . . ."

Aimée pressed on. "Who else can I talk to in your organization, please?"

"Can't this wait?"

"In news, nothing waits or you won't have a story."

Aimée saw videotapes stacked on a cabinet arranged by title and date of demonstration. Surely the demonstration against the oil agreement would have been taped like the others. "Who filmed the march last night? Please, it would help so much to convey the mood of the event. Will you give me the name of the videographer?"

"Sure," Brigitte said. "I'll tell you on the way out."

Out on Quai d'Orléans, Aimée ducked, but not in time to avoid receiving the Peugeot's diesel exhaust in her face as Brigitte gunned the motor and sped off. Notre Dame lay shrouded in mist on her right, and rain pelted the stone ramp angling into the Seine. She pulled her hood over her head, glad she at least had obtained a lead from Brigitte. Then she stumbled into a rut filled with water and her pants got sopping wet up to her knees. En route to the documentary filmmaker's studio, she'd make a stop and buy an umbrella.

South of Gare d'Austerlitz, once an industrial area, cobblestone-surfaced rue Giffard still held traces of small workshops. Near Les Frigos, the old refrigerator warehouses that had served the train yards, two-story buildings housed artists, musicians and — judging by the graffiti — an anarchist or two. She read CLAUDE NEDEROVIQUE — DOCUMENTARY FILM PRODUCTION by the digicode at his door.

The grillwork gate stood ajar. Aimée pushed it open and entered a narrow courtyard roofed by grime-encrusted glass resembling a train station. Rain pounded relentlessly overhead.

She shook and folded her umbrella, remembering the radio alert she had overheard: traffic advisory warnings and closures of lanes bordering the Seine due to record rainfall.

She knocked. Her trousers and sodden leather boots were soaked through. No answer. She knocked again. Chills shot up her legs. What she wouldn't give for a warm fire, dry clothes, and . . .

The door swung open. "Took you long enough!"

All she could see was a man's head in shadow, haloed by the bright lights of the studio behind him. Guitar licks of the Clash met her ears. "Claude Nederovique?"

"Who's asking?"

He wore torn denims and motorcycle boots. Wavy brown hair hung over one eye and the collar of his black leather jacket. She tried not to shiver, aware of the surprise on his face as he stepped back into the light. His dark eyes studied her. A bad boy, just her type.

Merde! The one time she forgot to retouch her mascara. Or reapply lipstick.

"Brigitte at MondeFocus gave me your address."

"Excuse my rudeness," he said, his voice low. "I'm expecting the AGFA film shipment. They're late. As usual."

"Do you have a moment?" She'd seize this opportunity before his delivery arrived. "I'm writing an exposé of violence at the Monde-Focus anti–oil agreement vigil. Brigitte said you shot some great videotape."

Stretching the truth never hurt.

Silence except for the rain. She tried again. "I realize it's a bad time," she apologized.

"You're shaking," he said, taking her arm. "Why your pants are soaked! Come in."

The studio was lined with a bank of high-tech equipment: videotape recorders, monitors, camcorders. In contrast, old film-splicing machines and reel-to-reel spools sat atop high cabinets. An inner door led to a small room bathed in red light, emitting the acrid smell of film developer.

"Excuse the mess," he said, shoving cardboard cartons aside with his boot. "But I'm glad to take a break. I'm editing my Rwanda documentary. The Hutus and the Tutsis: genocide, ghost villages, and no one cares."

Pain and determination layered his voice. For a moment he looked lost and then he turned away.

"I'll make it brief," she said. She edged

toward a strobe light, feeling awkward. "Here's my card. Again I apologize."

He glanced at it. "*Pas de problème.* I did shoot some video footage that might interest you. Can you give me a minute?"

She nodded, reaching into her backpack for a notebook.

He gave her a crooked smile, a nice smile, then took off his jacket and pulled a cell phone from his faded gray corduroy shirt pocket. Suddenly businesslike, he went to the red-lit darkroom to speak into the phone.

On the studio walls hung black-and-white blowups of barefoot African child soldiers in tattered uniforms, AK-47s slung over their shoulders. None looked more than ten years old. A shantytown — skyscrapers in the distance — a cluster of huts with cardboard and metal siding, dogs, garbage strewn on the dirt street. She looked closer, horrified to see that the dogs were sniffing at bodies. A baby, flies on its open mouth, lay next to a metal gasoline jerrican, ESSO printed on it. Her insides wrenched.

No wonder oil protesters like Krzysztof were passionate. Another photo titled *Sorbonne '68* showed a cloud of tear gas engulfing miniskirted and bell-bottomed students. A 1987 film poster for *Guido and the Red*

Brigade with a shot of the Roman Coliseum was inscribed *Claude Nederovique, writer and producer* in red letters below. She felt like a voyeur seeing the most brutal side of injustice. Just a shallow urbanite worried more about her lipstick than the suffering of the world.

"Quite a body of work." She didn't know how to express her feelings . . . her horror at these views of evil.

He pulled up a stool for her in front of another deck of video machines and monitors. He straddled another, turned down the stereo's volume.

"Why film, if you don't mind my asking?" Aimée said.

He sat back, reflective. "Because I don't have the words like you journalists do to express this." He gestured to the wall. "Suffering, injustice." He shrugged. "I'm bankrupt in that department. I envy you lot, if you must know. So I film, searching for the essence — the look, the gesture, a glimpse into a window that speaks volumes."

Some underlying pain drove him. She sensed it. And she felt even guiltier for impersonating a journalist.

She put that aside; she had to keep her goal in mind. A woman had been murdered, and Nelie was in hiding. And there was Stella.

He leaned forward, leaving a sandalwood scent in his wake. The warmth in the studio crept up her legs.

"*Et alors,* just raw footage, haven't had time to edit it yet. Bear with me until I find the march." He inserted a cassette into one of the two videotape recorders, hit *Rewind,* and switched on the monitor. The whir of winding competed with the spattering of rain against the windows. "Anything or anyone specific you're looking for?" he asked.

A dead woman. Talk about rewinding a ghost. A glimpse of the mother with her baby. Something.

She pulled out the photo she'd taken from Krzysztof's flat and set it on the smooth aluminum counter. His knuckles clenched so hard they turned white.

"Do you know them?" she asked. "Friends of yours?"

"What happened makes me sick," he said. "I've documented this movement from its inception."

"Do you know either of these women?"

He nodded. "Demonstrations, sit-ins. . . . I'm sure I've seen them." He pointed. "*Oui,* her."

Nelie.

"I'd like to talk with her."

"Me, too," he said. "She borrowed my old Super 8. Promised to give it back a few days ago. But I'm still waiting. Why do you want to interview her?"

"Were they both at the demonstration?"

He ran his fingers through his hair. "I think so. Bedlam, chaos — that's what I saw."

"Wasn't she involved with the roadblock at La Hague?" Aimée hoped this would draw him out.

Silence, except for the rain beating on the skylight.

Keyed up, she said, "I know she's in trouble. Hiding."

He studied her, the scent of sandalwood stronger, his teeth just visible between his half-parted lips.

"Journalists protect their sources, right?"

"Always." At least that's what Martine had told her.

"I have connections to the network."

"Network?"

"The network that helps people who have to lie low. Know what I mean? I can help Nelie."

She was about to tell him about the baby,

but something prevented her. She just nodded.

"But you need to keep this confidential;
it's a clandestine highway," he said. "If you
should make contact with Nelie, let me
know."

First she'd have to find her. "Did you see
any bottle bombs at the march?" she said.

"In every struggle, there are power shifts
within organizations. Right now," he said,
pointing his finger at the photo, "the MondeFocus people think this *mec*'s a saboteur."

Krzysztof. That fit with what Brigitte said.

"He planted the bottle bombs, right?" she
said.

She figured he'd shown up at the morgue
to see for himself if Orla's body had been
the outcome.

"Who knows?" Claude said with a shrug.
"I just document and record the moment."

The videotape clicked to a stop. He hit
Play. A rainbow bar code showed on the
monitor, then dots of candlelight, dark
figures. Blue light from police cars swept
the crowd. Faces were blurred. There were
shouts. Then a close-up of bushes, leaves,
sprays of water. Action too rapid to make
sense of. Feet, a leg. Truncheons raised in
the air.

"That's it," Claude said. "Water damage,

I think. Residue and condensation corrode magnetic tape."

Disappointed, she slumped back. Rain drummed on the roof harder now, the rhythm of the Clash bassist throbbing in juxtaposition.

"Can you slow the tape down?"

He nodded. Ran it again.

"Any way you could enhance this, magnify it, or go frame by frame?"

"Video's not like film, with twenty-four frames a second."

"Sorry, but does that mean you can't isolate images?"

"In a manner of speaking, yes," he said. "Unlike film, video's written on magnetic tape in interlacing lines of resolution, converted into an electronic signal like a wave written in odd and even stripes on the mag tape. Much faster than film, too, at sixty images per second. So it can't be isolated without capturing part or half of the preceding or following image as well." He hit *Pause,* then *Play,* adjusting a jog shuttle dial on the keyboard. "Look, notice the blue flickering, the gray line below?"

She nodded.

"That flickering, twitching effect shows the degradation. Really, it's showing part of the next image. It is impossible to isolate one movement. See what I mean?"

She did. The blurred tape showed her little. Another dead end.

He sat back, glancing at his watch. "Give me a few hours. I'll work on the color contrast and saturation, using a processor to boost the sound. I'll see what I can do."

A pool of water had dripped from her feet onto the hardwood floor beneath them.

"I'm so sorry," she said. Again, apologizing. She reached for a rag by the large porcelain sink and mopped it up.

"Any other proof that this Krzysztof sabotaged MondeFocus's demonstration?" Aimée asked.

"I like him. It's not my place to say anything." He paused, hands in the pockets of his torn denims.

Was this some code of honor not to tell on fellow activists?

"Did anything strike you as odd at the vigil? Did Krzysztof seem out of sync?"

He shrugged.

She figured he'd said as much as he would.

He switched off the video camera. Then paused. "It was odd the CRS knew about the bottle bombs but the demonstrators didn't."

More than odd. She filed that away for

later and tried another angle.

"Would any of the demonstrators know Nelie's whereabouts?"

"Ask Brigitte."

She was wasting his time — and hers — now. Better go.

"I'll call you later to get a copy of the enhanced tape."

Again, she saw that lost look. Vulnerable, at sea. A maverick bad-boy type looking for a life raft. Her.

"How about a *verre?*" He gestured to a bottle of Chinon, half full, and pulled out the cork. "Until your clothes dry." He jerked his thumb toward the window. Water ran from the gutters nonstop.

Thirty minutes until her next appointment if she hurried. His sandalwood scent and dark eyes were appealing. She stepped closer. Then caught herself. She shouldn't get involved. Couldn't.

"Merci," she said, accepting the *ballon* of rouge. She sipped it. Flowery, notes of juniper, hint of berry. Nice. Expensive. Out of her price range. Like everything else until the check from Regnault cleared.

She sat on the stool.

"You got me thinking, you know, why I do this. Film." He sat. "Call me a red-diaper baby, my mother did. So proud of it, too.

She was steward of the Lyon railway trade union."

Aimée nodded. Lyon, capital of unions, the staunch labor movement stronghold. She knew the milieu, figured he'd grown up in a working-class socialist household.

"Madame organizer, they called *Maman*. I crawled around her legs in soup kitchens for the workers. It's in my blood, I guess."

No wonder.

"And you? What compels you to write about causes?"

Startled, she ran her finger around the rim of the glass. Not many men asked her what she thought.

"I don't like injustice, real or abstract. My mother didn't either." She paused. She couldn't remember the last time she'd talked about her mother with anyone. And never about her mother's ideals, the causes she'd embraced. "A seventies radical. But I don't know much. She left when I was eight. To save the world."

He gave her a sad smile.

"That's young. Mine left when I was sixteen. Soon after, I stowed away on a freighter bound for Liberia. I came back years later but my father had passed away by then."

"I'm sorry."

He shrugged. "Maybe we're the same in some way, don't you think?"

Both scarred and searching.

"That and a franc, twenty centimes gets you the paper," she said, a half smile on her lips. She didn't want to deal with this.

"You have to face it sometime," he said, almost reading her thoughts.

As if she could and it would disappear.

She turned away.

He put his hand on her shoulder. Warm. "*Voilà,* done it again."

"What's that?"

"Brought down the burden of the world onto your shoulders . . . no wonder I'm not invited to parties." He shrugged. "My friends tell me to lighten up."

"Right now I've got a story to write," she said.

She pulled out her worn Vuitton wallet, removed two hundred francs.

"Of course, I'll pay you for the tape and your time. You're busy. You can leave it outside your door, and I'll pick it up or send for it," she said. "Will this cover your expense?"

"Forget the money," he said. "Journalists don't pay their sources."

Didn't they? If she didn't hurry, she'd miss her next appointment.

"I do. You're a professional."

"On one condition," he said, an amused look in his eye. "This goes toward more of that superb Chinon and you come by later."

Aimée skirted Place Valhubert. His words, the wine, the warmth. She'd wanted to stay. But mixing business and men never worked.

She heard a baby's cry and turned around to see a woman emerging from the Metro with a stroller, the plastic cover coated with rain, blue-bootied feet just visible. A shudder of guilt went through her. Stella. And those big blue eyes. She had to hurry to her appointment, then relieve René. An oil company seeking an injunction against an environmental protest group; Krzysztof Linski discredited as a right-wing plant and drummed out of MondeFocus; bottle bombs that the CRS knew about in advance while the demonstrators were ignorant: It didn't make sense.

Ahead, car headlights illuminated the wet pavement. She passed the Musée National d'Histoire Naturelle, a *belle époque* building Jules Verne would feel at home in — musty glass display cases of taxidermied tortoises from the Galápagos, two-headed fetuses curled in glass tubes from the year 1830. A place where she'd spent many a

Saturday afternoon with her grandfather, hiding behind him to peek at the more graphic displays.

She checked her watch again and ran. A raincoated *flic* directed traffic and by the time she'd made it down the bank, littered with sand and salt to prevent slipping, to the Brigade Fluviale's headquarters, she had less than a minute to spare.

Quai Saint-Bernard, home in the summer to evening tango dancing, glimmered wet and forlorn in the lights from Pont d'Austerlitz. The slick gangplank to the Brigade Fluviale's long, low-lying *péniche* swayed over the Seine's current. She clutched the gangway rope tightly, almost losing her balance twice.

On the left loomed L'Institut du Monde Arabe. And not more than a few barge lengths across the Seine from it lay Place Bayre, at the tip of the Ile Saint-Louis, like the prow of a ship. White wavelets lapped against the stone steps and brushed the deserted bank. She thought of the tire iron, of fleeing through the park, and shivered with fear as well as cold.

She tapped on the white fiberglass door. A blue-uniformed member of the river police greeted her, a snarling white German shepherd at his side.

"*Bonjour.* Aimée Leduc to see the *capitaine de police.*"

He pulled the leashed dog back. "*Arrêt,* Nemo!" he said as he motioned her inside. The brigade headquarters reminded her of a holiday houseboat except for the computers, the white erasable boards filled with assignments, the scurrying officers, the thrum of fax machines, and the smell of the river.

"This way."

She followed him and a now friendly Nemo, who smelled her legs and keened to be petted. The officer slid another door open and they crossed a deck to an adjoining *péniche.*

"*Bonjour,* Mademoiselle Leduc," said Capitaine de Police Michel Sezeur. Shorter than Aimée, he had brown hair combed back *en brosse.* He wore a Manhurin standard-issue revolver in a holster on the belt of his form-fitting blue twill trousers. "I regret that I can only give you five minutes." He gestured toward a row of blinking red lights on his telephone.

"I appreciate your making the time for me, Capitaine," she said and sat down on a swivel chair facing his crowded desk.

The *péniche* rocked in the backwash of a boat speeding past and her stomach lurched. Waves lapped over the steamed-up portholes and gray mist hovered in the distance.

"Commissaire Morbier confirmed your request," he said, handing her a stapled report several pages in length

Smart and quick. He'd checked with Morbier after her call.

"You'll find all the details in this report: our recovery of the victim at 02:47 hours, attempts at resuscitation by one of our paramedic qualified divers, the assessment of the inspector who arrived on the scene and decided upon the next course of action, and the victim's subsequent removal to the Institut médico-légal. Standard procedure as you will see."

"About the CRS involvement —" she started to say.

He kept a tight smile. "You know the CRS carry no bullets, their guns are sealed, and they can't attack the public unless provoked or for due cause."

"A demonstrator's in the hospital —"

He cut her off. "Due to illegal assembly, failure to disperse, and discovery of weapons. The CRS only react if demonstrators cross the line. Which, I believe, one of them did." He sat. "But that's not my area nor the reason you're here, correct?"

"How do this victim's circumstances correspond to or differ from those relating to other bodies you've recovered?"

"We find fifty to sixty bodies a year in the Seine. More often than not, they've been submerged a long time."

"But this one wasn't. Mind telling me the river's depth and temperature?"

"Usually four to five meters[*]." He gestured to a wall chart of the river confluences. The *péniche* rocked and her stomach lurched again. A door swung open, revealing a line of hanging wet suits. "However, the Seine can rise two to three meters more, as it has now. The current's strongest now. Temperature-wise, it's three to four degrees in winter, up to twenty[**] degrees in the summer."

"You mentioned that the corpses are usually submerged. How does that affect the body?"

"It's not rocket science, Mademoiselle. In winter, bodies sink, in spring, they bloat. Sometimes they blow up with body gases like a hot-air balloon. When they're black and swollen it's difficult to distinguish between a man or a woman. We've recovered bodies as far away as the *barrage,* the sluice gates south of the Tour Eiffel." He paused.

[*]Thirteen to fourteen feet
[**]Centigrade

"That one took three weeks to travel eight kilometers."

Curious, she leaned forward, though it had little to do with Orla.

"Three weeks?"

"The current, the time of the year, and water temperature all have to be taken into account. Plus the *silure,* the big-river fishes, and the *écrevisses,* fresh-water crawfish, had eaten more of the extremities than usual."

She shuddered, thinking of them feasting on Orla.

"Some fishmongers near Les Halles supplemented their income by selling *les écrevisses.*" He smiled. "Until we stopped them."

Aimée glanced at an array of rusted fire-arms and a collection of rope knots behind glass on the wall. "Artifacts from the river?"

He grinned. "Treasures. I found the Sten gun used by the Résistance on the river bottom. On another dive I brought up this revolver, from the 1930s. It had been a dumping point for gangsters from rue de Lappe. Amazing to find it, considering the murkiness of the water, Mademoiselle. We must use our hands; we can't see a thing down there. And twenty minutes in a wet suit is all a diver can take."

Interesting, but it got her no further. She had to ask him for guesses with respect to what she wanted to know. "Two more questions, Capitaine. How long do you think this woman's body lay in the water? And, in your opinion, how far could it have traveled from the point at which it entered the water?"

"The Seine's risen several centimeters since last night and will continue to rise due to runoff and rain. We're near flood levels." He exhaled. "Given the body's temperature and the lack of severe bloating or discoloration, I'd hazard three or four hours. The autopsy report should be more definite."

A knock and the door slid open. Two uniformed officers stood outside. "Ready when you are, Capitaine."

He grabbed his raincoat from the rack. "Regarding the body . . . well, I can only conjecture."

"I understand."

He flipped the pages of the report to the end. "On this diagram, you'll see, I've marked the place where the body was recovered from the sewer grate."

It was at a point just below Pont de Sully. "But wouldn't it be unlikely for her body to remain in the same spot at which she was shoved in, considering the river current, the passing Bateaux-Mouches and other barge traffic?"

"I've seen it before; it happens," he said. "A limb catches on a sewer grate, a body twists and sticks in the iron rungs or the underwater steps descending from the bank. Or it becomes entangled in an underwater pylon or with an old fishing line. Sometimes the currents from a Bateau-Mouche will push a body up to the surface."

"So what do you conclude, Capitaine?"

"Don't quote me." He walked to the door. "And I'll deny saying this, but I doubt she'd been there long at all. It's just a feeling, a sense, from my twenty years of experience."

"Can you explain what you mean a little more clearly?"

"I tried to reconstruct the scene. It struck me, well — a possible scenario would be that she reached for help, was struck, and fell back into the water, her lungs filling up then."

That's what Serge had intimated, she recalled.

"There's no way to be certain," the commander continued. "But it's almost as if she was trying to grab her attacker."

Or to grab something from the attacker? Serge had not mentioned any defensive wounds on her hands.

"Who knows? The attacker might have been frightened by the lights of a passing boat. He might have been interrupted and so he ran away not knowing if she survived."

He put his raincoat on. "And I never said that."

Interrupted?

Nelie Landrou had made the frantic telephone call to her. This made sense if she'd seen Orla attacked at the river, been chased in turn, and so feared for her life and the baby's. She had not even had time to put a diaper on Stella. Shaken, Aimée rounded the curve of Quai d'Anjou.

The rain continued to pelt down. She walked down the worn steps to the spot Capitaine Sezeur had pointed out. White and rust-colored lichen splashed with clumps of lime covered the stone wall; moss feathered the cracks oozing under her wet boots. A Bateau-Mouche glided past, so close she could hear radio static erupting from the deck, and sweeping gray-green water onto the bank and her shoes. Just as quickly, the water receded, trickling back over the weathered stone.

Here. Hunched over, she reached her hand into the icy water. Flailed around until her fingers touched a metal rung, invisible in the murky depths. A whoosh of colder subterranean water, putrid and scummed with foam, gushed forth and was swept away by the current. The capitaine's conjecture was right. Caught in and buffeted by the sewer stream, Orla couldn't have been here long or she would have been bruised all over.

Her hand, dripping by her side, tingled. Then the rain stopped and a warm, almost tropical wind whipped her face as she walked the few steps to her building. A weak moon struggled behind wisps of pearl gray clouds hovering over Pont Marie.

Orla had died almost outside Aimée's window. Capitaine Sezeur had confirmed her suspicions.

But her investigation had fallen short. Brigitte had revealed little about MondeFocus or Nelie. Claude's video held only blurred, unfocused images and would require painstaking processing to decipher. And then the tape might show only two minutes of dark chaos. There had to be more.

What was clear was that she couldn't juggle work and take care of Stella.

Yet she needed to sniff under the rocks Brigitte had pointed her at and to find Krzysztof. To focus, or — as the old dinosaurs in the force said — squeeze till the water ran dry.

She tried Brigitte at the MondeFocus office. No answer, so she left a message on the machine. She stopped at the *boulangerie* around the corner and stood in line behind a bent old man. He tipped his cap with a knowing smile. *"Bonsoir."*

She returned his greeting, searching her memory. Did she know him? He struggled to put his loaf of *pain au paysan* inside a plastic bag printed with the green cross of the pharmacy next door. She noticed boxes of bandages and dressings inside the bag.

The *boulangerie* doors stood open to the street where the few passersby were folding their umbrellas to save them from the wind. Meter maids in blue peaked caps checked car meters along the quai. She emerged, baguette in hand, and paused, sensing someone watching her. Her skin prickled.

Unsure of what to do, she ducked inside a doorway and scanned the street, but she saw only a meter maid writing a ticket in her little book and the bent old man shuffling to the stone stairs leading down to the riverbank. She had to control her nerves.

On impulse, she followed him. She wanted to ask if he'd seen anything unusual the previous night. The algae-scented breeze rustled the budding plane-tree branches.

The old man clutched the stone balustrade as he made his way downward with slow, painful steps. Odd. She wondered why he was descending since the Seine's gray-green water lapped over the bank and rose above the bottom step. No one else was out walking on the quai now.

Pont Louis Philippe arched ahead of her, decorated with carved stone wreaths of intertwined sculpted leaves. Buses trundled overhead, their green sides flashing above the stone wall.

When she looked down again, the old man had disappeared.

"Monsieur?" she called out. Anxious now, she took the steps two at a time, hesitated, then tiptoed through the swirling eddies of water. Useless. Her shoes were soaked. And she couldn't see the old man on the bank or in the river. Before she waded ankle deep in water to explore, she had better relieve René. She mounted the stairs. Her cell phone vibrated in her pocket.

"Allô?"

"Mademoiselle Leduc?" said a familiar voice. She searched her memory, came up blank. The guitar of an old Georges Brassens song played in the background, punctuated by an engine starting.

"Oui?"

"You asked about a tire iron. Well, one's missing from the garage stockroom."

Momo, the mechanic from the garage near Pont de Sully. Chances were the figure in Place Bayre had stolen the tire iron while Nelie was telephoning Aimée, and had then used it to attack Orla. Not a comforting thought.

"Momo," she said. "Can you remember anything more about the woman who used the garage phone?"

"No, I'm sorry," he said.

Too bad.

"But I thought I saw her," he said as she was about to click off.

She gripped the phone tighter. "You did? Where?"

"The scarf . . ." The sound was muffled as he put his hand over the phone, speaking to someone.

She controlled her frustration. "Her scarf, Momo, you're sure? Do you remember the color, the design?"

"Chic, you know," he said. "Never saw one embroidered like that. But I'm not sure. Just an old woman. They're like crows, you know; they go through the garbage —"

"What color?" she interrupted.

"Chic, with *papillons,* pink butterflies. I've got to go."

He hung up.

Inside her apartment, all was still except for the strains of a lullaby. From the doorway, she saw René sprawled on the *recamier,* eyes closed, mouth open. Miles Davis was curled on the floor by René and faint whistles of sleep came from the bundle in the hammock. She checked on Stella. And sat, watching her, lost contemplating the little balled fists and feathery eyelashes until she noticed a note in René's handwriting. It read, *Never wake a sleeping baby.* Nesting all right. And in this case, it was a tired René who was catching up on his sleep. The old lullaby on the tape deck played over and over again.

His laptop screen showed a program running a standard virus check. *Bon.* Again René had it all under control.

Still, she prepared a bottle, in case, then sat down, expectant. But Stella's little peeps of breath came measured and slow. She glanced at the clock, then tiptoed to her bedroom, riffled through the hangers in her armoire. A white military-style frock coat with a double row of buttons, over-the-knee boots, striped black-and-white trousers with a Left Bank mottled brown leather oversized doctor's bag? Or a more *soignée* Right Bank assembly of cropped wool Chanel jacket and rope of pearls worn over dark washed jeans and stilettos with a metallic python-skin handbag?

Neither. Her role was that of a concerned eco journalist. She chose the jeans, stilettos, frock coat, a T-shirt silk-screened with Che Guevara's chiseled face and her leather backpack, pinched her cheeks for color, and daubed a drop of Chanel No. 5 in the hollow of her throat.

"Santé." Aimée clinked her wineglass against Claude's. The bottle of Chinon sat open and breathing on the wooden West African manioc-kneading table. At least her pants were dry and she wouldn't drip puddles on the floor this time.

"I am so sorry the video didn't come out more clearly. But take it with you." Claude brushed his hair back. His long legs were clad in black leather pants and he wore a black V-neck sweater and a small silver hoop in his ear. "Did Brigitte help you reach Nelie?"

She felt stupid. He looked as if he had dressed for a date. She thought she had better leave now.

"Non, but I'll keep trying. *Merci."* She downed the wine in one gulp and picked up

her bag.

"Wait a minute — why rush off? I've got a joke to tell you." He threw his arms up in mock supplication. "I've practiced it all afternoon."

Was this part of his "lighten up" campaign?

"Sit down again," he said, refilling her glass.

"Do I have to laugh?" She took a sip. The wine slid down her throat, smooth and full bodied.

"In Dakar, a steamroller operator's at work flattening the dirt for the highway. He is injured. His friend goes to visit him in the hospital. 'What room's my friend in?' he asks the nurse. 'Rooms 15, 16, and 17.' "

Aimée grinned dutifully but she didn't find his joke very amusing.

"OK, I tried," he said.

She hoped he wasn't going to pull out some cowrie-shell game to teach her.

"Now it's your turn."

Jokes . . . she didn't know any clean enough, or politically correct enough, for a documentary filmmaker.

She pointed to the tattoo of a lizard on his arm. "Nice. From Africa?"

"Marseilles, on the dock. Young, dumb, and drunk," he said. He ran his hand up her arm. "Do you have any tattoos?"

She averted her face, blushing.

"Look at me." He grinned. "You do!"

She couldn't lie before that intense dark gaze.

"A Marquesan lizard," she said, "the symbol of change, with the sacred tortoise inside."

"*Et donc,* didn't I say we were the same? Both branded with lizards. Show me."

She took another sip of wine, shook her head, and stared at the tribal rug under her feet.

"From Marseilles, too?"

"It's a secret," she said, loath to admit that she had once had to hide from a *flic* in a Sentier tattoo parlor and wound up with one.

When she looked up, his face was almost touching hers, so close his eyelashes feathered her cheek. "We all have secrets," he breathed in her ear.

His finger traced her mouth. Soft and warm. The only sound in that moment was the patter of rain on the glass roof over the courtyard. She inhaled his sandalwood scent, stronger now, engulfing her.

A tentative look shone in his dark eyes. "What's in your mind right now?"

Her fingers explored his shoulders. "You

really want to know?" The wine was talking, she couldn't believe she'd said that.

Then his arm was around her waist. His hand dropped to the small of her back.

"I know what's in mine," he said.

His hair brushed her chin, his warm lips finding her neck.

"Time to see your lizard." His arms were tightened around her, pulling her toward him. His mouth was on hers, tasting it.

"Then you'll have to find it."

Wednesday Afternoon

Krzysztof sensed the presence of the plain-clothes *flic* leaning against the scuffed wainscoting of the engineering lecture hall before he recognized him. He'd noticed the man shifting from one foot to the other in his fresh white Nikes. It was the same *flic* who had showed him Orla's body in the morgue. He turned on his heel, suppressed a shudder, and merged with a laughing group of Sorbonne students heading out of the hall.

Brigitte had turned him in. And the *flics* had lost no time in tracing him here. He had to move fast, to get away. He broke from the group by the reception desk, eased down a passage toward a sign saying ÉLECTRICITÉ

BUREAU, and opened the door. Inside, he balled up his sweatshirt jacket, pulled a brown ribbed sweater from his backpack, and put it on. Then he studied the diagram on the wall that showed the exits from the building in case of fire.

Growing up under the Communists in Warsaw, where apartment blocks had been filled with informers and nightly ESKEK — secret police — visits were the rule had honed his senses. Some things one never forgot. His thoughts went back to the unfamiliar faces on the street; men sitting and smoking in their telltale Trabant sedans; the day his father was taken to Bialoleka, the political prison. All gulags were hell, but the Soviets had taken particular delight in torturing his father, an intellectual of aristocratic lineage.

His uncle never wanted to hear about real Warsaw life, which had been governed by the *kartki* — coupons. Standing in line for gas, sugar, and clothes, his mother had used her maiden name. A title had meant nothing without a *kartki.* Or *bony towarowe,* dollar bonds printed by the government and exchanged for goods only in special stores. Reality had been quite unlike the romantic vision of prewar Warsaw his uncle nurtured.

The physics lab lay at the south end of

the building; a nearby fire exit to rue Descartes was indicated in small red letters. Perfect. He avoided the electrical panel with its green lights and levers, opened another metal door, and found himself in a peeling brown stucco tunnel breathing warm, fetid air tinged with dry rot. Safe for a moment, he began to feel his anger mounting, overcoming the hurt and shame. After his uncle's accusations, the long hours of work, his commitment to MondeFocus, now he'd been accused of betraying the cause. He'd been disgraced and would likely be expelled as well, when all he'd done in reality was skip his engineering exam to organize the vigil! And Brigitte, whom he'd regarded as a mentor, had informed on him to the *flics*. His life was ruined. He had no hope of finishing his studies and obtaining a degree. Now he was being hunted, condemned to hiding.

And despite everything, the Ministry would sign the agreement with Alstrom tonight. If he didn't do something, they'd win.

Perspiration dampened his sweater by the time he found the physics lab. Empty. Lab classes were over for the day. The last rays of weak light reflected off the slanted slate roofs opposite. The hour of dusk, *entre chien et loup,* when a dog and a wolf were indistinguishable, as the saying went. He set his backpack down. Above him, arched ceilings were frescoed with portraits of the forebears of physics and science: Pasteur, Curie, Fourier. By the old stained porcelain sinks, beakers and test tubes had been rinsed and left to dry on the drain board. He stared at the liter bottles and vials of chemicals and reactive agents.

Bottle bombs? He snorted, kicking the cabinet. How primitive. On the Internet, recipes for destruction written by fourteen-year-olds were more sophisticated! They involved remote ignition triggered by cell phones, and the explosions packed far more punch. He could rig something twenty times more effective if he had a mind to.

But he'd been caught on video, probably laughing and singing, carrying the backpack with bottle bombs.

Not only ruined, he faced prison like his father. Except that his father, finally recognized for his work after the overturn of the Soviet regime, lay under a gravestone in Warsaw's Powazki Cemetery.

He took stock of the chemicals on the shelf, the solutions packed in the drawers. If a candlelit vigil against the oil-company negotiations had ended with Gaelle in the hospital after a beating, MondeFocus labeling him a saboteur, and now the *flics* hunting him, then what had peaceful means accomplished?

The heavy hand always worked . . . in Warsaw and here, too. Didn't they say the end justified the means? And now he had nothing to lose.

WEDNESDAY MORNING

Aimée reached out her arm. Instead of Claude's taut chest she felt something wet against her hand and she blinked. Light streamed through the window. Something was ringing near her head. Beside her, half under the duvet, Stella cooed like a little pigeon with a leaking diaper. Time to change the sheets. Again.

Warm air floated through the open window. She groped under the pillow, fumbled in the damp sheets, and found the phone.

She stretched her legs, inhaled the baby's smell and the sandalwood scent of Claude still on her skin.

She rubbed her eyes and pressed the answer button. *"Allô?"*

"Mademoiselle Leduc," Vavin said. "I'm concerned. Have any more firewall attacks occurred?"

She sat up, grabbing her father's old flannel robe, still dotted with spit-up. She was awake now. Not many heads of departments worried about this kind of detail once they'd hired a consultant.

"Un moment." She hurried to the laptop on her desk. Thank God she'd forgotten to turn it off last night. She clicked on Regnault's system.

"Right now we're working on your new workstations setup, Monsieur Vavin," she said. She had to act as if she was on top of the assignment and to be polite, she reminded herself. And enthusiastic, too; they were paying Leduc Detective big francs. "I'll check with my partner. Can you give me ten minutes?"

She'd come back so late last night. Stella, wide awake and hungry, had given her no time to discuss anything with a grumpy René but getting the formula temperature right. Not even the time to decipher the odd look in his eyes. "I'll call you right back," she promised.

"Meanwhile, there's another detail," Monsieur Vavin said, his voice tentative.

New user account configurations filled her screen.

"Of course, we're making great progress." She glanced over at Stella's kicking feet.

Slants of sunlight played over her pink toes.

"Glad to hear it," he said. He cleared his voice. The clinking of cutlery and the sounds of chairs scraping were in the background.

Some breakfast meeting?

"I'd appreciate a favor," Vavin said. "This involves accessing a colleague's e-mail. It's very confidential. Can you help me?"

As system administrators, she and René controlled the domain and e-mail server. Their clients often asked them for this kind of service: evidence of a colleague's wasting time in chat rooms or visiting dodgy sites. But spying on his colleague's e-mail wasn't her kind of thing.

"Monsieur Vavin, we're on a tight schedule," she reminded him. "We run on deadlines, you know."

"I appreciate that," he said.

Stella would need a bottle soon; the little thing packed away more than Aimée had imagined.

"Newborns lose weight, then gain almost a kilo in the first few weeks," René had quoted from the birth-to-one year book he'd bought. Thank God she could read up on breaks, try to get some handle on why babies spit up and what infant gas was all about and how to avoid it.

"It won't take but a minute for you, I'm sure," he said.

Her fingers typed at 120 strokes a minute; one didn't get much faster than that. His request seemed to be made with the assumption that she had nothing better to do with her time than snoop. But it would be impossible to refuse him.

"This sounds odd," he continued, "but certain negotiations . . . well, it's difficult to go into right now." He lowered his voice, she heard the sound of a door being closed. "I've heard some disturbing information. But I can't say anything until I know what's being concealed from the public."

This sounded cryptic and not like anything she wanted to get involved in. Probably some promotion blackmail or a hatchet job he wanted the skinny on.

"The e-mails I'm concerned with could have been read by hackers who got past our firewalls. Please, take a look. I'll hold on. The name's de Laumain."

She turned to her second laptop, which was already logged on. She hit some keys and entered a back door in systems administration mode.

In minutes she had accessed de Laumain's e-mail.

"So, de Laumain's a lacrosse aficionado?"

"How'd you know?"

"De Laumain subscribes to five lacrosse newsletters."

The baby's coos had turned into faint cries. She stretched her feet to touch the edge of the bed and began to bounce it. The cries escalated.

"You have a baby, Mademoiselle Leduc?" he asked.

She didn't want to sound unprofessional. "My neighbor had to rush to the pharmacy. The baby's got a fever, so I . . . I'm helping her out for ten minutes."

There was a pause. She sensed there was something else he wanted to say. There were shuffling noises in the background.

"De Laumain's the one," he said. "Look for the word 'Darwin' on the subject line."

She found two messages with "Darwin" as part of the subject.

"Copy them and send them to my e-mail account," he ordered. "Can you make their status 'unread' and exit without any traces?"

"Not a problem, Monsieur Vavin," she said.

"Of course you won't . . . read them."

"You said this was confidential, right? Is there anything else?"

"Let's hope not. When my meeting's over, I'll call you. We should talk."

He hung up before she could remind him of the system-design overhaul René ached to do.

"René?" Aimée shouldered her cell phone, left arm holding Stella, her right hand clicking away on the keyboard.

His voice mail answered.

Great. Firewalls were his *métier;* this job really should be his. She saved her work on a backup disc and sent a copy of the completed program to Regnault, as usual. Her laptop clear, she checked the firewall herself. She had started going through each protection system when her cell phone rang.

"René?"

"What have you found out, Leduc?" Morbier asked.

The last person she wanted to talk to. A click came over the line — someone was calling her . . . René? Vavin?

"I've got another call, Morbier, and I'm swamped," she said, irritated. "Real work."

"That can wait," Morbier said. "I can't. Have you run across Krzysztof Linski?"

Her fingers tightened. Stella moved and Aimée propped the baby on her hip.

"You there, Leduc?"

"Why?"

"He's been taped on video carrying bottle

bombs at the demonstration."

She hadn't caught that on Claude's tapes. But she'd been too busy in his arms on the leather sofa to watch the video again.

"What's that got to do with the student Orla Thiers?"

But she now knew — Krzysztof, Orla, and Nelie were radicals.

"He's at it again. There's another bomb scare at the l'Institut du Monde Arabe."

"How do you know it's him?"

"Nelie Landrou's a suspect," Morbier said, ignoring her question. "What aren't you saying, Leduc? You owe me."

She stared down at Stella. Was her mother a bomber?

"Too easy, Morbier. Simplistic. How can you fall for that?"

"Eh?"

"It's a setup. Orla and Nelie were taking part in a roadblock of trucks at La Hague's nuclear fuel processing site. . . . MondeFocus has disowned Krzysztof: they say he's a loose cannon and a right-wing plant."

Stella opened her mouth, her pink gums glistening. The key to understanding what was going on was Stella. Aimée had to find Nelie . . . make a deal, get the lowdown on Krzysztof, before doing anything else. Then she'd decide what to tell Morbier.

But to get Morbier off her back she'd have to tell him something more. "I checked Krzysztof's room, a *chambre de bonne.* He's gone, disappeared, sleeping bag and all."

"So?"

"Think outside the box, Morbier. Orla's murder could —"

"I try. We get witness reports all the time."

"Meaning?" What wasn't he telling her?

"The good news: your local secondhand goods dealer claims a *clochard,* an old woman, saw her being killed. The bad news: we don't know how reliable she is. She talks to an imaginary sister and thinks it's 1942."

"The *brocanteur* on rue des Deux Ponts?"

He grunted. She scribbled that on the back of a data report; she would check out this information later. Far-fetched . . . but who knew?

"Back to the point. Why would he set off bombs at a peace march and let himself be videoed carrying them? It doesn't make sense."

"I'll make sure to ask him once he's behind bars."

He hung up.

She checked her voice mail and found a terse message from Vavin telling her to meet him at his office at once. She couldn't bring the baby with her; she had to do something

235

with Stella.

Aimée handed the taxi driver an extra twenty francs. "Mind waiting?"

He grinned. "Take your time."

Her back ached as she climbed the red-carpeted stairs of the building, Stella in her arms, and baby bag dangling from her shoulders.

"Quite the modern *maman,* Aimée," Martine said, opening the door. "Juggling everything in designer wear."

She looked down at her agnès b. black dress, the closest thing at hand without spit-up, which she'd grabbed to wear to her meeting. "The babysitter's here?"

Martine nodded. "The location of tonight's reception has been changed."

"Due to the bomb scare?"

"Can't have all those sheikhs and oil execs in danger, can they? I'll call you later when I know it." Martine showed her to a luxurious children's bedroom decorated with Babar-theme murals, bunk beds against the walls, and Legos strewn on the floor. She introduced Aimée to Mathilde: tight jeans, big sweater, and gap-toothed smile.

"What a beauty," Mathilde said. "May I hold her?"

Aimée removed her finger from the hot,

wet little mouth and handed Stella to Mathilde. "I'm sure you're experienced," she said, half to reassure herself.

Her last view was of the flopping pink bunny-eared cap. All the way down the stairs, she could still feel Stella's warmth in her arms.

"Monsieur Vavin left this for you," said the smiling receptionist on the ground floor of the Regnault offices.

"I don't understand. Isn't he here?" Aimée asked.

The receptionist shrugged. "I'm sure whatever you need to know is all there. He's been called to a meeting."

Called to some meeting and she'd gone through hoops rushing here!

She walked to the tall glass window. She could see a few demonstrators standing outside with banners saying, STOP OIL POL-LUTION . . . NO AGREEMENT!

Inside the envelope was a piece of crisp white paper with 41 Quai d'Anjou written on it in Vavin's script.

Her hand trembled. The address was only a block and a half from her building. Why hadn't he told her to meet him there?

"*Pardonnez-moi,* when did Monsieur Vavin leave?"

"I didn't see him go out."

"Merci."

She walked past the bomb-removal squad truck parked on the pavement near l'Institut du Monde Arabe. Several Kevlar-suited men stood around, eyes narrowed at passersby.

"False alarm, eh?" she asked one of the women filing back into the building.

"Can't be too careful," the woman said.

"True. What happened?"

"A librarian found a backpack left in the library," she said.

The *flics* were jumpy. It made them trigger-happy and dangerous.

Forty-one Quai d'Anjou was the address of an upscale antique shop. A buzzer went off as she entered it. Her grandfather had haunted the Drouot auction galleries, scouring the sales for bargains. Her cluttered apartment was testimony to his hobby. She lived surrounded by antiques, his "finds."

She noticed a hefty price tag on a Sèvres porcelain figurine. Not her type of bargain at all. The shop contained château-sized armoires, stone statues, marble busts on faux fireplace mantels, and delicate Louis XIV desks. But it held no clients.

"Bonjour," said a middle-aged man with a

receding hairline. A smell of espresso clung to him. His eyes flickered as he sized her up, estimating the cost of her dress. Not couture but a good label. No way he'd know it came from the rack at her favorite second-hand stall in the Porte de Vanves flea market.

"Mademoiselle, how can I help *you?*" he asked with a smile.

"I'm meeting Monsieur Vavin. Perhaps he's here . . . in back?"

"*Non,* Mademoiselle," he said.

"I'll wait if you don't mind."

"But he has already left, Mademoiselle," he told her.

She was going around in circles. She should have ignored Vavin's message and kept working.

"Did he leave any word for me?"

"He left in a hurry, that's all I know."

"Where did he go?"

The man shrugged. "He's a client but I don't keep track of his movements."

"A client?"

"Such good taste." The man's face brightened. He'd thought of another sales tactic. "Mademoiselle, are you interested in antique children's toys, like Monsieur Vavin is? This is a delightful nineteenth-century rocking horse." He gestured to a miniature horse with a horsehair mane and leather

239

reins, its white paint peeling.

"It's just ornamental, isn't it?" she asked. It was so small that she doubted a child could ride it.

"Monsieur Vavin's daughter rides one very like it, he tells me. It's been repainted, of course. Monsieur Vavin's very particular. He never buys plastic or mass-market toys for her. He wants her to appreciate craft and tradition."

She let him ramble on, her mind elsewhere. Vavin might have stepped out to buy cigarettes, talk on his cell phone, or for a myriad other reasons. She'd wait.

". . . the MondeFocus petition . . . ," the man was saying.

Her ears perked up. "Pardon, Monsieur, what did you say?"

"Not that I'm against the environment, you understand," he said. "I signed her petition. Monsieur Vavin explained how important it is."

"Today?"

He tapped his forehead. "A few weeks ago."

Her mind raced. "Monsieur Vavin came here together with a woman who had a MondeFocus petition?" She had an idea. "Was it about oil pollution?"

"Saving the whales, I believe," he said.

"So important."

She pulled out the photo. "Do you recognize her in this group?"

He peered closer. "So polite. *Oui,* that's her."

Nelie Landrou.

"When she visited the shop, was she pregnant?"

He stuck his arms out and linked them in a big circle. "Like this."

The door opened to a rush of traffic noise from the quai. She looked up. Instead of Vavin, a couple had entered, triggering a buzzer.

"Monsieur, which way did Monsieur Vavin go?" she asked.

"If you'll excuse me . . ."

"Through your glass windows you can see the quai. Did he go left or right?"

The man stuck his thumb to the right. "Aaah, Madame *et* Monsieur Renaud, so good to see you. That cloisonné vase has your name on it." He'd already forgotten Aimée as he scurried toward the couple.

Vavin, the Regnault publicity head, and a pregnant Nelie, a MondeFocus activist . . . together?

She stood outside on the quai. The gunmetal gray sky threatened rain. She tried Vavin's number. No answer or message.

Then why had he summoned her here?

A Bateau-Mouche passed under the supports of Pont Marie more slowly than usual because of the rising level of the Seine. The slap of water against the stone mingled with the blaring horn of a taxi. Cars, unable to use the flooded road on the other bank, crossed the bridge at a snail's pace. Fliers advertising neighboring Théâtre de L'Ile Saint-Louis performances were caught up in the wind; they swirled around her ankles. She grabbed a handful, meaning to bring them back to the theatre. Inside the building, she set them down in a corner stacked with theatre notices and more fliers. She saw a pile of MondeFocus report pamphlets, identical to the one she'd found in Krzysztof's room and noticed in Vavin's office. She'd better check this out.

Her footsteps echoed in the damp tunnel-like passage that led to a seventeenth-century courtyard like that of her own building. The theatre proper and rehearsal studios were upstairs. She climbed a switch-back series of neo-Gothic wood-railed steps and heard a voice coming through a window that opened onto the courtyard. The words themselves were in old formal French.

I find that everything goes wrong in our world; that nobody knows his duty, what he's doing, or what he ought to be doing, and that outside of mealtimes . . . the rest of the day is spent in useless quarrels. . . . It's one unending warfare.

She recognized lines from Voltaire's *Candide.* Valid then and today.

Loath to interrupt the rehearsal, the first drops of rain pattering in the vacant courtyard, and with nowhere else to stand but the dank hallway, she entered the small theatre. Red crushed-velvet curtains were halfway drawn. The brightly lit stage was bare except for a throne-like wooden chair and a woman mopping the scuffed black-painted floor planks, humming, her bucket beside her.

"Madame, are any of the crew about?"

The woman looked up, squinting into the darkness beyond the stage lights. She pointed. "Rehearsal."

"*Merci,* I'll wait." Aimée pulled up a corner of the dust sheet that covered a seat, glad to take a rest, even in the cramped velvet *chaise* designed in the nineteenth century for a less statuesque person. She put her feet up, rubbed her calves. Checked her voice mail. No message from Vavin or René.

The woman finished mopping and left. Aimée tried Vavin again. No answer. She let the cell phone ring.

In the middle of a yawn, she heard a digitized ring-tone version of "Frère Jacques" from the stage. Then an ear-piercing scream made her sit up. It was followed by another, higher pitched.

She ran down the aisle and up the side steps leading backstage. The white-faced cleaning woman leaned, heaving, against an electrician's stage-light panel.

"Are you hurt?"

A salvo of Portuguese erupted from the woman's mouth. She crossed herself. "Maria Madonna" was all Aimée could make out as the shaking woman pointed to the partly open door of a broom closet.

A stout security guard arrived, red faced and panting. The ring tone was repeated. It was closer now.

"Not another mouse! Xaviera, I told you last time, old buildings have them," said the guard. Catching Aimée's glance, he rolled his eyes. "Answer your phone, Xaviera!"

The cleaning woman's hands were trembling, her eyes wide with terror.

"Non . . . telefono de mi . . . non ai . . . non telefon."

No phone, that much Aimée understood. She stepped over the fallen mop and opened the broom-closet door wider. The annoying ring tone was repeated.

Vavin's trouser-clad legs sprawled. His head was turned away and slumped onto his shoulder. The brooms and a tin pail were overturned next to him inside the closet.

"Monsieur Vavin?" she said. She knelt and gripped his shoulders. "Can you hear me?"

His body slid forward, limp. He was not conscious. She took his head in her hands, turned it to face her. His eyes stared up at her, lifeless. Then she saw the clotted blood on his temple and glimpsed the cell phone in his hand. No wonder he hadn't answered it.

"Nom de Dieu!" the guard gasped, knocking over a bucket and spilling ammoniated suds over the wooden floor.

"Quick! Get help." Aimée grabbed the guard's arm and they laid Vavin flat on the suds-soaked planks.

Xaviera backed away, crossing herself.

Vavin's phone tumbled to the floor. Aimée hit a button to stop the ringing and thrust the phone at Xaviera. "Call 17 . . . call the ambulance!"

Vavin's eyes seemed to stare at her. Watching her, he was watching her. The guard cleared Vavin's mouth of spittle, began mouth-to-mouth resuscitation.

Aimée tried to steady herself. Her fingers on Vavin's wrist confirmed that he was not even cold. His fists were clenched.

"How long has he been here? Did you see him come in?"

Xaviera shook her head. "I *non . . . non* see him."

No pulse. Lifeless.

Aimée looked around the barren backstage; there was no place for the attacker to hide. She didn't remember seeing anyone else in the theatre.

The guard said, "He's gone," and reached for his walkie-talkie.

She'd been too late. She wondered what he'd wanted to tell her. He'd left the message an hour and a half ago. Why had he asked her to meet him at the antique store?

To see Nelie? But a few weeks had passed since Nelie had accompanied Vavin there.

She heard the static of the guard's walkie-talkie. Her eye rested on the photo of a child amid the soaked clutter spilling from Vavin's briefcase onto the floor. A happy little girl sitting on a rocking horse.

The guard got to his feet.

Something glinted among the broom bristles. A key ring. One she remembered Vavin pocketing in his office. Had the killer, searching through Vavin's briefcase, missed it? Or had Vavin tried to hide the keys? She had to deflect the guard's attention.

"Did you check in the wings?" she asked him.

As he turned, she reached down and clutched the keys, dropped them into her pocket, and stood. She backed into the velvet curtain, then made for the stage stairs.

"*Attendez,* you know him, don't you?" the guard asked.

He was sharp, just her luck.

"Hold on," he called out.

And wait for the *flics* and a trip to the Commissariat to give a statement that would reveal her connection to Vavin? Not on her life. She had to work fast, use her sysadmin access, and read *his* e-mail before the firm turned it over to the police. She wanted to search his office before whoever did this got there first.

He'd wanted to tell her something. And was murdered before he could.

More crackling sounds came from the walkie-talkie. The guard spoke into it.

The implications spiraled, spinning in her head. Vavin's knowledge of Nelie, his desperation concerning a co-worker's e-mail, and the meeting, the fact that he was her boss . . . she'd mull that over later. Right now she had to leave.

"I'll show them the way," she said, edging down the steps.

"The location's been radioed in. What's your name?"

But she was already striding up the aisle. "*Non,* it will be quicker if I guide them."

"Wait," he barked.

Xaviera's sobbing and the guard's shouts telling her to stop echoed in the empty theatre.

She ran down the stairs, colliding with a man in a black turtleneck sweater who held a folded-back script. Irritation knit his brows.

"Pardon me."

The hall was full of people; conversations buzzed all around her.

"Point me to the restroom, please?" she asked him.

"Down there."

She rushed past him down the stairs to the street level, realizing she smelled of ammonia. The door to the ladies' room was locked. The mens' room door, too.

A siren wailed from down the passageway.

Morbier would give short shrift to her deepening suspicions. And so far, that's all she had.

Vavin . . . his eyes staring up at her. Why kill him?

She had to find a way out and get to his office fast.

Several doors lay ahead. She tried one. Locked. And the next.

A loud voice filled the courtyard. "No one leave the building, please." She looked back, saw blue uniforms. Talk about fast response! But since the nearby bomb threats, they were on high alert.

The third door opened. She ran inside a vestibule where hanging coats and damp umbrellas leaned against the paneled walls. The next door was locked, too. She took off her wet heels and found her red high-tops, emergency footwear, in her bag and laced them up. The door scraped opened.

Voices and dense cigarette smoke emanated from the next room.

"Entrez," someone said. "Sorry to keep you waiting."

Before she could stuff her wet shoes into her bag and leave, a man's face appeared at the door.

"Aaah, you're changing. But we've only got five minutes. You're the last one."

She nodded.

"After you," he said, gesturing her inside. "Here, I'll take your things."

"Wait . . ."

But he'd taken her shoes and the bag with her laptop and gone ahead.

Nothing she could do but walk in, make an excuse, and retrieve her bag.

Bright lights and a haze of cigarette smoke hit her.

"Mademoiselle, if you don't mind," another voice said. "Go to the right."

She turned.

"*Non,* face right. *Bon.*"

She felt like a deer caught in the headlights.

A murmur of voices: ". . . tall enough, what's with the shoes? *Non,* it's eclectic . . . androgynous look . . . too skinny?"

She could distinguish several heads through the haze of smoke and the burning orange tips of cigarettes.

"Dip, please."

What the hell did that mean?

"From the knees, please."

She took a step and tripped. An arm caught hers.

"We're making a video, not auditioning for a clown act, Mademoiselle."

What?

She bent her knees and kept her back straight, afraid to bump into anything else.

"Now lower, more *décolletage!*"

A porn video? They wouldn't see much of her in this agnès b. spaghetti-strap dress. She bent and thrust her chest out while peering through the haze for another door.

"Now jump in place once, then run over there — make space for her, please — as if you're afraid."

At this moment, that wouldn't require her to act.

Someone pounded on the door.

She jumped higher than she'd intended, heard the table vibrate when she landed, then kept running.

"Over here," someone said. She found herself by a group of women sitting on the edge of a small stage. Some filed their nails; one thumbed a *Marie Claire* magazine. All wore foundation, black eye makeup, and had platinum or dirty-blonde hair reaching below their shoulders.

A number was thrust at her.

"We're ready. Mount the stage, please, Mesdemoiselles."

She followed them, out of place except for the number that she — like the rest of them — held. Unlike the others, she had dark spiky hair, wore no heels, and had no *décol-*

letage to speak of. They stood on the stage like a lineup of Barbie dolls; she was the black sheep.

"One last dip, please."

What was with this dip?

She watched the others, mimicked them, and thrust her chest out even more. Several men had entered the room. She heard the static of a walkie-talkie. The *flics.*

She was caught in bright lights on stage.

"Number 13."

She waited for one of the women to step forward. Looked around behind her for a door. Saw a red lighted EXIT sign. But she needed her bag with her laptop, and the man had taken it!

"Number 13!"

"That's you," the blonde woman next to her hissed. And she shoved Aimée forward.

"We need to question everyone," a *flic* was saying.

Her hands shook.

The man who'd taken her bag clutched her arm and guided her to the table, behind which several men were seated. She saw a pile of whips and jackets on the chair. "I'm cold, do you mind?" Without waiting for a reply, she pulled the closest jacket to her — a hand-stitched feathered brocade affair further adorned with a vintage diamanté brooch — and slipped her arms into the sleeves.

"Your portfolio's not here," said a man at the table.

The *flics* stood in a circle by the strobe lights. "Auditions, I told you," a tall man was saying. "We've been here all afternoon, Officer. We rent this room by the hour. Now can we get back to work, eh?"

"Who's your agent?" the man asked her.

Aimée thought quickly. "Her card's in my bag. Can I have it?" She beamed her brightest smile at him. "I just switched to a new agency."

Her eyes stung from the smoke and the glare of the lights. Someone thrust her bag and shoes into her lap. She dug into her card case, picked one of her aliases with a Saint Germain address, and handed it to him.

"If you'll assemble everyone in the courtyard," the *flic* said, annoyance in his voice. "It won't take long."

They'd have a crowd to question with the actors, the women at the audition, and the crew. Before they could proceed, they would try to contain the possible witnesses while waiting for the medical examiner.

"I'll be in touch," the man with the tousled hair said, his gaze skimming her legs.

I bet you will, she thought.

"Feel like an aperitif?" he asked.

Fluff from the feather edging on the jacket got in her eyes and she blinked.

"Love to," she smiled. Glanced at her watch. Shrugged. "But" — she leaned forward — "this will take forever."

He turned around. *"Merde!"*

She grabbed her tube of Stop Traffic Red and swiped it across her lips.

"Unless we go out the back door." She licked her lips.

He grinned. "Bet you look good in just feathers."

"I need to make a list," the *flic* was saying. "Everyone who's here. Get your things, ladies." A *flic* gestured to them. "You two, now."

She lingered at the back of the line filing out, trying to catch the eye of the man with the tousled hair. But the *flic* clapped him on the shoulder and guided him to the front of the line. So much for her hope to use him as cover. What could she do? She leaned down as if to pick up her bag, got onto her hands and knees, and crawled under the table. She could see several pairs of black-stockinged legs and two pairs of solid police brogues just beyond her nose.

The damn feathers kept coming off. She

was molting. She crawled sideways, thankful for the dim light. If she could just reach the stage curtains and get behind them . . .

"Wasn't there another one?" a *flic* asked.

She reached for the loose change in the bottom of her bag and pitched the coins out onto the floor. They hit the surface, then rolled.

"*Et alors,* someone dropped a purse," a voice said.

Heads ducked, eyes focused on the coins, and she crab-walked behind the curtains. She stood against the wall and pulled the dusty curtains around her, trying to cover her toes.

She waited, praying they'd hurry and that she wouldn't sneeze. Her nose itched and she pinched it hard. The exit door lay behind her, stage left.

"I only count twelve."

"No, that's my ten-franc coin."

"I dropped it; give it back."

She had to take her chance right now!

She slid from behind the curtain and over to the door, pushed it open, and gently closed it behind her. The exit led to a dank passage, so narrow that her shoulders scraped the sides of the adjacent stone buildings. She broke into a run and found herself on the street next to the post office in a drizzling rain. Several blue-and-white *flic* cars on her right blocked the way to the quai.

Another pulled up to her left. A bus, wipers going, was stuck in traffic in front of her.

She grabbed a real estate journal from a newsstand, put her head down, and shielded her face with it as she put the stopped bus between herself and the theatre. Keep walking, don't stop, make it to the *brocante,* she told herself. A siren wailed on her right and she heard the squeal of brakes.

WEDNESDAY AFTERNOON

René fumed, tapping his short fingers on the Citroën's steering wheel in time to the baroque chamber music on France2. He sat stalled in traffic at Porte de Vincennes with no reception on his cell phone and looming trucks sending waves of rain over the windshield. His seat was customized for his height. He adjusted the knob that extended the accelerator pedal to ease his aching leg.

Five centimeters did it. Eased the twinge in his right leg. But nothing alleviated the low back pain radiating down his legs after the fall he'd taken at the dojo last week. Even though he had earned a black belt in karate, it still happened.

Not that he'd ever let on about that to Aimée. Or that he hoped they'd become more than partners. He repressed that thought.

He planned on buying a stroller in which to push Stella instead of carrying her. But looking at the dashboard clock, he saw that, due to the unexpected traffic, it was now too late to shop. And all this driving and dampness had exacerbated his hip dysplasia.

A sickening crunch and he lurched forward, feeling a sharp twinge in his chest as it hit the steering wheel.

"Merde!" Just what he needed . . . a fender bender. He punched the seat in frustration. Whoever had hit him better have insurance. He switched off the engine, took out paper and pen and his umbrella.

"Not even a dent," said a red-haired trucker in a rain-beaded slicker after peering at the Citroën's bumper.

He'd see for himself.

The trucker grinned at him as he took in René's height. "Where's the driver, *petit?*"

"There's a long scratch on the chrome." René pointed it out, containing his anger. His 1968 Citroën, specially customized, had a huge slash on its bumper. "See."

257

"I said, where's the driver, little man?"

"I hope you have insurance," René told him. "And I'm the driver." He wrote down the truck's license plate number and the model. "Your license and registration, please."

The truck driver bent down and peered under René's umbrella. "You must be a dwarf *flic!*"

Horns tooted in the pouring rain. Traffic had started to move. Angry shouts came from the cars behind them. The upright row of budding cypresses lining the highway glistened and swayed in the wind.

"*Et alors,* I only tapped you," the trucker said with a short laugh. Dismissively, he rubbed his hands, big meaty ones, the skin bulging over a wedding ring. "Quit making a big fuss."

René didn't relish arguing on the expressway in the beating rain, his Italian shoes and the cuffs of his suit pants getting soaked. "Have it your way. I'll deal with your firm and mention your rudeness to your supervisor. I doubt that he'll be happy to hear about the damage and your attitude, Alphonse."

The truck driver poked René's shoulder. "How do you know my name?"

"It's stitched on your jacket lapel. And I'll

know where you live, your hobbies, and your bank balance in an hour or so."

"That's harassment," the truck driver said. His eyes darkened. "What kind of freak are you?" He raised his fist and took a swipe at René.

René jumped back into a puddle and slipped. Pain shot up to his knee. Even though he was a black belt, with his leg pinned behind him at this angle no kick could save him. He clutched the bumper, made himself get up. He tried to will down his fear. A fight in the rain on the shoulder of the wet highway — no way could he win with his leg already throbbing in pain. Right now he couldn't afford an injury: the Fontainebleau contract, Stella. . . .

He darted a look at the truck's windshield and saw pictures of children hanging from the visor. Since childhood he'd had to learn how to deal with bullies. Now he fought back the only other way he knew.

"Alphonse, I'll find out your children's names, their school, the teachers you have parent conferences with," he said. "Computers, Alphonse, I work with computers and it's all there, if you know where to find it."

For the first time the driver looked unsure. Cars passing them in the next lane rolled down their windows. "A giant and the *petit* making a big jam," someone laughed. A siren wailed from the other side of the road, red lights from a police car reflecting in the puddles as it slowed down.

The truck driver hesitated. "Hey, let's talk this over. No need to get them involved."

René knew any trucker involved in an accident lost his job. Zero tolerance.

"So, Alphonse, I waited six weeks for this customized bumper. You want to hand over the eighteen hundred francs that I paid for it and call it quits?"

"What do you mean?" Alphonse's eyes narrowed at the mention of money. Scratch the surface and no doubt he was just one generation removed from the land belonging to a frugal farm household.

"Make it nineteen hundred, so it ships faster. Cash." René pulled out his dead cell phone. "Or I'll make a report."

The truck driver reached under his rain slicker, pulled out a wad of francs. "That's all I have."

"Not enough, Alphonse," René said, thumbing the wet bills.

"I'll check what I have in the truck."

René climbed back into his car with fifteen hundred francs in cash and four hundred francs' worth of *ticket de resto* restaurant coupons. Not bad; he'd eat out more often.

He took off his wet shoes and blasted the heater and defroster. At least he hadn't had to resort to a punch to Alphonse's middle. As if he could have managed it with his throbbing leg.

He tried his cell phone again. Still no reception. He'd canceled drinks twice this week on Magali, his sometime girlfriend and clubbing companion. He didn't think she'd understand why he'd rather change a diaper than go to a rave. He couldn't understand it himself.

Traffic moved, then halted. He turned off the radio and, to keep his mind off the pain in his legs, switched on the alphanumeric police scanner under the dashboard. A birthday gift from Aimée, only installed last weekend. He hadn't yet had time to crack the scrambled frequencies used for high alerts and terrorist attacks. So far, all he could decipher was the coded *flic* lingo on the unscrambled channel. They all watched American *télé* and liked to throw in veiled *Columbo*-style references. Or what they figured were *Columbo* style.

Horns blared behind him. A big space had opened up between him and the car ahead. He brightened up when he saw the cars on the off-ramp moving.

". . . bleeder . . . units in the area, respond

41 Quai d'Anjou . . . refresh that sir, victim . . ." came from the police scanner.

René let in the clutch, shifted into first.

". . . scene secured . . . awaiting the Big E."

The medical examiner, of course. He leaned over to turn up the volume.

"ID intact . . . Édouard Vavin, 32 rue Rocher in the ninth . . ."

Vavin . . . could it be *their* Vavin who lived in the now-gentrified old Jewish district near the Freemasons lodge?

". . . work address, according to ID, 6 rue des Chantiers . . ."

René's clutch ground, and the car jerked and stalled. Aimée had met Vavin there. That was Regnault's office address.

WEDNESDAY EARLY EVENING

"Bonjour, allô?" Aimée said, stamping her feet inside the doorway. She shut the door to the secondhand shop, feeling as if she'd been ridden hard and put away wet. Sodden feathers stuck to her black dress and glitter dust sprinkled her damp red high-tops.

This had to be the place Morbier had mentioned. She'd spied it from across the street. Vavin's keys jingled in her pocket.

She pulled out her phone and dialed Regnault's number. A message told her that the offices had closed for the day. So she might have some time. She hoped so.

She'd dry off and question the shopkeeper until the *flics* left and she could grab a taxi to Regnault's.

In the dim shop, she made out a hand-lettered sign: ESTATES PURCHASED AND CONSIGNMENTS WELCOMED — JEAN CAPLAN, PROPRIETOR. An old man was sorting through the contents of a cardboard box. Piles of yellowed newspapers tied in bundles with rotting twine, shelves of dust-covered salt shakers and the odd marble bust, old colored-glass liquor bottles, and a warped eighteenth-century desk. A pewter-tinged suit of armor stood in the corner, a collection of swords mounted on the wall behind it. A mixture of junk and treasure if one was to sift through it, she thought.

"Monsieur Caplan?"

"I'm closed, Mademoiselle," the man said. His voice was curiously high pitched for someone his age. White hair curled over his shoulders. A half-full glass of red wine sat on a small table next to an uncorked decanter. "Forgot to put the sign up. Come back tomorrow."

She recalled Morbier's conversation.

"I'd like to ask you something, Monsieur," she said, walking toward him and wishing he'd turn on the sagging chandelier. The gaslight fixtures and ocher-patinaed walls looked as if they hadn't been cleaned since the last century. A framed Honoré Daumier print of a laundress with her child on the Quai d'Anjou steps met her eyes.

"What's that . . . *alors,* Mademoiselle, I'm busy right now," he said turning around. "I've got this consignment to sort."

To sort and leave in the dust. She wondered how he did business.

"I'll make it quick." She summoned a smile. Sirens sounded outside on the street. She couldn't go out there yet.

He set down a packet of crumbling violet envelopes addressed in faded ink to "Commandant Sillot, Arsenal." Old love letters. Amazing the things people find in their attics.

Great-granny's hots for a regimental officer didn't interest her.

"In your conversation with Commissaire Morbier, you mentioned . . ."

"Who?"

"You reported to the Commissariat that an old *clochard* —"

His eyes flashed. "Her name is Hélène. I spoke with a young *flic* who treated me like a senile fool. Whether or not I am, I pay their salaries with my taxes and I demand to be treated with courtesy."

He took a swig of wine. She needed him to keep calm so he would recount the information that he'd reported.

"*Exactement.* That's why I'm here. We're checking every lead and I apologize."

"You're apologizing for the police?" He squinted at her. His wine-tainted breath hit her in the face. "Apologizing, the police?"

"We've got our best people on it, I assure you, Monsieur." She tried not to wince at the trite phrase.

"That's a first!"

A cynic. Not a typical reaction from his generation, but then perhaps she had laid it on too thick.

He stared at her. Red and purple feather fluff from her jacket floated up with the dust motes, then landed on a warped harpsichord.

"You're undercover, that's it," he said. "I understand."

She passed this man's shop all the time. Had seen him on the island, recognized his long woolen coat from the quai where she walked Miles Davis. Cut out of context and in her feathery outfit, he didn't seem to know her.

"You're a sleeper. That's what they call it, *non?*" he asked.

She glanced outside. More police cars and one lane closed to traffic. She was trapped.

She pulled up a stool with three legs, a chair for him. "Tell me about Hélène."

He glanced at the wall clock, a ticking period piece in need of a new glass face. "She comes by if she's hungry."

He blinked. A sad look in his long face. "It's a long story."

"I'm sure the pertinent details come to you. We don't have much time." She didn't know if this would go anywhere. Yet, as her father used to say, omit the smallest lead and it whacked you in the head later.

"I'm ashamed to say it. Life's treated Hélène hard. You don't know."

"Try me."

"They ridicule her. The young ones most of all," he pounded his fists together. The veins in his face more pronounced. "But what would *they* have done . . . how could they know what it was like?"

His gaze was far away, in another time, another place.

She had to pull him back, gently. Coax him.

"I'm listening, Monsieur."

"We lived next door. Her family owned

this shop," he said, his voice hard and abrupt. "What's left of it's hers, I tell her all the time. Take it. Go to court, make a claim, I'll give her legal rights. No one had the right to auction it at the end of the war. Least of all my father, to buy it for nothing."

She groaned inside. The story would come out his way. Painful and tortured.

"What did Hélène see?" she tried again.

He shrugged.

Great. "According to your report, she has conversations with imaginary people. So why did you call if you . . . ?"

"She talks to Paulette. But the last time I saw Paulette was end of September 1942. Right there." He stood and shuffled to the window. Pointed. "It was a rain-drenched day, like today. She was right there, in front of Fondation Halphen, only then it was a tenement."

Behind a fence, Aimée saw a soot-blackened building in the throes of gutting and renovation.

"An eyesore to the SS. They requisitioned the town house and its contents — art. Now it's the Polish Foundation."

Aimée focused on the *flic* cars, their blue-and-white lights flashing over the cobblestones. A man she recognized was getting

267

out of one. Morbier.

She moved back from the window.

"I don't understand, Monsieur."

His eyes glazed. "The *flics* came then, like now."

She had to bring him back to earth, to what the woman — the *clochard,* whoever she was — had said.

"Monsieur, how is this relevant?"

"Hélène bribed her little sister, Paulette, with nougat candy to pick up Hélène's homework from her classmate in Fondation Halphen," he continued as if she hadn't spoken. "*Flics* under Geheime Staatspolizei — Gestapo — orders rounded up Jews who lived there, forty of them children."

"You mean . . . ?"

"They dragged Paulette out with the others, still holding Hélène's math book. I saw them herded into waiting trucks. Now a plaque marks the building. You see, right there."

And she knew. She recalled the plaque on the wall. All 112 inhabitants, including children, had been rounded up. And deported.

"Paulette wasn't even Jewish. But they slammed the truck doors closed."

"I'm sorry."

"Sorry?"

She saw the pain in his eyes.

"But we all saw what was happening. We knew. People hurried off, trying to melt, to evaporate into the stone buildings. To avoid seeing or being seen. The shame, the fear. Hélène came walking down the street. She stood right there, holding her laundry basket."

How did that fit into this story? "Laundry, Monsieur?"

"It was cheaper if you did it yourself in the *bateau lavoir* near Pont Marie," he said, his tone matter-of-fact.

The old laundry barges had been moored in the Seine until the fifties. It was hard to believe the river had once been clean enough to do laundry in.

"Then Hélène was screaming . . . her basket fell from her hands, the white sheets lay on the cobbles as she stood on the street, pleading." He shook his head. "They had quotas, they told her."

Aimée hated these stories — the pain, the oozing guilt. The helplessness to alter the past.

"Every day Hélène and her father went to the Place de l'Opera and waited in line at the Kommandantur."

The former Kommandantur now housed a Berlitz center, the Royal Air Maroc office, and Aimée's bank, BNP Paribas. The bank manager had moaned to her one day in his office about the techs finding a rat-chewed cloth swastika while tearing up floorboards to install fiber-optic cables.

"All futile," Caplan said. "Paulette had left on the Auschwitz-Birkenau convoy number 37 on September 25."

Aimée couldn't speak. There was nothing to say.

"Hélène blamed herself. Her parents sent her to a cousin in Le Puy. What happened to them later, I don't know. But there was heavy bombing of the southern train lines . . . so many never came back."

He scanned the street and shuffled back to his chair. Sat down with a sigh. "After the Libération, my father bought this shop at auction. It would make me sick to hear him justifying his 'investment.' Then the store passed to me." He gave a tight smile. "I wanted to study medicine. But that's not your problem. A dozen years ago or so, Hélène reappeared. I'd thought she was dead. She wanted to go to sleep in her bedroom. Vacant eyed, she spoke to an imaginary Paulette."

Aimée wanted to know about the present, not this sad past, the shame clinging to these walls. Here in the dust, a miasma of the forgotten was almost palpable, though his words and the plaque were the only testimony to what had happened long ago in front of his door.

"To survive, you move on. But it's still here." He hit his chest. "No one likes remembering. Those who broke, like Hélène, live in a twilight of the past. She'll go for months, rational and even able to work, and then . . ."

He pulled a much-folded *Elle* magazine from under the cushion of his chair. An issue from the sixties with a young Catherine Deneuve on the cover, pert in Courreges boots in *The Umbrellas of Cherbourg.* Now a collectors' item. He opened it and took out a black-and-white class photo from the École des Garçons around the corner. Another photo showed a street scene with two laughing girls in school smocks, petting a puppy in front of the butcher shop; the butcher in his apron; people sitting in chairs on the street, fanning themselves. "See, that's how the island used to be, shopkeepers, the aristocrats, talking together, a village."

She didn't need a nostalgia lesson; she'd grown up here and heard it before.

"That's Paulette and Hélène."

Preserved in that moment of joy, playing

with a new puppy . . . too bad joy couldn't be frozen and thawed at will.

"I'm sorry," she said, "but getting back to the present . . ."

"You don't understand, do you?" he said, putting the photos away under the cushion. "Forget it."

She'd rushed him. Stuck her foot in it and he'd clammed up, changed his mind. Or his guilt had taken over. Whichever, she'd lost him. Yet this story was relevant somehow. She had to curb her impatience.

"Try to remember what Hélène told you while it's fresh in your mind, Monsieur."

"Hélène's confused," he said. "She had shock treatments that left scars. You know what that means."

Aimée recalled how widespread shock treatments for the depressed and deranged had been once. Now one took a pill.

"I shouldn't have called the Commissariat," he said.

"Monsieur, we need your help. No one's accusing her. Since you've told me this much, it's better I hear from her . . ."

He pulled back in his chair.

"Let me reassure you, Monsieur," she said. "No questioning at the Commissariat, nothing like that."

"Questioning, Commissariat?" His voice

shook. "*They* said that, too."

"Who?"

He gestured to the cobblestone-paved street outside. "The *flics* who rounded the people up. But no one ever came back."

"That happened more than fifty years ago. I'm talking about now. A young woman has been murdered and if Hélène was there —"

"She's not insane." He shook his head. "She can't be locked in Saint Catherine's with the loonies. She keeps herself clean and asks for nothing. If she did anything, she's not responsible."

Aimée's jaw dropped as she registered his meaning.

"Responsible! You're saying Hélène may have killed . . . ?"

"I said nothing. Get out!"

His words shook her. Hélène had to be in her sixties, or even older. And she recalled the mechanic Momo's words.

"Did she wear a scarf with butterflies, pink?"

He scratched his head. "Maybe. I don't know."

Big jump. Or was it? "You think she may have killed the person who threw the young woman into the Seine, that she may have confused the victim with Paulette, don't you?"

He turned away from her.

"She'd have to be strong, Monsieur. And then, where's the killer's body? Exactly what did Hélène say? It's important."

"She said, 'I took care of it.' "

"That could mean she acted in self-defense or even that she did nothing at all."

"*Exactement.* Forget it, I've got work to do."

"But there's been a second murder," she said. "A man was killed in the theatre. We can't forget it."

He clutched the armrest, surprised. "What?"

"I thought you knew why the *flics* surrounded the quai." She pulled out the photo. "Have you seen this young woman around?" She pointed at Nelie.

No recognition shone in his eyes. His body deflated. He looked smaller, as if his flesh was retreating into itself. Protected, in a shell.

And then she noticed the silent line of tears trickling down his wrinkled cheeks.

"Monsieur, please." She put her arm around him. His shoulders were so thin, like a sparrow's.

He shook her arm off, wiped his face with his sleeve, and sobbed. "Leave . . . just leave."

Guilt pierced her; reducing an old man to tears hadn't been on her agenda. Her ringing cell phone broke into his muffled sobs.

Torn, she didn't know what to do. She didn't even have a tissue. In her bag, she found a moist towelette pack, LÉON, BRASSERIE BELGE, with a green mussel imprinted on it. She tore it open and put it in his hands. Her phone kept ringing. Something wrong with Stella? Or Nelie calling?

"Allô?" she answered.

"It's on the scanner, Aimée. Vavin's been murdered," René said, breathless.

"I know, René."

In the pause she heard bleeps from the scanner.

"They're on the lookout for a woman with spiky hair, wearing a red feather-trimmed jacket. . . ."

That damn security guard! Her heart sank to her wet high-tops.

"That's me." She couldn't even go back to her apartment to change.

"What?"

"I found him."

"What the hell's happened? And Stella?"

"Later, René," she said. "Stella's with the babysitter at Martine's." She had to work fast. "I'm going to Regnault."

"And run right into the *flics?* I heard the

275

office address; that's how I recognized him."

"The *flics* will need to get a search warrant and that takes time," she said. "I figure whoever killed Vavin is en route to his office. But I have the keys. That should give me some advantage."

"Don't go there alone," René said.

"There's not much choice. Or time."

She heard the police scanner crackle in the background, glanced again at the wall clock. She'd have to hurry.

"I'll meet you," René said.

"You don't have to, René," she said, but she appreciated his offer.

"Where?"

"On the second floor," she said. "Women's restroom. Bring your laptop and a coat for me."

"In case you hadn't noticed, I'm a —"

"Then meet me by the fire door next to it. Hurry, René."

The old man had sat in the chair again and he was far away, lost in his memories. "Monsieur . . ."

"Leave me alone." He shrugged her hand off his shoulder and drained the wineglass with shaking hands.

She set her card down on the table, her fingertips blackened with surface grime. "I doubt that Hélène killed anyone, but if she witnessed the murder, call me. I'll use your back door if you don't mind."

In his galley kitchen piled with dirty pots, she opened the back door to a small courtyard. She looked back but he hadn't moved.

She took a headband from her pocket, pulled it over her hair, fished out big black sunglasses from her bag. Put the jacket on inside out, on the red-and-orange-fiber side. Not bad. She looped a scarf around her throat to cover the Christian Lacroix label.

Several doors opened onto the small courtyard. She tried the one labeled HÔTEL and walked through an even narrower passage — once the seventeenth-century tennis court of Louis XIII, who liked the fashionable *sport à l'anglaise* — that led into the lobby of the four-star Hôtel du Jeu de Paume.

In the restored medieval timbered lobby, tapestries lined the walls and tall floral arrangements in Lalique vases adorned the tables. A woman whose face Aimée recognized from an eighties Louis Malle film stared at her. There was no time to waste.

She smiled at the young doorman, wishing the old White Russian who'd worked here for years was standing there instead. "Taxi, please."

"You're a hotel guest, Mademoiselle?" he asked.

"A guest of a guest," she said. "I'm in a rush."

"Pardon, Mademoiselle, but service extends to our guests only."

That meant he wanted a big tip.

"He'll appreciate my disappearance," she said, palming fifty francs into the doorman's hand. "Before the photographers arrive!"

One-upmanship was the only way to handle his type.

After a blast of his whistle, she stepped in a taxi and sat back on the leather seat.

"Six rue des Chantiers."

She slouched down as the taxi sped past the *flic* cars.

WEDNESDAY EARLY EVENING

Krzysztof rubbed his goose-pimpled arms in the chilly lab. He stared at the row of labeled chemicals. Easy, so easy. He'd seen recipes for explosives on the Internet using HTH, the swimming-pool chlorination compound, Vaseline, and simple table salt. Concoct an explosive, plant it at the oil conference reception, threaten to detonate it unless they canceled the agreement. It should be easy.

Stop . . . what was he thinking? Violence against one of the hydra-headed corporations who polluted the world? Disable one and another would spring into its place. There had to be another way. He wished he knew what it was.

Night threw shadows over the farm compound as Krzysztof entered the dark kitchen. It was deserted. The only evidence of the red-haired *artiste* was her welding torch on the scorched floor by her twisted pipe sculpture. Art — she called that art?

He climbed into his sleeping bag in the corner, exhausted. His cell phone bit into his side. He took it out, turned it on . . . no messages. His mind drifted in the enveloping down bag's warmth.

Voices, guttural and low, invaded his dreams. "Explosives enough for a nice little scare." Then low laughter. He blinked. A dim light from the *artiste*'s studio cast oblong shadows on the table. He realized that he wasn't dreaming.

He sat up, rubbing his eyes. Saw beads of rain on the shoulders of huddled figures in raincoats. Craned to get a better look. Two men, crouching. The taller one stood and left. Krzysztof caught only the outlines of the other's face; he was blond and hawk nosed. The face looked familiar, he'd seen him before but couldn't place him. Then footsteps, the slam of a door, and the man was gone.

Krzysztof got to his feet, stiff from sleeping on the floor, and walked into the studio. The redhead, a shawl around her lace halter top, was stuffing something into the pocket of her torn jeans.

Cold drafts whistled under the warped window frames. Her welding torch was hooked onto a dark green gas canister, her protective visor was on the floor.

"Who was that?" Krzysztof asked.

"Quoi?" Her gray-speckled eyes darted from side to side. "How long have you been here?" she asked irritably. She put her hand over her jeans pocket but not before he saw the wad of francs.

Scattered pieces of copper wire snaked across the floor near metal pipes and smudges of black powder, like a clump of ants. He stiffened. Gun powder. How could he have been so naive?

"Long enough," he said. "You're making pipe bombs."

"What's it to you?" She combed her fingers through her red curly hair, caught it up, and twisted it into a knot. "You've overstayed your welcome."

"You made the bottle bombs, too."

"Art expresses itself in many mediums."

"And set me up."

"*Phfft,* not me. I manufacture to order only. Clients do what they want with what I make for them." She gathered her shawl around her shoulders. "Boring. Instead of a militant, you're just a scared little boy."

"You pay lip service to art and politics, *ma rouquine,*" he said, disgusted. "But you're just in it for the money."

"We're all in it for something." She grinned. "Nice photo of you in the paper. You're wanted, rich boy."

He clenched his hands in his pockets, felt the balled-up Metro ticket. What was it with women searching for thrills? The old Polish woman, and now her.

"We can't stop environmental pollution with pipe bombs," he said. "Those men — give me their names."

"Why's it important?"

"They framed me."

"Then shouldn't you be the one running?"

He pulled out his cell phone. "The Ministry of Sanitation's eager to shut this place down. By the time they arrive, I'll be long gone."

She bent and picked up her straw sack

from the floor. "Big talk. Good night, sweet prince."

He shuddered. "What?"

"Great piece in the paper. Says you're in line for the nonexistent Polish throne."

He grabbed her arms, twisted them behind her.

"I like it rough." She rubbed her denim-clad legs against him.

He snatched some wire from the floor and looped it around her wrists several times. She squirmed and twisted, trying to kick him. He dumped her bag out on the floor and the contents scattered over the clumps of black gun powder. Eyeliner, a copy of *Le Deuxième Sexe* by Simone de Beauvoir, and a Moroccan leather wallet. Inside it he found an expired École des Beaux-Arts student card; a receipt from Sennelier, the art store on Quai Voltaire; and a social services card for unemployment benefits. She was on the dole.

"Nice little side business for you."

"Not everyone lives off a trust fund," she said. "I couldn't buy supplies and live on the stipend they give me for art school."

And he was supposed to feel sorry for her?

"That's your rationale for making bombs?"

He took the wad of francs from her

pocket. Folded inside the fifty-franc notes he found a business card — blue, half torn. On it was written: *Wednesday 19:00 G.* He glanced at the ticking clock on the wall. Ten past seven. And took a deep breath as he noticed part of a logo on the card. Sloppy. Or arrogant. Or both.

"Halkyut Security bought pipe bombs from you ten minutes ago? *Ma rouquine,* you're big-time."

She kicked him in the shins.

He doubled over in pain. But he grabbed the copper wire, caught her espadrille-shod feet, and bound them.

"Who's G?"

"Haven't you heard of the G-spot?" There was mockery in her eyes.

He limped to the corner, stuffed his sleeping bag into his pack, and shouldered his rucksack.

"Last chance to tell me."

She twisted on the floor, thumping her heels.

He walked to the door, turned the doorknob.

"He's called Gabriel," she said, "that's all I know. A pickup man. Never makes a direct buy."

"Liar, you have the francs in your pocket! Where's he taking them?"

"Get these wires off my feet," she said. "Who knows? It's business, they don't tell me."

But she knew. He hit the light switch, plunging the studio into darkness.

"Wait!" Her bound feet kicked the floor. "Undo the wire."

He edged toward her. "I'm waiting."

"They're not even rigged with a timing device. They're just for show; they won't go off."

"He pays money for pipe bombs that won't go off? Right!"

"No one's dumb enough to light the fuse and stand there! That's the only way . . ."

"Good luck. As far as the terrorist squad goes, you're implicated. An accomplice."

Her lip trembled, her arrogance melted. For the first time, he saw fear in her face.

And it came back to him where he'd seen the blond *mec,* Gabriel: at the peace march. Of course, a security firm would use amateurs and handmade explosives to lay a trail leading toward MondeFocus.

"*Merde!* I'm squatting here, they cut my social service benefits. Where do you think I get money for food?"

The truth for the first time. For a moment he felt sorry for her.

"You won't tell on me, will you? I took

care of you, made you feel good."

Pleading. To think he'd almost slept with her. Disgusted, he set the francs on the floorboards out of her reach.

"I asked you where he went."

"You'll untie me?" Her eyes were on the money.

He nodded.

"A town house on the Ile Saint-Louis."

"Which one?"

"Hôtel Lambert."

He froze. He'd worked there at catered parties. The baron hired impoverished aristos as help. It amused him. And paid for Krzysztof's living expenses.

"You think I live on a trust fund? Titles don't come with trust funds. Get real, *ma rouquine,* you're not the only one who has to grub for money."

He slammed the door shut.

"Salaud!" Her voice echoed as he ran through the courtyard.

Jadwiga Radziwill, wearing a fifties-style cocktail dress that he supposed had fit her once, stood at her apartment door.

"Entrez." She held the Chihuahua in her arms. His teeth bared as he emitted a low growl. "Bibo, *arrêtes!*" she said. "Our prince has come."

Right, and he'd left his white horse out-side. "Mind if I pick your brain?"

The eye makeup crinkled in the crow's-feet of her powdered face. "Only my brain?" she asked, disappointed. "It wouldn't be the first time I've sheltered a political fugitive, young man!" Her blood red painted lips grinned. "A little excitement keeps us young, eh, Bibo?" She nuzzled the foul-smelling little dog in her arms.

Krzysztof stepped inside and was sur-rounded by the smell of dust and heat. Dark oil paintings hung between crowded book-shelves. He doubted whether she ever opened a window. The place needed ventila-tion, especially because of the dog.

A spinning Japanese candle-lantern on the table sent swirling stars over the velvet draperies and the fissures in the cracked ceiling. Second thoughts crossed his mind, but he didn't have many options.

"Your exploits sent your uncle into apo-plectic shock, I imagine, young man."

He didn't want to think of his uncle right now. He was too absorbed by the accusa-tions against him and by chagrin at his own naïveté.

"Like the old days." Her thickly mascar-aed eyes gleamed as she bent in a mock curtsy, her joints creaking. "Now sit down.

Put your hands over the crystal ball. I read the future, you know. My forte."

He didn't need his fortune told to know how bad things looked.

She wore calfskin gloves, like old *coquettes* did to hide their veined, age-spotted hands. And she kept her powdered face away from the light. He spied a black rotary-dial phone with the old prefixes on it. Like one he'd seen at a flea market.

"May I use your phone?" he asked.

"If you have a drink to celebrate," she said and headed to her drinks table.

He'd make it short so the *flics* couldn't trace it. He took a deep breath and dialed Hôtel Dieu, the public hospital. A nurse asked him to wait.

Several departments and clicks later, a sleepy voice came over the phone.

"Gaelle?"

"Oui . . . ?"

"I'm sorry. It should have been me," he said in a rush of words.

"Did you . . . ?"

Was someone there in the hospital room, listening?

"*Non,* the bombs were planted. But Brigitte accused me."

"They missed my skull, if you can believe it." He heard a lisp. "I just lost some teeth."

287

Machines beeped and wheels rolled over the floor in the background.

"I'd never set off bombs; you have to know me better than that. We're going to do this by peaceful means, but . . ." He paused. "The pollution reports, everything, all our evidence was stolen from MondeFocus."

"Tell Nelie. She'll know how to compile it again."

"I can't find her."

"There's a certain doctor's report. I don't know details. She went to her uncle's to get the proof."

He almost dropped the phone. "You didn't tell me . . . but she's disappeared."

"No time. Remember at the demonstration how she was trying to get our attention?"

He just remembered Orla shouting.

"Krzysztof . . . find Nelie."

Did she know that Orla was dead?

"Mademoiselle," a voice said. "Who's on the phone?"

The line went dead.

"You disappoint me, young man." Jadwiga stood next to him with two shot glasses of a cloudy drink smelling of licorice. "Your cause can only succeed if you make a big bang. A quiet protest is no use at all."

He took the glass. Sniffed.

"You like absinthe?" she asked.

Absinthe had been outlawed for years.

"The wormwood inside rots your brain," Krzysztof said.

"Na zdrowie." She toasted and downed the shot glass, a gleam in her eye. "Delicious. Gives one courage."

"And hallucinations," he said.

She tugged at her yellowing string of pearls. "Only if one drinks enough."

He had no intention of doing that. But courage, that he needed, and he drank it. His throat burned; his eyes watered and smarted.

"You've had too much of this," he said, setting the glass down. "A thug's taken pipe bombs to the oil conference reception at Hôtel Lambert —"

"*Aaah,* but you know, it's just as they say," she interrupted, "there are only three ways to get into society: feed it, amuse it, or shock it."

She poured herself another shot of absinthe, raising her painted eyebrows at his expression of disgust. "Not my words, Oscar Wilde's."

"With your anarchist background, you can help me," he said, scanning her bookshelves for *The Anarchist's Cookbook.* He trusted the Internet only so far. "You can explain how to defuse a pipe bomb!"

"Now why would I do that, young man?" Instead of the excitement he expected, she seemed disappointed.

"Adventure," he said.

She shook her head. "And miss the best catered affair in Paris?"

The old woman wanted to crash the reception.

"Bibo's hungry, aren't you, *mon chéri?*" She picked up the bulging-eyed Chihuahua.

Ridiculous, this old woman and her foul-smelling dog wouldn't get near the door while he might be able to blend with the catering crew and get inside.

"There's no time," Krzysztof said. "Look, I know the caterer, I can talk my way in. If you could diagram how to disconnect the fuses —"

"So naive, young man," she interrupted in a bored tone. "I can get in the side door unobserved. But I need an escort."

"Wait a minute."

"The concierge consults me. She comes for readings every week," she said, gesturing toward her crystal. "She swears by me." Jadwiga pulled out a compact, checked her face, and powdered her nose. "Everything's in my head, young man. We never wrote anything down about *explosifs.* Too dangerous, you know. We'll talk on the way."

She grinned, reminding him of a cat who'd swallowed a mouse. Sated for the moment but ready for more.

No time to argue. He shrugged. "Let's go."

"Not like that, you're not."

She took his hand, led him to an armoire, opened the creaking door that smelled of mothballs, and displayed a hanging tuxedo.

From an old lover of hers?

"A little loose in the hips, perhaps," she said, eyeing his waist with a smile. "But it should do."

WEDNESDAY, EARLY EVENING

Aimée pulled René's raincoat tighter around her. The hem hit her at mid thigh but fit across the shoulders. She and René stood under halogen recessed lighting in front of the reception desk to the beige office suite. Vavin's wing lay dark and deserted. She thought it unlikely that the *flics* had obtained a search warrant yet: even in high-profile murder cases it took hours. But she was afraid that Vavin's killer might have bypassed security down below and preceded her even though she had Vavin's keys. The sound of splashing and a muttered *"Zut"* interrupted her thoughts. She stopped in

291

her tracks, put her hand on René's shoulder, mouthed "Shh."

The secretary was watering a potted palm. Why hadn't she left for the day? Aimée racked her brain for the secretary's name. Naomi?

"*Bonsoir,* your terminals seem to be malfunctioning again," Aimée said. She noticed the secretary's name on a memo pad. She had been close. "Nadia, meet René Friant, my sysadmin partner. You're working late tonight."

Nadia, in stylish narrow black-framed glasses, blinked. She took in René's stature as she shook his hand. "But, Aimée, *my* computer's working fine."

"It's always like that," René said. "You won't notice any problem until you access the server database." He rolled his eyes. "By then, what a mess."

Nadia set down the watering can, confused. "Go ahead."

"We'll start with Monsieur Vavin's machine and tackle yours later."

Aimée paused, as if she'd had an afterthought. "Hasn't our tech associate called or stopped in yet?"

Nadia shook her head. "I've been here all day. Nobody called. Should they have?"

René said, "Don't worry. We'll take care

of it." They walked rapidly to Vavin's office.

"Smooth, René," Aimée said. "Still taking your PI courses?"

"If I had the time, I would," he said.

"Let's make this quick. Before whoever murdered Vavin pays his office a visit."

Vavin's subdued office overlooked the dark trees on the boulevard facing the Faculté des Sciences. Aimée's damp high-tops sank into the plush carpet. Nothing appeared to be out of place.

Aimée pulled out Vavin's key ring and studied it. Two Fichet house keys and a third, a smaller one, which might be to his desk drawer.

She inserted the key into the lock on the side drawer. The key didn't turn. She tried all the drawers. None of them opened. She scanned the minimalist-style office. No more furniture, not even a closet. The only place she hadn't tried was the top drawer, which opened without a key. She slid it open. Pencils, pens, stapler, and Regnault stationery. A dead end.

"Nothing, René," she reported.

A duplicate of the photo of Vavin's smiling daughter on the rocking horse stared at Aimée from his desk. She imagined the knock at the door, the excited little girl running to answer it, her mother's white face, and the girl tugging her sleeve, asking, "Where's Papa?"

Then she succumbed to thoughts of Stella and warmth filled her. At least Stella was safe.

Vavin wouldn't have hidden the key ring if it hadn't been vital. Think. She took out the stationery from the wide drawer and felt around the interior. Smooth plywood. Cheap for this type of high-end desk. Then in the back her fingers found a clasp. She tugged it, heard a snap, and the plywood panel loosened. She slid it out and saw another panel with a lock. The drawer had a second level.

She inserted the key; it turned and the hidden compartment opened.

"Look, René." Inside lay a laptop PC.

René consulted his notes. "His Mac's on the systems inventory you made but not this one. Let me check something."

He lifted it out and whistled. "Alstrom gave Vavin a new toy. See," he said, lifting the laptop up to show the asset tag near the serial number embossed with *Alstrom* on the underside of the machine.

Aimée's cell phone vibrated.

"Oui?"

"Stella's restless," said Mathilde, the young babysitter. "I can't get her to sleep."

Aimée gripped the phone. A fever?

"Please take her temperature," she said.

Stella's cries sounded in the background. René looked up, concerned.

"Loosen her shirt and the blankets, Mathilde," Aimée said, thinking of what she'd read in the baby-care manual. "Try a cold compress on her forehead. And give her a bottle with sterilized water. I'll wait."

"I only have two hands," Mathilde said, sounding flustered.

"*Bien sûr,* I'll call you back. If nothing helps, I'll take her to the doctor," Aimée said and hung up.

Her mind jumped ahead. According to the manual, fever in a newborn could mean meningitis. *Nom de Dieu . . .* she couldn't stay here and work if Stella's life hung in the balance.

"Aimée . . . you with me?"

René was staring at her.

"Wait five minutes, eh? You gave Mathilde the right instructions," he said, pulling out his car keys. "Wait a bit, but if Stella has a fever, take my car."

She nodded. René was right. She had to focus. She had to get a grip; nothing else would make it up to Vavin.

"Vavin had access to Alstrom's internal system via this PC," she said. "Can you get into their system on his machine, René?"

"More important, can I access it in time?"

She'd given René a quick overview in the hallway.

"Whoever murdered Vavin did a sloppy job. But I bet it was for this — something on his computer involving his colleague's e-mail."

"Aren't you jumping to conclusions?"

She didn't have anything else to go on.

"Well, it's a place to start, René," she said. "But I'd feel better working in another office."

By the time Nadia had opened the conference room, crowded with a suite of modern walnut furniture, René was right behind her, rolling in both computers on a wheeled trolley. Nadia paused at the door, a worried look on her face. "A *flic* just called. He wanted to visit concerning some incident having to do with one of our employees."

Aimée's shoulders tensed. Not standard procedure and they couldn't have obtained a warrant so soon. "Did he identify himself?"

"I didn't catch the name."

René looked up and met Aimée's eyes.

"I told him it's impossible," Nadia said. "He'll have to visit during business hours with Monsieur Vavin in attendance."

Aimée willed her hand to remain steady. "*Bon,* we'll work on the system, nail the glitches." She paused as if she'd just had an afterthought. "Did he mention any details? Or refer to a search warrant?"

Nadia's thin eyebrows shot up and she shook her head. "I told him no one's here; I was on the way out. Monsieur Vavin drops his daughter at her school on his way in, in the mornings, and arrives a bit late." She shrugged. "The *flic* can wait."

Aimée looked away. She couldn't face Nadia. Or lie anymore.

"Thanks for letting us know," René said, glancing at Aimée. "Have a good evening."

Nadia shut the door behind her.

Either Nadia's words had bought them time or whoever had called would arrive soon.

Aimée's fingers ran over the smooth conference-table surface, planks in shades of light to dark walnut. Disparate yet fitting together in one piece. Like Vavin with Nelie? She'd seen MondeFocus pamphlets here, found an empty Alstrom folder in Nelie's room, and the antiques dealer had seen them together. But she didn't know how these pieces fit together.

"I failed Vavin, René. If only I'd talked to

him . . ."

"Right now, do you know what's the best thing you can do?" he said. "Help me find the password for this PC. Otherwise, I'll have to use a brute force attack," he said. "We can't count on dumb luck; he may not have used the same password on this laptop. And what we'd need is back at the office."

"Let me scout around."

On Vavin's Mac she accessed his user account with her sysadmin password. She scrolled through his activities and the functions he used on the computer. Why hadn't she thought of this before? But then Vavin had been the boss. Why would she?

René tugged his goatee. "As I thought, he used another password. Found it?"

Appointments, meetings were noted on his calendar. All routine. Business lunches. No breakfast meetings, apart from one with de Laumain. No cache of passwords.

She shook her head. A big stumbling block and one they didn't have time to chip away at. "If it's buried in here, it could take hours to find."

Her mind kept going back to his early morning call, claiming to be concerned about the firewall protection, as a pretext for accessing de Laumain's e-mail. It all tied together.

She looked at her watch. Six minutes had passed. She hit the call-back button on her cell phone.

"Mathilde?"

"Stella's a thirsty girl," Mathilde said. "She drank a whole bottle."

"No fever?"

"Her temperature's normal," Mathilde said.

"You're sure?"

"Of course, I took it twice, Aimée," Mathilde said.

Aimée let out a slow breath of relief. "*Merci,* Mathilde. She likes to be held and rocked, try that. I'll stay in touch."

She hung up.

René had plugged into an outlet, powered up the PC, and was clicking over the keyboard. "Here's some good news," he said. "The *flics* use one tech for several units. They're overwhelmed, so my friend tells me."

A feeling she could relate to right now.

"So unless they suspect right away that the murder was connected to his work, they won't come for his Mac hard drive until tomorrow." He stared at her. "Whoever called Nadia wasn't a *flic.* They'd ask for the system administrators first to avoid shutting

down the system. That's us. In the meantime, Alstrom could cancel his access. And
if I do find the password and log on, they'll
know; there will be a record."

More complicated with every step.

"If Alstrom denies access, wouldn't that
mean they know he's dead?" René asked.

"We won't know until you try," she said.
"Your pager's on, René?"

He nodded.

She pulled up the e-mail she'd forwarded
to Vavin and opened it:

Regarding understanding reached in yesterday's meeting with the vice minister of
Interior and Alstrom's bureau chief, you
have the go-ahead to draft a public statement to that effect for Alstrom's review.
We're sending statements describing the
draft terms and expect you to set up a
campaign enlisting public and industry
support for the North Sea Oil Platform
Agreement.

"This makes sense if Alstrom . . . wait a
minute, sounds like they've already got the
green light from the Ministry."

She pulled up Vavin's next e-mail: *Regarding investigative reports you requested, un-
necessary until after agreement is ratified. No*

further action on your part deemed necessary.

"Or, in other words, quit poking around," she said. "They plan on inking the agreement before the investigation reports come in."

"Maybe Vavin had grown a conscience," René said.

His words hung in the air.

She stared at him and thought of Vavin's daughter's photo, his words — ". . . like every parent, I want my child to grow up in a clean world."

"Or he had a weight on his conscience and was about to blow the whistle," she said.

"Speculation, Aimée," René said. His fingers raced over the keys. "It's impossible to prove his biggest client had him killed over these e-mails."

True.

"Companies hire ex-military or former intelligence officers to do their dirty work," she said. "What if Vavin had found incriminating reports in the computer files at Alstrom?"

"Even harder to prove."

René had a point. He shook his head. "Alstrom wouldn't leave the minutes of these meetings in their system."

Her pulse quickened. "But what if they were in a rush and had a lot more on their minds than worrying about someone snooping in their secure internal system, René?"

De Laumain . . . Vavin's desire to read his e-mail had caused him to call her. And gotten him killed?

"The proof is on either his Mac or this PC . . . I have a hunch."

"Makes it like finding a grain of sand at the beach," René said.

Shadows slanted across the conference table. Outside the window, she saw the distant dark waters of the Seine. Cars crawled over the Pont de Sully, their red brake lights like a string of jewels.

They needed help, she realized.

"Isn't Saj back from his meditation retreat?"

"Good idea," René said. "Two of us will work faster for sure."

She rang Saj, heard the tinkling strain of sitar music on his voice-mail greeting, and left him a message.

"Looks like an all-nighter, René. Let's copy Vavin's hard drive and take the laptop PC with us."

"Take the PC?"

"Should we leave it for the killer?"

"How many laws have you broken so far?" He flicked a piece of lint from his vest.

Running away from the scene of a crime,

she thought, would be one. "We have the perfect cover. After all, we're Regnault's sysadmin and can plead ignorance concerning the PC."

René rolled his eyes.

She reached in her purse and her hand brushed a cotton ball that smelled like Stella's baby lotion. She felt a jolt in her rib cage. Somewhere there was a connection. She had to think.

How had Vavin known Nelie . . . how?

She ran out into the hallway to Nadia's empty desk. The hall was dark. She heard the elevator approaching.

"Nadia?"

She ran to the elevator.

"Nadia?"

And then the bathroom door opened to the sound of water flushing and there was Nadia, wiping her hands on a towel, having just changed into black yoga pants and a sweatshirt.

"I just wondered," Aimée said, choosing her words. "Nelie, this girl in the photo" — she pointed to Nelie's face — "she's with MondeFocus. Did she visit Monsieur Vavin this week?"

Nadia shook her head. "I've no idea. Sorry, I have to hurry to my yoga class."

The elevator door slid open and Nadia

stepped inside.

"There are MondeFocus fliers in Monsieur Vavin's office," Aimée said.

Nadia glanced at her watch as the elevator door started to shut.

Aimée stuck her foot in the elevator door. "Did she bring them?"

"Why would she?"

Aimée thought quickly. "I thought maybe she met with him here to express her concerns."

Nadia shrugged and pushed the button. "Maybe. She's his niece. *Bonsoir.*"

And the elevator door closed.

The connection!

Back in the meeting room, Aimée dumped out the contents of her bag. She rooted through her keys, a dog-eared encryption manual, a tube of mascara, her worn Vuitton wallet with her lucky Egyptian coin intact, and a disc of expired birth-control pills. She found what she was looking for on the back of her checkbook. Her copy of the ink marks she'd found written on Stella. Letters, numbers, like an equation. And part of a word . . . a name, a title? Then 2/12, part of a date.

She handed her checkbook to René. "Play with this."

"It's incomplete."

"Right now it's all we have to go on," she said. "And Nelie is Vavin's niece."

René's fingers paused on the keyboard.

Until they found Nelie, the numbers and word fragments would probably remain indecipherable.

Her cell phone vibrated on her hip.

"Did you forget, Aimée?" Martine said, her husky voice wavering. "We should be leaving for the oil conference reception."

She'd have to hurry. "Sorry, I'll meet you there. I'm running late."

"You're always late. But you're lucky; this time everyone else will be, too. They've moved it. Again."

"Not another bomb scare?"

She thought of Krzysztof and the bottle bombs. Was Morbier right?

"Alstrom picked a posh new venue for their reception."

Aimée grabbed a pen. "Where?"

"Where else would you entertain world-weary oil execs? It's at a shareholder's place, the most exclusive private mansion in Paris. And it's in your neighborhood. Hôtel Lambert."

A few town houses down from her on the Ile Saint-Louis.

"Can you handle this, René?" She stepped into her semi-dried high heels, swiped lipstick over her lips, and blotted them with a piece of computer paper. "Copy the Mac's hard drive and —"

"Why?"

She peered at her laptop. "With any luck, I'll be able to corner de Laumain at the reception and find out what he has to say. First, I'll get background on Alstrom from Martine's young Turk journalist."

"You're leaving right now?"

The dark blots of trees on Quai de la Tournelle swayed outside the window. The Ile Saint-Louis was a glittering cluster of lights just over the river. It wasn't far and this wouldn't take long.

"The Alstrom's reception is right across the river. Let's take the PC and leave together," she said. Shadows had lengthened; the office seemed ominously deserted. "It's not safe for you to work here alone."

"I'll leave as soon as I copy the Mac hard drive," René said, rolling up his sleeves. "Go ahead. Just leave Vavin's keys."

Myriad dots of light were reflected in the gelatinous waters of the Seine from Hôtel Lambert's tall windows, which were illuminated by glittering candles. Aimée passed the place every day. Once, long ago, the mansion had been owned by a Polish prince who had hosted recitals by Chopin. Now the tenant, a penniless baron and friend of the grand family who owned it, kept the place running and hosted select corporate receptions and celebrations.

Aimee's heel caught in a crack between cobblestones as she caught the attention of the broad-shouldered man wearing a headset. Strains of a cello faded in the wind from the Seine.

"I don't see your name, Mademoiselle." His heavy-lidded eyes were dismissive.

"Check the guest list again, please," she said, peering around his shoulder for Martine.

"Leduc, Aimée?" He shook his head. "*Désolé,* Mademoiselle, now please move aside," he told her, blocking the gate. A professional brush-off.

Martine appeared, breathless, flashing her press ID. "*L'Express.* Mademoiselle Leduc's with *L'Express,* if you notice."

He consulted the list again. "Of course." He smiled, a smile that failed to reach his eyes, and waved her inside.

"Nice jacket. I saw one with feathers just like that at —"

"Plucked most of them off," Aimée interrupted. "They made me sneeze."

"Another find?"

"You could say that."

Martine took Aimée's arm, steered her across the courtyard, and up the curving entry staircase. They entered an oval gallery under a painted ceiling lit by flickering candles in crystal holders. Waiters with silver trays of hors d'oeuvres wove in and out among men in formal black-and-white attire and the occasional robed sheikh. Pyramids of *fleurs de sucre* — lavender and rose crystallized flower petals — bedecked the white-linen-covered tables. Aimée spied vintage champagne magnums and headed in that direction.

"Merci," she said, accepting two flutes of champagne, noting the Dom Pérignon label as she handed one to Martine and dropped a sugar-dusted rose petal in Martine's glass. "But I still owe you," Aimée said.

The fizzing velvet purred down her throat. Not bad. This crowd expected and got the best.

"Where's your young Turk journalist?"

Martine scanned the groups of men in tuxedos conversing under a Louis XV chandelier that frothed with crystal. "Knowing him, upstairs with the big honchos."

"No time like the present," Aimée said. "I'll fill you in en route."

The walls of the wide staircase were

crowded with a profusion of Flemish old masters, a lesser Rembrandt, a Corot, landscapes by Watteau, and a handful of Impressionist canvases. Better appreciated in a museum, Aimée thought, not hung in a hodge-podge on the wall.

"The owner's great-uncle built the collection," Martine said, awe in her voice. "In his heyday, he bought a painting every day."

Aimée nodded. "But everything's bequeathed to the Louvre now," she said. "The baron, his tenant, rents the place out to help him pay the taxes."

They entered the second-floor hallway, which opened onto oval Galerie d'Hercule, which was lined by rectangular windows, Corinthian columns, and stucco reliefs of Hercules' exploits.

Aimée felt out of her league in this museum of a place. The talk around her was foreign, too. She caught snippets of conversation as they circulated. "Oil flow . . . black crude. . . . percentages."

The *L'Express* journalist Martine guided her toward looked to be in his thirties. A shock of black hair nearly hid his darting eyes, and he wore a black jacket with a white shirt, but no tie.

"Aimée Leduc," she said, extending her hand. "I'd appreciate it if you would let me see your notes."

"Daniel Ristat," he replied, enfolding her hands in his warm ones with a wide smile. "Get right to it, don't you?"

She figured his smile and manner took him a lot of places. And he knew it.

"Guilty." Next, she wanted to meet de Laumain. "Have you seen Monsieur de Laumain?"

He arched an eyebrow. "And you know the big players, eh? The old buzzard suffered an attack of gout. The disease of the rich."

"Meaning?"

Ahead of her, a sheikh in a white robe, holding a glass of what looked like orange juice, walked by.

"Meaning that de Laumain left before I could interview him."

Left after hearing of Vavin's murder? She wondered who else she could question. They all oozed power and looked alike in their tuxedos. Even the sheikhs with their fruit juice resembled each other.

"But Deroche, Alstrom's CEO, is standing right there." Martine nudged her. Aimée noticed a smiling silver-haired man at the edge of the crowd, an executive who exuded authority even across the wide room. "And the press attaché looks nervous." Martine indicated a woman with short hair in a severe navy blue suit, *publicité* pin clipped to her lapel.

Aimée was about to say that the press attaché's nerves might be attributable to the murder of Vavin, Regnault's publicity head, when the woman tapped an ivory-handled dessert knife against a champagne flute. "Attention, please."

As the tinkle died, a hush descended over the well-dressed crowd.

"Monsieur Deroche, Alstrom's director of operations, has asked me to convey to you his wishes for a wonderful evening." The press attaché flashed a bright smile. "He'd hoped to make the announcement that I'm sure you've all been waiting for. We expect that we will be able to make it tomorrow. However, I can tell you now that out of its continued concern for the environment and as part of its ongoing program to safeguard it, Alstrom has completed the dismantling of all its North Sea oil rigs in the Baltic. Its waste-management operations have been transferred to the La Hague facility and new sites will be explored."

The attaché waved her hand at Deroche, who raised his champagne glass. *"Santé,"* he said. "Enjoy . . . no one leaves until every magnum's empty!"

Ripples of applause and laughter greeted his remark.

But both Martine and Daniel seemed amazed.

"Rumor says that the execution of the agreement between Alstrom and the government was postponed due to a bomb scare," Daniel said, taking out a small notepad and jotting something down. "This sounds like a concession to the environmentalists."

Aimée's cell phone vibrated.

"Allô?"

"Turn around," a man's voice said. A familiar voice.

"Who's this?"

"Face the windows on the north side."

Bomb scares . . . all the bigwigs . . . a sniper? A *frisson* of fear rippled over Aimée's skin.

She pivoted on her heel. Saw the flash of a tuxedo jacket and got a brief look at the face of the man wearing it.

"The service stairs to the kitchen. Now."

She thrust her champagne into Martine's hand and crossed the creaking inlaid wood floor, passed the suave, smiling Deroche, opened a door in the carved paneling, and went down the steep sconce-lit winding stairs. She fished the miniscrew-driver out of her bag. Too bad the tip had broken off in Nelie's door.

She had a bad feeling as heat rising from the kitchen enveloped her.

And then he stood on the step below her. Krzysztof.

"You lied to me," she said.

"It's going down." His eyes bulged in fear.

"What's going down?"

"Coming through," said a waiter, passing them with a tray of toast slivers coated with foie gras.

"You have to help."

Unease filled her. "Me? Why should I? Orla was your girlfriend but you wouldn't even ID her body. You and Nelie planted bombs at the march and you're wanted by the police."

"You're wrong!" Krzysztof interrupted. "Orla was not my girlfriend. Nelie's hiding, but I would never expose her. I promised to keep quiet."

"So you know where she is?"

He shook his head. His words came out in a rush. "We didn't plant bottle bombs! We were framed. Saboteurs ruined the peace march."

"How'd you get in here with all this security?" She saw the tuxedos hanging in a storeroom off the kitchen. "Wait . . . you came in with the caterers, didn't you?"

He pulled at her sleeve. "Hurry," he said, his voice tense, as he tugged her downstairs.

A distant memory bubbled up. Aimée had been in this kitchen before. She'd gone to school with the daughter of the Hôtel Lambert's head chef. Sometimes, after school, the chef, who was from Brittany, baked Quimper biscuits for a treat. They'd been forbidden to wander upstairs but she remembered the white-tiled kitchen, enameled Aga stove, and the fragrance of hot butter. Now it was overrun by a crew of red-faced white-hatted chefs intent on adding decorative touches, sauce swirls, and radish florets to platters of dainty delights.

Krzysztof pulled her toward the walk-in pantry before they could be noticed.

"There are explosives here." He held up a piece of waxed fuse. "I found this on the floor."

Chills ran up her spine. Her first impulse was to yell, "Bomb" and get out. She was an idiot. Why had she followed him?

Before she could stop him, he had pushed her into a walk-in freezer and shut the door. She lowered her bag to the floor, pulling out her fist with the screwdriver in it, and confronted him. "You wouldn't talk to me before. What's your game . . . your demands . . . are you taking hostages?"

"I checked you out."

"So you're having second thoughts, feeling guilty?" She kept the screwdriver in her fist poised to defend herself should he attack her. "You've set explosives and now you want to stop them from going off?"

"What?"

"You'll use me as a cover —"

"Listen to me, Halkyut Security's involved," he interrupted, handing her a battered business card on which someone had written the initial "G."

She knew that Halkyut, a private firm, employed former intelligence officers and ex-military as security operatives. This situation was going from bad to worse.

" 'G' stands for this *mec,* Gabriel, who brought the bombs here."

"How do you know?"

"It's a long story, but I found out that he bought pipe bombs from a person who lives in a squat."

A high-level security firm buying bombs in a squat?

"And I'm the prime minister," she said in disbelief.

He waved his hand. "He saw me and he recognized me. He's checking out the kitchen. I know the explosives are here. I'm an amateur. I thought I could defuse the charge but . . ." He kicked an aluminum tray. "Look, I'm in over my head, I screwed up. I'm for peaceful protest, exposing the oil corporations . . . but not with bombs."

Maybe an operative employed by Halkyut had been clever enough to use unsophisticated explosives to divert suspicion.

She reached for her cell phone. She'd left it in her bag on the floor; she didn't want to bend down to rummage through it and give him an opening to attack her. "Let me use your phone. We have to evacuate everyone."

"They want to blame the bombs on eco-terrorists, extremists. On me. They'll forge a demand note and attribute it to me, create chaos, and blame the destruction on me."

"Why are you so sure?"

"They did it before, at our peace march. Now the oil agreements are ready for signature," he said. "It will happen unless certain evidence surfaces first."

"I don't get it," she said.

"What can't you understand? They want to silence all opposition. . . ." His forehead glistened with sweat. "The oil companies use Halkyut to hire infiltrators — wild men — so anyone who protests seems to be an extremist. Once this agreement is signed, there will be more contracts and the North Sea will be polluted further by nuclear wastes and other toxins."

"But they just announced that they've dismantled their North Sea oil-rig platforms."

"They lied. Nelie has the proof. It's in black and white. But they've gotten to her."

That corresponded with the statement by Deroche's press attaché. And now she knew that Vavin was Nelie's uncle.

"What do you mean 'gotten to her'?"

"I think they took care of her, like they did to Orla. She and her baby have disappeared."

Her pulse raced. "The baby . . ."

A man in a chef's apron opened the freezer door. "What are you doing here?"

Aimée said the first thing that came to her mind. "I'm checking supplies." She hit a side of hanging cured ham. "The maître d' needs more *jambon* hors d'oeuvres upstairs."

"When I'm good and ready. The smoked trout's on my mind right now, if you please! Give me some room."

They stepped back into the kitchen. The chef rushed over to a wire shelf, grabbed a package, and hurtled out past her.

Beyond them lay a box of Beurre de Breton on a wooden chopping block. Next to it, a sous chef was using a hand-sized butane torch to caramelize turbinado sugar on fifty or more porcelain ramekins of *crème brûlée*.

"*Zut alors,* Henri; hurry up with the *crème brûlées!*" a waiter shouted.

Bending, she saw pipes and wires encased in colored plastic, taped to the underside of the chopping block. Her heart stopped.

"There . . . look." She pointed, her hand shaking.

Krzysztof's eyes widened in terror. "The sous chef could set off the explosives by mistake. Distract him. I'll disconnect the fuses."

"Wait!" She tried to think. "There has to be a timing detonator," she said. Touching the wires or fuses could activate it. "Everyone must evacuate. I'll alert the bomb squad."

She felt for her bag. Where was it . . . where the hell was her cell phone? They couldn't risk everyone's life . . . My God, Martine was upstairs!

"*Non,* cut the waxed wires," he said.

"What?"

"No detonator. Keep it away from flame and static electricity; the old woman, the anarchist, told me. I'll snip the fuse near the base; it's the best way to prevent —"

"Mademoiselle, out of my way." A large man stood in front of her. "The garlic's burning, I need butter."

"Let me." Krzysztof moved in front of him.

He shoved Krzysztof's arm away. "Ridiculous. Who let these people in here?"

Aimée saw pushing, a fistfight erupting, then Krzysztof lay on the floor.

"*Et voilà*, the *crème brûlée's* finished." The sous chef turned, his torch still lit and emitting a blue flame.

"*Non,*" she screamed. She had to get the bombs away from the fire, from the hot kitchen. Or they'd blow to kingdom come.

Terror stricken, she saw her father in her mind's eye, the orange billowing heat and fireball explosion that had reduced him to charred cinders.

"Bombs! Get out," she yelled as loud as she could above the din of the kitchen. "Run!"

"What the — ?" A pan clattered. The hiss of escaping gas and steam filled the air, shouts of *"Merde"* accompanying it. Krzysztof had risen to resume battle with the chef while others stood, pots and knives in hand, paralyzed by annoyance and fear.

Panicked, she didn't know where to turn. A chef stood blocking her way, frozen in horror.

"Move!"

She ripped the tape that was holding the

wires to the underside of the chopping block and grabbed the colored plastic case. The only thing she could think of was to run to the service door. She shoved the door open with her hip and barreled onto the quai, bumping into a surprised group of white-aproned men who were taking a break, smoking.

"Eh, look where you're going —"

"Security! Stand aside!" She ran the few steps across the narrow *quai,* past a surprised man walking his dog, and took the stone steps, running as fast as she could.

She splashed over to the riverbank, ankle deep in the rising water, and threw the pipe bomb as far as she could into the Seine. Then she dove back to the steps, crouched, and covered her head with her arms.

She waited but the only sound was of the lapping water. She breathed a sigh of relief. A close call. Until she saw bright yellow-orange bubbles coming to the surface.

From the bridge she heard a baby cry. Stella's face flashed in front of her.

Then there was a deafening explosion, followed by a deep rumbling. The steps shuddered. Then the same thunderlike clap she'd heard in the Place Vendôme when her father was blown up.

She lost her balance, reached out, and her

fingers scraped across slippery moss. Water shot up in an arc, spraying the bridge; waves broke over her. She scrambled onto all fours, reached for the steps, trying to climb, her knees shaking. Another rumbling, followed by shaking, rocked the stones. Icy, stinking water burst over her, soaking her, and she was crying, sobs racking her body.

She became aware of people on the Pont de Sully shouting. Now billows of dark gray smoke rose from the surface of the Seine, forming a blanket of fog. Her shoulders were heaving; her dress clung to her dankly. Sirens wailed. She heard laughter from the bridge and then clapping. "Good show," someone said. "Where are the fireworks?"

Only candlelight illuminated the darkened windows of the Hôtel Lambert now as men in formal attire and elegantly gowned women stood on the dark balconies, a scene out of the past. Several other buildings had lost electric power as well from the explosion. Then a receding wave of icy water sucked at her, pulling her down again, and she gulped a mouthful of scummy water.

Choking and spitting, she lay on her stomach on the stones of the embankment and her arms flailed in the water as she fought against being sucked into the cold backwash of foam, twigs, and bits of sharp metal pipe. She tried to clutch the iron rungs of the ladder that led from the river to the bank. The current snatched her away. She had to swim.

She kicked, battling the current, but her eyes could make out nothing in the murky, dense blackness. She surfaced, sputtering, in the middle of the Seine. Shivering, treading the frigid water, she saw people running along the quai, and now lights blazing in the Hôtel Lambert. The electricity had been restored. A low toot and the black hull of a Bateau-Mouche loomed. The whirling blades of the engine had been revved up to battle the choppy current. Her adrenaline kicked in and she swam, desperate to get out of the path of the boat. If she was sucked under, she'd be sliced like meat in the rotor blades. She heard shouts, took a deep breath, and dove, her arms numb, her legs cramping. So cold. She remembered Capitaine Sezeur's words: twenty minutes in a wet suit was all the divers could handle.

The water, a foaming broth, swirled; the current seized her. Vibrations from the engine pounded in her ears. Now lights filtered through the dense greenish silt, and dead crawfish floated past her. She had to get free of the current; her lungs were bursting. Her feet hit something and she pushed off, away from the churning bubbles created by the motor.

She hit the surface, gulped air, and her head hit something hard. Her jacket sleeve caught and she was sucked down again.

WEDNESDAY NIGHT

René loosened his damp shirt collar. Vavin's hard drive and the laptop PC in its case hung from his shoulder. Just as he passed Nadia's desk, he heard a *ting* from the elevator and the slow *whoosh* of the door opening. He froze. Security guards or . . . ? He didn't wait to find out.

He searched for cover behind a potted palm, gathered his thoughts, and looked for the stairs. The last thing he needed right now was questions. He wouldn't be able to fight his way out carrying a several-kilo laptop case with his aching hip.

Palm fronds brushed his nose. The moist terra-cotta planter was exuding moisture. He saw the red-lit EXIT sign to his right and knew two flights of stairs led down to the foyer. And escape.

There was a soft padding sound on the carpet, then the flash of a man's blond head. He was going straight to Vavin's office. René held his breath, waited until he heard the office door open, and made for the exit. He wouldn't have much time after the *mec* discovered Vavin's laptop was gone.

He opened the door, stood in the stairwell, and held the handle so the door would shut silently, then raced down the stairs, trying to ignore the sharp pains in his hip. The laminated ID hanging from his neck flapped against the jacket he carried folded over his shoulder, under the laptop-case strap.

At the front desk he smiled at the security guard, praying he could get away with this. The last time he'd stolen anything was a car magazine when he was fifteen. And he'd been caught.

His shoulders were just at the level of the counter, where a sleepy security guard nursed an espresso.

On tiptoes, René reached for a pen with which to sign out. The guard eyed him, taking in his size.

A few more minutes and he'd reach his car.

"Before you go, open your bag," the guard said.

"I'm in a hurry, I'm sure you understand . . ."

The guard jerked his thumb. "You heard me. Standard procedure."

René opened the laptop case.

"What's that you've got?"

René debated fully waking him by telling him the truth.

"A rat's nest," René said. "Terminal malfunction in the hardware. I've got to repair this back at the office."

"No one informed me," the guard told him, one eye scanning the video monitors.

René followed his gaze. On the monitor labeled SECOND FLOOR he saw a blond *mec* standing at the elevator bank.

"Nor me! Just happened." René rolled his eyes. "Deadline, too! They need this back in a few hours."

"Eh, you can't take equipment without —"

"Look, this system needs to be up and running before the exec's conference."

"You need authorization."

Perspiration dampened René's collar.

"Then you tell the CEO why his computer doesn't work when he arrives at his meeting in a few hours." Sweat trickled down René's shoulders.

"Let me see your ID," the guard said.

René held up the extra laminated badge Aimée had given him. "I'm a network system administrator. Get it? If I can't deliver, it's your job on the line."

"Cool your heels, *petit*."

Several men and women in blue work smocks had lined up behind René, grumbling. "What's the holdup? We've clocked out."

Behind him, he saw the orange light of the descending elevator.

René reached for a pen. "Where do I sign?"

His upper lip still beaded with perspiration, René walked toward the budding trees in front of the Faculté des Sciences. He nodded to Saj, who was waiting under a lamppost, light gleaming on his bleached-blond dreadlocks, and opened the door of his parked Citroën, putting the laptop case on the leather seat.

"Namaste," Saj said, placing the palms of his hands together in greeting.

"Namaste." René returned the gesture. "Thanks for meeting me. Let's go."

"What's with the slash on your bumper?" Saj asked.

"A big rig near the Périphérique got too close for comfort." René's hands were shaking so much he didn't think he could drive. He opened the car door, leaned down, and somehow adjusted the seat controls and pedals for someone Saj's height. "Do you mind driving?"

"To what do I owe the honor?" Saj said. "You've never even let me touch the steering wheel before."

René climbed into the passenger seat. Lampposts shone on the bridge. He touched the floppy discs in his pocket for reassurance.

"Move it, Saj. Get us out of here."

"René, you just missed big fireworks downstream on the Seine." Saj gunned the engine. "You look nervous. What's up?"

The Citroën shot over the Pont de Sully.

"It's not every day I steal a laptop and a dead man's hard drive."

Seated in front of his terminal in Leduc Detective's office, René tugged at his goatee anxiously. He and Saj had copied Vavin's hard drive to a backup disc. Now for the tough part — cracking Vavin's password so they could get into the Alstrom files if the Alstrom system hadn't already shut down his access.

He lowered his orthopedic chair and checked the mail piled in front of the frosted-glass door of Leduc Detective. Bills and more bills.

Saj asked, "Got the software installed?"

René nodded.

Saj sat cross-legged in a white flowing

shirt and drawstring muslin pants, bent over the Alstrom laptop's screen.

Breaking into systems was Saj's specialty and he was a master at it.

Pain pulsed in René's leg. There was still no word from Aimée. He'd left several messages. He wondered if she'd spoken with de Laumain. Or, worst-case scenario, if she was keeping vigil at the hospital by the side of a feverish Stella.

"I'm running the password program. Brute-force attack, as usual. When it hits, we'll be in business. If we're lucky." Saj reached over and ran his fingers over René's neck, down the lumbar curve of his spine.

"Full of tension." Saj nodded with a knowing look. "Your chi's blocked."

René's biggest concern at the moment was if Vavin's access to Alstrom was blocked.

Saj sat on the wooden floor. "Time to center, René; it will clear your mind and do wonders for your spine."

Might as well; he'd do anything that might help. René spread his raincoat on the floor and joined Saj.

"Deep breaths. Think of the tip of your nose. Good, now notice the air entering your nostrils."

René tried to concentrate. He wished his hip didn't ache.

"Feel the in breath. Good. Now let the air out, let your breath go. Exhale."

René focused on breathing.

"Ommm." Saj's mantra mingled with René's exhalations. And then René grew aware of a buzzing. Deep and monotonous, at the edge of his consciousness. The creaking of the floorboards broke into his reverie.

"Got it on the 11,034th hit!" Saj was saying, rubbing his palms together in front of Alstrom's laptop. "Juliette. Probably his wife's name. Or what do you think, René, his mistress?"

René's mouth set in a tight line. "Or his daughter," he said, thinking back to the child's photo on Vavin's desk that Aimée had stared at.

Saj caught René's look and shrugged. "Anyway, you know what that means. We're in business. Now if the stars are shining on us, Alstrom won't have denied Vavin's access yet. I'll start the dial-up system for remote access and log on to their corporate account," he continued. "But when I do, we've only got twelve hours — maybe, at most, eighteen — before Alstrom finds out and traces the phone number." Saj rolled his swivel chair back and looked at René. "You're prepared for that?"

Should they take the chance? But what

other options did they have right now? He only had a few hours.

Saj stood up and stretched. "Has the travel agency next door moved out yet? You know, I'm thinking —"

"Brilliant, Saj!" René stood up, excited.

Saj grinned. "It's worth a shot."

René looked around in Aimée's desk drawer, found what he was looking for, and motioned to Saj. "Not only did I steal, now I'm breaking and entering," he said. He held up a lock-picking kit. "Pray the stars still shine, Saj."

Saj picked up the phone in the deserted, shadowed travel-agent office. The desks were littered with travel brochures for Istanbul and Tunisia. He winked. "Dial tone! Let's hook up."

In five minutes, René heard the welcome series of high-pitched beeps as they attempted to dial up via remote access. The question now . . . had Vavin been blocked yet? Two long minutes later, the PC with Vavin's password was logged on to the corporate account.

"Now we're in," Saj said, "but it still could take a day."

"That we don't have," René interrupted. He glanced at his watch, calculated the time. "Four hours. Tops."

Saj shook his head. "The system is immense. Of course, you've got a file name or word string?"

Another obstacle; why hadn't Aimée told him more? This was going to be like looking for a blade of grass at Versailles.

"Look under pollution, oil spills, toxic percentages, Ministry meeting reports," René said. "But they could have camouflaged it under something else."

Saj's fingers clicked over the keyboard. He shook his head as files filled the screen. A whole screenload of files to comb through; their long search had just begun.

"More than hours, this will take . . ."

"Time we don't have. Go to Vavin's home directory." René thought fast. It would be dawn in a few hours and he had to return the PC. "We'll try Vavin's recent files, say those created within the last two weeks." With that, and the info they'd copied from his hard drive, they should get somewhere. It was the best they could do.

WEDNESDAY NIGHT

"Open wider, *Mon Chéri*," Jadwiga Radziwill said, putting the foie gras-coated cracker into Bibo's waiting mouth.

Panic-stricken guests rushed past her down the Hôtel Lambert's wide stairway. Candles flickered, their melting wax dripping onto the linen tablecloths. But it was a shame to waste the trays of caviar-dotted blini and the endive shoots filled with *crème fraîche,* she thought.

"Madame, please allow me." A waiter offered her his arm. "It is time to evacuate."

She raised her eyebrows. Not bad, this one. What was it about a man in a tuxedo?

"A little late, young man," she said. "Like closing the barn door after the horse has been stolen."

"The bomb squad fears other bombs will, er, *may* have been set, Madame."

"Set?" She shook her head. "If they had been set, we'd have been vaporized into mist floating over the Seine by now. This wasn't a professional job, you know."

"Madame Radziwill?" Deroche, the CEO, bent and kissed her gloved hand. "You are a legend, and now I'm honored to meet you in person."

She knew him right off — suave, distinguished, and with the roving eye of a roué. And the man in power. Her favorite kind.

"Monsieur Deroche, my compliments on the hors d'oeuvres," she smiled. "Bibo approves, and he's very selective."

"*Merci,* at least someone's enjoying them. But in the interest of your safety, please, let this man escort you outside."

"The excitement's over." She sighed. "A little crisis, *non,* a turbulence like on the airplane when a minor bumpiness occurs and then, *voilà,* all is once more smooth. Wouldn't you concur, Monsieur Deroche?"

Deroche raised an eyebrow, giving a dismissive wave to the waiter. "Why do you say that, Madame Radziwill?"

She showed him her best profile and smiled. "Bombs, seeking attention, pointing the blame — aah, I recognize the hallmarks of my day." She sighed again. "But wonderful champagne. Vintage, *non?*"

He refilled her waiting flute.

"And you're still bewitching," he said. "Now, you haven't shared this observation of yours, have you, Madame?"

But of course he'd noticed the journalists hovering at her side, otherwise he wouldn't have bothered to talk to her.

"Chopin insisted that a shovelful of Polish dirt be placed in his casket at Père-Lachaise," she said. "We Poles birthed anarchism. Being contrary is part of my heritage."

"Won't you let me take you to dinner?" He glanced at the security force checking the room. "When I finish up here."

She took a deep swallow of champagne. Then another. "The journalists were fascinated when I explained that the danger had passed. Of course, as a former chemistry professor, I know that if a bomb in a hot kitchen had been meant to detonate it would have done so, and this landmark with us inside would have been vaporized." She fluttered her mascaraed lashes and paused for effect. "I'm dining with some of them later."

Deroche sat heavily in the chair next to hers. He was straight as a rod, but his eyes darted about. Her words had struck home.

She couldn't remember the last time a powerful man had squirmed in her presence. Or when she'd last felt this quiver of excitement. Now she'd make him grovel.

She fanned herself with a linen napkin. "We owned this hotel once, you know. It was Prince Czartoryski's former residence, the gathering place for Polish aristocrats exiled from Warsaw by corrupt mercenaries working for the tsar."

"That occurred more than a century ago, Madame," Deroche said in a frosty tone.

"Governments, corruption . . . some things never change, do they, Monsieur?"

She enjoyed his barely suppressed wince.

He'd love to throttle her, she knew, if he could have gotten away with it.

"But I am available for dinner tomorrow," she said. Bibo loved dining in four-star restaurants.

She noticed his calculating eyes as he gauged her potential value. Then she saw something else.

"Of course," he said. "But between you and me . . ." He leaned forward, his voice edged with titillation. "Is it true you persuaded your lover General Von Choltitz not to burn Paris despite Hitler's orders?"

She stifled a yawn. Always that tiresome question when people felt emboldened enough to ask it. "Semantics, Monsieur Deroche. The bombs were set. I just persuaded him not to ignite them. It is an important distinction."

She fed Bibo another foie gras–spread cracker.

"I'm sure you have to do — what's that phrase? — damage control." She stood, Bibo in her arms. "Merci, quite an exciting evening. Tomorrow then; somewhere we can arrive fashionably late?"

WEDNESDAY NIGHT

Aimée twisted her arms free of her jacket, and, kicking her legs in the Seine's sediment-laden cloudy water, rose again to the surface. Gasping for air, she was carried away by a swirling eddy. River grass entangled her arms.

She kicked with all her might against the sucking wake of the boat. Then a cold water current swept her away. She spit out the brackish water, inhaled and dove again. Her arms caught in the branches of a submerged tree, her breath almost gone. She struggled until she snapped the branches and shot to the surface.

Spluttering, this time she inhaled frigid air layered with diesel exhaust. Her leg brushed something hard, mossed stone, and she grabbed on. She realized she'd travelled down current to the stone legs of Pont Louis Philippe. On the bank, a yellow glow flickered. The fires of the homeless? Or of the clochards?

Shouts mingled with the sound of rushing water that filled her ears. A figure stood, calf deep in water. Then a cresting wave from the *Bateau-Mouche* slapped her up against the stone bridge support.

She had to try for the bank, battle the current, and pray she'd make it. She climbed partway up the support, slipping and scraping herself on its ridges, then dove. She kicked as hard as she could. The current seized her and she battled, kicking harder. Her hands hit something. She grabbed at it and missed. Someone held out a tree branch to her. She caught it and felt herself being pulled toward the shore. Her face smacked into the embankment and then arms held hers. Limp and spent, she was dragged, knees scraping, onto the water-filled walkway. She was soaked and freezing, in a little black dress that clung to her like her skin.

"Can you walk?" Krzysztof panted.

Where had he come from?

She heard the whine of a Zodiac outboard motor. Searchlights scanned the black turgid water. The Brigade Fluviale. This would not be a good time to renew her acquaintance with Capitaine Sezeur.

"Quick . . . kk." Her teeth chattered. She got to her feet, slipped, and grabbed Krzysztof's arm. She made her frozen bare feet support her. Licks of firelight came from one of the half-boarded-up arches of a sewer drain. Someone had to be in there.

Krzysztof pounded with his fists on a piece of warped board half covering the sewer's dank opening.

"What do you want?" The words were slurred. The board was scraped back. Smoke and flames haloed the face of a man with a white beard and flushed face. "Too late." He hiccuped. "I gave at the office."

"Hurry up and let us in." Krzysztof didn't wait for an answer and tugged the board away; he helped Aimée to step inside and climbed in behind her.

"You young have no manners!" the man said. "Eh, show some respect. Did I invite you?"

In the high-vaulted sewer cavern, flames came from a raised blackened-metal barbecue grill that radiated heat. Aimée waded knee deep in the cold water, then climbed an improvised staircase of wooden crates to a bunk made from an old door chained midway up the wall to iron rings. At least it was dry. A scratchy transistor radio tuned to the weather channel echoed through the tunnel.

She noticed the open can of Sabarot lentils bubbling on the grill, its odor mingling with the smoke and damp. It was like camping in flood conditions. Bottles of unlabeled wine sat on wet boxes near an old pair of rubber boots.

Her arms shook; chills ran up her legs from her numb feet. She'd lost her shoes.

Good Manolos, too. And she had to get out of this dress.

The old man squinted. "Make yourself at home, why don't you?"

Sweaters and blue work pants were piled behind her. "Sorry to interrupt your dinner, Monsieur. I'd like to buy this blanket and some clothes," she told him.

"Everything's for sale . . . except my *vin rouge.*" He grinned; his red-rimmed eyes were bloodshot. "Funny time for a swim," he said. He jerked his head back. "She's rising tonight. There is a lot of runoff because of the unseasonable heat. I've never seen her swell like this in February. The river will hit a record, for sure."

His words suggested he knew the Seine. An old sailor who lived under the bridge now?

Money, ID . . . her bag — she'd left everything in the kitchen of the Hôtel Lambert. All gone now. Her heart sank. She had no money with which to pay him.

"Here. I picked this up," Krzysztof said, setting her bag down. He climbed up next to her on the improvised bunk.

"Fast thinking." She pulled the none-too-clean blanket around her, peeled the wet dress off under it, and rubbed herself dry with the coarse wool. Her fuchsia silk Agent

Provocateur bra stank of the river.

"They'll be looking for you in that," she said, eyeing Krzysztof's dinner jacket and handing him the sweaters. "Give me the tuxedo jacket."

"You shouldn't have thrown the pipe bombs in the river," Krzysztof said angrily.

Surprised, she looked at him. "What . . . let the bombs blow up in my face?"

"All we needed to do was cut the fuse."

"What?"

"I tried to tell you — wax fuses are waterproof. But by plunging the pipe bomb into the water you must have set the explosion off."

"Your anarchist friend told you that?"

Krzysztof nodded.

Great. She'd never live this down, if she didn't freeze to death. She'd blown it in both the figurative and literal sense. Now everyone, from the bomb squad to the terrorist brigade, was after her.

Dampness oozed from the sewer cavern walls. She shivered, wondering if she'd ever feel warm again. Krzysztof took her cold hands in his and rubbed them, then wrapped them in a woolen sweater.

"It's already been fifteen minutes," he said. "If we don't get going, they'll find us."

Only fifteen minutes? It felt like hours.

And if the Brigade Fluviale took them in, she couldn't count on hot tea, a warm blanket, and congratulations. More likely they'd be sent for questioning by the terrorist brigade and make a protracted stay in jail.

"We have to get out of here."

She handed the man a hundred francs, looking at the lentils that were cooking on his fire.

"Food and wine's extra."

"Non, merci." How could he eat surrounded by the reeking sewer odor?

He sat on a box and raised his bottle, his dripping legs dangling. "*Salut.* Nice and intimate, eh?"

She heard squeals in the background. Rodents.

"All the comforts of home — dry, too — when she's not rising."

The man had to be desperate to live in an old sewer drain; the river reached a quarter of the way up the walls when it was in spate.

The blanket's warmth and her rising internal body heat kicked her mind into gear. The man's radio got reception; would her phone work? She had to check on Stella. She tried it. But she couldn't get through.

"Anyone else live here, Monsieur?"

He shook his head.

A loner. And the cavern reeked of drains and mold. But as they said, any port in a storm.

"What's your name?"

"Jules . . . first mate of the *Scallawag.* Drydocked. At your service." He made a mock bow and teetered on the door's edge.

"Aimée Leduc," she replied. "We appreciate your hospitality."

"Can always tell a lady," he said. His eyes closed and he nodded.

Engines whined from outside. Krzysztof leaned down and slid another piece of wood over the sewer opening. His eyes were anxious.

It occurred to Aimée that Jules would know the homeless people who were sheltering nearby and the local *clochards.*

"Jules, I'm looking for Hélène," she told him.

He snapped awake. "Eh? I keep to myself, I keep my distance."

Aimée nodded reassuringly. "Seen her around?"

"I don't fraternize with that bunch down there."

"Where?"

"Near the bend."

If only she could find Hélène, talk with her. "So, tell me . . ."

Jules shrugged. "I know nothing. I keep myself to myself."

"I have to get out," Krzysztof said before she could press the old man further. Fear shone on his face as he observed the rising water. "Now! I feel trapped."

Claustrophobic.

"I can't swim."

Aimée scanned the embankment walls for the opening to another drain. All these sewers crisscrossed under the island. They'd find a manhole exit eventually, but with Jules's help it would go faster.

"Jules, can you show us a way out?"

"That'll cost you," he said.

Their refuge was growing more expensive every minute.

"The package deal includes a flashlight," he said.

Several mismatched, cracked rubber boots were piled up over by the wine. "Throw those in, Jules?" she asked.

But he'd gone ahead, shining the flashlight beam over green fungal configurations on the walls that oozed slime.

She picked out a mismatched pair of right and left boots — one red, one blue — and stuck her feet into them. She draped the blanket like a shawl over her tuxedo-clad shoulders and lowered herself down the box staircase to follow the flashlight.

Scurrying and squealing came from the darkness ahead. Now the water level was lower as it was borne away by runoff tunnels that slanted toward the Seine.

Krzysztof hesitated.

"I don't do well with rodents," Aimée said. "You go first."

Compared to the rushing Seine outside, the water in the tunnel flowed slowly and steadily but it was putrid and foaming. Chill emanated from the lichen-encrusted walls. The sewer was divided; the main branch had secondary connections, all leading to a collection point. The tunnels, built partly of brick, partly of stone, formed a vast underground network.

Jules stopped, shone the flashlight beam, and pointed. Overhead were freshwater pipes, telecommunications cables, and pneumatic tubes. Rusted wire rungs led upward. All the sewer tunnels had access through manholes to the street.

"You'll need this," he said, holding out a sawed-off hook. "A deposit's required."

Without it they would have had no way to pry the metal gating open.

She thrust fifty francs into his hand. "You open it, Jules."

He stuck the flashlight in his belt and

hoisted himself up the rungs of the ladder. Krzysztof followed and Aimée heard the wrench of metal and then a clang as the manhole cover was raised.

"Can we get out here?" she called.

She heard the squeaks of rodents and splashing, then footsteps descending.

"What's wrong?"

"Not here," Krzysztof said, landing in a puddle beside her.

"What do you mean? It should be easy, once the cover's off."

"A *flic* car's parked right on top of the manhole!"

She shivered as a burst of frigid water gushed over her feet.

"I don't want to drown . . . I have to get out . . . it's too close down here." Krzysztof's breath came in short gasps.

"We'll find another exit," she said and thought hard. Hundreds of kilometers of sewers, quarry tunnels, and abandoned Metro tracks existed but they were honeycombed with water mains, and other substructures. Without a map or guide one could stumble into a warren of passages and be lost for days.

Yet the sewers followed the layout of the streets above: wide boulevards had wide tunnels and the narrow ones and the side streets were duplicated underground. All they had to do was follow the well-marked blue signs mirroring the streets above, then find another exit.

"I figure we're under . . ." The flashlight illuminated RUE SAINT LOUIS EN L'ISLE written in white paint on the stone. "See, we're close; we're just a few blocks from my place." She took Krzysztof's arm. "We'll get out there. It's just five minutes away."

"She's right," Jules said. But the *flics* were right overhead and the only way out was a sewer full of water and rodents. Two red eyes glared and a rat the size of a cat squealed as it struck her boot. She jumped as a rush of water hit her knees. "The freshwater valves opened," Jules said. "It will rise another meter, so hurry."

They slogged down the tunnel in cold knee-high water laced with chlorine and feces. The flashlight's yellow beams played across the rising water and the rivulets running down the walls. In a stone niche sat a statue of a saint, chipped and furred with moss. The saint of the sewers? With rats this big, they needed all the help they could muster.

Panicked, Krzysztof grabbed onto a set of metal rungs and started climbing.

"Come on, just one more street," Aimée

coaxed him.

He clung, unsure, his feet slipping.

"We're almost there." She reached for his hand and helped him down. "I promise."

They wound to the left and she prayed they'd find the sluice gate below her building. The ground juddered overhead. A car or truck had passed by.

"Quai d'Anjou," she said, pointing to the blue-and-white sign. "See."

She found openings — a few were bricked over; others were covered by ancient, decayed wooden doors, bearing almost invisible coats of arms. She counted them and tried the tenth, a medieval stone arch enclosed by iron grillwork. But bits of debris and plastic bags were caught in the grillwork and there was no way to open the doors. Next to it was a waist-high chute. "Here. Give me a boost. It's dry — feel the grit? Sandstone."

If she'd counted right, this was the aperture she'd explored as a child, and it led to her building's subterranean cave — the storage area in the basement.

"A marquis's daughter hid here during the Reign of Terror while the authorities searched the house for her," she told Krzysztof. That was building lore, anyway.

She found a wad of francs and handed it

to Jules.

"I'm going in, Krzysztof. You can stay here if you like; it's up to you."

Cobwebs caught in her hair and webbed her eyelashes as she crawled up the chute. She blinked and wiped them away. Grit got under her fingernails. But the flowing air was warmer and dry. She heard Krzysztof crawling behind her. And then Aimée was facing a pile of copper pipe and stacked plastic tubing.

She straightened up, stretched her legs, and climbed over the pipes. She shone the flashlight around and hit a light switch on the wall. A single hanging bulb sent harsh light over the cavern, which was lined with gated compartments piled with the stored possessions of the building's inhabitants. Her own bin lay open, a pit dug in its sandstone floor from which wires and pipes protruded.

"Nowhere's safe." Krzysztof's face paled under the stark light.

"My apartment's upstairs," she said. "And when we get there, you can tell me where Nelie's hiding."

"I don't know. No one knows."

"You're going to have to try harder. Make some calls, track her through your Monde-Focus connections."

He shook his head. Agitated, he picked at the cable-knit sweater he wore. "Fat chance. They think I'm spying for the right!"

She grabbed his arm and led him upward. She needed to think. And to find warm wool socks.

On her black-and-white marble landing, she saw cardboard boxes piled up and an old-leather tooled chest leaning against her door. *Cave #8* was written on it. A present from the concierge, no doubt. Just what she needed: to sort through her grandfather's forgotten auction finds and then make room in the closets in her apartment for them.

She unlocked the door.

"*Ça va*, Miles?" His wet nose sniffed her boots. She bent and he licked her hand, then growled at Krzysztof.

Together she and Krzysztof slid the boxes inside the foyer. The chest's leather bindings were crumbling, leaving a trail of brown powder on the floor. She needed to shower to get the sewer smell off her, and then to put on clean clothes. She pulled off the cracked boots, hung up the tuxedo jacket to dry, and motioned Krzysztof toward the kitchen. "I'll join you in a minute," she said and, barefoot, padded to her bedroom. First, she had to call Mathilde and check on Stella, then shower.

"*Allô*, Mathilde?"

"*Oui?*"

She heard irritation in Mathilde's voice and Stella's whimpers.

Aimée clutched the cell phone tighter. Mathilde was young, probably inexperienced. She shouldn't have just taken Martine's word that the girl was capable. So many complications could occur with newborns, according to the manual. She imagined Stella's face flushed with fever, eyes rolling up in her head, her limbs twitching, all the signs of a febrile convulsion.

"Does Stella have a fever?"

"Relax, Aimée," Mathilde said. "She woke up fussy. Now she's refusing the bottle but I'm coaxing her to drink, little by little."

Aimée took a slow breath and tried to remember what she'd read in the baby manual; terms like *gastric distress* and *viral infection* swirled in her head.

"Last night, too, Mathilde, she woke up every hour. I rocked her back to sleep."

Mathilde yawned. "That's what I'm doing. Are you coming back soon? I have an early morning class."

"Please, Mathilde," Aimée said. "It won't be much longer. I'll make it worth your while."

"I hate to charge you for staying overnight but I'll have to."

"No problem," Aimée said. "Of course, I'm giving you taxi fare and something extra for your trouble."

"*Oui* . . . shhh. See you when you get here," Mathilde said and hung up.

Aimée jumped in the shower, then toweled dry and checked her cell-phone messages. One was from René saying he and Saj were working at the office. The other, from Claude, said that he'd found more video footage, that she should see it, and that he had a bottle of Chinon waiting. She thought of the Chinon and Claude's warm arms, but before she could go to him she needed to know what light Krzysztof could shed on MondeFocus connections and the video.

She pulled on black jeans and the nearest T-shirt. No time for makeup. She slipped on socks to warm her numb feet and black patent leather-heeled boots.

In the kitchen, she spooned the butcher's scraps into Miles Davis's chipped Limoges bowl, which stood on the brown mosaic-tiled floor. The kitchen, in the throes of remodeling, stood with one wall open, revealing pipes and ancient lath and plaster. Disaster lurked every time the contractor went to work.

She found Krzysztof standing at the closed kitchen window. Below, searchlights shone and Zodiac boat motors beat the water. Divers, their masks catching in the light, bobbed in the Seine.

"They're looking for you," Krzysztof said.

She stilled her shaking hands.

"For someone," she said. "You took my bag; they don't know my identity."

She felt a cool breeze and realized she must have forgotten to shut the salon window.

"Hold on," she said. But when she checked, she noticed the baby blanket hanging from the chair, not on the *recamier* where she'd left it, neatly folded. And the box of wipes was on the floor, not on the table. Papers had been moved. Yet René hadn't been here; he didn't even have a key.

She sensed a stranger's presence. Someone had entered her apartment and not to sniff her underwear. Whoever it was now knew the baby had been here. It wasn't safe here for Stella any longer. She couldn't bring Stella back here. Aimée stuck her phone in her pocket, ran back to the kitchen, and picked up Miles Davis.

"We have to go. Now." She grabbed

Krzysztof's arm and pulled him down the hallway.

His eyes widened. "What the hell?"

She had to appear calm. He was already a bundle of nerves; she knew if she told him any more he'd bolt.

"Claude left a message. He's found more video footage."

"What do you mean?"

"We're going to check Claude's video of the march," she said, grabbing her bag and the first jacket she found, the damp tuxedo, as she led him out the door.

"Good," he said, his tense mouth relaxing. "You'll see the proof that we were set up."

On the staircase, she punched in the speed-dial button for taxi service. "Twelve rue Saint Louis en L'Isle, please."

Downstairs, Madame Cachou stood in the doorway of the concierge's loge, reading glasses pushed up on top of her head, chewing a pencil.

"Come to complain, have you?" she asked.

"*Mais non,* I want to thank you for bringing up the boxes," Aimée said, tugging Miles Davis by his leash.

"There's more, you know."

"Miles Davis loved staying with you. Could I impose again?"

Miles Davis cooperated by wagging his tail and licking Madame's outstretched hand.

Her face softened and she stuck the pencil behind her ear. "Such a good boy."

Aimée put a hundred francs in her waiting palm. *"Merci."*

In the taxi speeding through the dark Left Bank streets, Krzysztof sat beside her, his fingers twisting the loose yarn on his sweater's sleeve. She rubbed a clear spot on the fogged window so she could look back at the quiet streets. No one seemed to be behind them.

She couldn't put Stella in more danger. Whoever had sifted through her apartment had seen the diapers and knew she'd kept the baby. She couldn't lead them to Martine's either. As long as Stella was safe, Aimee's time was better spent getting Claude's video, which might give her a lead to Nelie's whereabouts.

With the bombs and Vavin's murder, the stakes had shot sky-high. She drummed her fingers on the window, wishing the taxi would go faster. Her fear was that the Halkyut operatives had already found Nelie. She tried to put that thought aside.

"You must tell me everything, Krzysztof,"

she said. "About Orla, the Alstrom files that Nelie found. And why Nelie's hiding. Who is she hiding from?"

"I don't understand your involvement," Krzysztof said. "You work for Regnault and they work for Alstrom. How can I trust you?"

"And I want to know why, when you saw Orla's body at the morgue, you didn't identify her. I have to have your answer before I can trust you," she said.

"I couldn't take the risk. It wouldn't have helped Orla anyway. If I had opened my mouth, the *flics* would have locked me up. I'm *wanted*. MondeFocus told the *flics* that I planted the bottle bombs at the demonstration. There was even an article about me in the newspaper." He rubbed his forehead. "All lies. We were just trying to stop the oil agreement."

"Nelie's uncle was my boss at Regnault."

"Is that why you had Regnault files? Did you find the reports about Alstrom's pollution of the North Sea?"

"My partner's working on it," she said.

"You still wonder about me, don't you?" Krzysztof said. "I assure you, I know we cannot achieve peace with bombs."

She had to trust him; he'd saved her life.

"I want to know why Vavin and Orla were

murdered."

Terror painted his face. "Nelie's uncle was murdered?"

"Like I said, I want some answers."

He hesitated. "Nelie's afraid."

"You mean she's afraid the authorities will take away her baby because she's wanted for her part in the demonstration at La Hague?"

"If her evidence isn't publicized, the oil agreement will go through," Krzysztof said.

"So the person who killed Orla was trying to get to Nelie, right?"

"But if she has the reports, why hasn't she given them to me?" Krzysztof asked.

And why had Nelie left her baby with Aimée? Vavin couldn't have been ignorant of Stella's existence; he was Nelie's uncle. Why not choose Vavin? Or was Aimée supposed to have met Vavin at the antique shop and turn the baby over to him to take to Nelie? He'd been murdered nearby. Again, another person murdered in place of Nelie.

Aimée tried to piece it together. Was Vavin killed because he wouldn't reveal Nelie's whereabouts? All she had was suppositions.

Krzysztof stared at her. "They're going to kill me, too."

"Who?"

"Halkyut," Krzysztof said. "I saw Gabriel

at our march. He was standing on the sidelines, watching."

"And he killed Orla? Is that what you mean?" She wanted to pry a straight answer from him.

"Maybe the killer was the baby's father," he said.

She hadn't thought of that before. As the taxi sped along the quai, she checked again. No headlights behind them.

"Maybe the baby's a pawn, think about that. He could threaten to obtain custody unless she shuts up about what she knows."

Was that what this was all about? Domestic drama? Aimée didn't think so, but who knew?

"You mean so Nelie won't divulge what it says in the Alstrom report?"

"Makes sense, doesn't it?"

"Then why do you think they want to kill you?"

"Nelie had a difficult pregnancy," he said. "She missed a lot of classes. Orla helped her."

What did that have to do with it, she wanted to ask. Instead, she said, "You mean Orla was protective of her?"

"Orla had to take care of the baby when it was born," he said. "Nelie bled too much."

She thought back to the bloodstains in

the baby bag. "Is she in the hospital?"

"She refused to go back to see the surgeon after her Cesarean. He had her name and she was terrified he'd turn her in. Nelie said she broke up with the father when he found out she was pregnant."

The rosebud mouth, mauve-pink eyelids . . . those minuscule fingers gripping hers. How could anyone not want Stella?

"That doesn't make sense," she said, her frustration mounting. "Would the father threaten to obtain custody if he didn't want the baby?"

"I don't know. Maybe, if it gave him leverage over Nelie. The last thing she said was that the father would be able to trace her if she went back to the surgeon."

Krzysztof was clutching at straws like she was.

"Who is the baby's father . . . can't you guess?"

"Nelie had nothing to do with him after she got pregnant. According to her, he was out of her life. She never told me his name."

"Don't you have any idea?" Aimée said, her patience wearing thin. "Someone else in your class or in your crowd?" And then it clicked. "You suspect that the father's a member of MondeFocus?"

"Who else?"

She pulled out the photo she'd taken from his room.

"You stole that." There was outrage in his eyes.

"I'm sorry," she said. "I was trying to find you — and Nelie."

"What else have you done?"

"Could any of these *mecs* in the photo be the father?"

"I'm getting out of this taxi. You're going to turn me in, aren't you?"

She put her hand on his arm. "I believe that you were set up. And we're going to see the proof of it in Claude's video."

Krzysztof subsided. "You're right." He stared at the photo, his shoulders shaking. "We were idealists, naive. That was taken two years ago. It seems like another world. Another time." He pointed to the men in the photo. "*Non.* That one's gay; this one's studying in Nanterre."

Another dead end. She thought hard.

"Tell me about the La Hague group."

"Why?"

She took a guess. "What if the father's one of them?"

"That protest took place two weeks ago. Nelie said the whole thing was bungled. Amateurs." He looked down. "Like me."

Something Krzysztof had said stuck in her mind.

"Hold on . . . you said the father might seek custody if Nelie didn't shut up. Shut up about what?"

"All I know is that Orla and Nelie were digging into reports that falsified pollution counts. They thought there had been funny business juggling the statistics," he said.

"Was her uncle helping her?"

Krzysztof shrugged. "Nelie told a Monde-Focus activist there was a doctor's report she had to find that would sew everything up."

"Did you get any details concerning this doctor's report?"

He shook his head.

She thought about Stella's father, whoever he was, infiltrating MondeFocus and sabotaging the demonstrations.

"The video will show that I'm telling the truth," Krzysztof said, hope in his voice.

She hoped he was right.

The taxi left them south of the Gare d'Austerlitz in a warren of small streets. An old metal streetlight illuminated peeling posters on the walls of Les Frigos, the refurbished refrigerator warehouses.

There was no answer to her knocks on

Claude's door. No light in his window. She checked the box for deliveries labeled NED-EROVIQUE PRODUCTIONS. No videotape.

One step forward and three steps back.

She heard the roar of a motorcycle, the scrape of the gates to the deserted warehouse courtyard opening. The headlights of a vintage motorcycle with a sidecar bobbed over the uneven cobblestones. The engine switched off.

Claude took off his helmet, then shook out his hair, looking more bad boy than ever in torn denims and a motorcycle jacket. Bad boys with bad toys. But the expression on his face, raw and vulnerable at the same time, made her think of his warm hands and the way he'd curled up, spoonlike, against her.

He nodded to Krzysztof, then pulled her close by the tail of her tuxedo jacket. Gave her a searching kiss. And for a moment all she knew was his stubbled cheek, his sandalwood scent. "Partying without me, Aimée?"

"Long story, I just got your message," she said.

"Too late," he said.

"What do you mean?"

"The *flics* took the video, the copy, and they even 'requisitioned' my tapes."

Outraged, Aimée said, "That's illegal.

That's a violation of procedure."

"Try telling them that," he said. "They said I'd get them back 'in due course.' Or if I lodged a complaint, I could spend an evening with them explaining why I hadn't brought them to the Commissariat in the first place."

"But if the police watch the tapes, they'll see the proof that I was set up," Krzysztof said, his voice rising in excitement. "The video must show the woman slipping the backpack onto my shoulder. You were there, Claude, you saw it."

Claude told him, "Humidity ruined a lot of the tape."

"But you said you found something," Aimée reminded him.

"I found Gaelle being beaten, *oui*," he said. "Orla was shouting; I caught that on the video."

"I heard her, for a moment," Krzysztof said. "Just before Gaelle stepped into the square."

Claude glanced at his watch. "Word has come down. The Direction Territoire de l'Interior is closing the net around all of you. It's just a matter of time until they tighten it." He opened a compartment in the motorcycle sidecar and pulled out a helmet. "Krzysztof, the network has arranged a safe house in the Bobigny suburbs for you. But I'm not supposed to tell you where it is."

Aimée saw indecision on Krzysztof's face.

"I can't leave. If we don't do something, the oil agreement will be signed tomorrow," he said. "And then we're back to square one. Nowhere."

"If you want to be safe, you have to go deep undercover, Krzysztof. We have to leave now. You can figure something out once you're in hiding where they can't find you. You'll come up with a plan."

The indecision faded from Krzysztof's face.

Aimée had to do something before they left. The warehouse courtyard was quiet, the only sound that of the occasional car passing outside on the street. The gleams of the sodium streetlight pooled on the cobbles. An idea formed in her head. Hadn't Morbier said, 'First you have to catch the wolf?'

"Krzysztof, may I see that Halkyut card?"

"Why?"

"I'll call Gabriel, and you'll talk to him. Say you want to meet him in thirty minutes or you'll give his phone number to the *flics*. Tell him, in return, you'll show him — *non*, you'll *give* him — Alstrom's disc."

"What do you mean?" Krzysztof asked.

"You know more about this than I do. All those oil statistics . . ."

"Of course," Krzysztof said. "The cover-ups on the Brent Spar oil platform, the falsified percentages with respect to the deep drilling."

"Right. Tell him that, in exchange, you want Nelie too," she said. "That will flush him out. Even if he doesn't buy it, he'll have to meet you if only to try to corner you."

"Corner me?"

"He won't. I'll make sure of that. If he brings Nelie, you'll tell him the disc is somewhere else."

Claude frowned. "A disc means nothing. The originals are in the computer. They know that."

"If Halkyut's working for Alstrom," she said, buttoning the jacket, "then it might work. All their techs would need to do is insert the disc in Alstrom's system, find the matching file, and erase it. Trash it. Then *phfft,* it will be all gone. No record will exist any longer on their hard drive either."

Except that René and Saj had a copy at their office. At least, she hoped they did. But there was no need to tell Halkyut about that.

Krzysztof nodded. He handed Aimée the

card. "If they're holding Nelie, it would explain why she hasn't contacted me."

If they had a chance of luring Gabriel into their trap, she'd call Morbier and have him waiting.

"Is it that easy to erase the information?" Claude asked.

That's how she paid her rent. "I should know, it's my bread and butter."

Claude stared at her. "As a reporter?"

She had a big mouth. But it was too late.

"Actually, I do computer security, Claude," she confessed. "I'm sorry to have lied, but I needed a cover."

She searched his dark eyes, detecting a flutter of hurt. She didn't want it to end with this man. She hadn't met anyone like him before.

"I'm trying to help Nelie, but I can't explain any more," she said, attempting to recover. "It's a lot to ask, but can you just trust me?"

"And if I do?" he asked.

She leaned against his leather jacket, felt the warmth from his body. "Wait and see."

"Do you have a better idea, Claude?" Krzysztof interrupted. He didn't wait for Claude's answer. "Give me your phone, Aimée."

She wrote down an address on a scrap of

paper and showed it to him. "Give Gabriel this information."

They would arrange to meet him on the corner by the boiler room of her old lycée. The safest place, just across the Seine. And she knew the door code.

She punched in Gabriel's number, which started with 06, indicating it was a cell phone, and thrust the phone at Krzysztof. She leaned close so she could hear.

"Oui?" a deep voice answered.

"Bring Nelie to rue du Petit Musc at Quai des Celestins," Krzysztof said, reading from the paper Aimée had given him. "Wait on the corner."

There was a pause. They could hear loud talking and music in the background.

"Who is this?"

"The Alstrom reports make interesting reading," Krzysztof improvised. "Especially in the right hands. I'll exchange them for Nelie."

"How did you get this number?"

"From *la rouquine*," said Krzysztof.

"She's a naughty girl."

"Thirty minutes. Bring Nelie," Krzysztof said.

"Why should I?"

But Aimée could hear curiosity in his voice.

"Otherwise I'll give the *flics* your number," said Krzysztof. "They can trace a cell phone in thirty minutes. Or less." He hung up.

"I think we've got him," Aimée said. She searched her pockets for some money. Paying Jules and the taxi had tapped her out. She turned to Claude. "Mind giving us a ride?"

He switched on the ignition and started up the bike.

"I'll open the gate and meet you outside," she said.

She hurried to the street, taking out her cell phone and dialing, while Claude turned the bike around.

"Morbier," his tired voice answered at the other end of the line.

"I'm baiting the wolf, Morbier," she said, keeping her voice low.

"The wolf responsible for blowing holes in the Seine?" He sounded more awake now. "Disrupting river traffic for hours?"

Her heart lurched. How could she confess that she'd been responsible?

"About time you found Krzysztof," he said.

"Wrong. I'm after a *mec* named Gabriel," she said. "But there's one condition."

"Always a condition with you."

"*Bon,* if you're not interested . . ."

"Difficult." Morbier sighed. "The terrorist brigade is involved, so there's not much I can do."

"What you do is take this Gabriel in. He works for Halkyut. Question him about the bomb he placed in the Hôtel Lambert kitchen."

"Why do I think you're hiding something?"

"You've got a suspicious mind, Morbier. You have to learn to trust."

"Every time I do. . . ." Another sigh. "You've infiltrated MondeFocus, right?"

She turned to make sure she was alone. She saw Krzysztof putting on a helmet and climbing into the motorcycle sidecar.

"Halkyut's the culprit."

"Eh?" Morbier was silent for a few moments. "No one can touch them with a barge pole."

"If they plant bombs, you can."

Claude's motorcycle engine sputtered and roared. She had to hurry.

"Afraid to take on the big guys, Morbier? You'd let them get away with this?"

"You're sure?"

"I'm only sure of death and taxes. As for the rest, I hedge my bets."

Even if Gabriel had Nelie, she doubted he would bring her with him. But with any luck, he'd come. He'd be curious. And if Morbier cooperated and netted him, Gabriel would provide them with the link to Halkyut itself.

"How reassuring!" Morbier said. "Now I feel better. And you want *me* to stick my neck out?"

"Don't blow my cover. Bring just a few men. Say you've got a witness to his bomb purchase, and that this witness also places him in the Hôtel Lambert's kitchen. Keep it intimate and question him in the back room. I'm sure you've done that before."

"Do you have such a witness?"

"Only on condition that he gets immunity for his testimony."

"Not if he's an ax murderer."

"He's not."

"Let's get going," Krzysztof shouted from the gate.

She kept the phone between her shoulder and her ear and leaned against a wall. "Wait a minute, there's a rock in my boot."

If Krzysztof knew the *flics* would be waiting, he'd flee. She wouldn't even have time to tell him she'd gotten him immunity. She whispered into the cell phone crooked next to her ear, "Is Nicolas still working the cameras at France2?"

Nicolas had been on staff there since her

father's time.

"You want a camera crew, Leduc? Forget it."

"*Non,* Morbier. Ask him to pore over footage of Monday night's MondeFocus march to l'Institut du Monde Arabe. The outtakes, raw footage, the whole thing."

Claude revved the engine; the noise echoed in the narrow street. "Aimée, you ready?" he asked.

She made a show of shaking her boot and putting it back on.

"France2 sent the tapes to the terrorist brigade," he said. "Sounds like a motorcycle there with you. You a biker now?"

"They can't have sent all the raw footage, Morbier," she said. "I saw a video made by a documentary filmmaker, but it's not enough."

"Eh, who's that?"

"Claude Nederovique. But it's too blurred. Just ask Nicolas. Deal or not?"

She put her finger in her other ear to hear better, heard his chair scraping over the floor and a sound like the snapping of fingers. If she wasn't mistaken, he'd stood, grabbed his coat, and signaled to some of his men.

"Better be worth my while, Leduc. Where?"

She'd hooked him. She took a deep breath.

"École Massillon, the corner of Quai des Celestins and rue du Petit Musc."

Her tuxedo tails flew behind her as she rode clutching Claude's waist, her knees clamping his hips. Those wonderful hips.

Krzysztof sat hunched in the sidecar. The engine revved as they passed shadowy Place Bayre. She caught the whiff of green vegetation, of damp grass, wet from the rain. A now dark Hôtel Lambert went by on her left.

Every pot has a lid, as her grandmother had phrased it. Meaning life was about finding the right mate. The right fit. She was attracted to bad boys in leather jackets. Ones who had been hurt, who were fierce inside. The ones mothers warned their daughters against. But in her case, there'd been no warning. And for a moment, Aimée wondered what it would be like with Claude, sitting in front of her fireplace, Stella taking her first steps. Together.

Stop. She'd gone soft, just as René had accused. She had more to think of than Stella and this man who'd once been abandoned, too.

She prayed Morbier would make good on

his agreement. That they'd nab Gabriel, link the bombings to Halkyut, and find Nelie.

The Brigade Fluviale's Zodiacs were trawling below the Pont de Sully. She shivered, thinking of the silt-laden, churning water below. And of Orla's waxen face in the morgue.

Claude slowed and turned into fourteenth-century rue du Petit Musc, the street of the strolling hookers. No working girls had lingered there for a long time but the name clung, though now only media types and the *branché* crowd could afford it.

Claude downshifted by École Massillon's side entrance, the rumbling of his motor-cycle engine reverberating off the walls of the blackened stone buildings. Aimée removed her helmet as Krzysztof climbed out of the sidecar.

"I'm coming, too," Claude said, taking her arm.

A dark figure stood in one of the doorways of the narrow street. Another figure sat in a parked car. Big mistake. Morbier's men were making their presence too obvious.

"It's the *flics*," Krzysztof said, wild eyed. "*Merde!* Let's get out of here."

"*Flics?*" Claude pulled her arm. "Get back on, Aimée."

"They're backup; it's all right," she said, looking for Morbier.

"I get it," Krzysztof said. "*You're* trapping me."

"You'll be given immunity from prosecution. I worked out a deal for you."

But Claude gunned the motorcycle engine and Krzysztof jumped on behind him, holding tight as Claude turned the bike around.

"We can't stay," Claude said, his eyes narrowed. "No *flics.* You don't understand." He popped the shift into first gear. "Get on."

She couldn't leave. She had to see this through, alone if need be.

"It's all right! Listen to the deal I made."

"A deal?" Krzysztof said. "I'll never risk a deal with the *flics.* You're crazy." Krzysztof pushed Claude's arm. "Get us out of here. Now!"

The motorcycle sped off down the rue du Petit Musc. The red brakelights' reflection wobbled across the stone walls of buildings. The motorcycle turned the corner, peeling rubber. Krzysztof and Claude were gone. They had deserted her.

What had she been thinking, she wondered. She'd been fooling herself, intoxicated by playing house with the baby and sleeping with this gorgeous, sensitive man. She shook herself and called Morbier, afraid now that his men would chase away Gabriel, too, if they hadn't already done so.

"Call off your dogs, Morbier. They're so close I can smell them."

"What do you mean, Leduc? We're on rue de l'Hôtel-de-Ville crossing rue de l'Ave Maria."

Four blocks away.

She heard a car door open, saw a man getting out of the car. Her hands trembled.

"Get prepared for a reception committee." She clicked off before she dropped the phone. And stood there alone, with her supposed backup blocks away.

Her heart skipped. The only thing she could think of was to press 34B51 on the digicode of the next building.

The massive carved seventeenth-century door opened. She slipped inside, into former stables that were now a delivery bay for school supplies. A ramp led to the lower playground gate, which could not be glimpsed from the street. She tugged at the door and it clicked shut behind her.

A few years ago the junkies had discovered this enclave but she didn't see any discarded needles among the tufts of overgrown grass. She followed the border of the enclosed playground to a back door where she counted on finding a key. From time im-

memorial, janitors had left one here for de-
liverymen, always in the same place. She
slid her fingers over the wall, located the
loose stone, and pried it out. In the dirt-
encrusted space she found the janitor's key
where he'd always kept it. She and Martine
had used it on occasion when they'd been
late to class.

She unlocked the door and put the key
back. Inside the school, she ran down a narrow low-ceilinged hall lined with bulletin
boards laden with notices of class schedules
and after-school club meetings. The smell
of paper, the dull luster of the linoleum floor
— nothing had changed since her day. No
doubt the cracked ceilings upstairs still
leaked puddles onto the marble floors.

This was formerly the residence of the
first archbishop of Paris. Later it had been
an outpost of Charles V, then Marie-
Thérèse's chancellor's quarters. It had
became a sugar refinery and then, in the
last century, a high school.

Perspiration dampened Aimee's collar.
She had to figure out what to say to Gabriel
when she found him.

Using the stairway, she descended into the
bowels of the École Massillon, to the blackened boiler room. The fourteenth-century
foundation emitted a dank chill, barely

combatted by the heat radiating from huge soot-stained boilers abutting the wall. They must recently have been stoked. The boilers were firing at full blast, and charcoal dust lay everywhere. Carved out of the thick wall was the half-oval window she remembered. It was not glassed in; it was needed for ventilation. This window was level with the sidewalk and looked onto rue du Petit Musc. Quai des Celestins lay beyond it, then came the Seine, and, across the river, the Hôtel Lambert on the Ile Saint-Louis. The Hôtel Lambert, again.

She leaned against the window's rusted bars. She could see a pair of brown walking shoes and the bottom half of khaki trousers passing by on rue du Petit Musc's pavement. The man was so close she could have reached out and untied his shoelaces.

"Gabriel?"

The legs turned and retreated. The streetlight illuminated a *mec* with blond hair, a barrel chest, and close-set eyes now scanning the building.

"I don't see Nelie," she said.

"And I don't see you. Why'd Krzysztof leave?"

She had to keep him talking until Morbier arrived.

He hunched over and peered down and inside.

"Don't you have something for me?" Gabriel asked. His gravel-edged voice was the one she had heard over the phone.

The light from the boiler illuminated her coat sleeves but she didn't think he would be able to get at her through the chipped and rusted iron bars. But her certainty was wrong.

With two swift kicks, he dislodged them.

She jumped back but thick fingers reached in and grabbed her, encircling her neck. Her face was wrenched hard against the gritty stone. She tried to bite his fingers but couldn't turn her head so that her teeth could find a purchase. Her hands were free, though, and she scratched his and tried to get away. His pressure on her throat increased and as she struggled, her face was thrust against the wall again. Where were Morbier and his men?

"You don't . . . have Nelie, do you?" she sputtered, her fingernails scraping against the stone as she sought something, anything, to fight back with.

Her hand caught the metal poker used to stoke the furnace that hung from the boiler door. Choking, she wrapped the tail of her tuxedo jacket around her hand, seized the hot poker, and slammed it against his thick knuckles, his hands, his arms. The air filled with the smell of singed hair and burning cloth.

"Ayyeee . . ." One hand relinquished his grip. She kept beating the other until it, too, fell away.

"You set the bomb —"

"Screw you." The blade of his Laguiole knife sliced through the air. She heard footsteps. Men were coming. "Where'd you take the brat?" he asked.

"So it was you in my apartment." She hooked the hot poker around his ankle. "Why do you want the baby?" He let out a piercing yell as the poker connected with bare skin. She yanked him against the building with all her might. She could smell searing flesh. "Why?"

His screams were the only reply.

And then he was surrounded by scuffling legs and the impact of punches, the sounds of thuds. She heard the wail of a siren, then shots, and still she held on, yanking harder. Now she could only smell coal fumes. Outside, a car squealed off.

"Leduc?"

She dropped the poker.

"Let go. It stinks." Morbier's face was above her, at the window. "Pretty messy barbecue, Leduc."

Morbier sat behind his desk, rubbing the gray growth on his chin. His jowls sagged and his eyes were red rimmed. He pointed at her soot-stained Che Guevara T-shirt. "Your new hero, Leduc?"

"Part of my cover," she said.

She took another sip of espresso. Her legs felt warm; the shivering had stopped. The ice pack she held to her forehead was already partly melted and sagging.

Smoke spiraled from a burning cigarillo in the Ricard ashtray. Aimée took another from Morbier's yellow Montecristo tin and lit it from the box of kitchen matches on his desk.

"Help yourself, Leduc, why don't you?" he said. "Didn't you quit?"

"I'm always quitting." She glanced around. "New office. You're coming up in the world, Morbier." Wood file cabinets, a computer screen with a blinking cursor. "I didn't think you knew how to use one of those," she said, pointing to the computer.

"I even type like a pro now," he said. "I've graduated from two-finger hunting and pecking."

Outside his office there was a large open room with vacant cubicles and computers.

Once it had been the incident room. She saw the adjoining office, the number five painted on the glass beneath the transom. Her father's old office.

"A real nice *mec,* Gabriel Leclerc," Morbier said, consulting some papers in a brown file folder. "Ex-military, low-level ops. I thought I knew him from somewhere."

She bit back her surprise. "So, he fits Halkyut's profile."

"Let's say he's a bottom-feeder, not their usual level operative." Morbier shook his head. "Seems like they didn't vet him with their usual thoroughness."

She figured Gabriel was someone Halkyut used for jobs that could go wrong.

"Any good news, Morbier?" After all, it was Gabriel who had set the bomb at the Hôtel Lambert. "Did he give you a confession?"

"The evening's young." Morbier smiled wryly. "But it seems that he skipped his parole appointment yesterday. So we've got all the time in the world."

Missing a parole appointment meant there would be no need for lawyers or an arraignment. Gabriel had a ticket to La Santé. He'd be arrested and then it would take several weeks or even months to process his case. With luck he'd end up in a maximum-security prison like Clairvaux.

There was a knock on the frame of the open door.

Aimée looked up to see a young policewoman wearing a blue cap cocked at a jaunty angle.

"Commissaire, a package for you," she said, with a Provençal accent wide enough to push a cart through.

"From whom?"

"France2."

Nicolas was on the ball.

"Do me a favor, Officer," Morbier said. "Set up the VCR for viewing a tape, *s'il vous plaît*."

Aimée blinked. Morbier polite? Not only did he type now, he also said please.

She stubbed out her cigarillo. "You got a fast response from Nicolas, Morbier. Must be your good manners."

"That, too. And Nicolas owes me at poker. Big-time.

"Nicolas says this Claude Nederovique made a splash ten years ago but hasn't produced anything in a while," Morbier told her. "Is he part of MondeFocus now?"

She shook her head. She didn't want to direct suspicion toward Claude even if he'd deserted her, abandoned her to those *mecs*.

"He's just helping out. He's filming, that's

381

all," she said.

She hit *Play.* The images flickered by, disjointed. There was more footage than what she'd viewed on Claude's video. He and Krzysztof should have gotten to Bobigny a while ago. Yet she'd had no phone call.

Now the video showed a smiling mix of students and Socialist types, milling about on a narrow street. The cameraman talked to an assistant about lighting, angles. Krzysztof and a woman in a red-and-white Palestinian scarf passed out candles. Bottles of wine were being shared in the loose ranks of marchers who were singing "The Internationale." The camera cut to a blonde with long hair. There was a close-up. From the remarks of the cameraman about her low-cut jeans, it seemed he was a derrière man. Then they heard his sigh as she put the strap of a backpack over Krzysztof's shoulder and pecked his cheek. Next they saw an unfocused blue glare. A wobbling handheld shot showed a limping woman shouting. Another woman grabbed her and ran toward the Pont de Sully. More wobbling. The first woman slumped to the ground.

Nelie. It was Nelie.

The next shot showed the woman in the red-and-white Palestinian scarf, which was now soaked with blood. Aimée didn't recognize her but seeing the scarf turning red with her blood made Aimée queasy. The cameraman's voice said, "Hurry . . . bomb squad's arriving." He zoomed in . . . then came a shot of a backpack out of which bottles and yellow rag fuses were spilling.

Watching the tape she felt relieved. The march had happened just as Krzysztof had described it. But the most important question was still unanswered.

Morbier said, "Great idea, Leduc! You've wasted my time. It's after midnight. I could have been halfway home, and not had to call in a favor."

"Wrong, Morbier." She hit the *Rewind* button.

"Important, eh? All I saw was a bunch of long-haired radicals partying, and the CRS doing its job."

Her shoulders tensed at Morbier's dismissive tone. It was all there, in blurred color. Why didn't he see it?

She hit *Play* once more, took the remote control, and stood close to the screen. "OK, see, here's Krzysztof." She pointed to him as he passed out candles. Then she fast-forwarded. "Here's the blonde."

"It's blurred; it's hard to see what's happening."

"Bear with me. You're seeing this at sixty images a second, not frame by frame."

"Quite the expert, eh?"

She was just parroting what she'd learned from Claude.

"Notice something else, Morbier?"

"I concur with the cameraman — nice derrière."

"The blonde's putting the backpack on Krzysztof's shoulder," she said. "She kisses him. And then she disappears. But see the blond man on the sideline?"

"Gabriel Leclerc," Morbier said. He scratched a kitchen match on the table's edge and lit up a cigarillo.

She fast-forwarded and hit *Stop.* "This woman . . . recognize her?"

Morbier exhaled a puff of blue smoke. "Orla."

"But do you recognize who she's reaching for? It's Nelie Landrou."

"So that's what she looks like."

In slow motion they saw Nelie limping. She had an anguished look on her face, and was almost doubled over as she ran. But there was no baby; Aimée didn't see Stella.

"Keep going, Leduc."

She forwarded the video in slow motion now. "Here's the proof the blonde gave the backpack with the bottle bombs to Krzysztof. It was a setup."

"You'd be a good *avocat,* Leduc," Morbier said. "It's easy to interpret the video the way you want, in your client's favor."

Aimée was frustrated. "Look at the video. The proof is right there!"

"Or it was an elaborate plan, and Krzysztof expected her to bring the bottle bombs in the backpack and to give it to him."

Aimée rewound the video to show Krzysztof's smiling face as the blonde was kissing him. "I think he's just a sucker for a pretty face. Doesn't it look like that?"

"It wouldn't persuade the tribunal."

She sat down, tired. "It doesn't have to. Gabriel Leclerc's off to La Santé anyway for a good long visit. Show him this in a *tête-à-tête.* Get him to spill. Tell him you'd appreciate his cooperation and you'll reciprocate, et cetera."

"Reciprocate?" Morbier snorted. "It's out of my hands. Out of my realm now." But he tapped his pencil, a sure sign he was thinking.

"Promise Gabriel a three-man cell instead of the usual one for six," Aimée said. Her temples were throbbing. She needed more ice. "Or say you'll try to get him assigned to the VIP wing. You know, along with the disgraced financiers and officials."

There was silence except for the whir of the tape rewinding. Aimée could smell the bitter dregs of her espresso. She was worn out. All she wanted to do was crawl under her duvet.

"He's pretentious enough to like that," Morbier said. "You actually think he'll admit that Halkyut is involved in sabotaging ecology groups and, in particular, MondeFocus?"

Smart. Why had she underestimated Morbier? He had to watch his back and he was always moaning about imminent retirement. And he didn't like taking on the ruling powers.

"Morbier, you won't lose your pension or anything else, and you'll just gain in self-respect."

"So you've got it all figured out, eh?"

"Figured out?" She shrugged. "It's up to you."

She didn't know what else to say. She stood up, buttoned the tuxedo jacket, shouldered her bag, and walked to the door.

"Still not going to tell me, Leduc?"

She froze. "Tell you what?"

Hiding the baby? Finding Vavin's body? There was so much she'd kept from him. She wished she could confide in him, like she had before.

"Leduc, you there?"

She turned to face him. But he sat shaking his head, in disgust or anger, she couldn't tell. When he looked up, she saw the redness of his eyes and the pouches under them. And, for a moment, she saw him for the hard-working, aging man he was. And the one constant in her life, her father's old partner, whose pigheadedness time hadn't tempered. Others came and went, but Morbier was always there.

"Leduc, I covered for you . . . the hole in the Seine . . ."

She cringed. So he knew about that. Would they make her pay for the damage?

"Don't ask me to go out on a limb. Again!"

"You're focusing on me, Morbier. Focus on that *salaud* Gabriel, who set the bomb." She fixed her eyes on him. "It's not Monde-Focus, not Krzysztof or Nelie. It's those who employed Gabriel. It's Halkyut and the ones who hired them."

"I know," he said, a thaw in his voice. "That's the problem."

She felt vibrations shaking the table. Noticed Morbier's hands clutching the edges.

"You OK, Leduc?"

Startled, she nodded. What had come over him?

"Remember the pool in Butte aux Cailles?" he said, a distant look in his eyes.

A faded image of cracked yellow tiles, spring water feeding into a pool. She hadn't thought of that in years.

"She insisted you take swimming lessons," he said, an unreadable look in his eyes. "She overrode your father's objections. She took you every week, even talked me into it a few times."

Aimée's gut wrenched as she remembered the smile on the carmine red lips greeting her as she emerged from the swimming pool and the feel of the dry towel her mother held to wrap around her.

"Maman?"

Her American mother, the woman Morbier never mentioned.

"For once in her life she was right," he said with a sad smile. "It's a good thing she made you take swimming lessons."

"Are you going to tell me something about her that I don't know?"

"She always said you had to learn to take care of yourself. And you can. But now it's time to stop."

"Where did *Maman* go, Morbier? I . . . if you know something, tell me. I can take it."

She clenched her fists and fought back tears. "If she's dead, just . . . can't you just say it?"

He stared. "Now's the time for you to step away, let us handle it. It's too dangerous, Leduc. Will you stop?"

Bargain . . . this was the bargain. The powers that be had warned Morbier off. He'd asked for her help in nailing MondeFocus, Krzysztof, and Nelie, but she'd tied Gabriel to the bombs and Halkyut. René and Saj would find documentation, proof, they had to. And now Morbier wanted her to back off.

"Even for you, this is low," she said, her shoulders tensing. "Going along with them!"

"It's for your own sake, Leduc," he said.

Even if she wanted to, she couldn't turn Nelie in. And she wouldn't hand Stella over to the authorities.

"Why don't you find a man, have babies, do what other people do?"

She averted her eyes. If only he knew. "That's rich coming from you, Morbier."

He'd lost custody of his grandson, Marc, to the other grandparents who lived in Morocco after his estranged daughter was killed in Belleville.

"Once and for all, will you do as I say if I

tell you what you want to know, Leduc?"

She yearned to know so much it hurt. But he was trying to manipulate her. Nothing came for free from Morbier.

"Not on your terms, Morbier," she said. "I don't negotiate about *Maman*. Either you tell me because it's the decent thing to do, or you don't."

"You make everything so difficult, Leduc." Morbier sighed.

"You're just dangling a carrot in front of me to get me to do what you want. You don't know anything more about her, do you?"

Morbier said, "Your swimming saved you. It's nothing to do with 'them' or this snake pit of an investigation."

But he was wrong. Abandoning Stella, turning Nelie in were too much like her own mother's case. She had to get out of this room, this Commissariat, with all the memories it held, before she broke down.

"You can't ignore the video, Morbier. You saw it. Someone trumped up a plan to brand Orla and Nelie as terrorists for blocking some trucks in La Hague. They want all the ecological protesters stopped, or denounced as violent agitators. I won't let it rest," she said, reaching for the ice pack. "I'm leaving."

He met her gaze full on. "I don't know if your mother is alive or not."

"That's all?"

Morbier tented his fingers. Again he had that unreadable expression in his eyes.

"Your father took you to the Klee exhibition in the Palais Royal on your fourteenth birthday, remember?"

A Sunday afternoon, the crowds, and her father's arm through hers, holding her tight. His nervous talk, none of his usual jokes about art. She remembered sitting in the café, looking out to the Palais Royal fountain, then blowing out the candle on a slice of chocolate *gâteau ganache.*

"She wanted to see you."

Aimée stared, speechless. And the walls seemed to shift. Her lip quivered. This talk of her mother . . . was it true?

Morbier's shoulders slumped. "She'd been deported, banned from reentry. It was dangerous for her. If she was in the crowd, he didn't see her."

Her mother had wanted to see her.

"That's it."

She found her voice, a whisper. "How did Papa know?"

"An arrangement, letters. He tore them up. End of story."

His words cut her to the bone. She

blinked, determined not to let him see her cry. Her mother had risked her freedom and had been in contact with her father . . . yet he'd never told her.

"I'll question Gabriel," Morbier said. "No promises."

"Merci."

Her throat tightened and she nodded. Morbier looked even older now.

She felt numb. She'd think about this later. She made her feet move. Now she had to protect Stella.

Aimée squared her shoulders and nodded to the policewoman behind the desk. She crossed the worn marble floor that smelled, as always, of industrial-strength pine-scented cleaning fluid. Each tap of her heels echoed off the limestone walls. Orla's face in the morgue, an injured Nelie on the video, Stella's flushed peach cheeks, and her own mother's almost forgotten face spun in her head.

A few Commissariat casement windows were lit, and a blue-uniformed *flic* guarded the courtyard door at street level. She needed to clear her head, to try to fit the pieces together as she walked along the quai. The last vestiges of the night clung to the sky. Warm wind, the gravel crunching under her heels, the muted cry of a seagull.

But she couldn't think straight. She'd been rocked to her core, set adrift, as the memories flooded her. She hunched down against a stone wall. The lone pigeon pecking on the gravel ignored her. She covered her face with her hands, tears wet her cheeks. Her mother had risked everything for a chance to see her and she hadn't even known. Her father had never told her. Nor Morbier.

And Nelie . . . what was she risking to save her baby?

She was still overcome, her thoughts jumbled, when she heard the whoosh of a street-cleaning truck. She had no idea how long she'd sat there but her face and jacket were wet with tears. Stella, she reminded herself, she had to get back to Stella.

Aimée grew aware of the cell phone ringing in her pocket.

She answered it, wiping her nose. She heard loud buzzing. "Where are you?" Claude's concerned voice was breaking up into static. "I'm worried . . . looked for you . . ."

He'd *deserted* her, left her with those *mecs*. She'd thought he was different.

"I made a deal and got Krzysztof immunity; why didn't you help me convince him to stay?" she asked. Why did you run away? she wanted to ask him, but she bit back the words.

"I couldn't, Aimée," Claude said. The line had cleared. "I'm involved with the eco freedom trail. People depend on me, a whole network. I cannot get involved with the *flics.*"

A chain of safe houses for ecoterrorists on the lam, she realized. But then why wouldn't Nelie have used it? Or maybe she had?

"Do you mean Nelie's there —"

"No," he interrupted. "She's gone underground but no one knows where."

The reason must have to do with Stella and the ink marks on the skin under her arm. She remembered Krzysztof's words — Nelie had told him there was a doctor's report.

"Let me talk to Krzysztof."

"He jumped off my bike and ran into the Métro. He said he'll take care of it his way," Claude told her. "I couldn't stop him."

He, too, had run like a scared rabbit.

The line was clearer now.

"Aimée, are you all right? What's happened?" he asked, breathless.

"Why did this *mec* Gabriel demand Nelie's baby?" she said.

In the silence she could hear the sputtering of the motorcycle engine.

"Who knows?"

"France2 has news footage showing Nelie and Orla at the demonstration."

"You saw it?"

"But there was no baby with them," she said.

"The march erupted into chaos. But . . . ," Claude paused.

"He didn't work alone, right? Now you may be in as much danger as Nelie and her baby."

He was right.

"Gabriel didn't believe that we would give him the disc; he wanted the baby. Otherwise why did he show up?" she said. "But at least we accomplished something: he's headed across the river to La Santé."

"What do you mean?" Something had changed in Claude's voice.

"Gabriel skipped a meeting with his parole officer, so he'll be locked up," she said.

Her head ached, the muscles in her legs had cramped, and tiredness flooded her body.

"Claude," she said. "I have to go."

"You've gotten under my skin," he said, his voice low and hesitant. "I've never met anyone like you. We're alike, you know . . .

we share so much."

She wished she weren't attracted to him.

"Stay at my place. At least I know you'll be safe with me," he said. "I'll make sure of that."

She pictured his warm studio, imagined his arms around her, his musky sandalwood scent. But with René and Saj working on the incriminating files and the babysitter having to leave, her duty was clear. She had to care for Stella; she had to protect her.

"*Merci,* but I can't, Claude," she said. "I'll call you tomorrow."

"Promise me you'll come to stay with me?"

How could she? With Stella?

"Aimée, you asked me to trust you. Now I'm asking you to trust me."

"I want to."

"Then you'll come?" he breathed into the phone.

"I don't know, Claude."

Before she could change her mind, she turned off the phone. Aimée stood and made her tired legs walk. A block later she found a cruising taxi. She collapsed against the leather seat and then realized her wallet was empty.

At the Paribas cash machine, with the taxi waiting on the curb, she took out half of what Vavin had given her. She had to pay Mathilde overtime. They'd barely limp by for the rest of the month unless René worked wonders and snagged the Fontainebleau account.

Conscious of the blur of the street lamps on the quai, the almost-deserted, rain-chased streets, the hint of dawn in the faint ribbon lightening the sky, she leaned back. At least she could tip the taxi driver who'd gotten her to Martine's in record time.

She took a deep breath, trudged up the red-carpeted stairs, and rang Martine's bell.

Martine opened the door. In a leopard-print silk robe, cigarette dangling from her mouth, relief in her eyes. "You've got more lives than a cat! You scared me, Aimée. I thought —"

"Next time keep your phone on, Martine," Aimée said.

"Damn thing's battery ran down." Martine hugged her hard and put the cigarette between Aimée's lips. "Want a hit? You deserve it. Believe it or not, Jadwiga Radziwill, the celebrated anarchist, provided an interesting take on your explosion."

"I thought she was dead," Aimée said.

"At first, with all that makeup, it was hard to tell. But Deroche broke a sweat talking to her, then summoned his minions to a hurried caucus. I love to see those CEOs . . . well, you can tell me about it."

All Aimée wanted was to see Stella and sleep.

"In the morning I will, I promise. And I need to meet with Daniel Ristat. But right now I need —"

"To sleep, *d'accord.*" Martine kept her arm around Aimée as she walked her down the hall and then helped her out of her clothes. "Mathilde's asleep. Shall I wake her?"

The last things Aimée remembered were putting francs into Mathilde's bag and then curling up on the Babar sheets next to a sweet-smelling Stella.

THURSDAY MORNING

He stared at the headlines of *Le Parisien* displayed at the news kiosk. MYSTERY WOMAN SAVES A HUNDRED LIVES — EXPLOSION ROCKS THE SEINE.

Merde! He flicked his cigarette onto the pavement, ground it out with his foot, and read the article. *The woman, who was wearing a feather-trimmed jacket, and claimed to be affiliated in an unexplained manner with the press, has not been found. The Brigade*

Fluviale continues to dredge the Seine. . . .

Another screwup.

He'd told Halkyut to quit recruiting low-lifes. Had they listened? Not according to the front-page article. *Le Monde,* a more news-oriented publication, said: *Oil conference: Alstrom presence plagued by eco-group militants, bomb scares, and oil platform pollution rumors.*

The man reached into his blue trouser pocket, took out a coin, and threw it on the counter.

"Genocide in Rwanda, impending Metro strike . . . but this . . . at least there's some good news in the world, eh, Monsieur?" the smiling vendor said.

"A real bright spot." He almost ripped *Le Monde* as he unfolded the front page, looking for the story and its continuation. He read:

Oil conference executives, attending a reception at the historic Hôtel Lambert, hosted by Mathieu Deroche, CEO of Alstrom, expecting to hear an oil rights agreement with the Ministry announced, watched in horror as a woman disposed of explosives in the Seine. The third bomb threat in two days, and the murder of an executive of Regnault, Alstrom's high-powered publicity firm, sent shock waves through the oil-producing community. The second bomb threat, a hoax, at l'Institut du Monde Arabe, was attributed to MondeFocus, which denied responsibility, and has now been blamed on a splinter peace group. However, insiders reveal that a bomb threat delivered to M. Deroche was meant to highlight the questionable practices of Alstrom, France's largest refiner of petroleum. An oil conference source expressed disbelief that a peace organization would use such "terrorist tactics," insisting an inquiry be launched into Alstrom's recent freighter accident in the North Sea. Preliminary explosive experts' findings reveal that the unsophisticated pipe bombs used lacked a timing ignition device, indicating that the danger was in part simulated. Unconfirmed reports indicate that static electricity was the cause of the ignition. An unnamed MondeFocus spokesman said, "Disinformation and bomb hoaxes were used by Alstrom to distract attention from the underlying issues of toxic waste and environmental pollution."

The man crumpled the paper, tossing it into a nearby trash bin. He had to fix everything himself. He patted the Beretta in his inside jacket pocket and blended in with the commuters rushing down the Metro steps.

THURSDAY LATE AFTERNOON

The café was crowded and noisy; Aimée held Stella in her arms. A few hours ago, she'd visited a pediatrician, who, after examining Stella, had pronounced her healthy and fever free. For two hundred francs more, he'd prescribed antibiotics for Aimée and asked no questions as to why she needed to ward off the Seine's microbes. She'd slept half the day, soaked in the tub at Martine's, and borrowed a black velvet pantsuit and cap. Rested now, despite an undercurrent of anxiety, she tugged the little hat onto Stella's head and scanned the other customers in the café.

A milk steamer hissed, competing with the conversations at the zinc counter. Delivery truck drivers in blue work smocks threw back espressos and *bières,* a pinstripe-suited Ministry type stood reading *Le Monde,* an office worker on a break in a pencil-thin skirt spoke on her cell phone, and a gray-haired, elaborately coiffed woman held a cigarette between her beringed fingers, Bon

Marché shopping bag at her feet, and blew smoke rings in the air.

The man she was waiting for hadn't arrived.

She sat back. This *café-tabac,* across from the Institut Océanique, was filled with locals. No one would look for them here.

The cell phone in her jacket pocket vibrated. With the phone crooked between her neck and shoulder, she laid Stella on the booth's leather seat.

"Aimée, what happened to you last night?" René said with irritation. "I left you messages —"

"Sorry, René. I set off some fireworks, then took a swim," she said. "It seemed better to lie low and call you when I —"

"That was you?"

"Let's say it was an alter ego," she said. "Has Saj found anything promising?"

"We used the dial-up system and accessed Vavin's password and account."

"Brilliant, René."

"I said I would, Aimée," René reminded her. "Now Saj is working from the PC's hard drive backup. But I'm working on the Fontainebleau contract again. One more time. They're ready to sign."

He meant he had a "paying" job; she heard the implied criticism in his voice.

"The computer's been put back in Vavin's office," René said.

She heard a pause at the other end.

"But my log-in using Vavin's password will show up, Aimée. It's just a matter of time until the techs at Alstrom discover the intrusion."

"Right, but they can't prove you did it," she said. She had to reassure him and so she said the only thing she could think of.

"Of course not," René said. "We 'visited' the travel agency next door and luckily their telephone was still connected so we used it to dial up."

René constantly amazed her.

"Worst-case scenario, we'll spin the break-in as 'in the public interest,' " she said.

"You don't mean that law whistle-blowers use, citing special journalistic privileges or whatever?"

"That's only if we get caught, René," she said. "And I'm about to meet a *L'Express* journalist."

"Saj tunneled into some Ministry meeting minutes in Alstrom's storage database. He's not sure but —"

She heard the clicking of keys on the laptop under René's fingers.

"We're looking for what exactly?" he asked.

"A doctor's report from La Hague. And pollution statistics. You know, like a second pair of books accountants keep. The real set." She had an idea. "Ask Saj to find Alstrom's file of independent contractors."

"Tall order, Aimée. He's slogging through their records and he says it's a huge job."

"What about checking Alstrom's accounts payable? See if Halkyut's on the list; no one works for free."

"Halkyut?" René said louder. "The spies for hire?"

"One of Halkyut's employees has been after Stella."

"What aren't you telling me, Aimée?"

"I made it hot for him," she said.

In the literal sense, but she didn't think it wise to give René the details. "He's in La Santé right now. I'll fill you in after I meet the journalist."

She eyed the *café-tabac* lace-curtained door again. He was late. He had to show. And if he didn't come? She pushed the thought away. If she'd read him right, he wanted to make his name, and a scoop like this would do it.

Something still bothered her.

"We have to find out what those marks I

copied from under Stella's arm mean."

Nelie must have been desperate; she hadn't taken the time to diaper Stella but she had scribbled letters and numbers on her skin. Yet she must have realized that the marks would rub off soon, or be washed off.

"What's the big secret, Aimée?"

"No big secret, René," she said. "Right now, those ink marks — the letters and numbers that were written on Stella — seem to be the key."

"Deciphering an alphanumeric strand is a big headache."

It could take an hour. Or twelve. Or forever.

She thought hard. "Say Vavin discovered proof that Alstrom had falsified their reports and it's hidden in this equation. What if he told this to Nelie . . ."

"And it got him killed?" René finished for her. "We went through this last night. Big stretch."

Stella began to cry. Aimée put the baby over her shoulder and patted her back.

"How's Stella?" René asked in a gruff tone that didn't hide his concern.

"The doctor examined her; she's fine," she told him.

A dark-haired man entered the café, working his way past those in line buying telephone cards, and waved at her. Finally.

"The *L'Express* journalist's here," Aimée said, waving back. "I'll get his fax number. When you find the reports, you can fax them, and if I play it right, he'll nail them in print."

"Play it right, Aimée," René said and hung up.

Daniel Ristat, cigarette hanging from the side of his mouth, edged through the line at the counter looking every bit the handsome Left Bank journalist and knowing it. More than one woman glanced up from her magazine and gave him the eye.

"Je m'excuse," he said, setting his laptop on the table in front of Aimée. His snobbism evaporated when he saw Stella. He ground his cigarette out and waved the smoke away. "The baby, smoke . . . I'm sorry. She's a beauty!"

He sat down, a smile in his eyes.

"What's her name?"

"Stella, meet Daniel Ristat."

He took Stella's fingers in his big ones and gazed at her. Stella wrinkled her nose, curled her finger around his, and gave a half-hearted cry. Amazed, Aimée saw that Daniel Ristat's face had changed. The trendy journalist was putty in her small hands. This little *ravissante* was a natural *coquette,* born to it.

"Martine never mentioned your child. I had no idea," he said. Amid the noise of conversations, the *télé* above the counter with horse races blaring, the clatter of cups stacked on the espresso machine, he only had eyes for Stella. "You're so lucky."

Aimée winced.

"My wife and I can't have children. We're trying to adopt but the waiting list is two years long. Or longer." He shrugged. "*Famille d'accueil* recommends we become foster parents to gain priority."

Despite his male-model looks and air, something about him told her he'd make a wonderful papa.

Should she tell him the truth to gain his sympathy? But the truth wasn't hers to tell.

"I'm just taking care of her."

"*Vraiment?*" He studied her. "You seem so natural, the way you hold her. Like her mother. I don't know that much about babies . . ."

She blinked. "Shall we get to work?"

For a moment he directed a laserlike stare at her that went right to the bone. Her heart raced. Was it so obvious she was head over stilettos with this thing that weighed no more than three kilos?

"Here are some of my notes," he said, businesslike, pulling out a folder. "Background on Alstrom's corporate structure, the North Sea territorial water disputes, environmental impact statement, and some very subdued eco groups' responses, which I found surprising."

She skimmed the several pages of notes. Went back and reread the first page. "Here you note Alstrom's funding its drilling project with a Ministry loan?"

Daniel Ristat nodded.

"Would you say they're in financial trouble?"

"Their last drill didn't recoup their investment, and then unsafe platform construction resulted in the deaths of several workers, for which they were liable. Not to mention the bad press engendered by eco-militants' campaigns."

She put Stella over her shoulder again, patted her back, and was rewarded by a loud resounding burp. She hoped no spit-up had been deposited on Martine's black velvet jacket.

"In essence, the proposed agreement with the Ministry means they scratch each other's backs," he said. "The Ministry gains new revenue sources, higher employment, increased industrial production: it all looks good on their reports. And Alstrom snags a secure base in the North Sea from which to expand. All funded by the government. Everyone wins."

Except the marine life and the coasts of several countries, she thought.

"Not according to your other notes here on environmental impact studies," she said.

He flashed a smile at the waiter, who'd appeared with a tray in one hand, rubbing his hand on a white apron with the other.

"Une noisette, s'il vous plaît," he said to the waiter.

So trendy journalists drank macchiatos now.

"My information comes from a reliable source," he said. "Deep inside. He must remain unnamed. I can't use this information or it will point to him as the Ministry leak. He told me Alstrom's last spill rendered parts of the North and Baltic seas toxic to fish. And then there's Alstrom's deliberate misinformation campaign: deny, dupe, and delay. Dupe the public into thinking it's an environmentally and socially responsible corporation. Have you heard yet of 'dead zones'?"

She shook her head.

"Algae die from pollutants, and in the process of decomposition they consume oxygen. The depletion of oxygen leaves an oxygenless dead zone on the ocean floor, the effect of which spirals up through the chain of marine life."

She thought of what Krzysztof had told her. "I was informed that the supposedly abandoned North Sea oil-rig platforms were being used for dump sites. This could be corroboration."

"But where's the direct proof?" Daniel said. "Everyone in power wants this agreement to go through. You know it's almost a done deal. So even though I'd like to, I can't help you."

Desperation surged through her. "I'm sure there are more reports that were suppressed. MondeFocus's protest was sabotaged. Will you expose Alstrom if I get you proof? If I get you minutes of their corporate meetings, will you blow it wide open?"

His eyebrow raised. "Like you blew a hole in the Seine?"

"Moi?"

Why didn't anyone blame Gabriel Leclerc?

"I read the papers." He grinned, opening his laptop. "Martine filled me in, too. I was counting on a dramatic interview at your hospital bedside. Instead I have a *tête-à-tête* with two lovely ladies. *Charmante.*"

"I need your help," she said. "The agree-

410

ment's about to be signed."

He shook his head.

"Like I said, I need evidence: reports, meeting notes," he said. "No one takes shots at an oil company or the Ministry without incontrovertible evidence."

A young Turk? He didn't need convincing, just proof.

"Give me your fax number."

He handed her his card, slipped some francs onto the table.

"Expect the proof this afternoon or tonight at the latest," she said.

"I'll believe it when I see it." He looked amused. "But Martine said you meant business."

Aimée nodded. "My best friend should know."

Now he'd turned the charm back on.

"She smiled." He nudged Aimée. "Did you see? Stella smiled at me."

"It's gas."

Out on the street she put Daniel Ristat's fax number in her pocket.

"À bientôt, mes princesses." He winked and ran down the Metro steps.

Shadows burnished the shop windows, passersby hurried along the street. The last rays of light illumined cottony puffs of clouds framed by the sloping tiled rooftops. The incandescent clouds were tinged with yellow, as though lit from within reminiscent of a Monet sky.

Aimée wrapped Stella tighter in the blanket that enfolded the baby in the carrier on her chest. She was about to hail a taxi for Leduc Detective when she realized that she was standing in front of the blue awning of Jacadi, the upscale baby store. The window display had a christening theme featuring a delicate christening gown trimmed with lace, surrounded by white sugar-coated almonds — *de rigueur* for a bourgeois baptism — that had been sprinkled among a phalanx of stuffed animals.

The shop door opened to reveal a young woman wheeling twins in a double stroller. The clerk, a middle-aged woman with her hair in a chignon and appraising eyes, held the door for her. Stella stuck out her little fists and Aimée could have sworn that she was pointing in the direction of a pink terry-cloth onesie in the side window.

"Looks like your daughter knows what she wants," the clerk said.

Newborns couldn't focus farther than a meter, according to the baby manual. Aimée stroked Stella's velvety ear. And in the next moment, she found herself standing inside the store, which was filled with every kind of infant clothing possible.

"You were born with fashion sense, too, Stella," she whispered.

She left the shop hoping Stella would wear the expensive onesie longer than it took her to sneeze. Stella seemed to grow a size a day. Horns honked from cars jammed in the *rond-point* evening traffic. The taxi stand lay just ahead.

"Aimée?"

Startled, she turned at the corner, bag in hand, Stella strapped on her chest, to stare into the face of Yves, her former boyfriend. In a pinstripe suit and long hair, he was more of a hunk than ever. She felt her face flush. A stream of passersby parted around them, as if they were rocks in the middle of a current, then flowed together again at the zebra crosswalk.

"You've been busy," Yves said.

She couldn't tell if the expression in his eyes was hurt, wonder, or both.

He leaned down and brushed her cheek with his lips, inhaling her scent. "You still wear Chanel No. 5."

"And you're still in Cairo." More of a question than a statement.

"I'm bureau chief now." He gave a wistful

sigh. "You're radiant, Aimée. Motherhood becomes you."

Words caught in her throat. She remembered the little mole behind his ear, how he hummed Coltrane's ballad "Crescent" when he cooked, the way his legs had wrapped around her under her duvet.

"What's your daughter's name?"

She stared at him, found her tongue. "Stella. Her name's Stella."

"Aaah, you always had a thing for the stars."

And you, she almost said.

"Remember this?" She felt around in her bag, found the lucky Egyptian coin, the one he'd given her on a street corner in Cairo when they'd said good-bye.

A beeping came from her phone, indicating a message. Yves stared at the coin, then at her phone. "Don't you think you should check that?"

She hit the voice-mail button and listened. One message. Jean Caplan's voice. "Hélène wants to talk to you about the girl. She knows you somehow. The side door code is 78C65. Come to the back of the store. She'll be waiting." And then the loud buzz of a hang up.

"Have to get home, eh? Your man's waiting," Yves suggested, watching her.

414

Claude. But she wasn't sure he was her man. She'd put Stella first last night and he'd given his freedom priority over her.

"*Non,* it's . . . it's business," she said. She wanted to explain, tell him everything, even on this busy street.

"Of course, you'd never stop working," he said. "But I always thought if I gave you enough babies, well, you'd slow down."

"You did?"

He pressed something into her hand. Another shining bronze coin covered in Arabic writing. "One can never have too much luck, Aimée."

His cell phone rang but he ignored it. His warm hands held hers, not loosening their grasp.

"Got to go," he said. "Another meeting. I fly back tonight."

"Look, Yves, I —"

He put his finger over her lips. "Don't tell me how happy you are, or that you've found the right one at last. It's wonderful; I'm happy for you. And quit batting those big eyes at me, Aimée. I understand."

But he didn't.

"If your daughter's anything like you . . . whoa." He stroked Stella's head, kissed Aimée long and lingeringly on the mouth. "You know, we've got to stop saying good-bye on street corners."

Then he was gone. People hurried past her, their shoulders hitting hers as the shadows deepened. And she felt more alone than ever.

As she got out of the taxi at Jean Caplan's *brocante,* she was astounded by the driver's opening the door for her even before she produced her usual big tip. She stood in front of the shop for a moment with the baby bag over her shoulder, Stella strapped in the carrier and holding a bouquet of yellow daffodils for Hélène.

"Hélène knows you somehow," Caplan had said. Like Nelie knew her "somehow"? Caplan had realized, seen the truth in Aimée's words and convinced Hélène to talk to her. For the first time Aimée sensed she'd get answers.

She figured Hélène witnessed Orla's killing. Then either Hélène acted in self-defense or she'd gone after the attacker. Perhaps Hélène had helped Nelie, and it was she who had written that note to Aimée. If Hélène knew where Nelie was hiding, she'd lead Aimée there.

On the pavement, a man in a blue work coat grunted as he carried a tall sheet of glass in a frame on his back. He winked at Aimée, paused, and wiped his brow with his free hand. A *vitrier* — a glass man — who hawked his services on the streets. One of the few who still made the rounds with their distinctive high-pitched cry *"Vi-tr-ier."* A fragment of the disappearing old Paris.

Dark green metal shutters covered the front of Caplan's shop. A dim light shone through the crack between the door shade and the glass. He'd said to use the side door; she tapped in the digicode number.

Inside, she followed the narrow brown scuffed hall to the courtyard onto which Jean Caplan's kitchen faced. Standing by the sealed-up well she saw lights in the galley kitchen, heard what sounded like the *télé* blaring news.

"Time we meet Hélène," she said. Stella answered with a wail.

She knocked, opened the unlocked door, and entered.

"Monsieur Caplan? Hélène?"

She patted Stella's back as she edged past the hanging beaded curtains that separated the kitchen from the shop. The once exquisite chandelier, with missing crystal drops, provided the only light. Scattered piles of yellowed newspapers cluttered the floor. Stairs to the right and dark heavy curtains in front of her partitioned off what appeared to be rooms in the back.

Two half-empty demitasse cups and a blue sugar bowl with tongs sat on the small table. Were Jean and Hélène upstairs? Or in the back storeroom? Stella's cries mixed with the evening news announcer's words. She turned down the volume on the *télé,* wishing she could turn down Stella's volume as well.

"Monsieur Caplan, I'm here," she said, rocking the baby in her arms, rubbing the soft rolls of skin on her ankles, leaning down to blow in Stella's ear.

And then she was shoved through the thick woolen curtains into the storeroom. Startled, she stumbled forward, throwing her arms out to protect Stella and break her fall. She grabbed a dusty wall hanging and righted herself. Aimée turned to see the glint of a gun pointed at the baby's head. And gasped. A Beretta 87, the hit man's weapon of choice, pioneered by the Mossad.

Fear coursed through her veins. Stella's cries escalated into screams. Why had she listened to Caplan? She'd been set up and she'd put Stella in danger.

"I'm tired of wasting time and manpower," said a man in a tone of mild disgust. He filled the doorway. Medium height, he had a broad, smooth forehead on a big bull of a head that joined his almost nonexistent neck. Taut muscles strained his blue work pants and jacket. A professional with dead, killer eyes.

"What do you mean? Who are you?" she blurted out.

But she knew. A Halkyut hired gun and she'd walked right into his hands. She ordered herself to play dumb and pretend, to buy time to figure something out. He wouldn't shoot Stella, wouldn't kill an innocent baby, she told herself. Then the realization sank in. He could shoot her, then take Stella. She tried to read something in his expressionless eyes. What if Caplan hadn't set her up? Maybe she had stumbled into something else. Maybe she could still get out of this.

"Shut her up," he ordered.

She stuck her finger in Stella's mouth as she rocked her. Frantic, she looked around for any way to escape, for some weapon.

One flickering fluorescent panel overhead revealed marble busts standing at haphazard angles on grimy shelves, shards of glass from cracked picture frames stacked against the wall gathering dust. Stella fussed, gumming her finger.

"She's got colic, I have to take her to the doctor. Let us go," Aimée begged.

The man patted his work-pants pocket, saying nothing. Was he waiting for reinforcements? He hadn't spoken again. What if he didn't know who she was? She had to take the chance. Get him talking, figure out some lie, try to make a deal. Concoct a story, a way to get out.

"We live in the building. Monsieur Caplan's been ill," she said, words coming fast and furious. "Monsieur, I've seen nothing. I don't know you. We will leave the way we came, of course, and say nothing. The baby's sick. We just came to —"

"Bringing him some flowers?" he said. "Nice."

"I swear," she said, shielding her eyes, at the same time scanning the black lacquered table, the pile of dusty carpets behind it, the ocher wall in back of it. She caught sight of the tarnished silver candlesticks on the table and a dust-covered sword collection lying near the carpets. She smelled something coppery. Like blood. "I haven't seen anything. If you let us go, I won't say anything."

"But that wouldn't be sociable," he said.

She heard a loud groan over the sound of Stella's cries. She looked closer and recognized that what she'd taken for a pile of carpets was a body. Jean Caplan sat slumped in a chair with his hands tied. She made out his black-and-purple swollen eyes, caked blood on his nostrils, and his sagging jaw. The coppery smell of blood mingled with that of mildew. His worn brown shoes dangled over the cracked linoleum floor.

"What's going on? He's an old man. What have you done to him?"

Think. Think. Sweat sheened her upper lip. She felt light-headed in the dust and blood-tinged air, with Stella on her chest radiating heat, shrieking now, as she looked at the old man who seemed half dead.

Caplan's feet twisted and he whimpered in pain, then groaned louder.

"Haven't had enough, *mon vieux?*" The man turned, edging closer to Caplan, and kicked him.

"Why don't you give him the flowers?" the man asked Aimée.

"What?"

"You heard me. And I'll hold the baby."

"*Non,* that's all right, I'll just —"

"Do it now! Did you hear me?"

Her hands trembled as she reached for the flowers. Caplan blinked at her.

"No more playing mommy," the man sneered.

"What do you mean?"

"Give her to me or I'll start with your knees," he said. "Then work my way up."

421

She stepped back, toward Caplan, and felt the table edge with her hip.

"But you're not listening; perhaps you don't think I mean it. So maybe I'll start with him," he said, his eyes never leaving her face, as he moved closer to her and to Caplan. So close she smelled his acrid, damp sweat. "I will shoot his hands off unless you hand the baby over and tell me where she is."

He glanced at his watch. What was he waiting for? He was stalling.

"You're waiting for someone, aren't you? So you can kill Nelie, like you did Orla."

Her chest was wet with perspiration from fear and Stella's heat. Stupid, so stupid. She couldn't even reach her cell phone to summon backup.

He gave a little smile. "Not my job. Sorry."

"Halkyut hired you," she asserted.

He didn't deny it.

"Nelie took the Alstrom file, found the proof they needed in it."

"Who?"

"But the writing's gone, the marks have rubbed off the baby," she said. Her eyes locked with his. "I'll show you. The baby's not important any longer."

"*Salaud,*" Caplan shouted hoarsely.

Moaning in pain, he kicked out with his

foot, connecting with the man's knee, throwing him off balance. And then Caplan kicked the table, sending it and everything on it crashing.

Aimée ducked behind the overturned table. She heard the thud of a shot, the tinkle of crashing glass. She saw the flash. She pulled the baby out of the carrier and shoved her between the table and the wall.

She had to move fast. She crawled forward, using the table as a shield. The reek of cordite filled the air. More shots were fired over her head. She heard the man cursing somewhere behind her. Her fingers scrabbled across the gritty floorboards as she groped for the antique sword blade. After she grabbed it, they moved to the cup-like handle.

The man sat on the floor, Beretta pointed at the table. She saw bright streaks of blood on Caplan's shoulder.

Now! She had to do it now. She crouched and rammed the table with her shoulder, toppling Caplan against the man. Struggling to raise the heavy sword with her shaking hands, she stood and swung it with all her might at the man's shin. His mouth opened in dumb surprise, and he screamed in pain.

She pulled the sword back. As he reached for his leg, he dropped the Beretta. His hand was covered with blood.

Before he could recover and pick up the gun from the linoleum where it had fallen, she kicked it away.

"What kind of hit man goes after old men and babies?"

"These days, everyone specializes," he said. Then he barreled into her, knocking her against the wall. His fists hammered at her chest. She yelped with pain. He grabbed her by the neck, yanking her closer. She twisted her body, tasted blood, felt a searing pain in her ribs and fell to the floor.

Her hip landed on the Beretta's grip. By the time she'd gotten her fingers around the trigger, he'd pulled her up by her hair, slamming her head against the wall. Through the waves of pain she heard Stella's cries. The light was fading. Sparks danced in the corners of her eyes.

"Amateur," he hissed.

You used what you had.

He didn't let go until she'd fired the Beretta three times at point-blank range into his chest. She could hear the hiss of air as it left his lungs in a burst of blood.

Lights danced before her eyes. Whirling spirals and flashes, Stella's cries . . . she had to reach Stella. The light faded and then she knew no more.

■ ■ ■ ■

She walked on a broad band of moonlight, Stella holding her hand. Stella was a toddler now, yet with the same baby face. Someone else was there. An old woman all in white. Then Stella was skipping away from her and she was reaching out for her, calling over and over, "Come back, Stella."

Pain throbbed in her chest; cold linoleum numbed her cheek. The smell of blood and dust filled her nostrils. She heard moaning and blinked. Her eyes opened.

Where was Stella?

The baby had to be here. Panicked, she staggered upright. The man lay slumped, dead on the floor, in a dark pool of blood among the blood-spattered daffodils. She'd passed out. Whoever this man had been waiting for must have taken Stella.

She'd failed. Someone had kidnapped Stella.

She found her cell phone. She had to call the *flics*.

"Untie my hands," Caplan said.

"Who took the baby?"

He shrugged. She took up the sword again and sawed away at the thick rope, strand by stubborn strand. She flinched as the rope broke and he cried out in pain. She sawed away faster to free his other hand, its thumb swollen and purple.

"Who took her?" she repeated.

"Hélène."

The crazy homeless woman?

"No *flics,* please. Hélène's helping . . . you." His voice cracked.

"Where did she take the baby? Why didn't she untie you?"

"She was too frightened. It would have taken her too long. I told her to take the baby before . . . there's another one coming."

She found a bottle of wine on the floor, uncorked it, and held it to his split lips. Blood still seeped from a dark red hole in his shoulder.

"He shot you," she said.

"Never mind that now," Caplan said. "Go into the shop and look in my chair. She told me it's there."

Aimée staggered into the shop to the chair where he kept his valuables. An envelope was wedged under the cushion. She picked it up. It bore quivering writing in violet ink that she recognized. Inside, there was a half-torn page from a magazine displaying a crossword puzzle. In the margin she could make out the words *"Ask Jules Pont Louis*

Philippe . . . H."

H must stand for Hélène, the *clochard.* The handwriting was identical to that on the note Aimée had received asking her to keep Stella. Hélène had written Nelie's message.

She remembered Jules's evasive answer when she'd asked him about Hélène . . . somewhere down by the bend, he'd said. Near the end of the sewer cavern lay Pont Louis Philippe and another drain sluice. Hélène might have taken Stella there.

She'd been close to Nelie last night. Vavin, her uncle, had been at the antique store nearby. Of course! Had Nelie had been here the whole time, hiding under the bridge? Right under her nose?

How long had Caplan known? Had this whole thing been a ploy, had they been using her? A sour taste filled her mouth.

"Why didn't you tell me?" But his head had fallen forward; now he'd passed out.

She found his shop phone and dialed 17 for SAMU.

"Fourteen, rue des Deux Ponts. There's a man bleeding to death, another dead of gunshot wounds to the chest."

"Who's calling?"

"Hurry!"

She hung up. She'd killed a professional,

one of Halkyut's hired guns, in self-protection. But she doubted the *flics* would see it that way. And she didn't have time for explanations or hours to spend in the Commissariat.

She stood holding onto the wall as a flash of dizziness hit her, then found her bag under the bloodstained tapestry by the Jacadi baby clothes bag. She realized that she hadn't found the saboteur, just one Halkyut thug. Was the saboteur Stella's father? That could make sense even though she'd relegated the idea to the back of her mind after talking with Krzysztof.

Dumb. Consider all angles, her father always said.

She searched for the Doliprane in her purse. Popped the dry chalky aspirin and chewed it so it would work faster. Her cell phone trilled.

"*Allô?*"

"You want the good news? Aimée, we found the real pollution reports in Alstrom's files," René said. "The bad news, we've deciphered only half of them. And none of it will make us money. But that's beside the point."

"Is what you have deciphered enough to nail them?" Her hands shook.

"More than enough, in the right hands,"

René said. "Sickening. A crime. Makes me never want to eat seafood again."

She read off Daniel Ristat's fax number. "Send it all through to that number. He's expecting your fax."

"One more thing," René said. "Saj figured out what the writing on Stella was all about. It's a file title. We opened the file and found meeting notes all right but not about Alstrom's corporate board meetings. The notes refer to MondeFocus meetings, discussions, timetables of planned demonstrations. Alstrom knew every step MondeFocus took."

Proof that there had been an Alstrom spy inside MondeFocus.

"Can you identify the sender?"

"Fancied himself — if it's a he — quite the comic-strip hero. He signed himself 'Stinger2'."

"Like the Stinger?" The slick hit man who'd infiltrated the workers' unions on the Marseilles docks, then sold his information to the highest bidder. The one who shut down the unions and took out the leaders.

"Nice role model." René paused. "Shall I take over babysitting Stella now?"

Guilt stabbed her. Her fault. She had to admit it and, somehow, enlist René's help. "I found Jean Caplan; he'd been beaten up and shot . . ."

"Is Stella . . . hurt?"

"She's gone. Hélène, the old woman, took her."

"What? You let that homeless woman have her?" he said, accusation and hurt in his voice. "All you had to do was watch her. How could you put her in danger?!"

"René, I didn't mean to but —"

"Playing Wonder Woman again!" He cut her off. "For once, I thought you'd grown up and would consider the risks and consequences, with an innocent child involved."

What about Nelie, Stella's mother, who'd left her in the first place, she wanted to say. Nelie had left her baby with a stranger. But he was right.

"You're right, René," she whispered into the phone. "I'm sick at what's happened. I was supposed to meet Hélène at Caplan's, but when I got there . . ."

"Aimée, I'm tired of wild-goose chases and your excuses."

"If I hadn't found him . . . But I think I know where Hélène took her."

"Took her? Why can't you admit that she kidnapped Stella?" he asked.

She'd never heard him so angry. "Hélène wrote that note on the crossword that was sent to me. She's helping Nelie. But talking is taking time. Please meet me at Pont Louis Philippe. I think that Stella's father must be the saboteur. The spy. He must have followed one of us; he's after Stella, too. In that case, Hélène is definitely on our side."

"Another one of your theories?"

"You have a better one? Suit yourself, René, I'm going."

"If I do this, I want to ensure that Stella is safe. We call the child protection services. Do you agree?"

"Pont Louis Philippe. Ten minutes, René."

She hung up. Avoiding the staring, dead eyes of the *mec,* she put one hand over her nose, and with the other reached under his lifeless leg for the Beretta 87. She slipped it into her pocket.

By the time Aimée reached Pont Marie, the metal lampposts illumined only the rustling branches of the trees that lined the quai and the glistening cobblestones. The nighttime quiet of the island was broken briefly as a couple emerged from Le Franc Pinot, a wine bar featuring jazz, the moan of a saxophone and the sound of cymbals following them.

She hurried beneath the wine bar's old metal sign that jutted from the building — the artisanal emblem of a winemaker: a wrought-iron, grape-laden branch pointing toward Quai Bourbon. At the corner of rue Regrattier she paused under the statue of a headless woman in a niche above the street. It, like the king, had been decapitated in the Revolution. Under it was carved the former street name, *rue de la Femme-sans-tête:* street of the headless woman. Island lore said it really was Saint Nicholas. But over the centuries, no one had proved it either way.

She searched for René's Citroën against the backdrop of lighted Pont Louis Philippe, trying to ignore the pain in her ribs. The bookstore partway down the quai was open late. She became aware of being watched. Again. The feeling of eyes, somewhere. She pulled her scarf around her and retreated into a dark doorway.

Waiting.

Show yourself, she wanted to shout. And then René's Citroën purred as he pulled up alongside the quai. He parked on the curb and opened the door, putting out one foot shod in a hunter green Wellington boot.

"Well, are you waiting for the moon to rise or . . ." He stopped, handing her his handkerchief. "Your head's bleeding."

Her hand rose to touch it and came back red. "A scratch. Did you and Saj find any payroll connections between Alstrom and

Halkyut?"

"Looks like they were using Tiscali," he said. "A shell corporation."

"I don't understand."

"Tiscali's an offshore corporation registered in Guernsey. Like many others, it's a company in name only, a front," he said. "Alstrom remits payments to this Tiscali. And — this is the interesting part — every month Tiscali makes a payment to Halkyut. I faxed this information to the journalist, too."

This was like unraveling knotted string. Now she had them: the real pollution reports, the copy of the notes under Stella's arm, the record of secret payments to Halkyut. But she didn't have Stella.

She motioned to the stone steps leading down to the bank. Took a breath and followed him, alert for any sound. At the top of the stairs, she heard footsteps and froze.

Another Halkyut thug? Or Hélène, carrying Stella?

Just then the figure of a dark-haired woman emerged, casting long shadows onto the cobblestones as she walked up the quai beneath the street lamps.

Down on the bank, Jules's sewer sluice lay in darkness, boarded up again. She wondered if the *flics* had rousted him for his own safety. On the flooded bank, the water level now was up to her knees. Her leather boots would take forever to dry. If they did. How could Hélène bring a baby to this place?

Sirens wailed. An ambulance's red lights flashed as it went speeding over Pont Marie. Her Tintin watch read 9:34 . . . not a bad response time. Jean Caplan was tough; if his luck held, he'd live.

René played his flashlight beam over the partially cemented-up arch. "You can't mean *this?*"

"The second one, there," she said, pointing to a stone arch farther down.

René shone the beam on it. Planks of wood were nailed crisscross over the opening. No access. The *flics* must have closed this one down, too.

Gone. She put her head in her hands. She'd felt so sure Nelie and Stella would be here. She wanted to kick herself. No Jules, no Hélène.

"Another wild-goose chase, Aimée," René said.

"They're here somewhere."

René just shook his head. Khaki-colored water flooded the deserted embankment.

They climbed back up the wet stone steps to the bridge. Directly across from them, light showed under the red awning of Libraire Adélaide, a bookstore, next to the dark window of a *coiffeur.*

"Go ahead — say it, René," Aimée told him. "I was all wrong. I should have turned Stella over to the authorities right away."

A questioning look appeared on his face.

"I should have ignored my gut instinct, right?" she said. "What's the matter, you think I can't feel any worse than I do? I agree, I have to call the child protection services. My hope is that Hélène may already have taken her to a homeless shelter."

He shook his head. "I think we're being invited to the bookstore."

"I'm not in the mood, René."

"That gentleman seems to know you. I think he wants to talk with you," he said.

She spun around. Jules, wearing a navy blue pea coat and a captain's hat, beckoned them from the bookstore's doorway. A sign in the window read JOURNEY TO THE PYRAMIDS, SLIDE SHOW AND TALK THIS EVENING. They ran across the street.

"Have you seen Hélène?" Aimée asked breathlessly.

Jules looked around and then nodded. "Quick. Follow me."

He appeared to be steady on his feet

despite the wine on his breath. Inside the dark bookstore, he walked behind the counter to the rear, gesturing for them to follow. "I know the owner. Shhhh."

Beyond a bookcase in the next room, bodies were packed together on chairs, viewing slides of golden sand and the Pyramids basking in the sun, accompanied by a droning voice . . . "In this slide we see the smallest of the pyramids at Giza built by . . ."

"Here." Jules opened a door behind the cashier's counter.

Aimée hesitated.

"Hurry, she's waiting." Then he put his finger to his lips.

Aimée trailed René down a narrow wooden staircase, lit by a single hanging bulb. Shelves of books and cardboard cartons filled the stone-walled cavern. A funeral wreath of dried flowers hung on one wall. Suspended from it was the blue, white, and red ribbon that indicated the deceased had been a war veteran. "An old Résistance hideout," Jules said. "A cache for arms."

"Funny how these days every place was a Résistance hideout," René said under his breath.

Jules took a bottle from his pocket, uncorked it, and took a swig. He passed the bottle to Aimée. "*Courage*, Mademoiselle."

"Merci." She needed it. She wiped the rim with her sleeve and took a gulp to take the taste of blood from her mouth, then handed it to René.

"Use this," Jules said, handing her the ribbon. She replaced René's blood-soaked handkerchief with the ribbon, wrapping it tightly to stop her bleeding, wincing.

Jules pushed a carton aside with his rubber boot. He bent, stuck his finger into a ring in the floor, and pulled up a trapdoor. "This is as far as I go. Ladies first."

Noise from the floor above sounded like a stampede of elephants. "Jules!" someone called.

"I have to go," Jules said. "Close the door after you."

Prepared for the damp, Aimée climbed down metal rungs and was surprised to find herself in a sandstone tunnel that was dry and relatively warm. Not at all like the sewer. She pulled out her penlight. It flickered and she shook it. She needed new batteries. A thin beam illuminated cables, red and yellow tubes running the length of the tunnel before they disappeared in the darkness.

"Where do we go?" René shone his torchlight beam alongside hers.

"Follow the yellow tubes," she said. She

noticed footprints on the loose grains of the sandstone floor.

"Is this part of the old quarries?" René asked.

Who knew what lay ahead? The mushroom cultivation industry had thrived underground in tunnels like this one until the end of the nineteenth century, a fact she remembered from science class. Even today, mushrooms were cultivated on a smaller scale under Montrouge.

"I'd guess this leads to the quarries." It was hard to believe they were almost under the Seine. They walked for a few minutes. Along the way she noted regular gouges in the sandstone, evidence of pickaxes. They turned a corner and a light bobbed in front of them.

"*Ça va?*" said a man wearing a jumpsuit and a utility belt. He was dressed in knee-high rubber boots and a miner's hat with a light on his head. She'd heard of these *cataphiles,* underground aficionados, who explored the quarries and sewers, held parties in them, and even camped out in them on the weekends.

"Have you seen Hélène, an older woman . . ."

"Not me," he said. He took a sip from a bottle of water and grinned as if he'd run into them on the street. "Try the next cavern. *Bonsoir.*"

They rounded more corners in the winding tunnel and finally came to an open space. The shuffle of footsteps sounded from deep inside the dark cavern.

"Hélène?" Aimée's voice echoed.

"Jean?" a woman's voice quavered in reply.

"Hélène, it's Aimée Leduc."

Aimée shone the penlight. An old woman, her white hair in two long braids, wearing a white wool jacket, stood in the shadows up against the wall. Aimée saw violet eyes and a young face, incongruous with the woman's white hair and stooped posture. Then the woman shielded her eyes with her hands. A Pharmacie Leclery shopping bag sat on the floor at her feet. "You're blinding me."

"Jean's hurt, Hélène. I came instead."

"*Oui,* I know. Put out the light. Paulette's sick. . . ."

Paulette?

"Please, Hélène, we can't see without light. Where's the baby?"

Aimée heard a hiss as a gas camping lantern went on, flooding the chiseled walls with light. She saw a camping stove, a metal pot, plates, a broken chair, several shopping bags. Not much. In the corner, Hélène, crouched near a metal cot. On it lay a young, hollow-cheeked woman covered in brown sheets and green army blankets. Her brown hair was plastered to her face in wet strands.

Aimée recognized Nelie. They'd found her at last. And stood paralyzed with horror as she realized that the sheets Nelie was wrapped in were brown from dried blood.

"The bad man's coming to hurt Paulette." Hélène's eyes were wide with panic. She grabbed Aimée's arm. "Did he hurt you, like the other girl?"

Hélène was living in the past; she'd confused Nelie with Paulette. And because of that she'd saved Nelie's life.

"You mean Orla . . . the girl he threw into the Seine?"

"But I took care of Paulette, I thought I'd done for him."

So that's what she'd meant in her words to Jean Caplan.

"I saw him —"

"Hélène," Aimée interrupted, putting her arm around the thin, shaking shoulders. "Where is the baby?"

"Shhh," Hélène said, her eyes fluttering in terror. "The bad man's here."

"Nom de Dieu, we have to get this girl to the hospital," René said. "Now!"

Aimée bent over Nelie, whose face was

sweaty and pale, and whose breath was labored. She was hemorrhaging by the look of the new bright red stains on the sheets. She must have lost so much blood. She looked like a broken bird.

"Call for the ambulance, René."

She propped Nelie's head up, took a bottle of water from the floor, and raised it to Nelie's lips. Hélène stood in the shadows by the wall again, wringing her hands.

"After my C-section," Nelie said, "there were . . . complications. . . . I became so weak that . . . I couldn't take care of my baby. I had nowhere else to go . . . but I knew . . . you were working with my uncle; he told me. Then one time . . . on your street . . . I saw you. I looked up your telephone number."

The effort of saying so much exhausted her and she closed her eyes.

So that was it. . . .

Nelie made an effort to go on. "At the march, I . . . couldn't walk; the incision had beome infected. We hid in your courtyard but I heard noises. Orla ran the other way, to distract him . . . then I . . . I know he's after me . . . but now I can't move," she said, then whispered, "Hélène thinks I'm someone else . . . but she has been feeding me and hiding me. Otherwise . . . he would have found me . . . by now."

"We'll get you to the hospital."

René had his cell phone out and was muttering at it. "Bad reception," he said.

"My baby, she's . . ." Nelie continued haltingly.

"But Hélène has her, doesn't she?" Aimée asked. "Hélène?" She called. But there was no Hélène, just the sputtering camp light.

Aimée panicked. What had Hélène done with Stella? She ran to the mouth of the cavern. "Hélène, come back!"

And then she heard noises from the nest of blankets near Nelie.

"What's that?" René said, going over to the blankets.

A gurgle. So familiar an ache of longing filled her. Please, she prayed, let it be her.

René leaned over and rose with Stella cradled in his arms. He draped a blanket around her and gave Aimée a meaningful look. "I'll take Stella to the bookshop and call SAMU from there. Can you manage?"

"Go." The sooner the better, she thought. "Take the camp light. Go, René, hurry."

René took off with Stella in his arms; his footsteps echoed from the tunnel.

Aimée rested her palm on Nelie's forehead. She was scorching hot, but she shivered in the damp blankets, burning up with fever.

"The doctor told me . . . I have proof," she said, her eyes bright and wandering. "They framed us. We were running like fugitives . . . but I couldn't run anymore."

"I understand. Tell me about the proof in the doctor's report."

"Alstrom loaded an old tanker with toxic waste, sent it out to the oil platform . . . and they sank it there. The crew all died . . . drowned . . . except for the captain. He's dying from uranium poisoning."

"How do you know this?"

"I found out in La Hague," Nelie said. Her eyes fluttered. "I saw the captain. He admitted it. And the doctor's examination notes . . . symptoms of uranium poisoning. That's proof that Alstrom lied."

She had to get Nelie out of here right away. But Aimée's ribs ached and she knew she couldn't carry Nelie through the quarry tunnels and up the rungs of the ladder to the surface.

"Nelie, I'll tie you to the blankets and pull you, OK? We have to get you help." Aimée laid a blanket on the sandstone floor, reached under Nelie, and lifted her onto it, then folded another blanket over her and tied it around her.

"Your uncle found the files, didn't he?"

Nelie blinked. Then her eyes closed.

"Stay with me, Nelie," Aimée pleaded.

"Everything . . . the doctor told me," Nelie said. "But it's all . . . report."

They heard footsteps. "Hélène?"

No answer.

And then her penlight went out.

THURSDAY EVENING

Krzysztof's knees shook as he sat in his uncle's study under the framed chart showing the Polish royal lineage. Next to it was the Linski escutcheon. Beneath it his uncle's Légion d'Honneur medal was displayed.

"I need your help, Uncle."

"No more places to hide, Krzysztof?" his uncle asked. "And now, as I hope you realize, not even from yourself?"

Krzysztof winced internally. It had been even harder than he had imagined to put himself at the old man's mercy.

"We can still stop the oil agreement —"

"Not that again!" his uncle interrupted. "After the bomb incident, police everywhere, the registrar from the Sorbonne and reporters besieging me all day!" he said, shaking his head. "Have you gone mad?"

"I'm wanted by the police. Won't you just

444

listen —"

"To what? You can't escape your heritage, Krzysztof. Yet you persist in trying to throw everything away."

"But there's nothing to throw away!"

His uncle buttoned his sweater vest and straightened his tie. His position as *chargé d'affaires* was in reality a sop thrown to a decorated war veteran with connections and aristocratic blood.

"That's your heritage." His uncle pointed above his head to the 1791 article in the constitution declaring Princess and Infanta Maria Augusta Nepomucena Antonia Franziska Xaveria Aloysia of Poland and her successors in direct line for the throne:

Frederick Augustus, present-day elector of Saxony, to whose male successors de lumbis [from the loins] we reserve the throne of Poland. Should the present-day elector of Saxony have no male issue, then the consort, with the consent of the assembled estates, selected by the elector for his daughter shall begin the male line of succession to the throne of Poland. Therefore we declare Maria Augusta Nepomucena, daughter of the elector, to be Infanta of Poland, reserving to the people the right, which shall be subject to no proscription, to elect another house to the throne after the expiration of the first.

Krzysztof wanted to tear it up. A faded piece of paper couldn't create legitimacy.

"You refuse to remember that the Polish Parliament ended the monarchy in 1945. I'm not holding my breath until it returns. And neither should you."

He stood and began to pace back and forth on the creaking wood floor.

"Why can't you listen for once?" he said, his voice rising. "Forget this prewar romantic nostalgia. Everyone hid their titles during the Communist regime. Or they'd risk being imprisoned as 'poster relics of decadent Western royalism.' We were anathema to Stalin, Khrushchev, all of them, and most of all to the puppet Polish government. A five-zloty bribe, not a title, got one a larger bowl of soup in prison. Ask Papa. A name like mine in Russian class didn't endear me to the teachers. Papa took a stand but he fought for freedom. Not a forgotten title."

"You don't have to shout, Krzysztof."

"I'm sorry."

Krzysztof watched his uncle. For the first time he noticed that his uncle looked unwell. The gauntness of his long face exaggerated the size of his eyes.

446

His uncle sighed. "You think I didn't know privation in the war? It was worse than anyone imagines."

Krzysztof stared. His uncle never spoke about his experiences in the war.

"It was worse than any Stalin-built concrete housing block, worse than standing on long lines for food."

Krzysztof looked out the window, at the cones of yellow light shining on the quai.

"You glorify this country, Uncle," he said. "But here people look down on us . . . call us dirty, lazy Poles, behind our backs. Only good enough to work as plumbers. I've heard it. You have, too, but you look the other way."

"You forget, I joined the Polish government in exile," his uncle said. "In London, I fought with the Free French forces and thanked the stars every night that de Gaulle let me." He stood and leaned on his cane. "Colonel Lorrain let me out of his jeep at the Libération. Right here." His uncle pointed to the quai. "I walked into this shell of a building. Paintings were tossed on the floor, and there was rubble left by the Gestapo everywhere. Like garbage." He shook his head. "Only the French helped us. Never forget that. The other Allies let the Germans defeat the Warsaw uprising, starve the fighters, and flatten Warsaw. They let the Vistula run red with Polish blood."

War stories. But that was past. The world faced new problems; he had to make his uncle understand. His uncle was his last hope.

"The Vistula runs with pollution now," Krzysztof said. "In your day it was the Nazis. Now it's globalization and the destruction of the ozone. Poland is democratic. They're dealing with today's issues, like everywhere else. But the North Sea and the Baltic are being ruined by toxic runoff. That's why we must expose oil companies like Alstrom. Can you say it's so different, Uncle?"

His uncle's shoulders drooped.

Useless trying to talk to him. The cordovan leather chairs, the carved bas-relief in the ceiling, the crackled mirror — nothing ever changed here, least of all his uncle.

"You think I don't understand?" his uncle asked. "You're passionate. Good, I was, too. Yet tradition and beauty, they have a place. For me, that's all there is left." His chin sagged. "I want to clutch them, grasp at the ephemeral while I still can. A fragile thing of beauty — a painting, a strain of music — outlasts destruction. I want to celebrate that. And this country gave them back to me. I'm grateful."

Krzysztof took his uncle's arm. "How is it so different? Beauty exists in clean oceans, pristine mountains. And if we don't stop the polluters, it will be gone. Forever. But you can change that."

His uncle sat again. "A masterful plea, worthy of a young monarch. Not unlike Frederick Augustus, who mounted the campaign against the invaders."

What did that mean? "Uncle, you'll help me?"

His uncle leaned back in his chair. "You tell me I'm lost in the past, can't move with the times. Krzysztof, I fought my war. I'm old. Too old to do anything."

Krzysztof shook his head and pointed to a framed photo of his uncle receiving the Légion d'Honneur. "But your old comrade, Colonel Lorrain, is still in the Ministry."

His uncle nodded. "So? He's about to retire, at least that's what he told me at dinner last week. Wants to bow out of all those committees he's on. His wife serves a Boeuf Bourgogne cooked to perfection."

"I want you to talk to him, to explain Alstrom's cover-up and why the agreement must not be signed."

"What do I know about that?"

"There's nothing for me here," Krzysztof

said, shaking his head. "I'm wanted. I can't finish my studies. If you won't help me, I'm leaving."

"It's not like you to give up. You're stubborn, like your father. It runs in the family."

From somewhere on the quai, leaves rustled. The moon, half obscured by threads of clouds, shone outside the window.

"You're the son I never had, Krzysztof." His uncle's jaw trembled. "Don't leave."

Krzysztof took his uncle's age-spotted hand and held it. He felt its slight tremor. He reached over and hugged the old man, his strong arm clasping the thin shoulders.

"I'm sorry, Uncle."

Krzysztof imagined taking the night train to Amsterdam, the crowded second-class compartment, anxiously waiting for a tap on the shoulder, then dawn breaking over the narrow canals and his search for a squat. He'd find another ecological group and try to make a difference. He'd start all over again. With nothing.

His uncle gripped Krzysztof's hand as it rested on his shoulder. "Now what should I say to Colonel Lorrain — that is, if he's there?"

Krzysztof stared at his uncle. Then he bent and kissed the withered cheeks.

"I suggest you invite him for an early dinner." He pulled up a chair, took some paper and his uncle's old nib pen, and dipped it in the black inkwell. "And here's what you'll tell him. We'll craft it in your language, an appeal to an old comrade-in-arms. Get him to use the old boy network."

A small smile played over his uncle's lips.

"I have a feeling you're dragging me into the new world, Krzysztof."

"Into the new Poland, Uncle. Built on tradition, but embracing the present." Krzysztof grinned and handed him his cell phone. "Together."

THURSDAY EVENING

Aimée stumbled in the dark, feeling her way along the gritty floor of the sandstone tunnel. She tried René again. Miracle of miracles, the cell phone worked . . . but his line was busy.

If only her penlight worked. Or Hélène would come back.

Nelie stirred and mumbled, "*Non,* Claude . . ."

"Tell me, Nelie," Aimée urged, leaning against Nelie's wet, matted hair. "Quick."

"Relied on you . . ."

"What do you mean?" In the dark, Aimée

451

put her arms around Nelie and propped her up.

"Don't let him take my baby."

Him? Her hand quivered. "You mean *Claude? He's* the father? The spy?" Her surprise turned to panic. She remembered Vavin and his ringing phone and how she had found him in the closet and now Hélène's words — "the bad man's here" — and her disappearance.

He was here.

She felt Nelie go limp. Her arms ached but she had to pull the blanket faster; she had to reach the ladder.

Claude's high-tech equipment, the flashy motorcycle he rode — all too upscale for a filmmaker who hadn't had a film produced in years. A documentary filmmaker, sympathetic to MondeFocus, who offered a safe house. The safe house Nelie hadn't taken advantage of.

Claude had the perfect cover. He filmed MondeFocus demonstrations; Brigitte knew him. He probably attended the planning meetings for the demonstrations. Of course, that's where the information and meeting notes would have come from. Idiot . . . she should have figured it out sooner. The perfect informer. The saboteur. Claude.

"I can't believe I found you." And he was

standing over them. "That old woman's sadly confused. She ran away," Claude said. Light bobbed from his miner's helmet, a walkie-talkie was clipped to his belt, as well as some tools. His motorcycle boots crunched over the sandstone.

"My God, they hurt you!" he said, looking at the ribbon bandaging her forehead.

She wavered. His dark hair curled over his leather jacket, his sandalwood scent wafted over the cool limestone, his intense eyes stared at her.

"Are you all right?"

Had she got him wrong?

He shone a flashlight on Nelie. Now the blanket was becoming soaked with bright blood. "Can we move Nelie? I've got gauze for a tourniquet."

"She needs more than a tourniquet, she needs a hospital," Aimée said. "My God, she's hemorrhaging, losing blood fast. How did you find us, Claude?"

She hoped he hadn't heard the sound of panic in her voice.

"Stinger2, mission complete?" was the message that came from the walkie-talkie.

Stinger2. It was certain. He was the one who'd sent Alstrom the MondeFocus meeting notes.

He clicked off the walkie-talkie. "Aimée, I

told them not to hurt you. Not you," he said. "I'm so sorry."

"What?" She felt sick, dirty. She'd slept with him, for God's sake. And liked it.

"We'll get Nelie to a safe place," he assured her.

Like he'd taken Orla to a safe place?

"René's getting help." Or had he taken care of René and Stella, too? Her stomach lurched. "A rescue squad's coming, the *flics* are on the way."

"You asked me to trust you, Aimée. I do. We're good together. We fit; you feel it, too, I know."

She worked her fingers on the cell phone, hit speed dial. René's number. Then her shaking hands dropped it. *Merde!*

"Where is she? Where's my baby?" he asked. "We can make it work."

"Make it work?"

He sighed. "I have an apartment in Zurich, a new state-of-the-art studio, contacts. You could help me raise my daughter the right way."

Psychotic. But hadn't that crossed her mind, too, riding on the back of his motorcycle? She, he, and Stella. Her fingers tensed but she worked them inside her pocket.

"What do you mean, Claude?"

"You've had my daughter all this time. You can keep a secret, you'll keep this one."

She gazed in horror at the hammer hanging from his belt as he reached for it.

"Nelie's had a massive loss of blood. She won't recover, you know. The surgeon and I tried to find her to help her, but it's too late now. I'm going to put Nelie out of her misery and pain. It will all be over in a second."

Like putting an animal down. Sick, he was sick. Did he actually think she'd stand by and watch him bludgeon Nelie to death? Nelie, the mother of his child? He was a monster. Why the hell hadn't René picked up when she'd tried to phone him? Where was the SAMU?

"You followed Hélène here, didn't you? You could have taken the baby from her. No one would have paid attention to what she said. . . ."

"Aimée, you're not listening." His voice, his tone, were soothing, reasonable. "Nelie knows. She knows too much. She's the only one who can prove that I spied on Monde-Focus and informed Alstrom about their plans. I have to dispose of her so we can have a life together. So we can take care of my daughter together."

But wasn't he forgetting something? Now

she knew, too.

The tools hanging from his utility belt were silhouetted in the light. There was a heavy-duty flashlight in addition to the walkie-talkie and the hammer. It would be so easy for him to pound Nelie's skull to fragments. And then hers. He'd escape, disappearing in the vast warren of tunnels and quarries that lay beneath Paris. And surface somewhere . . . but not in Zurich. No one would ever catch him.

"What about your documentary?" she asked, saying the first thing that came into her head. She had to distract him until help came. "Were those all lies you told me?"

"The money's come through," he said. "Now, with what I've been paid, I can make it happen. It's taken years, but I'll be able to finish my video and begin work on new projects."

"You did it for the money? But everything you said about your mother — a committed Socialist, a union organizer . . ."

"Did you have holes in your shoes when you were a kid? Did you grow up with your neighbors jeering, 'Commie, Commie' at you? They recruited me, but it wasn't too hard."

"Halkyut recruited you?"

"I didn't go looking for them, Aimée. At

456

first, they just asked to see my footage of the environmentalists' demonstrations. Their money helped me keep going. Then they asked me to do a little bit more, to document who attended and who the leaders were. I realized I could live like the other half. Now I won't have to scrounge in commune kitchens, licking the pot after the others have eaten. Neither will my daughter."

She had to keep him talking. "But why did you have to kill Orla?"

"I didn't mean to. You have to understand that," he said. "She argued, she wouldn't listen to reason. She ran away, then she slipped off the quai."

"Slipped, Claude? I think you threw her into the river after hitting her with a tire iron."

His eyes narrowed. "Never mind about Orla. It's you and me now. We're alike, Aimée. Each of us was abandoned by the one person who should have put us first. I know you could be a wonderful mother. I've seen you with the baby. Don't disappoint me."

Nelie was moving, struggling, the blanket falling open. He was holding a gun. Where had that come from?

She saw Claude aim at Nelie's head.

"Stop, Claude, the *flics* are coming. You

don't have to do this." She reached for the Jacadi baby clothes bag.

"I can buy my baby everything she wants now. We can both live the way we were meant to."

"We've all had crap in our childhoods, Claude. Get over it. Her mother's right here."

"I grew up without a real mother. Just a woman wrapped up in causes, dragging me to strikes. Never home after school. No father. No real home. My daughter won't be brought up like that, poor and ashamed and lonely."

He was playing his vulnerable card again. But he'd said the wrong thing. She hated men who whined.

"Do you own that copyright, Claude?" she said. "I don't think so."

"You refuse to understand," he said, aiming at Nelie, pulling back the safety.

"Wrong, Claude," she said. "I do understand."

She fired the Beretta through the Jacadi bag. The first shot hit his shoulder; the second, his kneecap.

She let him live. After all, he was Stella's father.

Saturday Afternoon

Aimée clenched her fist around the sponge, watching the slow trickle of her blood dripping down the clear plastic tube. She cleared her throat and read aloud from the special edition of *L'Express:*

"Colonel Lorrain of the Ministry of the Interior has called for the cessation of the Alstrom oil negotiations and for an immediate inquiry into toxic substance dumping. Certain reports with respect to an oil tanker crew and to uranium poisoning have come to light . . ."

She paused, glancing at the occupant of the hospital bed.

"Nelie," Aimée said, "did you hear that? Alstrom's finished."

But Nelie, eyes closed, was asleep. With satisfaction, Aimée saw that there was a flush of color in her cheeks.

"Half a liter, Mademoiselle Leduc," the white-coated attendant said, pulling the needle out of her arm. "But we don't know if your blood will match."

"I understand," she said. "I just wanted to do something."

"Someone will benefit," the attendant assured her.

"Thank you for letting me come up here to do this so I could spend time with her."

"What my boss doesn't know won't hurt him." The attendant winked. "Pretty tough, eh?" He pressed the gauze down over the needle site with a firm hand. "And you with stitches!"

He cocked an eyebrow as he taped the gauze in place. "Are you all right?"

She wished she were.

In L'Hôpital Necker's linoleum-tiled hallway, laced with the odor of alcohol, Aimée joined René at the nursery window. A row of swaddled babies lay in white Plexiglas tray tables. Some were connected to tubes.

"Our girl's a trouper," René said. He pointed to the far right.

Stella's toes kicked the blanket. Her little balled fists flailed. A basket of stuffed pink pigs sat by her.

"She loves pigs," René said. "She laughed when I went oink, oink."

Impossible for a two-week-old, the manual said, but Aimée let that pass.

René slipped his arms into his Burberry raincoat and picked up his briefcase. "Got to rush, Aimée. Now that I've got your signature on the Fontainebleau contract, I'll

460

messenger it to them from the office."

"Fantastic." He'd made enough to pay the rent and much more.

"Me, I've got a network to monitor," Aimée said, glancing at the time. "Talk to you later."

René paused and shot her a look.

"Feel up to a rave with me and Magali tonight?"

"*Non, merci.* Magali must wonder what's become of you." She couldn't meet his eyes. She knew he'd cancel his date and hold her hand if she asked him to. But he had a life of his own and she couldn't intrude on it.

"Stella will be raised by her mother," René said. "You made that happen. You did a good thing." He took her hand and rubbed it. "It's for the best, Aimée. You know, I'll miss her, too."

He looked away.

Aimée swallowed. At the hospital door, René turned and stared at her as if he were reading her thoughts. "A baby would slow you down. Not your style, you know that."

She summoned a grin. "All those drycleaning bills, not to mention the cost of diapers!"

At the hospital gate she watched René's Citroën turn the corner onto rue Vaugirard, then she turned and walked back. One last

461

look. That's all.

She stood at the nursery window until a nurse appeared and picked up Stella. Aimée waved good-bye as they left the ward. She waved good-bye to those little pink toes.

Long after Stella had gone, Aimée's breath clouded the glass. Of course, Stella should be with her mother. But deep inside she ached for that warm bundle beside her on the duvet. Those blinking blue eyes filled with wonder. Somehow it could have been her style. People did it all the time. She would have managed. She would have been the mother she'd never had.

She made herself walk down the chilly corridor. She could do this. But the ache inside wouldn't go away. She collapsed onto a waiting-room chair, sobs choking her. A hand began stroking her back. She looked up into the eyes of a nurse.

"Lost someone?" the nurse asked.

I've lost her forever.

Aimée rubbed the tears from her face and sniffled.

"I'm sorry," the nurse said. "Trite as it sounds, every day the pain will lessen. It never goes away but you'll remember the good things."

Aimée nodded, took a deep breath, and hurried down the hallway.

■ ■ ■ ■

She climbed the steps to her apartment and opened her door to Miles Davis's wet nose pressed into her palm. But the high-ceilinged rooms were empty of a cooing Stella.

She washed the streaks from her kohl-smudged eyes. Dotted eye cream, for puffiness, in circles beneath them, using the last squeeze of Dior's fine-line concealer. At this rate, she'd need extra-strength putty.

Concentrate. She had a network to monitor, systems to check, work, there was always work to be done. At her desk, she booted up her laptop; Miles Davis nestled at her feet. Outside her open balcony doors, the Saint-Louis-en-l'Ile bell chimed the hour and leaves scuttled in the rising wind.

She performed routine maintenance, monitored the router connections, the firewall design. Yesterday's cold espresso sat forgotten by her keyboard. That done, she hit *Save* for the backup copy. Not bad — only ten minutes to get the system online once more.

Someone was knocking at her front door. She hit *Send* and grabbed her scarf from the duvet. The faint odor of talcum powder rose from it. She chewed her lip trying not to think of what could have been.

At the front door she peered through the keyhole and saw the hem of a blue smock and the legs of her concierge encased in their support pantyhose.

"Another box, Mademoiselle," Madame Cachou said, frowning with disapproval as Aimée opened the door. "You're lucky I didn't throw the others out, but the —"

"*Désolée*," Aimée interrupted. "I forgot, deadlines . . . I know, the plumbers complained."

The box sagged open, contents spilling over the parquet — letters in her grandfather's scratchy handwriting and something white.

"Not the plumbers, Mademoiselle," Madame Cachou said. "This was on my steps today, blocking the way. A lady left it."

Curious, Aimée bent to peer closer.

In the box lay a long lace christening gown smelling of cedar. On top of it was a color photograph protected by plastic, the colors still vivid. In the photo, a smiling couple held an infant by a baptismal font. She recognized the dark brown wood font of Saint-Louis-en-l'Ile and a younger version of her father in his good blue suit, her grandfather with a black mustache, a slimmer Morbier, and the woman who must be her mother.

Her stomach knotted. She hadn't seen a photo of her mother since her father had burned them, right after she'd left them.

Young, hair in a simple knot, a light in her eyes that the camera caught. Those carmine red lips. And for the millionth time Aimée wondered what had happened to her mother.

"Beautiful," Madame Cachou said. "You don't see many christening gowns like this anymore. Friends of your family, Mademoiselle?"

Aimée's thoughts returned to her dim hallway and the flushed face of Madame Cachou. She felt stupid, sifting through memories, wallowing in self-pity. But she couldn't help thinking that the christening gown would fit Stella.

She nodded. Her grandfather must have saved this and it had gotten mixed up with other people's boxes in the basement. She had better make nice, keep Madame Cachou on her good side.

"I'll have to apologize and thank the tenant who left this. Which floor does she live on?"

"No tenant that I know of," Madame Cachou said. "*Et alors,* the way people come and go these days, it's like the Gare du Nord."

"What do you mean?"

"The lady said you might need this."

"Need this?"

"For your baby," Madame Cachou said.

The hair rose on the back of Aimée's neck.

"You modern career women!" Madame Cachou sighed, hands on her ample hips. "Rushing everywhere. No time to cook." She glanced into Aimée's hallway. "Or clean. At least someone respects tradition."

But the baby's not mine, Aimée almost said.

"What else did this woman say?"

Madame Cachou shrugged. "She wasn't French. That accent, eh, I could tell."

Her mind went back to the woman's figure on the quai and the feeling of being watched. Hope battled against disappointment as she took a deep breath, a little girl again.

"Of course, you wouldn't have noticed, would you?" Aimée paused. "She didn't look like this woman, did she? Older, I mean."

Madame Cachou scratched her arm. She shrugged, pointing to Aimée's mother in the christening photo. "Too hard to say."

"Of course." Hopes dashed, Aimée got to

her feet.

"Same carmine lipstick, though," Madame Cachou said. "You don't see that shade much anymore."

Just then a warm breeze swept through the balcony doors. The breeze enfolded Aimée, like a pair of warm arms.

ABOUT THE AUTHOR

Cara Black lives with her husband, a bookseller, and their son in San Francisco. She frequently travels to France. This is her seventh mystery in the Aimée Leduc series.

The employees of Thorndike Press hope you have enjoyed this Large Print book. All our Thorndike and Wheeler Large Print titles are designed for easy reading, and all our books are made to last. Other Thorndike Press Large Print books are available at your library, through selected bookstores, or directly from us.

For information about titles, please call:
(800) 223-1244

or visit our Web site at:
www.gale.com/thorndike
www.gale.com/wheeler

To share your comments, please write:
Publisher
Thorndike Press
295 Kennedy Memorial Drive
Waterville, ME 04901